I ONCE MET A GIRL
WHO PAINTS THE LINES ON ROADS

Kira Fennell

"Rivers and Roads" by the Head and the Heart

Editors: Kayla Drahos and Sara Fennell

Book & Cover Design by Kira Fennell

Photos & Art by Kira Fennell and Kess Fennell

ISBN: 9781976726514

for Anyone who will listen, and for Everyone who cares

WHERE YOU'LL LIKELY STOP

=

A SMALL EXPLANATION

=

Natural disasters. New diseases. Baby animals. Cliffhangers with no sequel. Scary stories you try to convince yourself aren't real. Faulty politics. Technology we could never imagine. Pizza of any sort. Sex. Really fucking good music. Sleep: long, lustrous, fully-devoted, no-alarm-clock, making-up-for-the-past-month sleep.

They advised me to get your attention – warning, that if I didn't, you wouldn't be interested in reading, and you'd view this as a waste of time. But I will ask, if you're wasting your time by voluntarily reading, are you really wasting your time?

After being bombarded with rules, points, and evaluations, I came to the conclusion that it doesn't quite matter in this situation. Everyone knows that the best part of a book is the middle. The beginning and the end are just for the convenience of clarification and closure. I could write anything I wanted right now and you'd probably forget it by the end of the book.

Do I have your attention? Would you continue if I didn't?

Would you admit that you really do judge books by their covers? I do.

Often times, the mere pressure for an "attention getter" is enough to discourage even a brilliant mind from spilling its mess onto paper. So in honor of my abiding habit of avoiding problems at all costs, I'm going to skip to the middle. Here is an excerpt from my life that I would like to share with you: a time where I didn't know better, and I didn't know *something* better; a time that gave me a spirit of inquiry, and a better capacity for depicting grey areas in the towering contradiction we've somehow summed up with four letters: life. (I wonder who picked that word.)

The one I deem responsible for initiating this mess is Dylan Rivers. Despite the misleading name, you'd be wrong to label her male – not that she would mind – it's simply that she is a girl, and quite the valiant one at that. I owe her gratitude because if it were not for her, I wouldn't be able to fill this entire book with our sublime (and not too sublime) encounters.

Reader, I'm going to tell you this story and I'm not going to ignore the fact that you are here. This is written in second person despite the unjust rule of never addressing that, in all reality, I'm talking to you. So by all means, I say hello and thank you for picking up the book (for whatever reason it got your attention), and deciding to read my repetitive twenty-six letters. I appreciate it profoundly.

~ JUNE

A LARGE BROWN SCARAB BEETLE [1]

=

The teacher takes attendance as we find our assigned seats. To this day, our seating arrangements are projected on the wall, allowing the entire class to openly view our horrendous school pictures. I find mine with haste (not that that will make it magically go away). I happen to sit in the back, which is exactly what I prefer. My seat is out of everyone's direct view, and I'm able to observe rather than worry if the back of my head is annoying to look at, or if it's blocking someone's view.

"Kyle Otis?"

"Here." He's a dick.

"Lily Paulson?"

"Present." She tries too hard when she doesn't need to.

"Dylan Rivers?"

"Yeah," she curtly replies, causing me to break the comfortable stare I have going to look at the person to whom the new name belongs.

She's sitting three rows up and two seats over, so I can only see a sliver of her face, but it's enough for me to deem her "attractive" in an alternative sort of way. Although I'm ashamed of this, I say it because attractiveness is one of the first natural judgments we make. However, my attention doesn't linger long as the teacher continues the drone of roll call. Being averted, I notice a thin crack in the window which alters the light just enough to create a faint rainbow. This small beauty almost distracts me from the fact that my school is shit, because indeed, the window is broken.

This florescent-lit, dust-infused classroom is devoted to the study of World History, (as if we could actually learn the entire world's history in the span of a trimester, yet we get years to learn America's history). It's a subject I've always liked, but only for the knowledge of the outrageous things people did in the past. Humankind has always been cruel and naive which is why I find it ironic for us to claim we've improved, when, realistically, we've merely systematized our cruelty and have learned ways to be discreet about it. However, that conversation has a time and a place, and although it may belong in this room, it doesn't belong on this page. This page is devoted to organizing this jumbled introduction, and making sure you don't regret your decision to start reading.

So let me explain: Dylan is new to school this year, and this is the first class I've shared with her. I know no more than her name and her seat, but I've heard the inevitable gossip brought up in conversation because, god forbid, how could anyone miss the new girl in town? The childlike quality of being mesmerized by something new is magnified when the new happens to be a person. We view them as some foreign object, even if they're only coming from the next town over. At the very least, they're something to keep us occupied, and perhaps the only type of change we'll actually approve.

Have you ever been the new kid? To me, it sounds the least bit appealing. You're forced to undergo a week or two of continuous glares as people calculate their immediate judgement of you, and decipher where you might belong in this crosshatched society that is high school. (I promise this isn't going to be a yet another book about a teenager surviving high school, but this story does start here, so I might as well say what we all think of it.)

Few can deny that high school comes with categories that if asked, could easily be applied to every student within its walls. But I will admit, they're not quite as drastic as depicted in high school movies. Considering I'm aware of this, I try to associate little meaning to them. And despite the ancient hierarchy that has been drilled into our heads since we were first capable of understanding it, I know that people are dozens of things rather than one broad thing. I believe a lot of people know this, we're just not yet accustomed to giving others a chance to prove it.

All in all, stereotypes ruin our thinking. I encourage you to ignore their precedence, but I also encourage you to have your own opinion. As my first and foremost warning, I must tell you that I'm going to contradict myself. I do this because everyone does it. In this book, I will be honest, and technically speaking, a book is simply writing everything the silent voice in your head says as it comes to you. This means that there will be times where I'll ramble about side-note thoughts, implore my opinion on things I don't understand, and possibly even consult with you, Reader. And although it may be more of a one-sided conversation, I hope that you don't mind, and ultimately, I hope you can relate.

Since this is the first day of the new trimester, we start with the basics and go over the syllabus. It's the same in every class, so it's always a bore. But before the bell rings, my teacher talks about an upcoming group project that should be an easy introduction to the Hundred Years' War (it's sad to think that that's the best name they could come up with).

Teachers persistently attempt to push us out of our comfort zones by making us do projects with our peers – claiming it'll help us in the future. But their theory is flawed because we're allowed to pick our partners, and everyone goes with their closest friend in the class. It's basically a neon-lit arrow pointing at the few who are left awkwardly stumbling around, trying not to stand out for their lack of a partner. What's even worse is that the teacher won't let them do it alone, even if they'd prefer to. They proceed to ask, out loud, if anyone else doesn't have a partner or would be willing to allow that person into their group – certainly a self-esteem booster there. Most of the time I manage to get a partner before that goes down, but I feel for the ones who don't – secondhand embarrassment – plus, no one needs that extra stress.

I had assumed that this kind of situation would have gone away by the time I was a Senior, but I've been proven wrong. I remember in middle school I used to look into the daunting classes with older students, and I'd get a sinking feeling in my stomach as I anticipated how school would be at that age. I used to think that childish things like worksheets that require coloring or caring about an awkward seating arrangement would go away, but they didn't. With each year that came, I never felt older. I never felt like I was entering a new or elite part of my life. It merely felt like we kept adding layers over the things we already knew, and I'd only notice how much we'd all grown by looking back at old photos. But my god, are those photos horrendous. I know you know what I mean, Reader. I know you've had a Facebook littered with pictures you once thought were cool, but now can't understand what you must have been thinking to post something like that online.

Although it's hilarious (or perhaps mortifying) to look back on, it's made me realize something other than how much facial hair the boys have managed to grow in one year: it's taught me that there's a reason we revisit those photos and don't like what we see. There's a reason we look into the mirror and wonder why nothing has changed, yet we hate who we were a year ago and for a different reason than why we hated ourselves the year before that; nothing's ever consistent, so I hope you're never content.

I'm thankful that in regards to Dylan, I have a clean slate, so I make it my goal to somehow end up with her for this project. Even though it's unlike me to seek out a partner myself, I know that my acquaintances in this class all have a better friend present, so they won't initially pick me as a partner. Plus, I do take part in the interest of a new peer and usually succumb to my curiosity easily, especially when it's towards someone with the looks of Dylan.

Over the next week, I conclude that she dresses like she has more to say, and her hair falls in a way that looks as if it holds secrets. She wears neutral colors that still complement each other and fit her slim body. She usually dresses in skinny jeans with some sort of 80s-esque, indie top. She has dark brown eyes that match her wavy hair that falls all the way down to where her belly button would be. She has many faint freckles that stretch across her rounded face, and I have to admit, I'm jealous of her makeup skills. She's a bit taller than I am, which is slightly intimidating, but intimidation seems to be her goal as I observe her throughout the days. She never says much and keeps to herself, but she

4

never looks belittled. Maybe it's confidence or the lack of caring, but it grabs my attention, and on the day the project is officially assigned, I approach her in hopes that she'll say yes to being my partner.

(I now realize that I sound excessively creepy with all the observations I just made, but that's probably because I don't typically write out descriptions of people. I bet I'm that creepy with everyone. Are you?)

"Hi, I'm June. . . just wondering if you've got a partner?" I ask even though it's obvious that she doesn't or is even bothering trying to get one. Maybe she assumed someone would come to her.

"No," she quickly answers, but then takes a-bit-too-long-of-a-moment to analyze me. She continues after making eye contact with, "Junebug. . . I don't, but if you'd like to be mine, then sure."

"*Junebug?*" I ask. It appears she has given me a nickname within the first few seconds of officially meeting me, and I don't know how I feel about that – especially if that's the name I receive; June Bugs aren't particularly smart.

"More personal. I'm Dylan, but that's all," she says very casually while packing her few belongings into her bag.

"So you don't get a personal name?" I question as I ungainly play along with this unexpected conversation.

"No, I don't need encouragement to be personal," she replies matter-of-factly, but still manages to sound uninterested.

I'm sure you know, Reader, that this is not how teenagers talk upon first meeting. I was expecting a hi-yes-when-where-agree-bye sort of conversation, so I'm surprised at her blunt personality. However, I must admit that I find it refreshing.

"Okay?" I half-question, half-say, deciding to leave it at that. I proceed to ask, "Should we meet up sometime?"

"I suppose we'll have to. My house? I live on Alan street, eight-fifty-five, but that's about all I can tell you. I'm new."

"I've noticed. But that's okay, I can find it."

She stands and slings her backpack over her shoulder, forcing me to now look up at her.

"Um. . . Sunday at noon work for you? I work on Saturday," I ask.

"Sure, see you then."

The bell rings and I go back to gather my things, making sure to exit behind her. I don't want her to see my quizzical face that is a result of my now running mind.

I wasn't expecting that kind of encounter. Although brief, it was offsetting and dominance was defined quickly. I'm usually good at compromising with people, but from her firm initiation, I'm not sure what to expect when we meet to do our project, and that makes me anxious. What did she mean personal? Why does a history project have to be personal? Why did she call me Junebug? That's not how you greet strangers.

I decide that it's simply her preferred demeanor. Perhaps she likes to be superior and that's how she accomplishes it: taking control so far as to even control my name. Maybe I want to be personal now. I've got a lot of questions, but if I'm being honest, I probably don't have the balls to ask them.

I go to my next two classes but find that I'm paying little attention to the words my teachers want me to hear. Dylan is on my mind. (Wow, that sounds creepy too, but it's unfortunately true.)

Maybe that was her goal: to be present in my head for the rest of the day. Maybe because she's new she wants to make a name for herself. Maybe she had expected me to ask her and wanted to keep things interesting. Maybe she was curious about me too, and that's why she gave me a "personal" name. Maybe she wants to be the girl everyone's slightly afraid of because you never know what she'll do. Maybe I'm overthinking this. That's true, I am. Did she want that to happen? Does she even care? Probably not, because that's ridiculous. And although I know that it is, I'm a paranoid person when things don't go the way I expect them to.

(I don't care if you're 8, 18, or 80, books are always better with pictures)

MERELY MUMBLES [2]

=

Sunday: I wake up at 9:27 with an anxious knot in my stomach. It's frustrating because it's there before I can even process why. I've never been an outgoing person, but a school project shouldn't produce disquiet to this extent.

Perhaps the only pro to anxiety is that it's a good motivator. I get out of bed with more haste than normal, determined to fully prepare myself for the day – as if that were possible. Black leggings, a pair of Toms, and my floral print t-shirt is what I decide to wear. I figure it's casual but not unappealing.

Now, Reader, I don't know a clever way to divulge my physical appearance when writing, so I'll just take this time to describe myself. (And I'll be amused at the fact that none of you will have the same mental image of me.)

I'm about 5'4" and thin – bone bumpy. I've got dirty blond hair that I usually put in a messy bun for the convenience of it. Green eyes, long face, narrow features, and pouty lips. I'm not overly fond of my looks, but that's only because I live in my skin. Mirrors have learned to reflect the negatives more profoundly than the positives – perhaps because they're tired of everyone looking at them. I'd get sick of it too.

I do, however, know that I'm not necessarily unattractive. Although glad that this is true, I'm not without flaw. If my life were to become a movie, the actress that plays me should not be flawless. That's an inaccurate portrayal of life. They also shouldn't be twenty-five, which seems to be the average age of actors who play teenagers in high school. *Accurate.*

I exit my room in search of food.

My mom's in the living room and says good morning as I pass. I try to say it back without sounding grumpy. I'm not a morning person.

You should know that my parents are divorced and that my dad lives elsewhere. I only see him periodically. I don't mind it much anymore because I've gotten used to it, but as one could imagine, it wasn't the thrill of my childhood. I'm an only child.

Cereal rocks, never forget that.

I lounge around my room and dreadfully keep an eye on my clock. I hate the feeling of waiting for something you're not excited for. I can't tell if time is moving too fast or too slow, and it turns inside my stomach. Do I want it to move slow so the event doesn't come and I've got time to prepare? Or do I want it to move fast so I can go and get it over with? I'm too nervous and impatient for either way to be okay.

At 11:47, I decide to hop in my car to find 855, Alan St.

I'd die if it wasn't for GPS.

My initial observations of the day includes the sky. It's dense with clouds, which I've always loved. I don't fancy sunny days because they accompany pressure. Everyone expects me to be outside and happy, as if to mimic the sun. It makes me feel as though there's someone watching me in the bright and open environs. It gives me a bad vibe of no security. However, I can say the same about the night because of the dark. Maybe it'd be acceptable to just label me paranoid and call it good.

But nevertheless, I prefer clouds because 1) clouds are extremely entertaining to look at. I mean, they're practically big puffs of stagnant smoke, and 2) the town light looks beautiful. When the world is lit from different angles of light that casts elegant, abstract shadows, it can give the atmosphere a whole different feeling. I think the town is gorgeous with a grey overcoat, and a painting of street-light colors underneath. Rain just adds; perspective makes a difference.

After fifteen minutes of driving, I make a right onto Alan street and turn down my music to concentrate on finding the too-small-to-read-from-all-the-fucking-way-over-here house numbers that are posted in the most inconvenient places. After finally getting a glimpse of the nearly-falling-off, gold address that reads 855 in an unusually fancy font, I park on the curb in front of Dylan's yard.

I sit for a minute, observing her neighborhood. It's beaten down, old, and dingy just like her house. It's rusty blue and dirty white, long grass with dandelions, and nervous steps to the door, a doorbell, a ring, an awkward wait, and an answer.

"Hey," I say as she steps aside to let me in. I notice that she's wearing "comfy clothes" which includes sweatpants and a loose shirt. She obviously didn't feel the need to impress me while getting dressed, which makes me feel embarrassed for trying.

"We'll be downstairs in my room," she says as I take off my shoes and wait for her to lead the way.

Her house is relatively clean with dull walls and small rooms. There's not a lot to look at but there's a faint smell of tobacco in the air. It makes me wonder what kind of life she lives. However, I have no room to talk on that matter.

It's silent as we walk, and I anticipate how we'll start our project, but the word "personal" stays in the back of my mind. When we get downstairs, the walls become brick and the room is set to a darker lighting. Down the hallway, and she opens the door to her room. Rooms always make a statement about the one who dwells in them because they have the freedom to personalize, and Dylan's room certainly says a lot.

She has a few posters hanging up: one displaying Pearl Jam, a good band. Another is for the movie *American Ultra*. I've never seen it, but I recognized the actors. There's a pile of books in the corner. I start reading the titles: *To Kill a Mockingbird, The Realm of Possibility, Life of Pi, It's Kind of a Funny Story,* and so on. They all seem respectable. I put books on a pedestal, so I'm pleasantly surprised that she reads. I suppose it was unfair of me to assume that she doesn't, but who does if not required these days?

Her bed is small and messy. There's a desk with miscellaneous papers (including a couple of drawings), there's a red stain on her carpet near her dresser, lights that hang around the perimeter of her ceiling, a mirror with lipstick prints and sharpie writing that I can't decipher from where I'm standing, and a dream catcher complete with feathers that hangs over one of her windows and cast shadows from the slight daylight sneaking in.

"My room," she clarifies.

"It's nice," I concur, and meant it. Sometimes I wish I had a room like this, although, I don't know where to stand. Should I sit? This is awkward. I hope she says–

"So should we get started?" she interrupts my worried thoughts.

"Um, yeah. I brought my book. I can start with the research and you–"

"But I don't know you," she cuts me off. Which is true, but I don't consider that a requirement with school projects considering we're forced to do them with someone. My mouth opens in attempts to respond, but when nothing comes out, I close it again, so she steps in.

"I'm new, you know that. I haven't talked to a lot of people yet." She pauses once more to see if I've managed to come up with a response. I haven't. "I can start with you," she states, as if I were the project. I do understand her desire to make a friend after moving to an unfamiliar place, so I decide not to question her frankness. Plus, we have a long time to do our assignment which isn't very time consuming.

"Okay. Well, what do you want to know?" I ask without confidence.

"First, your middle name." Okay weird?

"Um, it's Rae. Why?"

"Because if nothing else, you at least know someone's first and or last name. But the middle name they get to keep for themselves. That's much more valuable to know. It's more personal. So, June Rae Blackfield?" she casually asks.

"Yes. How 'bout you?" I ask in reply, failing to admit that she does have a point. I've never viewed middle names as a particularly important piece of information, but they do have an air of confidentiality considering they're usually only an initial on documents.

"Dylan Lee Ann Rivers," she proclaims.

"Lee Ann?" I ask, genuinely surprised. The name doesn't seem to suit her at all, too girly. Although she is a girl, she doesn't dress to a gender or look the title.

"Yeah, I don't like it. Dad said it made up for naming me a 'boy's name.' But oh well." She leans up against her desk. "Do you care if I be blunt, Junebug?"

I don't know what more she has to be blunt about, and honestly, I'm slightly afraid to find out, but I can't refrain from my curiosity. It's the same curiosity that compels us to like the status of someone who posts, "*Like for a tbh!! :)*" like we used to do in middle school. Who doesn't want to know what others think of them?

I also don't bother to ask about the nickname, might as well just let that happen.

"No, say whatever," I encourage.

"I'm gonna' try to be real with you, and I would like for you to let me, okay? And maybe I'll get you to loosen up a bit in the process." She gestures at my body. "I'm tired of bullshit friendships. I'm tired of small talk and meaningless relations that are nothing more than convenient. You asked me to be your partner, so that's what I'll be," she rants, and all the while she takes a step and a half, back and forth, as she paces in place.

When I asked her to do the project with me, this isn't what I was signing up for. But the tone in her voice is almost helpless, so I feel slight sympathy for what I assume to be a history of bad relationships. Plus, I don't mind a new friend. It actually sounds kind of intriguing because, thus far, she's not like anyone else I've met before.

Due to her originality, I reflect on people I've previously known. I realize I haven't given much thought about "bullshit friendships," but I suppose Dylan is right. I can admit that I've been a part of many. I mean, what qualifies a friendship as real?

From what I have gathered in my short time with friends, I think you have to love them – like the kind of love that lingers in your stomach. The kind that feels as if you've got mechanical cables attached to one another; where if you were to break them, your electrical wires would be exposed, and you'd short circuit from the tears you'd be crying. Does she want this kind friendship with me? I've only ever had one friend like that, and he had to move away two years ago. Maybe it's time for a new one.

What I can tell is that whatever Dylan wants, she's going to take a very direct approach in getting it. This means no awkward deciding whether I should invest time into her, or wondering if she likes talking to me too. No seeing her down the hallway, anticipating the walk by, and debating whether to smile, or pretend like I didn't notice her from the start. She wants to skip the intro and go straight to personal, like she said.

"I'll try to be straight with you, then," is all that I can come up with as a response. It seems to satisfy her however, for she continues with, "Well, then let's sit down. We can start the project later. We should talk."

The requirement of talking always makes it much harder to talk naturally, so I try to prepare myself. I don't want to disappoint, but I'm not sure what her expectations are because of how unusual this situation is. I can't tell if she's being mature or plainly weird. Or perhaps this is normal, and my life experiences so far have been sheltered. I can't tell which I'd prefer to be true.

I guess she meant that we'd both be sitting on her bed, for she grabs my wrist and pulls me over. Her hair bounces as she sits down with her knees to her chest, leaning up against the corner. I sit leaning on the adjacent wall to avoid direct eye contact. She has powerful eyes. They're big, and bright, and intimidating, as if they'll get inside my head if I'm not careful. But why do I have to be careful? Why does this feel like such an uncomfortable thing? It's just talking.

SHIT [3]

=

"So are you a virgin?" Dylan asks with a completely casual face, to which I reply with only the widening of my eyes. Seeing my intense hesitation, she adds, "It doesn't matter. You're not a slut if you've had sex and you're not a prude if you haven't. Just want to get that question out of the way because it's viewed pretty high on the totem pole of typical teenage curiosities."

I appreciate some of the pressure being lifted. "I've had sex," I answer at a minimum.

"Care to talk about it?" she asks, just as casually, but I still feel inclined. I don't exactly know what she wants me to elaborate on, so I keep it simple. "I was fifteen and dating a guy for a while, just seemed like the thing you do. Broke up a little later actually."

"Do you regret it?" she asks, and I start to feel like I'm being interviewed. I've never really thought of that before, so I reply, "I guess I don't."

"Did it mean a lot to you?" she asks after. Once again, I haven't given much thought on that either which just proves that no, I guess it didn't mean a lot to me, which is what I tell her.

She doesn't make an expression that reveals her opinion of my replies, but instead states, "Virginity is stupid. I think it's more of an idea than a penis up your vagina. Just gotta' be careful when you know you're not ready for a kid." She pauses then adds, "With love though, I bet it can be more than an act."

"I suppose you're right," is all I reply with an awkward tone and an expression somewhere between confused and uncomfortable. Usually I'm better

15

at this, but I don't expect the majority of what comes out her mouth, so I'm not fast to react.

However, If I had to take a stance, I would agree with her. What would you say about rape victims whose first time "having sex" was not under their consent? To say they lost their virginity to their rapist is a cruel bag they'd be forced to carry around for the rest of their lives. And I do suspect sex would be a wonderful thing if you truly had passion for your partner, but I don't predict I'll be experiencing that any time soon. Maybe it's something to look forward to.

Why didn't I reply with something like that?

"Where are you at with virginity, then?" I ask instead.

"Lost it a while ago, but not the first time I had sex." She takes "virginity" away from virginity and makes it look prettier.

"So when was it?" my curiosity compels me to ask.

"When I couldn't be a kid anymore," and without a pause she adds, "What kind of person are you, Junebug?" She directs the attention back to me.

I think about it for a while. "I'd say I'm the kind that's. . . mature enough to know how to live my life." That's the first thing that comes to mind, although I don't know what it means or if Dylan could view it as insulting.

"Good, because I'm the kind that's *immature* enough to know how *not* to live my life. Maybe that's the same thing."

Damn.

I open my mouth for a response but it's interrupted by the slamming of the upstairs door. It echoes in her room, and when I look back at Dylan, her face morphs from worry, to anger, to apology.

"I didn't think she'd be home this early, I'm sorry but you'll have to go," Dylan quickly says and hurries me up off her bed.

"What?" I desperately ask as I hastily grab my things, looking down the hallway when Dylan opens her door.

"I didn't think this would happen," Dylan says, still leaving me with absolutely no explanation as to why it's a bad thing that someone's home, but then I understand.

"Who the hell is in my house!?" comes an angry woman's voice ringing down from the top of the stairs. She must have seen my shoes.

"Fuck," says Dylan. "Just come up behind me and I'll let you leave."

What is happening? My stomach drops.

I hesitantly follow her up the stairs, not asking any questions. I immediately feel bad and embarrassed for being the one that the woman is addressing, and I'm dumbfounded at the fact that this meeting has managed to get even more unusual.

When we reach the top of the stairs, a woman, who I assume is Dylan's mother, is throwing her jacket and purse on the couch, waiting for us to approach. She looks old, but not with time. She's tall with long hair like Dylan's, and she has eyes that could kill.

"Did I ever say you could bring people here?" she asks slowly and quietly, like she's holding something in but with confidence.

"No," Dylan replies with hatred in her eyes but a relatively calm demeanor.

"Then why the fuck did you!?" she triumphs, voice as loud as a train, and makes a grab towards Dylan. Dylan dodges it, and before her mother can try again, she runs to the door as I quickly snag my shoes.

"You do not have the privilege of inviting people over!" her mother yells as she watches Dylan quickly open the door for me and my ungraceful departure from this horrifying encounter. I have a wrenching feeling in my stomach as I get one last look at this reproachful women who has abruptly interjected her hatred on a simple school-oriented meeting.

The door slams behind me as I run to my car. My backpack, half-open, slips off my shoulder and hangs like a purse in the middle of my arm while I fumble with my shoes. One drops to the ground. I stop running and turn around to face the house, still shocked at what just happened. As I breathe heavily and squint at the window, I get a glimpse of Dylan's hair being held tightly above her head while her mother administers a hard slap across Dylan's face. I am appalled.

I drop the rest of my belongings and contemplate going back – what I would do is not apparent to me, however. Time slows, a second becomes an hour, and I watch the incident of her mother's tight grip on Dylan's arms, and her face, inches from Dylan's, in a furious rampage of spitting words. Dylan struggles with her grip but fights back. She pushes her mother across the chest, and trips slightly as she makes it to the stairs.

My legs decide without consulting my mind, and I find myself back on her steps, wrenching on the doorknob. It's locked and I don't know what to do. I pound on the door, intending to yell, but nothing comes out. I tug on the handle a few more times, breathing hard, but no one comes to the door. I can't see or hear either of them, for her mother has followed Dylan down the stairs.

As I hurry back to my car, I get out my phone thinking I should call the police. She can't do that, that's her child, abuse, it's illegal!

I don't call. I don't know why.

I mindlessly start my car and drive fast, but not home. My mind is racing. Dylan and I are still strangers in my opinion, but I have never gotten the impression that she is anything but strong. Maybe this is why.

How long has this gone on? How bad has it gotten? Does anyone know? Where is her father? I need to know these things. I don't have her number. I don't know what to do.

After nearly twenty minutes of driving without a destination, and the repeating image of her mother's abuse flashing across my mind, I decide to go home. I can't tell my mom at the prospect that she'll get way too involved. I don't have all the details, and I have a strange feeling that this should remain a secret. But it shouldn't! This is not something you hide! Yet I can't bring myself to enter my mom's room and share with her the new-found story of a friend I barely know.

VENERABLE FUME [4]

=

The night fails me as I wrestle with my thoughts and my blankets. Finding a comfortable position proves to be an impossible task, and my unanswered questions consume me before I manage to fall into an uneven sleep.

At school, Monday morning, I don't spot Dylan throughout the time roaming the halls between classes. I half-expect not to see her in her desk upon entering World History, but as if life is completely normal, there she sits, slouching as always, in her scribbled desk. This time I know her hair really does hold secrets.

No one knows. No one can tell. There's little resemblance of anything relating to abuse because slaps don't typically bruise. I wonder if it's ever been worse. She still doesn't look belittled.

Throughout the class, she never once makes eye contact with me. When the bell finally rings, and I start to gather my things with intention to catch her at the door, I look up to find her standing at the end of my desk.

"Are you doing anything after school?" she asks, too casually.

"Uh," I stutter, "no, I. . . I guess I'm not."

"Good, take me somewhere?"

Take her somewhere? She's asking me to make up plans after she initiates them and after what happened at her house? I guess she doesn't know a lot of places here, but still, it feels odd.

"Ahh. . . sometimes I hang out in the Antique store downtown, could be nice." It's the first place I can think of that isn't full of people and can allow us space to talk (plus, they're cool ya' know, old things can be cool, people).

20

"Sounds good, I'll meet you on the stairs after the last bell," she informs me, and then turns and leaves with no further communication either verbally or through body language.

Two more periods of anxious anticipation.

I hate the school bell. It's as if they try to find the most obnoxious sound possible, yet they make us love hearing it, how ironic.

The stairs look too grand for our dismal school. It tries to be something it's not and ends up feeling pathetic.

I sit for five minutes on the steps, playing a game on my phone to make it look like I'm occupied. I then see Dylan push open the door with a blank stare, and she walks my way without waver in her pace, inciting me to get up and start walking with her to my car.

We get in with no words, and I start the engine. I don't know what to say and she doesn't acknowledge that this is weird, so I play music to fill the empty space.

I know it takes around eight minutes to get to the Antique store, so I estimate two songs can be played in that time. Now, Reader, I don't know about you, but I find it extremely satisfying to discover that someone likes the same music as me. Music says a lot about a person, so this is the first test of our compatibility. I know the two songs that are going to play because I have my Spotify connected to my radio: "Roll Me Away" by Jack Symes and "Water" by Jamaican Queens. They don't fit the mood, but it'll have to do.

However, I'm left disappointed. It's not as if I expected her to low-key sing along if she knew either of the songs, but throughout the drive, I received no feedback that indicated her opinion of my selections. *Encouraging.*

Once parked, I notice that there's only one other car in the lot, and it belongs to an elderly man who comes here often (therefore implying that I also must come here often in order for me to know that. Maybe that's lame, but I don't care). I know that this man won't come over in attempt to start a conversation like some old folks do, and for that, I appreciate him. I am generally a fan of old people, yet I fear to be one. Sidetracked.

We silently get out of the car, and as Dylan turns to look at the store, she comments, "Nice," and proceeds to walk with me to the door. The store is long and white, and you can tell just by looking through the windows that there isn't an inch inside that isn't covered.

Upon entering, the cashier looks up, smiles, and says, "Evening, June," pauses then adds, "and friend." I reply kindly with, "Nice to see you, Carl," and he gives me his signature old grin as I walk to the back of the store. I prefer to be out of observation, even here.

"You like old things?" I ask as we pass a case of necklaces I would never care to own.

"In moderation," she replies as she prods at a particularly old jewelry box. God, she really likes to make things stressful.

I start to get anxious. What if bringing her here was a stupid idea? I mean, it's not like antique stores are today's hot spot for teenagers looking for an after-school hangout. But whatever, right? She asked me to pick a place, and I did. If she doesn't like it she can find a new friend – but how can I say that after what happened at her house?

Too busy thinking, I don't realize that she had stopped a while back to pick up an acoustic guitar. I turn around and walk back down the narrow pathway, asking if she knows how to play.

"No." Pause. "My dad was teaching me, but it never progressed very far."

Her dad. She has a father, but where is he? He's civil enough to teach her to play the guitar, unlike her abusive mother. Do I ask about her father? Her life? Would you?

"I wish I could play an instrument," I offer as a continuation of the conversation, but she doesn't look up, just continues to strum some strings that vaguely resemble a possible rhythm. She looks sad, and I take advantage of that.

"Why didn't it progress very far?" I nervously ask. I finally receive her gaze and half-regret prying, but for once, she finally looks small.

"I moved here. . . because my dad died while working at a construction site." I stare into her eyes as the heavy weight of this news sinks in.

She continues, "My grandparents are dead, and my dad has no siblings, so I was sent to live with my mother. The kind and caring woman you encountered before," she remarks, sarcastically. "She agreed to take me into custody again because she knows I'll receive my father's inheritance, and I will, but not until I turn eighteen. I'm assuming she's hoping that she'll somehow get what I'll inherent, but there's no way in hell I'm letting her take it." She looks back down at the guitar. "No matter how many times she hits me."

I shouldn't be surprised at her willingness to tell me her story, because she did promise to be personal, but I'm taken aback as I try to process the severity of what she just said.

The sadness I had seen before turns back to her blank expression as I stumble in place. I don't know what to say, so I say what everyone says, "I'm really sorry to hear that." And I am, I say it sincerely, but I know it means nothing.

She continues to look down and declares she knows that I am, that everyone always is, but it is what it is and she doesn't want any pity. And in that case, I just won't show that I have any for her, but it's considerably inevitable with that kind of life.

The realization of the complexity of her situation makes me think. Why does everyone have a shitty life? Why is there one horrible story after the other, yet no one is expected to have one? You meet someone new and I bet the first thing you question isn't: *Wow, I wonder what's the worst thing that's ever happened to them.*

Wow, I bet their beloved dog for ten years had to be put down. Wow, I bet their boyfriend cheated on them, and now they have a hard time trusting new people. Wow, I bet they tore their ACL during the game before finals and didn't get to play the end of their Senior year. Wow, I bet their parents got a divorce, and after a childhood of fighting, they see them on alternate weekends. Wow, I bet they were put up for adoption and now must deal with the question of *why didn't they love me?* Wow, I bet their parents couldn't afford a house anymore so they rent a one room apartment while working two jobs. Wow, I bet they were molested as a child whenever their addict mother got a new boyfriend. Wow, I bet their sister got cancer and all their time and money went into a hopeless and painful search for a miracle. Wow, I bet after two suicide attempts they finally ended up in the mental hospital, but I assume they'll be dead from their own hands by the time they turn twenty. *Wow, I wonder.*

And do you want to know what baffles me most? The one in the mental hospital doesn't also have to be the one with a terrible life; they could be the one with the beloved dog that died, yet have a fucked-up brain that doesn't allow them to enjoy simple pleasures – making them envy that dog. What is that? What is right with any of that? Why does Dylan's dad die and in return she gets an abusive mother? Why don't I have a terrible life, but can still get sad for weeks at a time? Why haven't I responded to Dylan yet? Why does it look like they never dust in antique stores? Why in movies, does no one ever have to pee during the inconvenient times? Why do I keep asking questions?

Here's another, "Why haven't you reported your mother hurting you?" She puts the guitar down, stands, looks at me, and states, "Because I'm not taking the easy way out." She says it as if it would be cowardly to work on fixing that part of her life. I don't understand. I need to understand.

I decide right then to put aside my anxiety and do something without care. I grab her wrist and turn around, pulling, encouraging her to follow.

Often times I don't buy anything on my trips to this store, just enjoy the collections. So I bring her towards the back, past the typewriters and the assortment of old knives, the wooden chairs and vinyl records, the genius polaroid's and endless dust filled trinkets – all the way back to my favorite corner obtaining hundreds of monochromatic, no-pictures, no-hope-of-ever-being-sold books.

"Do you read?" I ask, assuming the answer is yes considering she had a stack of books in her room. And I'm right. "Of course," she states, but nothing else. I'll take that.

We sit down, backs against the wall, with a bookcase to our right and a small bathroom (that I doubt anyone notices for the lack of a sign or much light) to our left. I reach under the bookcase and pull out a little bowl that I render as my ash tray. After I use it, I always flush the remains down the toilet, so Dylan doesn't get an idea of what I'm doing until I reach into my jacket pocket and pull out my pack of Marlboro cigarettes.

"You smoke?" she asks, sounding surprised.

"Yeah, I do. Carl doesn't mind, he does too. And he doesn't have any smoke detectors in here because he figures if one thing were to catch fire then everything would, and there'd be no time to put it out. So he doesn't bother." After I receive a blank stare, I add, "Do you?"

She adjusts her position and replies, "I have." Pauses. "I typically smoke something else, though."

"Weed?" I ask, more as a statement.

"Yeah, have you ever?" she asks. I haven't, and I tell her that, but what I don't tell her is why I haven't because it's kind of embarrassing.

I have wanted to smoke weed, but I have no friends that do. I honestly don't know how to ask. Don't you typically know who smokes, who sells, and who does neither in your school? I have an idea, but I never figured out how to go about asking someone for pot. Do I flat out say it, or are there code words? Do I do it in person, or over Messenger? Then what do I do about meeting up with them? And I don't own a bowl or piece or whatever term they use, so there's that problem too. It's stupid I know, but I don't have the "connections," and I'm too awkward and unmotivated to try. I can get cigarettes because I have a friend who works at the gas station and doesn't card me, plus, I'm seventeen and can almost buy them legally, so what does it matter?

"Would you want to?" she asks without sounding forceful, which I appreciate.

"Would be nice to try," I concur.

"Well great, I'll take your virginity some time."

It makes me smile purely because I wasn't expecting her to phrase it that way. I pass her a cigarette, she accepts, and we light them.

I have always loved the soft, yet bright, burn of a cigarette: slowly watching it fall away, rolling back, proceeding color, long drag, french inhale, relaxation. However, I know that it's a false relaxation and an addictive killing device, yet I let it kill me because time is anyway. I know I shouldn't say that, and I do plan on quitting, but just not yet.

I let it rest in my mouth, occasionally breaking the corner seal of my lips to release the smoke. While doing so, I pick up a random blue covered book. It's titled *The Full of the Moon* by Caroline Lockhart. I have never seen it.

I open to a random page, take the cigarette out of my mouth, and read out loud in appropriate voices:

"'Mr. White is so anxious that you should have a class in the Sunday School, Nan, and I'd do it to please him. Of course after you are married he can't expect you to give quite so much of your time to church work but at present there's no reason why you can't take them. They are nice little boys and they adore you.' Mrs. Galbraith fastened a glove clasp and surveyed the result. 'Nice little boys!' exclaimed her daughter with heat. 'They are little devils. Don't I know them?' 'Nan!' reprovingly. 'Imps, then, if it sounds better, but I mean devils.'"

I take another drag and look at Dylan. She looks back with a questioning yet intrigued expression.

"Hand me a book," she says. I exhale. She inhales.

There's no doubt that smoking suits her aesthetic. She holds it like an accessory, like she picked it out and it's doing its job, so she knows she can disregard it. The smoke gently rolls out of her mouth and up past her lips, making slow turns around the contours of her face, and eventually dispersing in the air. She fully exhales as I pass her a book, also unknown to me, titled *The Man Who Was Thursday: A Nightmare* by G.K. Chesterton.

She opens to random pages and reads:

"'I seem to remember only centuries of heroic war, in which you were always heroes-epic on epic, Iliad on Iliad, and you always brothers in arms. Whether it was but recently (for time is nothing), or at the beginning of the world, I sent you out to war. I sat in the darkness, where there is not any created thing, and to you I was only a voice commanding valour and an unnatural virtue. You heard the voice in the dark, and you never heard it again. The sun in heaven denied it, the earth and sky denied it, all human wisdom denied it. And when I met you in the daylight I denied it myself...But you were men. You did not forget your secret honour, though the whole cosmos turned an engine of torture to tear it out of you.'"

I'm jealous of her fluent reading ability, how one word casually flows into the next. She then looks at me, and I look back.

"Junebug," she once again addresses me with my officially assigned nickname, "you have an odd sort of entertainment," her pause - that I'd now classify as a mannerism, "Thank you for letting me be a part of it."

I smile and lightly laugh, for it flatters me. I take the last drag of my cigarette, say, "Sure thing, Dylan," press the remains in my rendered ashtray, and am captivated by its smolder.

BLANKET PROTECTION [5]

=

I take her home afterwards, or rather, I regrettably take her back to the dreadful place she's forced to call "home." We didn't talk further about the importance of her situation, just trivial topics, which I suppose were unconventional, yet significant after review – probably because I've never talked about them before. I guess it just takes a new person.

Tuesday comes and I have to work after school. It's also the last day Dylan and I have to do our History project because we've procrastinated, so we plan to meet at my house at 8:00.

My job for over a year now has been at the local movie theater. It's a job that has perks but is still a minimum wage job. Most of the people are great, the endless free popcorn is awesome, and I get paid for doing very little for hours.

After the usual, manageable rush (unless a huge movie like the umpteenth *Star Wars* comes out, making it a bit more unmanageable) of show times and minimal required cleaning afterwards, there's the two hour long waiting period of free time while those movies are running. That means that I get paid to either stand, talk with my coworkers, consume the concessions, or even do some homework if time permits. However, if you're like me, standing with one other person in a small area with no objectives can sometimes get uncomfortable, and it subjects me to more anxiety than I'd like. But the obvious benefits of some good friends and unlimited amount of free movies, are enough to keep me at the job.

On this particular day, I find it difficult to pretend like I care about the establishment because, again, I'm nervous to see Dylan. I wonder when the nervousness will subside, it's the annoying "friend" who can't take a hint.

7:38 and I get to go home.

Once getting there, I tell my mom my plans. Her only commentary is, "Okay," in her typical *sounds good, do whatever* tone of voice. My mom has always been lenient towards my everyday actions (although she doesn't directly know any illegal activity I partake in, such as smoking) and I've always appreciated it. As a sum, she's the mom of all moms.

After I quickly toss any obvious ailments to a clean room into my closet, the doorbell rings, and I notice there's no car in the driveway. When I let Dylan in, I ask why that is.

"I don't have one," she plainly states.

"Well, did your mom drop you off?" I ask even though it feels uncomfortable addressing her mother in relation to typical motherly actions.

"No, I walked."

Well, now I feel like shit. I could have given her a ride, and I tell her that, but she pushes it aside as if it were nothing. She tries to convince me that it's no big deal, when really, she lives nearly an hour away, walking distance. I don't understand why she didn't ask for one, and I make it clear that I'll be giving her a ride from now on. She gives a hesitant agreement.

We make it to my room, and I can't help but feel self-conscious based on the clear contrast of my room to hers. Mine is painted light blue with an organized desk and a half-assed, made bed. I have very few objects hanging on my wall besides a string of Christmas lights I mantled around my bed frame. I have a worn, carpet floor and white appliances with a standard, nightstand lamp. I wonder what it says about me.

I turn on the Christmas lights and my lamp because I prefer that over my obnoxious ceiling light. I tell Dylan we can sit on my bed and suggest my plan on approaching the project.

I'm not going to bore you with the details of the assignment, they don't matter. What does matter is that when I ask Dylan what type of music she wants to listen to, she replies, "Anything alternative." I'm relieved at the potential of us having a similar taste in music, so I simply hit shuffle on my saved Spotify songs, and we start our project.

We're about halfway through and our conversation topics have been limited to our class. I can tell by my inability to focus on what I'm reading that I want that to change. However, stuck in cycle of not knowing boundaries or which ones to push, I struggle to form sentences. So, let me paint the scene: "17" by Youth Lagoon is muffling out of my speakers, and our books are tinted blue from my lights overhead. The music fills the empty space in the room, so the moment feels more profound as we're "diligently" working. At a glance, no one would be able to tell that my mind is anywhere but on my project (that's the beauty of thought).

Reader, I will periodically inform you of the music that plays in the background of these moments (or the music that I wish was playing) because that's the closest I can get to you hearing them. I will do this because I believe that music is essential to a story. Everything we do seems amazingly more significant if it has a soundtrack. Isn't that the reason why when we're little and in a car while it's raining and a slow song is playing, we rest our head on the window and pretend we're in a sad movie? Isn't that why we add music to our picture slideshows at graduation parties? Isn't that why we listen to the type of music that reflects the mood we're in? I mean, listen to "A Punk" by Vampire Weekend while observing your joyous, energetic sports team on a bus ride home after a win. Or lose yourself in "Kettering" by The Antlers when ya' just wanna' not.

I'm sorry that we're restricted to the mere, silent voice in your head. It's "17" that gives me the encouragement to even initiate this topic to Dylan, so it's important that I include it with gratitude, and paint the scene that forces books to envy movies.

"Dylan?" I get her attention.

"Yeah?" She doesn't look up from her textbook. I don't want to be rude or put her in a bad mood, but I know that after this project is done, there's no guarantee that I'll be seeing Dylan outside of school again. I'm starting to hope that I will. If I want to get a serious discussion in, I better seize my opportunity of required time together, so I get right to the point.

"How long has your mother been abusive?" I hesitantly question. I don't think she was expecting me to ask something serious, but it doesn't surprise her enough to get her to look up at me. She continues to stare down at her History book, as if it were actually interesting, and ponders over my question for a while.

The silence is long. Have I overstepped?

Right as I'm questioning whether or not she'll even reply, she finally develops an answer and states, "Ever since I was little." She glances to the side, trying to recall her childhood, and her expression never wavers from firm. She finally makes eye contact and continues with, "My dad was so pathetically in love with her that he was constantly in denial of her mental state. I've never understood love like that. She'd come home and drink until the sun set, and then she'd get angry and abuse my dad. He always sent me to bed, but what's a kid supposed to do when all they can hear is their parents fighting in the next room over?"

Her tone suggests no sadness, and she speaks as casually as if she were reading from the textbook in her hands. Her attitude reveals no such thing as a troubled past, but her words and her body language make up for it. By the contradiction of her words to their meaning, I can't decipher what she considers her life to be. A sad story? A fictional tale? Insignificant? Ordinary? Simply just life?

She continues, "My mother only really hit me a couple times back then. My dad was a good protector. And when I turned fourteen he finally got the balls to leave her. We had a simple life until he died, and now I'm here."

My level of curiosity has never been an equal match to my level of well-developed responses. I decide to look into her eyes and mimic her trivial tone. "You got dealt a shit hand, and I can't help but apologize."

She looks down and I think something changes; she doesn't seem like such a robot with her emotions anymore. She purses her lips, makes eye contact again, and says, "I appreciate your intentions. . . . I forget that a shitty life is supposed to hurt. I guess I just hate admitting it."

"I admire your ability to push it aside," I confess. "Not many people can."

"The other options didn't seem too appealing," she replies. "Might as well deal with what I've got and suck it up. Things will be different someday, and that's what I'm counting on."

I can't tell if she thinks "different" means better by the tone of her voice, but it's clear that she's certain of it, whatever it is.

"How are you going to deal with your mother, then?" I ask, in search of a summary or plan that I can interpret as closure on the topic.

"I'm just going to live with her, deal with her shit, try not to piss her off, spend as much time as possible out of the house, and wait it out until I turn eighteen. Then I'll graduate and move away, never letting her get any of the money that I'll receive from my dad." She seems confident in her plan, and I reply, "I hope that I can help you achieve some of that," to give the impression that continuing this project-oriented friendship would be something that I'd condone. I figure if I take more initiative between the two of us, I'll feel more confident when we're together. Maybe the "friend" will finally get the hint.

"I'd love the help," she smiles, and I return one, and then she asks if I've finished the profile on Edward III, and I tell her I have, so we move on.

I come to the conclusion that she has her situation under control, and she wouldn't appreciate me being constantly concerned. I tell myself that the only way I'll get involved is if she asks, or if the abuse is even more severe.

Am I a bad person for not reporting this? Would you?

At this age, it feels as though we can handle our own lives; that confiding in our parents would be near insane; that it wouldn't be our life if we didn't face it alone. I can't make an adequate judgment on if that's right or not – because that's something you figure out when you're older – but I know that Dylan's life should remain a secret. Secret in the sense that it's hidden in plain sight, so that maybe I won't feel so bad when people realize it was simply overlooked. At that point, who's to blame?

Once we finish our presentation, I ask if she would like a ride home. It's 10:11. I'm slightly surprised at her reaction as she hesitates to respond and fiddles with her fingers like she's anxious.

"Actually. . . I was kinda' wondering if it'd be okay if I slept here tonight," she says, cautious about making eye contact. "It's just that. . . my mom was on her second drink when I left, and I don't really want to see how far she got."

I feel a surge of anger regarding her mother's decision to put her own daughter in such a situation. I repress it to kindly tell Dylan that it's entirely reasonable, and that she can spend the night. She's grateful, but in a casual way.

It then dawns on me of what I've just agreed to. My stomach drops as I realize I now have to direct the night. I find her some sweatpants to change into and point her to my bathroom. I've rarely had a friend spend the night on a school night, so I'm anxious about what's expected to happen. Are we supposed to stay up talking or doing something? Do we go to bed right away? I don't know what time she normally sleeps. I usually sit on my phone for an hour or two before I even try to sleep. What if the light from my phone annoys her?

I hope she gives me some input.

Once she comes back from changing, I give her the options of sleeping on the floor or bed. Of course, she picks the floor. Who wouldn't pick floor out of courtesy? I suppose I asked merely to feel less guilty about sleeping in my bed while she's on the floor; people do strange things to gain comfort with their emotions.

I gather miscellaneous pillows and blankets from around the house and fix a nice little nest that I present as her dwelling area for the night. She thanks me and hops in.

I start to feel uncomfortable about the absence of objectives to complete. Presumably, there's nothing left to do but sleep or potentially talk, so I decide to go to the bathroom to gain some time to think about it.

A routine that I insist upon is to pee before I commit to my room for the last time, but when I sit down, I start to feel self-conscious about the possibility of her hearing me pee. It's pathetic, I know, but I run the faucet while I go. Have you ever done that? I want to know that I'm not entirely lame. But If it is true that Dylan can hear me peeing, then it's likely that she can also hear the water running. In which case, she must consider the pattern of water-flush-water to be strange. *Or*, she's a normal human being and doesn't pay attention to the noises coming from the bathroom, considering it's kind of creepy to do that in the first place. Maybe it's just me that worries about this, but what can I do, I'm awkward and pee shy.

After I get over that mess, I realize I haven't even thought about what this stalling is meant for, so I quickly decide that I will ask a question about the presentation if it starts to get uncomfortable with Dylan. I hope it goes well from there.

I return to my room, and before I can decipher the ambiance, I see that Dylan is holding a book that was previously resting on my nightstand. The book is titled *Get to Know Yourself: 300 Thought Provoking Questions*, which is exactly what the title says: a book filled with three hundred questions, some lines to answer them, and some notes regarding your answers.

"This is cool," she states as she flips through the pages.

Out of all the questions I've only answered about a dozen of them. I meant to answer more, but I'm usually not in the mood when I get into bed. In which case, I don't know why I keep it on my nightstand.

Nevertheless, I'm relieved that she started the dialogue and I reply, "Yeah, I got it as a gift. It's a good way to learn conversation starters."

"Or awkward situation fillers," she smirks, which implies that she's acknowledging the fact that this has the potential of being weird if we don't initiate something, so she flips to a random page and reads the printed question.

"Question two fifty-six, '*Do you have a recurring dream, and if so, what is it?*'" She then looks up at me, waiting for an answer.

"Oh. . . um, yeah I do actually. I haven't had it in a long time, and it's very short, but I remember it. Um," I make it to my bed and sit down, "I was at a house where people were doing construction, I don't know why, but I would walk into the garage to look around. I saw these weird, bright, blue-green flies, and I'd follow them to a piece of plywood that was resting up against the wall. Then I'd pull back the wood and there'd be a mountain lion just sitting there, minding its own business. And that was it."

Dylan seems mildly surprised, and I'm glad she started with an easy one so I can work my way into more pressing questions. I still don't want to disappoint, and it seems she expects something of me, I just don't know what yet.

"Wow, I have no idea what that means," she says and hands me the book, stating that it's my turn. I, too, turn to a random page and read, "Question ninety-eight, '*Would you be willing to give up the luxury of socks for three years, if it meant you could have any job you wanted for the rest of your life?*'"

"Hmm. . . I can't say I enjoy cold feet, but I bet I could cope," she answers.

"But what about when you have to wear shoes? That just feels gross," I point out.

"Any job I wanted," she quotes. "I think I'd do it."

"I guess I would too," I concur and pass the book back.

"Alright, number two-oh-four, '*If someone you love was murdered, and you were given the opportunity to kill the one who did it, would you do it?*'"

How much do I really know about myself? I think for a second and can only reply with, "I think I would need to get revenge, but I'm not sure I'd be able to flat-out kill them. I'd probably be convinced I could do it until I was face to face with them. How about you?" I ask.

"I'd at least severely injure them, like the type of injury that prevents them from getting a job, and they'd spend all their money on medical bills, and it'd ruin their life. I think that'd be even worse," she says, sounding absolute.

"I admire your determination. I'd like to see what type of injury you'd be choose to inflict."

"I'll let you know if it ever happens," she jokes. "Now read another."

I blindly flip the pages and land on one ninety-two. "*If you embarrass yourself, does it bother you to be laughed at?*'" I'm curious about what her answer will be, but I bet I already know what it is: it wouldn't bother her because her hard shell – built from her mother's abuse – can also protect against critical judgment, but I'm not entirely right.

"I hate the fact that people would laugh, but not because I'd be embarrassed or hurt by their opinions, but because of human indecency." I give her a look to continue. "I don't understand why we have to judge people or care that they've embarrassed themselves. It's pointless and cruel."

"I completely agree, but it's inevitable that we'll be judged, either intentionally or not. So really, I just wish I didn't care what they thought," I give my input.

"It's easy, Junebug, you just simply *not care*," she tells me this as if saying "simply" actually made it simple. She continues, "They only laugh because whatever you did was deemed unnatural, but really, if everyone does unnatural things, then it's pretty natural to do them, don't you think? And if they had the audacity to make you feel bad for it, then they really don't deserve your worry because they're probably a dick."

She has a point, but changing my thought process is simply unrealistic, so I sarcastically reply, "Oh yeah, I'll remember that next time."

"You should, Junebug! Things will change," she assures me.

"Okay, sure." I fake a grin and toss her the book. She leans back in her nest, rests her feet up on my bed, and reads, "Twenty-three, '*Have you ever detested someone for being more successful than you?*'"

"Only if they're like self-centered, narcissistic, or snotty about it. If they worked hard and deserve what they have, then no, but if they've been handed everything and don't appreciate it or know what it means, then yes."

"Well said. I agree," she says and turns the pages again.

"One fifteen, '*Do you believe in ghosts? Could you spend a night, alone, in a deserted house that is said to be haunted?*'"

"Oh, no, definitely not."

"No to which question?" she asks.

"About staying in the house, I'm too much of a wimp. I don't know if there are ghosts and shit, but even if there wasn't, I'd let my mind get to me and be scared shitless."

And Reader, I don't care if that makes me sound pathetic, how many of you would actually do that, regardless of your beliefs?

She laughs. "Ya' wuss."

"What!?" I exclaim, wide-mouthed and playfully defensive. "Don't tell me you'd stay in a big house, alone, in the middle of nowhere, that's supposedly haunted."

"Well, would I get a blanket?"

"What?" I question. How is that relevant? But I answer, "I would presume you could bring a blanket, yes. Why?"

"I'm a firm believer in blanket protection. If I had a blanket, I bet I could remain calm enough to stay there a night," she claims.

"Seriously?" I question her logic.

"Yes!" She laughs. "You know how when you're a kid and you're scared in your room, and you hide under your blanket?"

"Well, yeah, but that doesn't actually keep you safe." (Yet I still do that today.)

"Let me finish," she continues. "Every time I did that, I convinced myself that I was protected, that nothing could get me if I was under my blanket, and did anything ever get me? No. No fake creature I've ever been afraid of has come and got me in the night while I was under a blanket. I know it's stupid, but considering there is a flawless reputation for blankets, it has continuously instilled my belief in them. I'd create the illusion that I was safe if I had a blanket in that house."

"You're crazy."

"Yes, but it works. Now if there really are ghosts, and they did come for me, I'd be screwed and my blanket protection would be ruined, so I guess I'd just hope they were nice ghosts."

She grins at the pleasant thought of nice ghosts, and I compliment her illusion and ask for the book.

"My turn, question one sixty-four, '*What's your biggest insecurity?*'"

She replies instantly with, "My eyes. They're too far apart."

"Na' ah." I take a second to examine her eyes. "I promise, I have never once thought that," I assure her.

"Well, if you look close enough, they are," she says, undoubtedly. She then adds, "And my mouth. It's too big."

"Now you must be joking," I insist.

"Well, maybe I meant what comes out of it," she slyly suggests. "How about you?"

I think it over, but I can't pick one. "Can I just say my face in general?"

"No, because then everyone would just say that."

"Well, fine, then my ears because they're also too big."

She glances at my ears. "I think they're cute."

I can feel them turn red, and I don't know how to reply, so my face gets awkward and I try to say thanks as I flip to a different page. "Two seventy-seven, '*Whose death would most affect you?*'" She pauses to think about it, so I answer right away, because I assume my response isn't as personal. "I'd say my mother, but I know you wouldn't."

"Yeah no, I would have said my dad, but ya' know – so I guess I'd have to pick my two best friends, Tate and Tanner. I had to leave them when I moved here, but we'll never not be friends. I bet they'll come visit me at some point. Maybe you'll have to meet them."

"That'd be nice," I say but secretly feel a jump of anxiety at the idea of meeting people who are, presumably, much like Dylan. I move on by asking another question: "Number two twenty-one, *'What has been your best and worst experience with drugs or alcohol?'*"

"Ooo, care for a longer story?" she asks with an answer already in mind.

"Of course," I assure her.

"Okay then I'll start with my worst. It was a long time ago, I was fourteen or fifteen maybe, somewhere around there. Anyway, me, my two friends that I just mentioned, Tate and Tanner, and two other friends at the time, not really important, were going up to Tanner's mom's house that she got with her new husband."

I nod to reinforce that I'm listening.

"We went up with Tate's parents, and we drove in their little RV. It was really pretty up there, and it was one of the first big trips I'd ever had with my friends, so we were pumped. We did stupid things like wrestling in the grass and light fireworks. It got to be late and all the adults were in the garage and front yard, drinking. The cool thing was that they let us drink, so we all filled a cup. It wasn't hard liquor, but I was still excited considering it was one of the first times I actually got to drink, and the situation had absolutely nothing to do with my mother.

"As time passed, it rained and we danced in it, had a fire, walked around, drank some more. It didn't get bad until us kids decided to go inside to watch a movie. Halfway through, we saw Tanner's mom crying as she passes the room. It took a while to know what was going on, but eventually we figured out that Tanner's stepfather was drunk on Jack Daniels, the kind of drink that made him angry and destructive. He started smoking cigarettes around the house and pushing Tanner's mom around. We were forced to go outside, and the last thing I remember before everything was chaos, was the stepfather grabbing a hold of Tanner's oldest sister and throwing her out the door and onto the concrete steps.

"Tanner then decided to run. I really don't know why, but he ran forever into a big field, and we ran after him, but couldn't catch him. It was dark and he was gone, so we returned to the RV to stay while the adults tried to figure things out.

"The stepfather was inside with all the doors locked. The problem was that they had a safe full of guns in the house, and no one knew what he'd do, so someone called the police.

"By that point, Tanner had come back crying, and his little sister was having a panic attack. His oldest sister explained that after she saw that their stepfather was going after their mom, she pulled a knife on him. He got her against the wall, blocked the knife, and threw her outside.

"They calmed her down and we all waited in the RV with Tate's father. He was buff and was trying to take care of the situation. The police eventually showed up, and everyone came to their fricken senses and realized that letting the kids drink was illegal, and they were doing breathe tests. We literally had to hide in the camper as they tested some other kids who were there who hadn't been drinking. We got really lucky, and after some more time, the stepfather left the house, and although we didn't know where he went, we were able to go back inside.

"We tried to sleep, but Tanner couldn't. We found out that his stepfather had slept in his car overnight, and then he came back the next morning to apologize sincerely. He swore he'd never drink like that or be abusive again. The funny thing is, we actually went out on the lake tubing with him that day like nothing had happened. It was fun. It's crazy to think about that now, though."

She finally looks back at me. She had been in a different place while telling the story.

"I'm sorry if I didn't explain that well. It was just awful for one of my first experiences with drinking. Didn't stop me from doing it again though, I guess."

The whole time I have been listening intently as she fell deep into her memory. I reassure her that there's no need to apologize and that that sounded like a traumatic time. I silently wonder what it means for me to never have had an experience like that. Although it's certainly not something to hope for, I can't help but wish that I was able to tell a story with an equivalent shock factor. But ignoring my internal contradiction, I tell her that I'm glad she shared the story with me.

"Of course," she replies. "I'll always answer a question."

"Well, then what was your best experience?" I ask, excited to hear something positive.

"That one's short and easy. It was again Tate, Tanner, and I, but this time at my house with my mom out of the picture. We were in my room with the TV on in bed. We took pills and were simply talking. I felt light and heavy at the same time. We were purely and plainly happy," she reflects.

"Pills are kind of serious," I say, half-concerned about how far she's ever gone with opioids. I would hate to find out that she takes after her mother and has an addiction.

"I know, so we don't take them often. They're just nice once in a while."

"I wouldn't know," I truthfully state, and am relieved to hear that she scarcely abuses them.

"Would you like to?" she asks, not sounding forceful, just curious.

"I'm really not sure."

"No worries. I wouldn't pressure you into anything, but if you do ever want to explore, I'm the friend to call."

I look down and give her a pleased nod, and she laughs and adds, "Guess it's official now," she smirks and waits for me to look back up at her, "We're friends. You can finally stop worrying about it."

Oh god, she addressed my anxiety which makes me even more awkward. I feel my face turning red, but I smile and play it off with, "Yeah, yeah, good to know," and we continue passing the book back and forth until I vaguely hear, "Question two sixteen. . ." and my eyes start to stare at the backs of their lids.

UNNECESSARY NECESSITIES [6]

=

I feel bad for falling asleep on Dylan, but I find her completely out when my alarm goes off at 5:59.

I reach over and slip on my glasses (I only wear them at night and in the morning because they look hideous on me) and am jealous of what I see. Dylan looks peaceful with her face nestled in an old square quilt and covered with surrounding pillows. She doesn't look ugly at all; she looks utterly normal.

When I sleep, my mouth hangs open, I snore, manage to drool all over the place, and I never stay still. I really hope she didn't see me like that before she fell asleep, but I would never ask if she had or not. Instead, I drowsily drag myself out of bed and wiggle her shoulder a few times to get her to wake up.

After the fourth time trying, she realizes what I'm doing and is slightly frightened upon coming to her senses and being in an unfamiliar setting. She takes a moment to gather herself and slowly stands up.

"You okay to go home?" I ask as she finds her original pants.

"Yeah, just a second."

I expect her to head to the bathroom to change, but it appears that our new status as 'friends' gives her verification to change right in front of me.

She has on blue underwear, and her legs are surprisingly as tan as the rest of her body. She does a hop-skip into her jeans, and states, "Okay, ready. My mom should've already left for work by the time I get home."

Instead of commenting on her confidence to change in front of me, I direct her to my car and take her home. Luckily, there's no sight of her mother upon reaching her house, so I head back home and get ready for school, but this time, a little more diligently.

Today is our presentation day, so I'm more nervous than usual when walking into class. Because, like most people, I prefer not to stand in front of a bunch of peers and talk about something I've just made while also keeping in mind the overbearing do's and don'ts of presenting, which are as follows:

- If you have note cards, use them! But don't use them *too* much.
- If you have a slide show, don't read the slides word for word.
- In fact, don't read them at all.
- Memorize everything.
- Make relentless eye contact, but try to ignore the fact that everyone is staring at you.
- Don't sweat.
- Don't shake.
- Don't make repetitive movements or pace.
- But don't stand completely still.
- Be natural, but also be very proper, and use elevated language that you would never use in normal situations.
- Don't talk too loudly, too quietly, too fast, or too slow.
- But don't forget to talk.
- While managing all this, also remember to watch the clock because there is usually a time requirement.
- And last but not least, know your shit because if you don't the teacher and your peers will know, and all the previous pressures will be for absolutely nothing, and you'll be disappointed, embarrassed, and sad.
- Oh, but "have fun with it!"

As you can tell I have a huge bias against presentations, but surprisingly, it's not because I'm bad at presenting. I'm actually pretty good at it, and have

45

never received a bad grade on one. However, this is because of one reason and one reason only: I am terrified of doing poorly.

I study the shit out of what I need to say. I make a slightly-better-than-average slideshow (so it looks like I'm trying, but not trying too hard), and I suppress my nervousness into my chest, so that my heart is beating faster than a freight train, but you can't actually tell that I'm majorly freaking out. I've perfected the art.

Once I'm done, I have one problem that I don't know if anyone else can relate to: I can't, for the life of me, remember anything I just said. Do you have this problem? I'm left sitting in my desk as the next nervous person dreadfully trogs their way to the front, trying to recall if I hit all of my bullet points. I'm left convincing myself that I must have, otherwise I wouldn't always receive a good grade. But honestly, I have no idea, so I sit back and try to enjoy the fact that I'm done presenting, but for some reason, I'm never relieved.

And yet, here's the real kicker: everything I just said doesn't actually matter because while you're presenting, your audience is only half-listening and half-caring because they're sitting there, just as anxious as you were, trying to go over their lines in their head and mentally making sure they don't forget anything. So basically, everyone is on the same level and no one should have to worry about presenting. But that's also bullshit, so who knows?

What I do know is that it's our turn, so Dylan and I trek to the front of the room and find our presentation.

Due to our previous conversation about Dylan not caring what people think of her, I expect her to be calm while talking, and she is, and so am I. I mean, at least on the outside.

Once we're done and receive the mandatory, awkward clapping, we both agree that we hate presenting, and we watch the next people hate presenting.

The day is easy from there on out, so I find it appropriate to now fast forward.

As you can see, Dylan and I are starting to manifest into normal friends, doing normal friend thing. Dylan becomes my carry-on luggage on the trip to surviving the struggle of everyday life. Or rather, I become her luggage, for she is often the one in control of what we do. Mind you, it's not because we are cheap that we don't check our bags, but because we prefer to keep our luggage close.

The best friend I had before Dylan, unfortunately moved away. His name is Oliver and today we converse only once in a while, but every time we do it's as if we were never not talking. Needless to say, we are still great friends, but I never made a new best friend since he moved – only acquaintances or friends that don't actually hang out one on one. So the reason behind the entire beginning of this chapter is to officially establish that Dylan has now taken that place. She's a friend that does all the trivial, unnecessary to mention, things that normal best friends do together.

For instance:

- Watch TV/movies for hours while on and off talking
- Find hair tutorials and attempt to do them on each other
- Find cooking tutorials and make a huge mess
- Play video games and playfully become very mad at one another
- Have dork ass *Harry Potter* marathons
- Eat a lot of food
- Find new places even though I've lived here for seventeen years
- Go to the store together because independent shopping is scary
- Help each other on homework assignments (a.k.a. copy homework assignments)
- Go to free movies
- Go to the Antique store
- Go to the lake
- Go Anywhere because we're bored

Although these things are indeed sublime, they would make for a very boring story. But I would like you to know, Reader, that no matter how many stories you hear about people's lives that are amazing, inspirational, wildly fulfilling, or meaningful, they all include these uneventful yet essential moments that make up the majority of life. Movies never show the boring parts but that's only because they need our attention for two hours. I consider these moments very important to a friendship, and now that Dylan is officially that friend to me, I can skip ahead to the things that hopefully sustain your attention, and give me a reason to write any of this in the first place.

(What better way to describe the simplicity of coexisting with someone than the casual use of Snapchat?)

HOW HIGH ARE YOU? [7]

=

I'm going to start with my first time smoking pot.

For some reason, the event of me smoking weed has moved itself up to the top of my *Need To Do To Be Cool* list, but I hate admitting that. I suppose it's because of the people who make a big deal about it, as if it's some sort of milestone that everyone needs to experience, like getting your license or having sex. I feel pressure from movies and peers, but the biggest persuasion is actually Dylan. She never verbally encourages me to smoke, but I don't fancy being sober while she's seeing the world in a different light, so I join in.

To set the scene, I'm accompanied by Dylan while sitting in my car at the parking lot of a deserted baseball field/park. Despite us being the only people here, it being dark out, and the fact that I've never even seen this park before, I'm still nervous about someone showing up.

I'm also nervous about this being my car. Dylan packs the bowl and it's as if she has a can of air freshener labeled "WEED" and decided to spray it on everything. It amazes me how quickly my car is filled with its distinct smell. I guess that's why stoners are always so easy to identify. That and the fact that smoking seems to be the only topic they know how to talk about. I'm being stereotypical however, I do know druggies who get straight A's and manage a respectable life. I'd want to be that kind of stoner, if any.

I relax a bit when Dylan pulls out an actual can of air freshener labeled "BREEZY UNDERSEA." I've never understood where they come up with those names.

"You want to take the first hit? Greens are the best," she asks, holding out the bowl.

"Um, I'm good. You can. . . thanks though," I reply, nervous about what to expect.

Dylan then puts the bowl to her lips and lights the greens. She inhales, inhales again, and then finally lets out a line of foggy smoke that reinforces the displeasing smell.

"See? It's easy, just like smoking a cigarette, just remember to hold the carb."

"Hold the what?" I feel stupid asking.

She smiles and says, "The hole on the side, hold it when it's lit." She passes it over and I ask her not to watch. She playfully makes fun of me, but agrees not to. I then put the end of the bowl to my lips and think about how many germs must be on it from anyone else who's toked from it.

I look down as I light it and see the green turn to bright orange and then to black as the flick on my lighter diminishes. As I inhale, I realize the second reason, after the smell, of why you should be secretive if you smoke: you will cough so much that bystanders would think you need an ambulance.

"Holy shit," I manage to get out in between coughs, "Do you have something to drink?"

I think the whole situation makes her happy. She laughs at everything I do, like she's teaching me a new skill and I'm clumsy and making mistakes. I hope for a day that she's not superior.

She reaches into her bag that held the air freshener and pulls out a bottle of soda. I thank her, manage to get a couple of swallows down, and ask what else she has in her bag.

"All the essentials," she replies as she pulls out a bottle of tea, the grinder she had used earlier, a little carrying case for all things drugs, a bag of Doritos, some perfume, a little notebook, some pens and pencils, a couple of double A batteries, her phone charger, wallet, headphones, a pair of socks, a bag of Jolly Ranchers, some basketball shorts, and finally a small brown cow figurine.

"Jesus dude, it's like you've got Hermione's never-ending bag over there, and why the cow?"

She frowns and replies, "Did you really just make a *Harry Potter* reference?"

"Yes," I answer with no shame.

She rolls her eyes. "Tanner stole me this cow when he was wasted at some convenience store one night. I don't know what's so convenient about a cow, but I've kept it with me since I've moved."

"Well, do you really like cows or why did he steal you that?"

"He's a vegetarian, so I bet he was trying to give me shit about eating meat. I think he did it so I'd have a reminder of the cute things I enjoy 'killing.'"

She did the air quotes, and I laugh and pass back the bowl because I know it's some kind of unspoken rule of not taking two hits in a row when sharing weed – not that she would care, however.

"When do you think I'll meet them?" I ask, more as a timescale for when I need to prepare myself rather than simply being curious.

"I've been talking with them and they said probably in early summer, around my birthday. They need to save up a bit more so they can stay as long as they want."

I then realize that if they do come down, there would be no way in hell that Dylan's mother would allow them stay at her house, so I ask what their plan will be when they come. She says they'll probably stay in a motel. That will cost a lot of money for teenagers; they must really value their friendship together. I admire that.

Dylan takes another hit and passes it back to me. She exhales out the window without coughing a single time.

"When does the coughing go away?" I ask.

"Depends on the person, you'll be alright."

"Speak. . ." another coughing attack, "for yourself."

We spend another fifteen minutes in the car, and by this time it's obvious that I'm feeling the effects. My chest is tight but everything else is very loose. Dylan had told me that I may not be affected considering it's my first time, but I'm certainly far from normal.

I become intensely focused on the one thing I happen to be doing and nothing else. It's very easy to forget what I'm doing the second after I do it, so I find myself talking way more than I usually do because I don't have a good sense of time. I think Dylan is finally satisfied with my level of participation and carefree demeanor. Everything becomes more humorous than I would have thought sober, and everything that I enjoy sober feels even better.

"Obstacles" by Syd Matters fills the car, and I experience a new feeling of riding the music. I can feel it tingle through every inch of my body, and when I close my eyes, I'm immersed into that world. I can listen to any music and it has the same effect on me. Next is "White Ferrari" by Frank Ocean, and I'm everywhere his words are.

I suddenly want to taste something.

"Could I have a blue Jolly Rancher?" I ask Dylan.

"But they're my favorite and they never put as many blue ones in the bag."

"But you love me," I plead like a child.

She sighs, but it's enough to convince her to give me one.

If food tasted this good normally, I'd be obese.

You know, I've never understood the flavor "blue raspberry." Raspberries aren't blue. My theory is that they already had cherry and watermelon, so someone was like, "Man, there's too many red colors, people won't be able to tell them apart without reading. You know what we should do? We should make it blue! People like blue, and it'll stand out over all others. Man, I'm so smart," and that's just how it went.

You know who my role model is? A well-kept house cat. They sleep for eighteen hours a day, spend the rest of the time just laying around or eating, have no responsibilities, and are smart enough to understand humans but sassy enough not to listen to them. I'd love a life like that.

Sometimes I think our world is just a big experiment like those dozens of dystopian movies. Like there are people or unimaginable beings somewhere beyond us trying to see if our society will work. If that's not true, I don't know what to consider our existence to be.

This is how my thought process and our conversations go for the rest of the night: spontaneous and somehow meaningful. Perhaps they're just meaningful because I'm seeing them from a different perspective, or perhaps I'm not, but think I am.

Dylan is the one to drive us back to my house because she's much more experienced with driving while high, and I'm much too nervous. She has her license just not a car. It turns out Dylan had totaled her car after her dad died due to a mental breakdown while driving. Luckily, she had no major injuries, but she confessed to me, late one night, that she'd been disappointed that she didn't. It's hard to get that thought out of my head some days.

Once we get back to my house, we quietly gather up miscellaneous food and make it to my bedroom. I then become paranoid that my mom will find out, so I make sure that our entire house smells like "BREEZY UNDERSEA." Dylan laughs at my persistence and paranoia.

I conveniently have a TV in my room, which is why it's the location we can most commonly be found when in my house. Over the months, it's become a normal matter that Dylan spends a lot of her time here. She spends the night whenever she can, weekends or weekdays, and keeps some of her clothes in a drawer I cleared out for her. She usually sleeps in my bed with me (my blanket nests got less and less comfortable), and sometimes she hangs around at my house alone while I'm at work. It's almost as if we're a couple in the awkward process of deciding if we should live together or not.

I realize that this makes her sound rather clingy, but it's only because she's avoiding her mother, and I'm usually the one that suggests she stays here in the first place. My mom doesn't care because Dylan never gets in the way. Half of the time my mom is unaware that she's over, but if I did explain the reason behind it, she'd be just as supportive.

Dylan's mother has gotten worse lately. Dylan doesn't like to show me, but I've seen some of the bruises across her face, neck, and down her arms. They're faint, but whenever I point them out she says things like her situation is fine, that she's handling it, that it'll only be until she turns eighteen, and she doesn't want child protective services involved and to be placed somewhere else. She even tells me that I'm overreacting.

I've seriously considered telling my mom and getting the police involved, but I know that Dylan would never forgive me if I did. Plus, our Senior year is almost done, and a few months later she'll turn eighteen and have plans for her life. I count the days until that comes.

It turns out I'm actually older than Dylan. I had my birthday in February and hers isn't until July. I wish they were reversed so that Dylan could already be free of her mother's grip, figuratively and literally, but we're still waiting.

My eighteenth birthday was pretty chill. Dylan and I went to a movie, my mom made a cake, and we hung out at my house. It was a school night, so we didn't drink until the weekend.

The only advantage of having a parent who is an alcoholic is that they have enough alcohol to not notice when some is missing. They're always too drunk to keep track, and it wouldn't be a challenging task to convince them that it was they who drank it. But even with that advantage, we don't drink that often; the last thing Dylan wants to do is follow in her mother's footsteps. However, it's too bad her mother isn't also a druggie because Dylan has taken on that role pretty fast – at least too fast for my taste, anyway.

The Foo Fighters were right, it's a long road to ruin, and I'm taking my first step by smoking pot. I'm not saying that drugs will ruin my life, I won't let them. Dylan on the other hand, doesn't have enough self-respect to realize that making the decision to do drugs, doesn't put her in control. I think her self-respect goes away with every beating she gets from her mother. Having a constant reminder that you're a worthless inconvenience every time you come home can only teach you one of two things: that you are or that you aren't exactly that. But name one person who was born with enough dignity to never give in to the opinions of others. I thought Dylan could be a close exception, but everyone cares at some point. I feel bad for her, but I know she'd shame me if I ever told her.

I'm getting ahead of myself, however. It is a long road, and this is only the beginning.

Later, we go to bed comfortable in every way. Weed amplifies the feeling of moving, so it's no surprise that the feeling of laying is endlessly enjoyable. It feels as if I'm falling into my bed or glued to its surface. Everything is perceived more intensely with my eyes closed, and we fall asleep with ease to the background fuzz of my low-volume TV. I know I'll want to do it again.

In the morning, there's no groggy awakening, annoying headaches, or being sensitive to bright lights or loud noises – it's waking up like any other normal day. The absence of any god-I'm-fucked hangovers leaves me pleasantly surprised at the outcome, and I decide that it's worth dealing with the smell and burn of my throat.

Dylan is happy with my experience, and when she asks if I'll ever want to do it again, I easily say yes. I want to walk down that road with her. After all, she is the one who paints the lines.

HIGH, HOW ARE YOU? [8]

=

Once we gather enough motivation to leave my bed, Dylan declares that she wants to "actually do something today," and after much debate on what that something will be, we decide to go to the small amusement park two towns over. Neither of us work, so we have plenty of time to get there and back.

Oh, Reader, I forgot to mention that in the last couple of months Dylan actually managed to get a job at the Antique store. After a bit of convincing, Carl had agreed that he could use a little help here and there, and Dylan was thrilled to get the job. It turns out they actually do dust in antique stores. Who would have thought?

We leave for the park an hour after we decide to go, and we get there two hours after that. It would have been an hour and a half but there was road construction, and we spent thirty minutes trying to get the detour signs and the GPS to stop lying to each other. It was quite the mess.

Once we get through the lengthy process of parking, the long walk to the entrance, and the endless line to buy a ticket, we go straight to the bathroom. No, we don't immediately get on a ride and have slow-motion fun while there's a lit song playing in the background. We pay, go through the gate, and find the dingy line to the restroom because we've been sitting in the car for the last two hours and really have to pee. Why be unrealistic?

After that, however, we do have moments worthy of slow-motion clips with lit music playing in the background because it is fun. It's the kind of fun you have to pay for, not the self-invented, humble kind. Sometimes it's hard to decide which one is better, but for Dylan it turns out to be pretty obvious.

We've already gone on a few mellow rides, like the ones that spin or the small ones designed only to make your stomach drop, but I want something more exciting. My favorite rides are the classic roller coasters simply because they're fast, they're tall, and they're long. Most of the other rides are fairly stationary, but a roller coaster can take you all around the park.

When I'm high above the ground, the world feels small, and with that, my problems do too as I marvel at the view. (I hate that that rhymed. I also hate that I can have a sentence with "that that" and it makes sense.)

Sidetracked.

I enthusiastically express my desire to ride the roller coaster to Dylan, but she doesn't return my enthusiasm.

"Why not?" I ask, actually surprised.

"I don't know, they're not my favorite," she pauses and glances at the line entrance and then back at me, "But we can ride it if you want."

"You sure?" I question. I don't want to make her do anything she's uncomfortable with.

"Yeah, it's fine," she grabs my arm and pulls, "Come on."

I naturally follow.

The line takes too long, as they always do, and Dylan gets increasingly quiet as we get closer to the front, which is out of character.

"You alright?" I ask as we're one group away from getting on the roller coaster. I notice that she's blankly staring at the tracks. I assume it's just a comfortable stare, but it's still concerning.

"What?" she asks after realizing she's been addressed, and continues with, "Oh, um yeah just thinking. Hey, would you want to get food after this? I'm hungry." She quickly changes the subject, and because I realize that that's purposeful, I respect it and reply, "Yeah sure, food is always good."

"Great."

The cart then pulls up, and as it's vacated the gate opens and we get on. I get in first so she's on my left.

The only restraints to keep us in the cart is a thin strap that stretches across our laps, and a bar that hangs over our legs. Dylan struggles with the strap due to its overuse and stubborn tendencies. The man who has the job of coming around to check if we were actually able to get it buckled, and if the bar won't fly open when we take off, approaches our cart.

"Hands up, please."

We do as he says and he easily buckles the strap and pulls on it near the middle to make sure it's secure. Then the annoying but mandatory safety announcement that we've already heard ten times comes on, and I look at Dylan. She has on that same blank stare as she did before.

"Dude, seriously, what's up?" I persist.

"I don'--ant t- -ide."

"What?" I have no idea what she said because she's barely audible.

"I don't want to ride," she declares a bit louder this time.

"Well, dude! Why'd you come on here then?" I instantly feel bad, but I did give her some opportunities to say no.

"I knew you really wanted to."

"You didn't have to come, I'm sorry." I rustle with the strap but she stops me.

"It's fine, really. I'm just severely afraid of heights."

"*Thank you and enjoy your ride.*" We hear the loud speaking turn off, and the cart juts forward, too late to stop now.

Of course, the first thing to a roller coaster is a huge, slow climb with the loud repetition of metal clicking and flicking into its place. I've always liked that sound, it usually makes me excited as I anticipate the drop to follow, but now that Dylan fears it, I hate the sound.

"Can I help in any way?" I ask when I notice her breathing pick up. I then realize that that's a lame thing to ask. I should actually be helping, not looking for tips. Either way, she doesn't respond, so I improvise.

"It's only for a second," I try to calm her. "After the peak you're fine."

She starts breathing heavily as we're halfway through the climb, so I awkwardly put my hand over hers and remind her that it'll pass. I haven't had a lot of experience with panic attacks, especially in this circumstance, so I don't know what more to do, and I feel like I'm failing some aspect of being a good friend.

A third of the way up, she clutches the bar in front of us and closes her eyes. She hasn't said a word. The repetition of clicks has increasingly slowed, while her breathing has increasingly gotten faster. Now comes the moment where we can't get any higher: my favorite moment – her least favorite moment.

For reasons oblivious to me, at this moment, she opens her eyes. She takes one last breath, her eyes well up, her face constricts as if to brace herself, and we slowly pass over the peak of her fears and plummet to her relief.

Her eyes let loose of her tears, and they dig a line across her temples as they whistle away from the speed. She lets go of the bar, and a smile cracks across her face. She then lets out a big scream as if to release her anxiety, and her breathing turns back to normal as we speed down the dip and twist into a new section of the park.

The ride eventually comes to an end, and we get off. As we walk out of the gate she asks, "So whatcha' hungry for?" as if nothing had happened.

"I want a hot dog, but are we not going to talk about that?" I persist.

"I'm afraid of heights, there's nothing more to it," she plainly states.

She seems adamant about ending the conversation, so I reply with, "Well, okay then, there's hot dogs around the corner," and we proceed to said hot dogs.

Reader, I tell you this story because I can count on one hand the number of times I've felt more in control than Dylan. And even then, I wasn't confident. I was just more mentally and physically stable than her, and considering the rarity of this happening in our friendship, it's hard to forget.

We buy our food, and our day of carefree, expensive fun eventually turns into a night.

"Sits down, submits to feet, bursts into flames," Dylan narrates.

62

"You know, I feel ya'," I say, mostly to myself. Dylan is watching a couple that's a bit too clingy walk past as she says, "I don't understand the whole dinner and a movie thing for a first date.

"Why's that?" I ask.

"Because I don't think eating is attractive, and for that to be the first thing you do in front of someone is a lot of pressure. Plus, you're expected to talk, but not talk with your mouth full. And then you go to a movie where all you do is sit in the dark together. You can only do minimal talking, PDA is unacceptable and awkward, and holding hands is just plain hard with the armrest and cup holder in the way."

"You've thought a lot about that," I comment.

"I've tried it and it wasn't fun."

"Really? You don't seem like the traditional dating type."

"We all go through phases, don't judge," she replies, jokingly defensive.

I throw my hands up as if to be passive.

We've gone on nearly every ride besides the ones that are "too high." The roller coasters and the Ferris wheel are her least favorite. I love them all.

Right now, we are sitting at a small table across from a karaoke stage where a little girl is trying her hardest to hit the big notes in "Let It Go." I swear I've already heard three other kids try the same song; their cuteness makes up for their pitch.

"Can anyone do that?" Dylan asks, gesturing towards the stage.

"Yeah, you just put your name down and pick a song."

She watches as the little girl bows, and the few audience members present clap enthusiastically.

"I think I'm gonna' do it," she states while watching the girl leave the stage.

"Seriously?" I'm genuinely surprised.

"Why not?" she shrugs with a casual face.

"I can think of many reasons," I truthfully state.

"Well, convince me then."

She gives me no time to however, for she's already up and walking to the sign-in booth. This is daring, even for her. She has a *do anything* personality, but I never pictured her singing in front of strangers. That being said, I never pictured her being afraid of heights either.

She walks back with a smile on her face.

"What'd you pick?"

"You'll see."

"Can you even sing?" I hesitantly ask, because I've never truly heard her sing, just goof off to popular songs. In fear of secondhand embarrassment, I really hope she can sing.

"Of course I can, I have vocal cords don't I?" she smarts off.

"You know what I mean."

"Chill, you'll be fine. I'm the one that's going up there. I'm going to prove to you that you should take a chance once in a while."

"Don't think this will inspire me or anything," I warn.

"You know, I think your comfort zone would expand if you did uncomfortable things," she declares.

"How do you figure?"

"Because, realistically, you can always do an even *more* uncomfortable thing than what you just did, which makes the first thing you did not as uncomfortable. But in order to do it, you need a good starting point. Does that make sense?"

I think it over for a second. "Logically, kind of, but you have to get the balls to do the first uncomfortable thing, and mine just don't grow that fast."

"Well, you better get some *miracle grow* because you're up next."

"What!?" If she's not joking, I'm going to punch her.

"And next we have," the announcer looks at his sheet, "June Blackfield singing 'Sweater Weather' by The Neighborhood."

I die.

I immediately turn to Dylan and she has a sly little smirk across her face.

"What the fuck? I'm not going up there! They don't know that's me, they think it's you." I have a reserved freak-out as the announcer sets up the microphone.

"I'm not going up there, I'm not–"

Dylan cuts me off, "Fine, fine, fine, but get used to that feeling, Junebug."

She stands up and walks the distance to the stage as I stare at the back of her head with my mouth open. I can't believe she scared me like that. I was about to get up and run away, just avoid my problems with a quick sprint out of sight. She's really going to do it. She's going to sing.

She hops up the stairs, makes her way to the microphone, and looks at the DJ. The smooth, recognizable beat of the song starts, and the audience goes quiet. "*And all I am, is a man. . . '*" comes out of Dylan's mouth, and I'm pleasantly surprised. She doesn't force it or overdo it; she simply sings, and it's actually kind of beautiful.

Reader, I don't know how to describe to you the impression I get from her singing. It's really something you have to be here for, because we could have completely opposing opinions. (And yes, I'm sorry, don't you hate it when people say, "*Oh, you had to be there.*" Like, thanks for the completely useless insight while also managing to make me feel left out.) However, I can honestly say that I'm not the slightest bit embarrassed to see her up there. She has her eyes closed for most of it which looks kind of odd, but I can tell it helps her focus. She genuinely impresses me, and when she sings the closing line, "*It's too cold, the hands of my sweater,*'" she deserves the applause.

She doesn't have the type of voice that belongs on a singing show, it's more of an easy-listening, modest voice that's meant for quiet times alone. I wonder if she knows this. I wonder if she would have gone up there if she thought she had a bad voice. Don't we usually only flaunt it if we got it? I decide to confront her on this.

"Dude, that was actually great," I congratulate her as she walks back with a content grin on her face.

"Don't sound so surprised," she jokes.

"So you knew you could do that?" I ask.

"Well, I wasn't about to embarrass myself, but I've always wanted to do that."

"Why'd you put my name down then?"

"Because you should get out of your shell. I figured you wouldn't go up, but I gave you the opportunity." I stare at the ground, contemplating what would have happened if I had gone up there.

"What's something you've always wanted to do?" she asks, sincerely. And I sincerely think about it, but disappoint her with a lame shrug.

"See! That's my point. Where's your ambition?"

"Maybe I just hate setting goals."

"Maybe? *Maybe* isn't an answer, it's an excuse."

"Why are you getting on my case about this?" I ask, partially defensive.

"I just want you to want something, you know?"

"Yeah I know, and I do, I'm just different than you," I pause, "*You know?*" I mock her tone.

"Oh, shut up," she replies as we head out of the karaoke setting.

By this time, the sun is starting to set, the air is getting chilly, and the night is peaceful despite the busy atmosphere. We have done nearly everything we could have here, even the mirror maze which was extremely hard to navigate and screwed up my vision for a while. I think it was worth the money however, and the night feels complete, so we decide it's time to head home.

We stop at a gas station on the way out to pick up some snacks, because who can afford a whole day's worth of food at an amusement park? Not this teenager with a minimum wage job, but oh well, I'll eat gas station food any day.

While in line, I scan the ground for any too-much-effort-to-pick-up change left behind by lazy people. Not to my surprise, I find a dime resting in the corner of the counter and the wall.

Adding this dime to the collection of change I've found throughout the day makes 87¢. That's a successful day in my book, and here's an explanation of why: for the past two years I have been collecting change I've found on the ground and keeping it in its own jar. I don't consider this a piggy bank because I don't plan on spending any of the money for a long time. My reason for doing this is to show the value of something so small. Unless you are homeless, most people walk past loose change and have no intention of looking for it in the first place, which is honestly surprising considering we live in a world which revolves around money.

Nevertheless, I've decided to value the penny, and by making that decision I have found $23.76 in the past two years in change. I know that's not a lot, but it is the only completely free money I have ever gotten. And to think, all I had to do was pick it up off the ground. To me, that's worth it.

"Have a good night," says the drowsy cashier who doesn't look like he means it.

"You too," Dylan and I awkwardly reply in unison.

We then leave the gas station, and as I hear the chime of the small bell that rings every time the door is opened. I get a whiff of the cold, musky, gas-tinted air, making me very nostalgic.

My mom and I used to go on long road trips over the summer. We'd either pick a state or visit relatives. We'd be in the car for hours, and sometimes I liked that better than the actual destination.

I thought it was endlessly easy to sleep in cars. I'd lay in the backseat and watch the simple passing of the trees or the pattern of illumination from city lights. I loved the receding sky and every type of cloud I could imagine. I'd slowly doze off to the music that filled the car and the soft vibration of 70 mph on a smooth road. Of course, I'd wake up a couple hours later because the position I was in got uncomfortable, but I'd just pick up on the next CD that was playing and quietly sing along until I got tired again.

Eventually, we'd watch the sun set and we'd still be driving. We'd stop at a gas station to restock our snack pile. I'd force my legs to unfold, hop out of the car, and experience the same smell that's here now.

I'd then go in and find the bathroom while my mom filled up the car, and I'd be blinded by the lighting of the room. I'd roam the aisles like I hadn't seen what they displayed five other times that day, and then I'd pick out something I hadn't tried yet.

As we left I would hop over the small puddles from the aftermath of rain, and avoid the worms that had surfaced. I'd notice the hundreds of bugs hopelessly circling around the fluorescent lights, and then I'd notice the dark abyss behind the lights that hid the roads we had left to travel.

We'd drag ourselves back into the car, distribute our snacks, and continue the ride. It was so simple, but I couldn't get enough of it.

I feel that way right now with Dylan, so I know that it's something worth remembering. Only now, I can't remember what else I've said that to – funny how that works.

A MESS OF A CHAPTER [9]

=

After that day, our lives start to revolve more and more around drugs. Time passes like the flow of "Devil May Dance" by Aj Roach, and I'm too involved to realize I'm not happy with where we're going.

Let me tell you, though, the small-town drug world is not what I expected. I hope you don't mind me vomiting some observations onto you, because here I go:

The most unsettling surprise is the age of the drug dealers I encounter, for not a single one of them has been older than me. I know I'm still in high school, but these guys are tiny. I'm sure there are some drug dealers in my grade, but the obvious ones that always get away with it are like twelve. I'm being dramatic, but only because I should be.

Dylan and I were chatting with our guy during a pick up one night, and he flaunted that he was on shrooms (I wasn't jealous). But what left me dumbfounded was the fact that he proceeded with, "Yeah, it's super trippy, but we have to hurry because I have to beat my mom home."

How ridiculous. I know we all do this behind our parents' backs, but that put doing shrooms on the same level as being at a friend's house or party that you shouldn't, and having to get home at a certain time. I feel like it shouldn't be this casual. He respected his mother enough to abide her rules and be home before her, but he was still fucked up enough to be on shrooms on a Tuesday night. I don't understand; too many things have become normal.

Another disappointment from high-school-level drug dealers is a side effect of them being twelve, and the fact that they're always on something: they are *never* on time and their packaging is awful. It's my fault for not expecting that, however.

We once got a gram that was wrapped in a piece of notebook paper. Like damn kid, you better be using that paper for school or you're not going anywhere. If you choose the life of being a drug dealer, you at least better be a classy one. I'd respect them more and they'd have better business - simple as that, do your job well.

That's it for my rant. I've grown accustomed to the conditions fairly quickly, and I know what to expect. I've never gotten used to the annoyance however, though it doesn't seem to bother Dylan that much.

+

Reader, I feel like we need a plot update. I apologize for my sporadic organization, but honestly, chronological order doesn't apply in the real world. If it did, how come we tell people that they're living in the past, or why is it only sometimes that we feel like we're living in the moment? Point being, sporadic is a state we live in, so right now, Dylan and I are sitting at the last month of school - the last month of our Senior year to be specific, and boy, are we ready to be done.

I've never understood Senior year. For many people, high school simply becomes a stepping stool to get into college. The agenda of most is to apply the summer after Junior year and get accepted far before one graduates. But if colleges know they want us after our Junior year, why stress over Senior year? I promise, I'm not.

I busted my ass Junior year, got accepted to three of the four colleges I applied to, and am doing the bare minimum this year (yet maintaining my GPA). I don't see the silver lining if my hard work is going to be awarded with harder work. Dylan doesn't have the same mind set, however.

Despite being a semi-stereotypical, downbeat home life, stoner, Dylan's more studious than I am. Or rather, more accurately, she's smarter than I am, for none of her time is devoted to studying. Although it provokes a quite shameful shade of jealousy, we don't let it get between us, because her being smart is merely a perk: Dylan wants to go to an art school. On top of being effortlessly intelligent, she's also very talented.

Her plan is to graduate, turn eighteen, and move far away from her mother where she will get a job, work for a year, manage to find a place to live, eventually apply to a cheap college and get a degree. It's a lot to take on as an eighteen-year-old with no outside support besides some money left from her father. Naturally, I'm worried about her. Naturally, she's confident about it, so I try to trust her.

Right now, Dylan's working on step one, and I'm confident that she'll graduate with a GPA close, or even above, a 4.0. Perhaps she was given brains in return of her shitty upbringing. But I don't believe that there's anyone or anything worthy of *giving*, so it must be chance.

Either way, fact is fact, and the fact is that Dylan has a high probability of pursuing a brighter future than her past, and with a month left of school, I'm excited for what's to come.

+

"What does that sign say?" I ask while squinting (as if nearly closing my eyes will help me see more clearly).

"'*Private Property, No Trespassing,*'" Dylan easily replies.

"God, I need new contacts."

I instinctively rub my eyes for no reason.

Reader, by my nonchalantly mentioning that Dylan and I are approaching private property, I present the one type of figurative language that almost everyone is able to identify: foreshadowing. This suggests that we are likely going to uphold the old stigma of "reckless teenagers" who do reckless things just for the sake of being reckless, and trespass on private property. But I'm tired of that story, so that is why I'm declaring, right now, that we are not a cliché.

However, you are technically right. Eventually the sign comes into focus, and we walk right past the warning that tells us not to. The only reason we are not being a cliché is because our intentions for being here are far less reckless.

Dylan is going to take some photos of me and our surroundings for her art portfolio she's working on. Adamant about having work from all types of media, I let her borrow my mom's fancy camera for our venture out here.

It's unfortunate that this is private property because it's a beautiful location. It's so vast that there aren't any buildings or residents in eyesight. There's only the setting sun and an opportunity for Dylan to have a good future, so I put aside my awkwardness and try to pose to the best of my ability. Luckily, her artistic aptitude makes up for my discomfort.

I'm not going to write about the photoshoot. It goes how I assume they all go. She ends up taking "posed-candids" which couldn't get more ironic (but honesty is something that's easily modified, so I don't object their origin).

"You look amazing in this one," she says as she holds out the camera while we walk back to the car.

"I suppose," is all I muster. It's a strange feeling to see myself on camera. I feel as though I'm not looking at me, but a faraway version on me that's been painted over a few times because the first attempt didn't quite look right. It feels like I've become my reflection – that I'm the one in the mirror, 2D, staring back at my 3D self.

This probably means I have issues, but who doesn't have issues?

The dirt path we've been following continues to widen, and we eventually reach my car. The sky is a perfect gradient of all colors, and in this moment, I consider it the most beautiful thing I've ever seen, but then I remind myself that I think that every time.

We get in the car, start playing "Holy Toledo" by Vundabar, and make our way home with the painting of color trailing behind us – slowly but surely fading to black, but remaining just as beautiful.

It's nights like this one, plus the surreal fact that I only have a month left of this chapter of my life, that makes me reminisce on all the things I've already been privileged to see or do. It also reminds me of all the things I wish I could have avoided, and that is why this chapter is going to get even messier.

The ride home is a perfect environment for me to reevaluate my life. For me, a car ride with good music is equivalent to a hot shower, so I find myself staring out the window with stagnant eyes, but a running mind, the entire time.

The overall conclusion of my thinking is the realization that I have lied to you, Reader, and for that I must apologize. I have declared Dylan and myself not to be clichés, but I can't think of a scenario where that is true. I blame this on modern society.

Today it has practically become a cliché to try not to be a cliché, and that is a dark hole of paradoxical shit. So really, all I can say it is that being completely original is one damn hard thing to accomplish. No matter what we do, no matter what abiding clichés we think we defy, we can all be categorized.

This is probably because, in this day and age, equal rights have jumped to the top of the *Social Issues We Should Actually Address* list. It's as if everyone has finally found their voice, and our only fathomable solution to it is becoming increasingly more politically correct. This mentality has dribbled all the way down to the way we view the ancient clichés of the dumb jock and the loser nerd, and the fact that I bet you pictured both of those examples to be men. Today we know that the captain of the football team can also be valedictorian. And that those with brains are respected and will likely have a brighter future than our own, rather than dweebs who wear suspenders and can't get girls.

We live in the era of mile-high pride which has transformed any combination of characteristics to be mainstream; therefore, the examples of clichés have only broadened. I am now a cliché for being an awkward, half-confident, comparatively intelligent, blond athlete with chill clothes and a mature mind. I bet there are thousands of me, and thousands of Dylan's: the adventurous, wildly talented, free spirit with a bad past and a degree in sarcasm. We are not new. We are only a subcategory in a sea of previously told stories, yet we take pride in our individuality. So that is why I am declaring, right now, that we are all a cliché.

As a positive outlook, all this really means is that the little details who make us, us, are now more important than ever. So when the car ride come to an end, I have become okay with this thought. I feel no reason to object and have no energy to try to challenge it. But my mind never switches out of its debunking mode, so the rest of my night is devoted to reliving all the moments I ever deemed worthy of remembrance. This is when, Reader, I'm going to list some of. . .

Those Sublime (and not too sublime) Encounters I Mentioned At The
Beginning Of The Book
Did you remember?
(Chronological order is intentionally ignored)

+

1) i once went to the Library

My wheels made an obnoxious noise on the half-gravel road that made my feet feel like they'd fall off from the deep vibration that almost tickled. But it didn't last long. We took a right onto a long, newly tarred road that smoothly lead us nearly all the way to our destination.

I had considered this the best road to longboard down because it was at a slight decline that allowed us to casually coast, but not too fast, so we were still able to slow down at an intersection.

Halfway down the road, the blur of the trees had broken to a view of an open sky. I felt liberated as the scene switched and the sun finally reached as far as my eyes could see. I threw up my arms and smiled at the refreshing breeze and swiveling ground. I could have lived in that moment. I could have lived in that moment with the chorus of "You Keep Me Hangin' On" by Vanilla Fudge filling my ears.

Dylan had been longboarding in front of me the whole time, and I think she felt the same way because she turned around, enthusiastically smiled, and yelled, "What ever happened to skateboards!?"

She didn't expect an answer. She laughed and turned back around. Her hair flew back from the speed, and she crouched down and extended her hand inches above the ground. I wasn't confident enough in my balance to do so, and it was yet another example of the contrast between our personalities. It didn't make me any less content, however.

I used to own a skateboard. I endlessly tried to perfect an ollie, but could never do any tricks more advanced than that.

The perfect road came to an end as we approached a trail leading into a wooded area. We eventually managed to stop, hopped off our boards, and headed down the trail.

The path had become as familiar to me as my backyard. We had traveled it what seemed like hundreds of times because it was the "red carpet" to our accustomed hangout.

We took a left at the broken tree, and a right at an ordinary rock that we had learned to recognize. We then arrived at a big pine tree that didn't have branches on its lower half. I'm not sure why it didn't, but it turned out to be very convenient for us: the upper branches hung low and provided a semi-hidden, chilling area. Although, considering it was a pine tree, the underside was anything but comfortable, so we improvised.

I went digging in my attic and eventually found an old air mattress that we must have forgotten about, because we now own two others. I took that as verification to take it without asking. I brought it, and a pair of scissors, to the tree. I spread out the deflated mattress and cut a line to the middle, then cut a circle the size of the tree trunk. It was easy to move and we couldn't feel the pine needles underneath, so it did the job.

To make it more inviting, we moved over some reasonably-smooth rocks for a place to sit and a place to set our things. Our things mostly consisted of weed, our backpacks, and Arizona tea.

We called this place the Library. We called it that because when there, we mainly did homework or read books. Dylan did this while high. She claimed it helped her focus and opened her mind, but she got the same grade regardless of being sober or not, so I figured she simply preferred an altered mindset.

For me, however, being high took away a part of me being real – if that makes sense – so doing homework was an exceedingly hard thing for me to comprehend while in that state. It was as if I didn't know what was going on, and any sort of reading became an impossible task of *what am I doing?* I stuck to getting high when I was done with school work, where I would play music while lying down and search for meaning in my surroundings.

One day at school, Dylan managed to steal the *Drop Books Here* sign form the media center, so we nailed it to our tree.

I must have read a dozen books under that tree by now. Maybe one day this will be one of them.

2) i once chased a sunset

"It should be around that building," she persistently pleaded.

"Dylan, if we actually want to see it we have to go like ten minutes out of town," I reasoned.

"Then let's do it. I've got forty-five minutes before my mom leaves for her night shift, and it doesn't pay to spend that time just sitting at your house if we're already out and about," she reasoned back.

"But I have chem homework."

"Screw chem, are you going to be a chemist? No. You'll do fine, you always do."

"Easy for you to say."

"Please? I promise it'll be worth it. I mean, look at that." She pointed to the sliver of sunset we could see in between two buildings. I could already identify at least five colors, so I knew that she was right, but my priorities didn't agree.

"We'll find a spot, you'll have a smoke, and it'll be a grand little evening," she gave her final coax.

I've always had a hard time saying no to her, probably because I have a hard time saying no to anyone, so of course, I put the car in drive and off we went.

She grinned the kind of grin that made her face scrunch up, and she reached over to give me an awkward, over-the-armrest hug. "Thank yooouuu."

"Yeah, yeah." I batted her away to make sure we didn't die before we got there; she seems to forget that driving requires focus.

I secretly thought I was wasting my time as we took our fourth turn out in the boondocks on an annoying, gravel road. But Dylan continuously assured me that we would get there soon.

The problem with chasing a sunset is that you're chasing time, and time is the fastest thing in the world. So no matter what path we went down, the colors only seemed to get further and further away. You're left thinking, *but it must be right up there* - right around that corner or right over that hill, but once you get there, you realize you were wrong, so you think *then it must be over there.* But it's not over there.

"Get past those trees and then we'll stop," she instructed, and I did just that.

I hate the bitter taste of being proven wrong.

"God!" she exclaimed. "Would ya' look at that!?"

The view made me temporarily forget about my chemistry homework, but not long enough that it wouldn't bite me in the ass when I got back home.

I drove past the trees and parked on the side of the road. By then, we had driven a decent way into the country, so the chance of there being passing cars was very slim.

Once parked, I opened my trunk and spread out the emergency blanket that I kept more for my convenience rather than an aid to an emergency. We sat on the ledge of my trunk, turned up the radio, and observed the sky while I smoked a cigarette.

To the left was a storm. There was a distinct slant of grey from the heavy rain, and random flashes of lightning that never struck when I anticipated and only when my camera wasn't pointing at it.

To the right was the sun set, or what was left of the sun set. In the time it took us to venture out there, clouds had condensed over the color, but the sliver that remained told us all that we needed to know.

Straight ahead was the wondrous mixture of heaven and hell; that's where I want to go when I die.

Dylan and I talked on and off while we wasted time with the beautiful sky. I had only a few puffs of cigarette left, but a lot more time to kill, so I decided to reach for another. Before I could, Dylan stopped my hand and abruptly turned my shoulders towards her. She then grabbed my face with a hand on either cheek, leaned in, and forcefully kissed me on the lips.

I took a second to recover.

"Um. . . what was that??"

"Do you know what kissing is for?" she asked in a tone that suggested she was going to teach me something.

I didn't bother the effort to think of a reply. I flashed her a quizzical look and she continued with, "It's for fun, and it can be intimate, yes. But it's also just for people you love."

I could have answered that.

"So you love me?" I asked, half-laughing.

"Yes," she replied.

"And you had to kiss me to get that message across?" I further questioned.

"Well, you don't need to shame me for it. I just wanted to broaden our boundaries and officially thank you for all that you've done for me."

I took another second. "Well, in that case. . ." and before I finished, I took the last puff of my cigarette, tossed it to the ground, grabbed her face, and kissed her right back. It certainly wasn't romantic or smooth in any way, but I was satisfied with the performance.

Dylan leaned back and laughed, but when she came back up, she flapped her lips with a face of disgust.

I was instantly embarrassed, and my hands naturally cupped my mouth as I said, "I really wasn't trying, but was I actually that bad?"

She reassured me with, "No, hun," she brought my hands back down, "I did that because you should really quit smoking, Junebug."

That's not what I was expecting. I sighed and said, "You smoke all the time."

"I smoke weed, it's different. Yours can actually kill you."

"Yes, I'm fully aware. I'll quit one day, I promise."

"I'm going to hold you to that, you know."

"Good," I replied, and decided not to pull out another. Instead, I laid down with my head on Dylan's lap and continued the evening by viewing the sky form a new angle.

She will forever go down as the first girl I kissed.

3) i once witnessed love

It was a night my mom didn't feel like cooking, but one where we had enough time to waste that we'd feel guilty if we had gotten fast food, so we went out to eat.

Restaurants always strike conversations that feel like they should have happened already, but that's not what this story is about. This story takes place on the way to the bathroom:

"I'll be right back," I told my mom, and got up from the table.

I don't know why bathrooms are always so hard to find. This one was a small door that led to a hallway with two more doors. Obviously, one was men's and one was women's (because our society has not yet evolved to undo its gendered constructs). When I reached the hallway, I noticed an old man standing against the wall, minding his own business. The hallway was rather small, so I awkwardly squeezed past him to get to the women's door.

I knew they were single stalls because the doorknobs were ones that could lock, so I was apprehensive about going in due to the fear of walking in on someone. But I grabbed the handle, and before I could figure out if it was occupied or not, the old man addressed me and said, "My wife is in there at the moment, it'll just be a minute."

"Oh, okay," I replied and backed up against the wall, now forced to wait in silence for his wife to emerge. It didn't take long, and it turned out that I was actually glad she had been in there.

Once she got the door open, I quietly stepped to the side and looked at her face. Her eyes were a cloudy grey; it was obvious that she was blind. She then reached out her hand for guidance, and the old man gently reached back and lead her down the hallway stating, "This way, darling."

I watched them walk the length of the hall, slow, but side by side. He opened the door for her. I watched until I was the only one left in the hallway.

She never knew I was there. It was a normal situation for her, but a heartwarming encounter to me. I've always viewed old couples as extremely endearing, but seeing them made me a little more comfortable with the fact that one day, I'll be that old, maybe blind, and unable to function alone. But now, there's a little hope that I'll have someone there to do it all with me – that growing old doesn't mean growing alone or restricted. Maybe one day, I'll accept the fact that looking back on my life will be an everyday event, and I can remember that moment and discover the validity of my predictions. Maybe those will be the years where I truly experience love.

I hate the fact that I had those thoughts while peeing.

4) i once grew young

I have other friends. Yes, this story's focal point is Dylan, but that doesn't mean she's the only person I ever associated with. I play soccer in the spring and fall, and I'd consider being in a sport, or other activities, the best way to make friends. I love the people on my team sometimes just as much as I love Dylan. And considering they knew that I'm friends with her, she was at least an acquaintance to them. I wanted to make that clear so it didn't seem as though Dylan and I were total loners.

Also, knowing Dylan does poses a semi-charismatic personality, she managed to become popular in the "party-boy" group. Although not something I necessarily approved of, it broadened my boundaries throughout the year, and I convinced myself it was a good thing. Plus, it was like pre-game college, so I tried to participate.

Now that we're on the same page, this might make more sense: there were a few guys in both the soccer and the party groups whom Dylan and I were quite familiar with. We and a few others who mixed groups were invited to a party. It wasn't a real party by any stretch of the word, but it reminded me of my youth.

The host's house was huge, just like all the others – like Legos down the street. It had a backyard that was more like a park and a hot tub that was more like a pool. The contrast between that lifestyle and the one that I'm used to, shocked me. I couldn't help but wonder what it was like as I crossed the threshold.

His grand house provided us ample room and more for the childish activities he had planned. Despite that everyone present was at the age where our toys had become merely a pile of dusty boxes in the basement, we managed to dig out a dozen Nerf Guns and what seemed like hundreds of bullets that had accumulated throughout the years.

As I grabbed a small yellow gun – for its convenience and easy handling – I felt like I was seven and at my cousin's barn, hiding behind a big piece of plywood with a grin that touched my ears; anxious breaths of trying to stay quiet as I waited for my victim to come around the corner. I was enthused that everyone was okay with being a kid again – that we weren't embarrassed. I had always wanted my own Nerf Gun as a kid. I never got one.

"Upstairs is off limits!" someone yelled from behind a couch.

"First team out gets last dibs on the hot tub!" announced the boy who lived there, and with that, the first brave soul stood and took a shot at a not-so-hidden boy who was using a chair as a shield. Fortunately, the chair worked while the boy who first stood was promptly shot in the chest by a girl on my team. He regretted his bravery while the rest of us were giddy with the initiation of war.

Not to brag, but I'm pretty boss at this game. It took nearly half an hour to widdle everyone down, and I was one of the few on my team left standing. It was me and the host against a girl and a boy who happened to be dating; they worked well together.

Dylan was on my team, but she had gotten out early on since she attempted to hide in a spot before realizing someone else was already hidden there. Needless to say, she was an easy target.

Those that were out went upstairs to eat the variety of foods that were presented to us. I was starting to want to get shot just for that reason, but my sports-driven sense of determination overruled my hunger.

The other team's mistake was making the first move. They had split to either side of the room in an attempt to spread us apart, but it put them each in a corner. I got the girl and he got the boy. We made a good team.

He high fived me as we went upstairs. It made me feel special, but I should've felt that way without his approval. He announced that our team had won and the others were welcome to eat or go on the trampoline, but we would be in the hot tub. In reality, the hot tub was big enough to hold everyone, so we all ended up there anyway, he just wanted to revel in the fact that we had won.

Even with this wonderful distraction of a strange party, it didn't stop the real world from leaking through our ageless bubble. It was like your seat at a stadium that would've been perfect if it wasn't for the sun that was shining directly in your eyes, and the person in front of you who wasn't quite tall enough to block it. There's always something that could be better.

It was time to go change into our swimsuits, so Dylan pulled me aside to talk.

"Are you going out there?" she asked.

"Yeah, aren't you?" I questioned.

"Uh. . . I don't really have a swimsuit that. . . covers." She gestured at her torso.

Being reminded of her situation angered me as if I'd just found out about it. Being abused never leaves her; being aware that she might not be able to do everything others can, or that she'll need to put in extra effort to hide, was a constant state of being. But I didn't want her to be restricted that day. I didn't want them to ask why she wasn't joining us, so I suggested that she keep on a shirt. I had brought a cut off, and offered it to her.

"They're gonna' think it's weird," she insisted.

"No, they won't. It's either that or you don't go in at all, and that they *will* think is weird," I tried to reason.

She thought it over. "Fine, but we're going out there at the same time," she declared.

"Of course," I concurred as we headed towards the bathroom.

Once changed, I could tell that she was self-conscious, so I tried my hardest to treat the situation as normal and draw no attention to us (as if I would've anyway). When we got outside, I took notice that all the girls were in a typical bikini. So as much as I'd like to say it didn't matter, Dylan did stand out, and I wasn't the only one that thought so.

"Why don't you take off your shirt?" asked a girl.

We got in water and her shirt stuck to her stomach as it got wet.

"I forgot my top," Dylan lied.

"I've got one you could borrow," offered another girl.

"No, it's okay, I don't mind. Thank you, though."

"Alright," the girl concluded, and that was that. Everyone moved on and no one questioned it again. I don't know why I was surprised, but I was certainly relieved, and so was Dylan. I marveled at the fact that a simple lie can cover up a life-altering secret. I appreciated our ability to conceal the truth, although I wished Dylan didn't have to.

The rest of the afternoon was weird (for lack of a better word), but it allowed us to forget about Dylan's position. As you may have realized, Reader, today's "pop" music has essentially manifested into rap. In regards to me caring, I'm pretty indifferent on this transition, although it has forced me to find "good rap" to at least be a part of this movement. But anyway, following in the trend of the aspiring small-town dreamers, it was apparently time for rap battles.

The boys sat on the edge of the hot tub and took turns playing their beats. Each was different and they all had lyrics that they had been working on for a long time, so it wasn't improv, and it was moderately well written. I was genuinely surprised and pleased to listen to each of them have a go. There was even a girl who went, and she did just as well (but I shouldn't need the disclaimer).

We all cheered when they finished, even at the ones that weren't the best. We all respected their ability to show us something they actually valued. I think my favorite part was that their songs weren't just about "fucking pussy" like the majority of the stereotypical rap songs I learned as a kid. Of course there were some "bitches" thrown in there, but it was all in good taste. I secretly wished I could rap. I'd own that shit if I could.

The rest of the time we remained in the hot tub. The host had his playlist running and we just talked. Once the water turned lukewarm due to how long we had been sitting in it, someone decided to switch it up. A popular game at the time was What Are The Odds (if we wanted to be mathematically correct, it should be What Is The Probability, but that doesn't sound as catchy). For those of you that don't know, What Are The Odds is a simple game. Someone proposes a dare, and the one who is being offered it must chose a range based on how willing they are to do the dare. For instance, 1 out of 15 is a typical range. It is then up to chance to see if the person dared must carry out the dare. Both people then count down from three, and after "one" they say a number at the same time within the given range. If they both say the same number, the person offered must do the dare.

I normally hated this game because I'm a pansy, but that time I chose to participate. Luckily, my low-key demeanor saved me from being chosen often, which I was grateful for. Dylan on the other hand, ended up having to 'ask the neighbor for sugar in what she was wearing', and 'try to chug a whole can of soda' (it would have been beer if we hadn't been doing it during the day).

Others had to 'make up their own dance' or 'lick someone's body part'. The weirdness progressed, but eventually no one could think of anything new, so it basically turned into *how many combinations of people can we get to kiss?* I don't know why teenagers always resort to this, but I didn't necessarily object. In my mind, and maybe yours, Reader, I was secretly self-conscious about how low the number of people I've kissed was. Before that night, it was only two, and for some reason I thought it should be higher. So when I got dared to kiss a boy named Tyler, I said, "One out of five."

This wasn't me being daring, however. As the afternoon went on, we had set the maximum range to be five, so we were much more likely to have to do the dare. I was okay with it.

"Three. Two. One. Four," the one who dared me and I said at the same time.

The group then gave a unanimous "oo" and "ahh," and I got nervous. Considering I was the one to get dared, I had to initiate the kiss.

Tyler was across from me, so I slowly made my way over and leaned in. There weren't any hands involved, and there wasn't any tongue. It was simply just a kiss, and not a very good one. Considering we had been sitting in the hot tub for a couple hours, our lips felt damp and almost pruney, but I was satisfied that my list had just gotten a little bit longer. (By the end of the evening my list had grown to eight.)

I don't know why we continued this predictable process of having everyone kiss each other, but we did, and eventually Dylan was dared to kiss everyone present (as if she hadn't nearly done that already).

At that time, we had lowered the range to three which was basically saying *we all want to see everyone kiss, but we don't want to feel weird about it, so let's act like it was part of a game.* It was no surprise that they said the same number, but before Dylan went for it, we had to make sure everyone was okay with it.

There was one guy present who had refused to participate in the game thus far, so we asked him once more if he'd join in.

"I don't know," he sheepishly said.

"Why not?" asked a girl, but he only shrugged in reply.

"Come on dude, it doesn't hurt," another guy joked. I felt bad that they were pressuring him, but I did want to know his reason for refusing.

"I just don't want to," he stated, defensively. His persistence without explanation persuaded Dylan to get involved. She observed his shyness and moved over to his side. After making eye contact for longer than he liked, she asked, "Have you ever kissed anyone?" She said it in a gentle tone, making sure not to sound accusatory, but he didn't reply, he simply looked down at his lap as if he was ashamed. Dylan then put her hand under his chin and lead his gaze up until they were staring at each other. We all watched in silence.

He looked nervous and flustered as he tried to construct words. Dylan then put her other hand on the back of his neck and leaned him closer. They kissed for longer than the mere pecks we were doing before, and they didn't stop until Dylan pulled away and ended it with kissing him promptly on the forehead. He blushed as she returned to her spot. The hot tub erupted in cheers.

He was patted on the back and couldn't help but smile. It was actually really cute, and I gave Dylan a nod of approval. She grinned and we all decided to end the evening at that as we emerged from the water and split up to find our clothes.

I don't really know why I remember that event with such content, but it was certainly a reminder that I'm still a kid - that we all are. And to that end, I believe we should try to remain in our youth for as long as we can, because with each year to come, we'll only wish we had.

5) i once overestimated the underdog

It's hard not to let the fans get to you.

Despite the fact that our team had had practice every day, sometimes twice a day, for hours, followed by countless pep talks, rallies, constructive criticism, and just genuine hard work, the other team managed to score. They managed to not only score, but to score the winning goal, and sometimes their fans were as viciously prideful as the team they were supporting.

The score was 2-3 and I was fully aware of the fact that my thirteen years of playing soccer had lead up to this game: the last game I'd ever get to play with the team I'd loved for years.

I dreadfully walked back to my position with only thoughts of how I could have prevented what just happened. Whether it was true or not, I couldn't help but believe that it was my fault.

I turned around and looked across the field to see a scoreboard that presented a time that nearly guaranteed our loss: four minutes and thirty-one seconds. My chest welled up, and as I tried to catch my breath, I started hyperventilating because I was trying not to cry. I felt embarrassed, but I shouldn't have.

The other team's excessive cheering sent a knot to my stomach that was compliant only to anger. *They don't deserve it*, I thought to myself, *we're clearly the better team.* And truthfully, we were, but our team had a history of coming up short.

This was our first sections game of the season, and we weren't expected to lose, but we also weren't expected to ever do well as a sport. In my school, soccer was as good as not existing. We had never gone to state, and our fan base was made up of 90% parents. That being said, our team would have been a perfect example of an underdog. I used to think that meant we had a chance.

There are several iconic stories of underdogs overcoming unimaginable obstacles, but we only put faith in them because we'd lose a lot of hope if we didn't. We feel obliged to cheer them on because we can sympathize and even relate, but how often do they actually come out on top?

With three minutes left, I fantasized about one last scenario that I tried to convince myself could happen: we'd score in the last few seconds, tie the game, and go into overtime where we would victoriously take the win and give justice to our underappreciated team, but that didn't happen. It wasn't like the movies. It was like life, or at least the majority of life.

In the last six seconds of the game, with no hope left to spare, the other team managed to injure one of our players. They were just a hair outside the goal box, so the one opportunity of getting a penalty kick to tie the game, and actually become one of those amazing stories, was blown over. They simply blew the whistle that queued the end of the game.

My teammate that was injured tore a muscle and had to be carried off the field. But without checking if she was okay, our opponents joyously got in line to shake hands to show their sportsmanship.

A ref admitted that they wished we would have won.

It didn't feel like it was over, probably because it didn't feel justified.

6) i once knew fear

Dylan forgot her homework at her house. It would have been fine, but it was worth a lot of points and she never turns in anything late. She was planning to spend the night at my house, like she usually did when her mom didn't have a night shift, but this forced her to stop home before she could.

"In and out," I told her when we pulled into her driveway.

"Yeah I know, it'll be fine," she tried to convince me. I wasn't convinced.

The fact that Dylan was never home but her belongings always were, angered her mother. It wasn't that Dylan left a mess, it was more of the reminder that there was a part of her life that she royally screwed up, and it came back to live with her. In my mind, she deserved to feel that guilt, but not if it made Dylan a target.

I started to worry once three minutes had passed. Three minutes doesn't seem like a long time, but it is when you're waiting for something. Three minutes is the length of a song, it's the time it takes to cook an egg, it's how long you're given to "discuss with your neighbors" in English class, and it was certainly enough time for her to grab homework and come back out, so I didn't know why she hadn't yet.

I decided to text her once five minutes passed.

"*Is everything okay?*" I asked.

I waited what felt like an eternity, but she eventually replied, "*Yeah. Staying here. You should go.*" I knew she didn't say that by choice. She was trying to protect me from whatever was happening in that house, and I wasn't about to accept it.

"*Why? I'm not leaving. Is there any way you could sneak out?*" I questioned, but after that text, I received no others. I had never been so conflicted in my life. I wasn't one to get out of my car and knock on their door, but I also wasn't the one to leave my friend behind.

I waited three more minutes for a reply. I then called. No answer.

What would you do?

I started to feel nauseous trying to think of a solution. I knew that I would be forever ridden with guilt if I didn't at least try to help her, so after convincing my body to move, I hesitantly pulled my door handle and exited my car.

The air was still and the trees didn't move. The world seemed untouched, yet anything could have been happening behind that door. I felt lied to.

I cowardly walked up to their front step and looked inside. I saw nothing that indicated that anyone was home. The last thing I wanted to do was further anger her mother, so I chose not to ring the doorbell. Instead, I went around the back of their house to see if I could somehow reach Dylan through one of her windows.

Their back yard looked even worse than the front. There was a brown fence around the perimeter that was broken in several places, and a single tree that was surrounded by a poor excuse for grass. There was no successful plant growth, and no indication that anyone spent any time back there. I wondered if Dylan's mother cared about her appearance enough to at least maintain the grass in her front lawn, or did she just get lucky?

With Dylan's room being in the basement, I had to climb down her window well in order to actually see into it. Once I managed to do so, I crouched down and looked inside.

Luckily, her blinds were up, but her lights were off, so my level of visibility was very low. I could only tell that there was someone in the bathroom because of the light that reached the hallway. I prayed that it was Dylan.

I waited a second eternity with anticipation building in my stomach to see who was going to come around the corner. To my utmost relief, when the light flicked off and there was movement in the hallway, it was Dylan who filled the frame. My hand naturally went to the glass as I watched her walk towards her room. She was holding a bloody rag under her nose.

When she was just a few feet away, she turned on the light, causing her to finally look up and notice me through the window. She jumped at the unexpected sight of me, and I vigorously pointed at the lock, coaxing her to let me in.

She put down the rag, unlocked the window, and thrusted it open. But before I could go in, she half-whispered, half-yelled, "What the hell are you doing here!?"

I ungracefully shoved my way into her room. Once stable, I matched her volume and replied, "I wasn't about to just leave you here." I said it like it was obvious, but I was slightly offended that she was surprised to see me.

"Well, you have to go. You shouldn't be here." I hated when she looked worried.

"No Dylan. Look at what she does to you." I picked up her bloody rag and waved it in her face. "You're the one that shouldn't be here!"

I gave her back the rag because her nose was still a mess. This time it wasn't something she could hide.

"What happened?"

We slowed down.

She closed the door and we sat on her bed. I felt like I was back at the first day that she showed me her life. We sat in the same spots, only this time, I wasn't afraid to make eye contact; I insisted upon it.

I'll summarize. She explained that her mother had stopped her on her way up the stairs, blocking her way out. She was drunk as usual, and told Dylan to give her her phone because she wasn't going to pay for it anymore. Of course, Dylan being Dylan, she refused. They then got into an argument, and when Dylan turned to go back to her room (also the only time she was able to get a text out to me), her mother pushed her from behind as she reached the last step. Dylan fell forward and her nose was smashed against the wall. Her mother managed to take Dylan's phone while she was distracted with the blood. After that, she simply walked back upstairs.

Her mother displayed no sign of guilt besides the small and pathetic gesture of going to get the rag that Dylan has now, throwing it down the stairs for her. After that, she remained elsewhere while Dylan was in the bathroom cleaning herself up.

I was seething. I wanted nothing more than to hurt her mother, or see her put in jail, but I convinced myself that I wasn't capable of making either of those things happen. Instead, I resorted to the only other form of protection I knew: to remove Dylan from the house.

"We're leaving," I demanded.

"She'll know, and that'll only make it worse for when I return," she reasoned, although I could tell she was surprised at how determined I was.

"Then you'll never come back. Dylan, I will not let you stay here tonight."

"She got what she wanted, she'll leave me alone now," she insisted.

"You don't know that! My car's outside, can we please just go out your win-"

She cut me off, "Your car's in my driveway?" she asked, obviously worried.

"Well, yeah, I didn't move it before coming in."

"Then we have to go," she urgently informed me. "She doesn't allow anyone over. If she sees that-" she stopped at the sound of heavy footsteps on the stairs. We instantly looked at each other with wide eyes, for we both knew what that was, and we both had the same idea of how to avoid it.

Within seconds, Dylan had her homework and any other necessities in her bag, and we were at her window. We could hear her mother down the hallway as I climbed through the opening. I don't know why I went first.

Getting out of the window well was harder than getting in, but once I did, I turned around to help Dylan up after she managed to close the window. The second she reached level ground, her mother wrenched the window back open and yelled, "You fucking brat! You'll be sorry for this!" as we sprinted to my car. I fumbled with my keys but eventually managed to start the engine and drive away, breathing heavily.

"What the fuck was that?" I asked as I blankly stared forward. "That type of thing doesn't happen!" I said this to myself. I was thinking out loud, not talking to Dylan, and I think she knew that because she didn't reply.

We didn't talk or play music, we just drove, and I purposely took the long way home. Dylan looked in the vanity mirror to examine her nose. It was bruised. It looked like stained strawberry juice - piled veins with nowhere to go, but she managed to get rid of all the blood. I wondered what lie she'd come up with this time when everyone asked what happened.

After that, she didn't return home for four days, she never saw a doctor about her nose, and she hasn't had a phone since. She never cried, and of course, she still didn't look belittled.

7) i once knew anger

I hate it when a class is ruined simply because the teacher sucks. For my third block class, that was the case.

She was the kind of teacher that was so clueless it forced you to wonder how she even qualified to teach the class in the first place. She was the kind of teacher that treated us like we were in kindergarten. She was the kind that took too long of a "dramatic pause" in between words she was trying to emphasize. She was the kind that explained the same, simple concept in twelve different ways, and didn't know what time management was, and couldn't work her own equipment, and was so innocent and *fluffy* that if I slapped her in the face with real life, she'd only shrug it aside and offer me one of those cheesy life quotes you see posted on some bullshit landscape picture on the internet. I couldn't stand her, and she caught me on a bad day.

She didn't do anything in particular that was any more overly annoying than her typical irritating tendencies. I was just pissed going into the class simply because school sucked that day. You know what I mean, Reader.

I sat with my arms crossed and my head down the entire time. I wouldn't give her the courtesy of looking at her when she spoke, and I didn't care that I was being rude. Eventually it came time to watch a video, and I was relieved to be free of listening to her pointless rambling. It took her at least five minutes to find the right scene.

I didn't pay attention. The video only reiterated what she had just drilled into us for thirty unnecessary minutes. Instead, I kept my arms crossed and

94

stared at the vacant table in front of me. I then went into a mindset that I think (or hope), that you, Reader, can relate to and prove that I'm not insane.

It went like this: I envisioned a scenario where I could fully release my anger and annoyance. I pictured myself kicking over the table in front of me. It'd be loud and disruptive, and her stupid, fluffy face would be appalled. I'd then stand and flip over the next table. I'd destroy her projector, rip out her computer, and clear off her desk. I'd confront her on all of the useless teaching methods she'd obnoxiously bestowed upon us and question the reasoning behind all of her annoying habits.

The students would be speechless, and I think she would be too. In which case, I'd simply pick up my bag and walk out the door. I wouldn't turn if she told me to stop; I wouldn't regret what I'd done. I would smile at my spectacle and leave the building.

But that didn't happen. It never happens.

I was still staring at the table when the video ended and the lights came back on. She asked the class if we understood. I didn't see how there could've been a single person who didn't understand, but because I wasn't the only one who viewed this teacher that way, no one responded. This prompted her to then explain it again, so I envisioned myself standing up and simply decking her across the face.

I realize that that is all very aggressive and would never happen, but don't you ever get those moments? Those moments devoted to the realization that you could cause a huge scene or a terrible accident? You could be driving in your car with passengers and randomly consider running the next red light to T-bone a car at 60 mph, which would kill everyone in the crash. Of course you would never actually do it, but man, it could happen.

I got an A in that class.

8) i once knew stress

I don't understand the stereotype that implies teenagers are lazy, immature, disrespectful, assholes who do nothing but text. Yes, we text. Yes, we can be lazy, and immature, and disrespectful, and an asshole, but so can any other age group. I think people sometimes forget that the majority of teenagers actually have busy-ass lives.

We have to find time to manage a school life, a sport life, a work life, and a social life. Some kids can be in sports, or multiple sports, or band, or both. They can be in other clubs, or things that "look good on a college application." They can have one job, or two. I even know some kids with three. I'd consider the most time consuming part of life to be school.

School life is essentially an everyday thing. I know we're only required to go five days a week, but how often do we actually end up with a completely free weekend? It feels as if teachers are under the impression that the weekend is equivalent to two extra full days of work time. Bullshit. Weekends are for work, or college visits, or extracurricular activities that figure they can be on the weekend because it's our "free time." When in reality, our free time doesn't start until midnight, so of course we're going to use it to stay up for hours watching Netflix, because who doesn't want an escape? That part is our fault. I'll give the type-casters that.

What I won't give them, is the assumption that we are not hardworking. When you're a Junior or a Senior your time can *always* be devoted to doing something more productive. That realization can send me into a depression. I feel guilty for devoting time to just relax; I feel guilty for writing this very sentence because I could be applying for another scholarship or figuring out how a grant works. But that thought reminds me of another reason to feel guilty:

In this day and age, we can literally graduate high school with an associate's degree. I could have started my Junior year as a full-time PSEO student. I could have abandoned the high school scene completely and went straight to college at age sixteen, shaving off two years of my presumed monstrous pile of college debt. But I didn't. I opted to have the "high school experience" and live out the last two years of the "best time of your life." Isn't that thought encouraging?

I know there are people who will read this and think, *wait until you become an adult,* and scoff at my pathetic complaining, but I think that just proves my point. We are encouraged to work our asses off in order to "have a successful life." If every adult I know is telling me that it'll just get harder, and that their life wasn't all that successful, doesn't it just prove that our work is practically pointless, and no matter what I do in these years, life will be hard? Of course it may be harder if I were to drop out of school, but me getting a degree does not guarantee success. Me getting grades no lower than a B- my entire high school career only provides me with the thought that huh, maybe I'll be able to get a decent job. But really, I'll probably take the first offer that comes to me because I'm scared I'll never get a better one, and I'll be stuck there for years, low-key hating my decision to accept it, and regretting my useless hard work in high school and college.

Not everyone makes it big.

Not everyone even *makes* it. I frequently try to remind myself of this.

That's just the school life. When and how will they know that we've reached our limit? But with that, I have one more thing to feel guilty about: I am extremely privileged to have these types of problems, so I better just shut up and deal with it.

9) i once knew serenity

Dylan introduced me to a new friend. He was smaller than I expected and very pale. He kind of scared me at first, but after about fifteen minutes, he grew on me. His nickname was Oxy, and I ended up seeing him on the weekends a lot. (Reader, what type of figurative language am I using??)

For those of you that aren't exposed to any sort of drug life, I'm talking about OxyContin, the semi-synthetic opioid used to relieve pain. How convenient and inconvenient that people generally get their wisdom teeth out when they're teenagers.

Dylan managed to get two pills from a friend and offered me a chance to experience yet another form of mind/body alteration. I have to admit that I was hesitant.

Opioids scared me. They've always been the thing you hear famous people got hooked on, and then you'd hear about damaging addictions or overdoses. I didn't want to be titled an addict or have to deal with the constant contradiction of wanting drugs but not wanting to spend the money to get them. Addictions aren't cheap, but I think that's a fair consequence. (I didn't count my cigarette habit as an addiction because I was in denial.)

Overall, I didn't want to be taking the first step to a huge problem, so as I stared at the little pill that could potentially control my life, resting in the palm of my hand, I hesitated as I brought it to my lips. The seconds before deciding felt like minutes. I can't remember what convinced me to finally throw it back, but in the end, I was happy that I did, and I think Dylan was even happier.

Twenty minutes later, I had transported into a different body and a pleasant mind set. I didn't feel out of control whatsoever, quite the opposite actually. The distinct difference between weed and pills was the type of lens I was forced to look through while influenced by them.

Weed provided two layers over my eyes. The first one stayed still and the second moved side to side, but it didn't distort what I was looking at. Instead, everything was thick and my mind usually convinced itself that I was stuck, yet my body convinced itself that I was moving. It was quite contradictory, whereas pills elated me. I knew exactly where I was and what I was doing. I was right there. Right at that moment. And talking became the most eye opening endeavor possible. My lens has never been as clear as it was after taking Oxy, and that thought scared me.

"What tattoos are you gonna' get when you're old enough?" I asked Dylan while lying next to her on my bed. She had talked about getting them before but had never specified what they would be.

"I don't really know," she started. Our responses were on the slow side because we were fully devoted to everything around us. The show on the TV had our attention, the comfort of the blankets had our attention, the soft glow of my candles had our attention, and we had our attention, and there was no one greater than the other.

"My first one will probably have something to do with *Winnie the Pooh*," she finally claimed.

"Seriously?" I asked in a nonjudgmental tone but was obviously still surprised.

"Yeah. My dad used to read it to me before I went to bed sometimes. It was either that or I tucked myself in while they would fight. I loved the nights that he would read. Plus, *Winnie the Pooh* is the best. Did you ever read it?"

"No, but I watched it."

"Not the same," she stated, and then turned back to the TV for a moment. "Would you get any tattoos?" she asked.

"Probably a few, but I don't know what," I answered, and that caused us to consider my possibilities. We discussed it for the remainder of the show and never lost interest. We never lost anything; we jumped topics and explored all that there was to know, or what we thought we knew, or what we wished to know, and eventually we reached God.

"I'm an atheist," she claimed and I wasn't surprised. "I don't understand how people can devote their life to something with similar qualities as the tooth fairy or Santa Clause." I let her continue. "It's not that I shame people for believing. I actually envy them because I just can't bring myself to do it. He's never felt real to me." I remained silent to see if she had anything else to say, but when she didn't continue, I asked, "What do you think happens when you die, then?"

She didn't hesitate. "You're gone. It's dark, and you have no knowledge of existing or having existed, and you're incapable of having an opinion about it because you're gone."

I was afraid she was going to say that, so I stepped in with my opinion, "Well, I'm agnostic, so I kinda' agreed with you until there, but I refuse to accept that my life is completely over once I die."

"Then what do you think happens?" she asked.

I took a moment to reply because I'd never actually committed to a single answer for that question. I've always loved – and despised – the fact that it could be anything, and I didn't want to limit the possibilities, but I knew I had to present a counterargument in order for Dylan to be satisfied.

"Well to start, I don't believe in heaven or hell. I feel like if there was a God, he wouldn't have the time to sift through everyone's life decisions and make a good or bad list. Plus, if God truly did love each and every one of us, how could he be so heartless as to send some of us to hell?" I questioned, and she nodded.

I continued, "I also don't fully believe in reincarnation, although I wish I did." I paused because I didn't know where I was going with my answer. "Um. . . I don't think we become ghosts or spirits that live amongst everyone because if that were true, there'd be a way bigger amount of spirits fucking with people just for the fun of it." I stopped again, and Dylan didn't comment because she was still waiting for an actual answer, and she could tell that I was failing to prove her wrong.

She then gave me the *I'm right and you know it* look and I broke. "Fine!" I exclaimed. "I don't have an answer. I can't prove you wrong, but you can't prove that you're right either. Yes, it makes sense that we're nothing after we die, but I will always refuse to believe that."

"That's because you're afraid," she calmly proclaimed.

"That's not true," I defended myself.

"Sure it is. Everyone is. We rely on religion because it's our safety net. We are scared shitless of becoming nothing. We're scared to die because we don't know what will happen, so we convince ourselves that we'll be saved. Because if we don't believe in something, we believe in nothing, and if that's true, then what are we doing here?"

Generally, I would have considered this a depressing conversation, but because my lens was clear, I was profoundly happy to be discussing it. And at that moment, I wasn't afraid at all.

"We're living," I answered.

"That's all you've got?" she sincerely asked. "You know, just because you say it like that it doesn't make it meaningful all of a sudden. The human race has been living for hundreds of years, yet all we've done is find a million ways to try to be okay with dying and avoid considering the possibility that, you know, maybe it truly is all for nothing," she ranted, and I could tell that she was genuinely concerned about the possibility of a meaningless life followed by a meaningless death, so I confronted her about it.

"I'm not the one who's afraid, Dylan, you are. You're afraid that you're right. And you envy religious people because they've somehow been able to put faith in the thought that we're living for a reason."

"But what if they're wrong?" she suggested.

"So what? Then they die and cease to exist, and like you said, don't have an opinion about it because they're incapable of it," I reasoned. "Isn't that better? Wouldn't you rather have a positive outlook on dying instead of fearing it like you do?"

"Not if I'm going to end up disappointed in the end," she claimed.

"Dylan, you wouldn't know that you'd be disappointed. If you truly believe that there is nothing, then you wouldn't have the opportunity to be disappointed. All you would have done was live with a better attitude towards death, and I can't see how that's a bad thing," I gave my last argument, but it didn't convince her.

"I just can't do it."

I wished that she could. I didn't want her thinking her shitty life would be rewarded with nothing. Even if nothing would end up being a better option than living, I could tell it wouldn't be her ideal, so I flopped my arm over her torso and gave her a squeeze.

"It's okay. We'll find out eventually." We looked at each other with the eye that wasn't squished on our pillows and smiled. I then presented my final thought on the subject, "You know what I think?"

"What?" she asked.

"If every religious person is able to be fully devoted to their religion, and are wholeheartedly convinced that what they believe in is true, then that makes someone wrong. So maybe we're all wrong." She continued to look at me. "That's what I believe in," I decided.

She stared at me for a while longer and then said, "Or maybe we're all right."

She never failed to offer a rebellious mind.

We then devoted our attention to what was on TV, and then we devoted it to the monochromatic room that resulted from turning off the lights, and then our attention was devoted to sleep, and there was no one greater than the other.

10) i once went to my first party

I was nervous. I had never gone to a "legit" party before which was pretty sad considering my age. Not to mention that it took someone who didn't even grow up here to get me to go to a party in my own town. But nevertheless, Dylan made me comfortable enough with the idea to go along. So we got in my car to head over to a college boy's house. Apparently, it was normal for high schoolers to attend college house parties, but I was still considerably skeptical.

Upon arriving, my skepticism was proven wrong, for I was surrounded by an odd selection of fellow Seniors, a couple of Juniors even, and the majority of the remaining people graduated from my school a year or two ago. The only thought I could manage was *weird.*

From that point on, most of what I thought I knew about parties was refuted, and I took another step forward in broadening my education on what it meant to be a "true teenager."

"This is weird," I vocalized my thoughts while whispering to Dylan.

"It's okay," she stated, and headed toward the island in the kitchen that showcased a wide assortment of alcohol. Dylan added her three-quarters-full bottle of vodka she had managed to sneak out of her house to the heard. This was a *bring your own or leave it alone* type of party, so her vodka was "a ticket to a good time" as she stated before we arrived. At that point, I thought there was enough to go around, but as the night went on, more and more came through the door. (I need to stop rhyming things.)

Dylan then took two of the cliché, red solo cups from the pile and filled them full with a mixture of three different drinks. Don't ask me what it was because all I'd be able to tell you is that it worked, and worked fast.

With the first sip, I nearly threw up.

"Oh my god, that's disgusting."

Dylan laughed, "You'll get used to it."

"I hope so," I pleaded, and took another drink which caused my face to scrunch up and resulted in a big sigh once it was down. That wasn't my first time drinking by any means, but I usually didn't drink a mixture of hard alcohols. I then noticed that most of the other people present were simply drinking beer. I silently wondered why Dylan chose to drink this, but I never bothered to ask.

We found our way into the living room and were greeted by a couple of our friends who admitted that they were surprised to see me, but that it was nice, and that I would have fun. It was reassuring to hear, but I never shook the feeling of not belonging. I only grew more comfortable with the idea that none of us really did; the only thing that truly united us was a common goal of feeling different.

I allowed that thought to ease my nerves a bit. But it still didn't feel natural to be surrounded by people I grew up with who now had bottles in their hands and joints to their lips. I swore just yesterday we were all playing tag on the playground. Now, we were playing in a different sense, and our hands were just as involved as they were before.

Dylan knew how to act. She could talk to anyone and instantly knew what type of humor they liked. It allowed her to flawlessly joke around with them, which is a quality that most people value. I was only good with a couple of people, and I viewed everyone as intimidating which I didn't understand. Why did I view people who got drunk and acted immaturely as people who were superior to me? Yes, I'm a teenager who values fitting in, but why did I feel like I needed to fit in with those types of people? Did they feel the same way? Like many things, I never bothered to find the answer. I only accepted the fact that they probably didn't care.

I managed to finish my drink. I knew before going into it that I was a lightweight, so one drink was all I needed, yet everyone else almost constantly had a drink in their hand, so I too, got another. Although this time, I didn't let Dylan make it. She was on her third drink before she lost her controlled, sarcastic demeanor. It was nice to see her fumble a bit, which is selfish of me, but no one liked her less for being drunk. If anything, everyone became more accepting as the night went on, and therefore, I did too.

In the time span of an hour, I had moved from the wall, to the couch, to the kitchen, to the bathroom, and to the living room floor. With each destination, it felt as though the new one was placed, instead of replaced, over the previous one. This system of overlapping settings made them all blend together, and suddenly, everything felt familiar. That familiarity allowed me to let go of my safety net (Dylan), and discover what I now perceive as a "real" party.

First of all, don't expect the movies. Although some are accurate, I wouldn't consider them a reliable source for you to base your expectations on. I, personally, was very surprised to find out that when playing beer pong, you don't actually fill the cups with beer: you fill them with water.

Perhaps I'm lame, and although it's logical, it never occurred to me that the movies weren't accurate. I thought that once someone got the ball in the cup, they were supposed to chug the beer inside, but really, there was no chugging at all. They filled the cups with water because, truthfully, everything got wet after a round or two, and it would have been a waste of alcohol. So when someone's ball did land in the cup, they simply removed it from the table and casually continued drinking at the rate that they desired.

The reason for playing the game was not for the players to get hammered, but for the players to have fun. And I now acquiesce, it actually *was* rather enjoyable, and I ended up playing, and winning, two games. (I also didn't know that there are specific names for the positions of the cups and some legitimate rules, so that made me feel stupid, but I was also too influenced by alcohol to really give a shit.)

Regarding my list of realizations, my next one came essentially the second I walked through the door: they aren't always as big as they're depicted. There was a total of around 40-50 people who could easily move around the house and occupied their own space, rather than be right on top of one another.

That being said, not every room in the house was full, and we didn't need to go outside in order to spread out and have some privacy. There also wasn't a pool in the backyard, or a bouncer in the front. If you didn't know the host, or someone close to the host, you didn't go to the party. I don't know why movies think that if one person sends out a text, suddenly the entire school knows about it, and everyone shows up within ten minutes. First of all, no matter how popular you are, you do not have everyone's number, and not everyone cares enough to spread the word. Second of all, not that many people are just sitting around waiting to hear about a party. It's usually something that's planned, and they don't only occur when "my parents are out of town."

Lastly, we didn't destroy the house. We were still (generally) civil people who didn't go around knocking shit over the second we got a drop of alcohol in our system. If that actually happened, no one would want to throw a party, and we'd truthfully be very apologetic rather than blow it off and destroy more shit. Give us some credit.

What I will say, however, is that it was very loud. I was often nervous about neighbors hearing, but then I would remind myself that I couldn't hear the music before I had entered the house, so it was unlikely that they'd have heard it then. I also worried about someone finding out, but I couldn't think of anyone who would care besides the police, and even then, it wasn't a big enough party for anyone to be suspecting it.

Once I came to those realizations, I hadn't a care in the world, and it was to my utmost relief that the night was genuinely fun. I legitimately felt as though I prevailed through a falsely promoted rite of passage, and I was happy about it. I was proud of myself. That's such a weird thing to be proud of.

11) i once went to my eighth party

It became pretty routine. With the handful of people that we knew who threw parties, there seemed to be one every weekend, and Dylan was always okay with attending them. I never opposed because I didn't see a point. They always had the potential of being fun, and it wasn't that they weren't, it was more of me getting used to it. I started to question what they were doing for me.

Dylan didn't care that much. Once we had attended multiple parties, I noticed that she was more so high than drunk, and would be content with doing next to nothing. I think she enjoyed the simple pleasure of forgetting what it meant to be sober, and embracing what it meant to be influenced. Often times, she'd have her never-ending bag on her, and she'd pull out a little sketchbook and a pen, and she'd draw what she observed, or an interpretation of what she observed.

She now has a collection of nearly twenty sketches, and she calls them her *Assisted Will* drawings. She claims they'll never become anything more than a sketch even though I've tried, on multiple occasions, to convince her to develop them. But she likes what they are in the simplest form, so I respect that.

This time, we were at a barn/shed that was bigger than it needed to be and had lights strung around the framework of the building. Some of them flickered, some projected, and some were constant. The low light with loud music promoted more dancing than usual, but the only type of dancing teenagers know how to perfect is grinding. Needless to say, I was okay with sitting that one out as I smoked a cigarette while sitting on a hay bale against the wall. (Now that I think about it, that had the potential of being very stupid.)

Dylan was high and dancing amongst some other single friends. I admired their ability to dance and not look like complete fools. Not that anyone would have cared in that setting, but I would've never joined them.

Reader, I bet this sounds like I'm the sad loner observing the party from the side and forever living in the shadow of my adventurous best friend, but I want to assure you that that's not true. Yes, I was jealous of the things that Dylan was comfortable doing, but my envy remained as envy rather than transforming into self-hate. So I wasn't sad to be alone, sitting on a hay bail in an atmosphere that suggested just the opposite; I was simply uninspired to conform to its suggestions, and I didn't view that as a bad thing.

Once I finished my cigarette, (I never allowed myself to have more than one) I poured myself a drink and returned to my spot.

Halfway through drinking it, I felt different. I couldn't tell if it was the placebo effect or if I really was that much of a lightweight, but I was happy that I didn't have consume copious amounts of alcohol to feel something. (I've never understood why being a lightweight is something to be ashamed of. Like, it just means I have to buy less alcohol. I'm saving money and having a better time faster than you. Fuck off, bud.)

Once my drink was gone, I continued to sit, and as I sat, I started to feel philosophical because, you know, that happens sometimes. So when I started to notice that the hay bail was hurting my butt, I distracted myself by trying to simplify my surroundings. I did this to remind myself of what was happening, and how small I really was.

Once more, I took notice of the lights. There were so many and not one set was the same. My favorite was by far the strobe light. It only went off periodically because at some point, it was too much to handle, but when it did, I was compelled to move.

With each flash, I felt liberated because the darkness that followed was enough of a camouflage to convince me that moving was okay. The split second of pure emotion that was displayed on everyone's illuminated face, and the shadows that were cast around the contours of their features, assured me of nothing but the fact that they were free. Or at least that they felt that way, and I couldn't help but let it rub off on me.

However, I didn't display the feeling of freedom in the way that they had. Instead, I remained sitting, and I closed my eyes.

I once had a friend explain to me that he had a "movie moment." That once, at a concert, he met a girl, and as they danced they faced each other, and he swore to me that the music started to fuse together. He no longer heard the lyrics, but a unified note that allowed him to devote all of his attention to that girl. "It was as if the world had stopped," he said, "yet I was certain that everything around us was moving."

I imagined that that was how I felt then. Instead of listening to rap, I was listening to the build of "666 ʇ" by Bon Iver, and each significant layer of the song was an individual there who contributed to the atmosphere. I felt immersed in the idea that it was all conditional, and that each aspect of the party was merely an innuendo for throwing one. If even one aspect was missing, everything would be different, so I took the time to notice them all.

The people. I didn't like them all, but I didn't have to. They posed as the most important part of the whole thing, so a few that didn't belong only made it more authentic. I noticed how each one was dressed, and how they wore their hair. I noticed that their level of comfort was expressed through the extent of their motions, and that that was mostly dependent on the number of drinks they had downed. Each one was different, yet as a group, their differences blurred together. I wondered what they would have been doing if they were alone.

The alcohol. The thing responsible for this entire event. It sat at its own table in glasses that disguised its intent. They were tall and sleek or short and thick, yet they all did the same thing. The table never went unattended, and its contents were always replaced when emptied.

The stereo. The thing that inspired an outlet for our emotions and a reason for our body state. Without the music pulsing through our bones, we would've had no inspiration to move, and everything we would've been doing would've become awkward. It was what made the event an event; the party now had an agenda, and everyone knew what they were supposed to be doing. It was the clarification that we all needed in order to come.

The walls. They were what gave the event a "space." Without them, we'd lose our sense of security. We'd lose our confidence to attend, and there'd be question of whether or not it would have happened in the first place. But the walls also served as another form of security. They were a safe zone for those who did not feel they belonged in the middle, amongst those who felt free enough to move. They were a symbol of stability and viewed as a way to not stand out. But really, they had acquired a bigger magnify glass, for they were not the majority. What a lie the walls told.

The smoke. This was viewed as a side effect to a cause that promoted change. With every blunt, butt, or bong, there was a trail of ghosts to follow. I could tell that no one minded, it was none of their concern, but I knew it had to go somewhere, so I watched as it rose. From every streak of light, I could see its cloudy state. It was what gave depth to the lights, and therefore, gave depth to the room.

The floor. The floor was the one thing I gave no doubt to count upon. Despite the dozens of feet pounding on its existence, it remained stronger than us. The floor was the first to come, and was what allowed the rest to follow. At that time, the floor was dark, unless a strip of light was able to venture to its surface. Then the floor was all sorts of colors despite being concrete. That was what brought me home. I imagined the floor with the main lights turned on. I imagined it with no people to stomp, and no stereo to vibrate. I imagined it for what it was: a smooth, compact surface that held everything above it, up. I imagined its eerie kenopsia, and in that moment, I viewed it as an opportunity. I knew that the party could only amount to being considered one that was seized.

I didn't feel the need to classify the event as anything more than the aspects it was made of. I didn't feel the need to justify me being there. But once the party ended, and I knew that there would surely be another to follow, I couldn't help but wonder if I actually had a desire to be there in the first place, or if I was satisfied with my decision to not oppose it.

My conclusion was simply *I don't know*, and I think that influenced my opinion of every party to follow. Eventually, my list for opposition grew longer, but so did my will not to, so I didn't. However, I got so used to the routine and so overcome by the expectations I didn't feel like meeting, that "Here" by Alessia Cara soon became my theme song.

Dylan didn't know that I didn't want to be there, so you can't blame her. But you can blame me, because I didn't try to change anything. Like I said, I didn't see a point, but that's probably the worst excuse I could have used.

12) i once was mortified

i once was telling a story to a group of people and realized halfway through that it wasn't funny.

i once waved back to a person who wasn't actually waving at me.

i once ended a song one note after everyone else.

i once returned a fist bump with a high five.

i once, twice, three time, four times, FIVE times, walked in on someone peeing.

i once walked in on someone having sex.

i once was walked in on while having sex.

i once spit on someone while talking to them, and they acknowledged it.

i once ended up in the background of someone's Snapchat while hardcore eating.

i once didn't understand what someone was telling me, so I pretended like I did and continuously nodded until I was asked a question about the topic. My bull shitting skills were at an all-time low.

i once was drinking a beverage and I missed my mouth.

i once called my teacher "mom."

i once stepped on the back of someone's shoe while walking, and when they looked back to glare, I acted like it wasn't me. We were the only two in the hallway.

i once did the thing where you're trying to pass someone but you both end up moving in the same direction, four times in a row.

i once had a planned joke in a presentation and no one laughed.

i once farted in class. I don't care who you are, you know. You. Know.

You know about all of these, really. We've all had our fair share of embarrassing or awkward moments, but despite that, we fail to consider them any less awkward even though everyone can relate. Why can't we all just get together and agree to never shame anyone for carrying out one of these terrible moments? They're completely normal if you think about it.

13) i once mattered, and so did you, and so did everyone

Starting now:

Did you know that there are 1.8 deaths per second? I cannot wrap my head around that for the life of me.

Bam.

Now that took you approximately 5 seconds to read, which means that right as you read the word "bam" about 9 people died.

Bam.

Another 5 seconds, 18 people. Do you feel guilty? As you're merely reading about people dying, those people actually are. Think about how many people die in the length of time it takes you to read this book. Sad, isn't it? But help them out: give your condolences and acknowledge their death.

Bam.

39 people, acknowledge them. They died while being in at least one person's mind, yours, and that's actually pretty significant considering that each of them were merely one in the ever growing population of 7.3 billion people. It means a lot that their time alive doesn't go unnoticed because it certainly wasn't wasted.

I can't stand it when people declare themselves meaningless in the grand scheme of life. Yes, it is inevitable that the world will end and everything in it, on it, whatever, will die. Yes, you as an individual will most likely not make a universal impact in the time that you're alive. Yes, it's likely that your name will not go down in history. And yes, there will be time where there isn't anyone to remember the names that somehow did. Yes, it's depressing to think about. But no, that does not classify you as meaningless.

Who decided that to be worthy of an everlasting, impressionable, elite legacy you had to be famous? A name known by millions and therefore a death acknowledged by millions. Why does that qualify the life you lived to be any more special than the life you would have lived if it wasn't posted on the front page of a magazine or gossiped about by people in need of small talk? I understand that we all like to be liked, but I wish we didn't live in a society that defined our worth based on if we were or not.

If you think about it, we live for the potential of having a good day, or to help someone else have a good day, or simply because we think we have to. But what if we didn't? What if we didn't have the natural instinct to survive? Would we want to live? In my opinion, the answer would be no - if it weren't for people. Considering it's a universal goal to be remembered, mourned over, or acknowledged, it's not hard to live a life worth living.

(Warning: I am about to sound like a cliché inspirational speaker.)

If you've impacted even a single person's life for the better, then your life has been justified. And that's because our lives are lived through the perspective of others. If we were to never have human contact throughout our life, we would have no desire to live, and that's because our lives revolve around people. Not plants, not animals, people. And there's no way around that. You can say our goal is to save the environment or to achieve world peace, but how do we accomplish that? People. So in order to keep people around, we need to encourage them, which is a very easy thing to do. And if we've done that, then we've done our job. And if we've done our job, then our lives are, therefore, justified.

However, that feels very mechanical, so let me make it pretty: if one does not prolong the life of another, then they may not be inspired to do the same. And if no one does, then who will? We are natural copy cats in a world that promotes individuality, yet we feel ostracized if we don't fit in. We are a foundation built on irony, and a corporation based on integrity. When have those ever proven to be stable?

We were doomed from the start. When living, we are provided a single guarantee: we will die. Such a low starting point demands the strength of billions in order to redeem our lost ground. When it comes down to it, we're all the same damn people on the same damn earth, trying to get the same damn thing. So it's simply not fair that some people get a head start if we're all running the same damn race. But the fact that it is a race, provides us with an opportunity: embrace our ironic tendencies and encourage our opponents. If we don't, then what was the point of having a race in the first place?

14) i once met

i once met a girl who didn't know the difference between positive and negative
attention, or rather, she didn't have a preference.

i once met a boy who was valedictorian. He got there by punching out all of his work on Friday, and then getting wasted the rest of the weekend.

i once met a girl who was both socially awkward and outgoing. She once admitted that footy pajamas were her ideal comfy wear.

i once met a boy who loved movies, but they never gave him a chance.

i once met a girl who could make anyone laugh, but she struggled to hide the scars on her thighs when her shorts were just a little too short.

i once met a girl who thought she was never wrong, but couldn't pass a class.

i once met an ordinary boy and an ordinary girl, and they were an ordinary couple.

i once met a girl who never spoke unless directly addressed, and she came from a bad home. But she snapped her fingers when she was mad, and had the kindest voice I'd ever heard.

i once met a boy who got all the girls, yet he was able to convince each of them that they were special.

i once met a girl who was brave enough to show her boobs at a parade that was made for that sort of thing, and she received nothing but applause.

i once met a girl who's only talent was her face.

i once met a girl who suffered from major depression, but had the most beautiful smile i'd ever seen.

i once met a boy who swayed when he walked and painted his fingernails black. He never failed to have a deck of cards, with which he performed wonderful tricks.

i once met a girl who loved the idea of a smile so much, she became a dentist.

i once met a girl who would give herself away before considering if it was worth it or not.

i once met a boy who I barely knew, and it saddens me to think that I never had the chance to learn something he loved better than the tight grip of a noose.

i once met a boy who had a smile that touched his ears.

i once met a boy who was a girl.

i once met a girl who was a boy.

i once met a person who didn't care about gender.

i once met a person who inspired me enough to talk about them here, and now.

i once met these people, and I'll never forget.
I don't know how I could.

15) i once kicked a single rock nearly two miles back to my house, only to have it fall down the sewer on my last kick. I couldn't tell if I was happy with that or not.

16) i once spent six hours on a puzzle only to realize that another puzzle had mistakenly been mixed into my box. i once wasted six hours.

17) i once went out to eat with five members of my family and they all ordered eggs benedict except me. What is that? (Side note, later that year that restaurant was voted to have the best eggs benedict in the state. No joke.)

18) i once took a shower and was so devoted to my thoughts, that I forget what I had and hadn't put in my hair. I had to start over.

19) i once watched a spider struggle to climb up its web. I viewed that as being equivalent to someone struggling to pay rent.

20) i once was labeled "lazy," but that's only because I put effort towards things they didn't deem worthy.

21) i once wrote this sentence simply to get you to read a pointless sentence.

22) i once realized that that wasn't a true sentence because I didn't capitalize the "I."

Oh well.

I consider each of these moments to be just as important as any other, because in the end, none of it truly matters, and I think that's the perfect excuse to let everything matter.

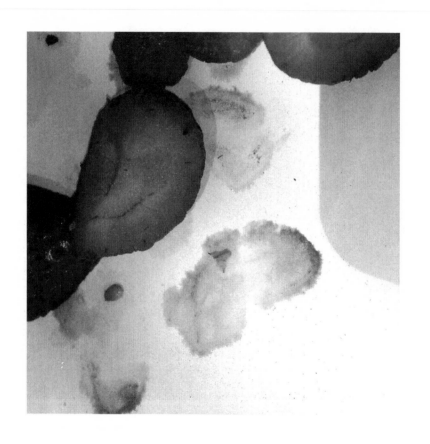

THE END IS OUR BEGINNING [10]

=

(Wow, that was a long chapter. Now back to me, laying in my bed, trying to decide which side is more comfy to lay on while contemplating my life, like usual.)

My thoughts and nearly-full memories ramble on, but I eventually fall asleep, and the night progresses like any other. I've always felt bad for people with insomnia. I absolutely adore sleep, and have no problem doing it. I can't imagine not being able to every single night. I used to have a friend who struggled with it. Her daily schedule was bizarre.

Anyway, the next few weeks advance in a constant state of *this is the end.* As a Senior, I attend multiple grad parties, and participate in many school-funded Senior activities that range from grill outs to giveaways. At this point, I don't care about my classes. I count the days of when they'll be done, but really, I don't need to, because it feels like it's going faster than I can count. It's going so fast it doesn't give me time to let it sink in, until I hear them call my name, and I get up to walk across the stage.

I'm going to graduate high school in one sentence because that's basically how it feels to get my diploma. Four years of work on one sheet of paper, and we're done.

We threw bouncy balls at our principal.

I nearly tripped.

Dylan is excited, genuinely excited, which is refreshing to witness. Her mother didn't come to the graduation ceremony, but I think I would have died of shock if she had. Dylan is mainly excited about being one step closer to leaving. With a month and half before her birthday, she's trying, to the best of her ability, to lay low with her mother who is getting even worse.

In the few occasions I've actually encountered Dylan's mother, I learned that she has multiple minimum-wage jobs that often require early mornings and late nights. This is a problem for many reasons, but two that stand out are the fact that she doesn't get much sleep, which causes her to be tired and crabby all the time. The second is that considering she is an alcoholic and doesn't have a lot of free time, she ends up drinking at work. This has caused her to be fired from multiple jobs which makes every new one she manages to get even harder to keep. No wonder she takes it out on Dylan, she's probably tired of taking it out on herself. But I can't feel bad for her, because she deserves the majority of the blame. She handles every situation in the worst way possible, and the outlet to her feelings should never be to harm her daughter. I just don't understand, but I wish that I could.

Dylan doesn't bother to figure it out either because right now, she's focused on the wonderful news that Tate and Tanner should soon be visiting us, and boy, am I anxious upon hearing that.

"When exactly?" I ask.

"They said they'd stay for the two weeks leading up to my birthday, and then I'll go stay at Tate's house until I can find a place of my own," she replies.

I think it over: that gives me a month of Dylan to myself, two weeks with the four of us, and a summer together that ends early because Dylan will be off searching the cities for a suitable dwelling, and I'll be anxiously waiting for college.

It's a lot to take in. Even though I'm longing for the day that Dylan can restart her life, I do wish that things would slow down a bit. It's hard to fathom that I'm standing in a crowd full of celebration amongst peers, who I've literally grown up with, in a sea of graduation gowns. I put it in perspective and realize how far we've come, but I know that it's barely a sliver considering I still have at least four years of schooling left to accomplish – as do most of the people present. This is merely the start, and I suddenly resent how long it's taken to get here, but I secretly wish that I could stay a little bit longer.

My parents greet me with proud phrases as they give a tight squeeze around the shoulder. My dad, who I haven't seen in nearly a month, makes me pose for multiple pictures. He always makes a point to take a picture when we're together, no matter what we're doing, so he thoroughly enjoys having an excused to take many now.

"One more," he pleads, and I give him my last effort for a smile. He's satisfied and gives me another tight hug around the shoulder. He then notices that Dylan is standing next to my mom, and as I walk to her side he asks, "Who's this?"

"Dylan," I answer. "She's my good friend."

"Pleasure to meet you, Dylan," my dad states as he holds out his hand.

"You as well," Dylan replies as she returns the handshake.

It's strange to think that Dylan is such a big part of my life, yet she hasn't met my dad before now. Although, I've never met her dad either, and it's a shame that I never will.

We chat for a short time about dates and what I'll be bringing to college. My dad is invested in everything I have to say, and he makes sure that I'll be fully prepared when I leave.

He then turns to Dylan and asks where she'll be going. My stomach instantly sinks because I know my dad won't approve of her loose plan. Dylan declares that she'll be taking a year off to save up some money, but later will attend an art school. My father gives his best impression of being excited for her, and concludes our meeting with yet another hug. My parents then walk back to their separate cars, and Dylan and I are left alone together (my favorite oxymoron).

"I'm sorry he asked that," I say.

"It's alright," she replies, unconvincingly. "It was expected."

Before I have a chance to say more, our favorite math teacher – who's more of a friend than an authority – approaches. He stops in the middle of us and flings his lengthy arms around our shoulders.

"Glad to be out of here?" he asks, and we smile.

"Done with your classes? Please, I've never been happier," Dylan jokes. Relationships with teachers always require an odd form of communication.

He grins. "Well, I'm certainly not. It was a pleasure to have the both of you. I suspect you'll do great things." He gives our shoulders a squeeze and then turns to face us.

"So what is it that you want to do when you're older?" he asks. "I don't believe you've told me."

"You know, I find that oddly offensive," Dylan states, and this time it's obvious that she isn't joking.

He throws up his hands. "I didn't mean to offend you," he sincerely states. "I just meant what job–"

Dylan cuts him off, "You know what I want to do? I want to put something out in the world and have it mean something to someone. And you know, I think I've already done that, but I can assure you, *age* had absolutely nothing to do with it." She then storms off in a very dramatic manner, leaving our teacher with a confused, apologetic look on his face.

"I'm sure she didn't mean to direct that at you," I insist and apologize as I run off to find her. I know that her anger has been misplaced. I can't imagine she's actually that mad about age discrimination, but I guess you never really know with her.

I eventually find her sitting alone on the curb adjacent to the school. She notices me approaching.

"What was that about?" I question as I sit down next to her.

She takes a moment to reply. "God, that was stupid. I should go apologize."

I stop her before she can get up. "I'm sure he knows, but seriously, what's up?"

She looks at the ground and says, "I wish he could have been here."

I instantly feel bad for my dad being flaunted in her face. I think of what I could say. I've never been particularly helpful on this topic, but I do manage to come up with, "I'm not going to tell you some bullshit like *I bet he's here in spirit* because I don't know that, and you don't believe that. So what I will tell you is that he would be proud, very proud, Dylan." She manages a smile. "Valedictorian and everything," I continue. (Oh yeah, I forgot to mention that Dylan managed to beat out everyone in our grade and graduate with a 4.8 weighted GPA. I almost couldn't believe it myself.)

I give her shoulder a nudge and she smiles a humble smile.

"You know, they probably hate you," I say as I gesture towards our peers. "You show up, halfway through the year, and knock everyone down a level."

Her mouth drops as if she's offended. "That's a terrible way to cheer me up." She laughs.

"What?" I sarcastically question.

"Telling me everyone hates me. Best friend of the year, right here."

We both laugh and I'm pleased with myself for easing the mood. We then stand and head back to my house to change and get ready for the school-hosted Senior party. After, we go to the peer-hosted Senior party, and I don't know which one I liked more because I wasn't in the mood for either. But I participated, nonetheless, and it finally hits me that I'm now done with all of the stigma that has ever been associated with my high school years, and it's time for me to start my life. I'm offended that the eighteen years which it took me to get to this moment is deemed a part of my life that has not yet been started.

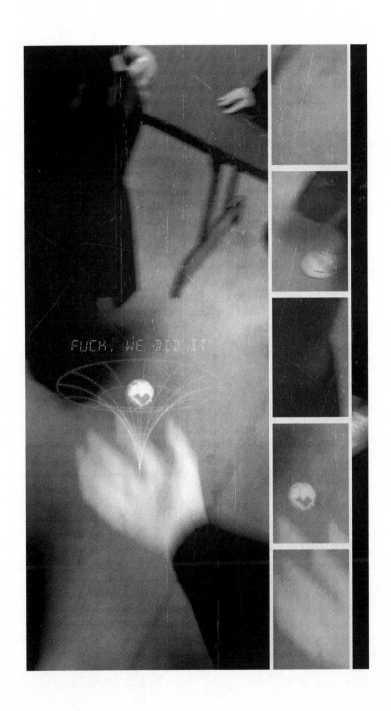

UNSTEADY [11]

=

We discover after a couple times of going to the Library that when we continue down the path we take getting there, it leads to a dingy, abandoned "beach" with a cracked boat landing and a little dock. It's positioned on a popular river, but not one that's made for swimming, so in all the times we've been here, I've never seen another person. Today, Dylan and I are sitting at its stiff end with our pants rolled up and our feet in the water. Dylan has a bowl in her hand that is soon to her lips as she continues her regular routine of getting high.

Dylan's only rule when it came to smoking weed was not to smoke it before going to school, but since school is over, she doesn't mind if she could be deemed a stoner by bystanders. I mind, however. I don't care that she's high because usually I can't tell the difference. What I mind is the hassle that accompanies getting high: the time it takes, the shitty dealers, the chance of getting caught. I haven't been high in nearly three weeks because it started to make me abrasively paranoid, and that's not something I can handle on top of my usual nerves.

Dylan doesn't get paranoid, probably because she thinks she has nothing to lose. But sometimes I wish she would, so she'd be more careful, and I could relax.

"I'm going to need to get more tonight," she states as she adjusts the remaining greens. "This is my last bowl."

"Okay," is all I care to say at the moment.

"Are you going to want any?" she asks, looking at me.

"No," I plainly answer. I never flat out told Dylan that I want to take a break from smoking, but she always respects my decision when she asks.

"You alright?" she questions as she puts down the bowl. I then realize that I had been staring at the water without realizing that I was staring at the water, which means I had been thinking. It takes me a second to reply.

"Ah- yeah. . . . Hey, can I ask you something?"

"I'll always answer a question," she states like she does every time I ask that. It always makes me smile.

"Why do you like being high so much?" I don't know why I don't know the answer.

"It's a distraction," she tells me. "It's a distraction that I don't realize is acting as a distraction, and that's nice."

That makes sense; I figure it works the same way as me staring at the water.

"I wish that worked for me," I admit.

"It's not made for everyone," she gently states and dumps the remaining ashes in the river. She then stands, does a little jig to dry her feet, and extends her hand to me. I promptly accept, she helps me up, and we make our way off the dock.

My feet hit the poor excuse for sand, and I instantly regret getting them wet in the first place. It takes too long to try to cleanly get my feet back into my socks and shoes. Wow, do I hate this process.

Once night rolls around, Dylan and I head to the abandoned park to meet our guy (I think "our guy" sounds stupid, but I learned quickly that that's what everyone says when talking about drug dealers). Dylan drives. Dylan almost always drives; we both prefer it.

We sit for nearly thirty minutes with no word from said guy. I bounce my leg as I view the distant headlights come and go. Every time I hope it's him so that we can get this over with, but every time I worry that it's a cop. I seem to convince myself that they all are, because in the dim light, it's always a possibility.

"Relax," Dylan says as she notices my leg, "you're making the whole car move."

"Can you text him again?" I ask.

"You know him, Junebug, five more minutes and he'll be here."

"*Why* do we come this early if we *know* he'll be late?" I complain.

"Because if he were to be on time, and we weren't, he wouldn't wait this long."

I glare. "That's stupid." I don't have the motivation to think of something better to say.

"I agree."

But just as she said, five minutes later I watch the distant headlights get closer and closer, but this time they turn into the parking lot.

"Finally," I say as I block his blaring lights from my eyes, but he then does something I don't expect: he turns and skims the edge of the grass with his car, shining his lights on our surroundings. Wait a second. . . as the car turns, I notice its color: black and white. That's not our guy.

"You have got to be kidding me," I say aloud.

"What?" Dylan asks. I don't know how she hasn't noticed.

"That's a cop car, Dylan."

"Oh shit," she says in a voice that doesn't suggest she means it.

I start minorly freaking out as the car continues to sweep the grounds. As they reach the end of the parking lot, they turn in our direction, and I lose it.

"What are we going to do?" I frantically ask Dylan.

"Calm down, they have no reason to interrogate us," she insists.

"You're still a minor. It's past curfew. They'll find anything to see what's going on. Dylan, we have drugs."

"No, we have drug paraphernalia," she corrects, "and the worst they'll do is confiscate it. But they'd have to search us first, and why would they do that?"

"I don't know! But don't you think it's strange as hell that we're just sitting here?"

"I'll tell them we came to star gaze," she casually suggests.

134

I look out the window. "It's cloudy, Dylan."

"I'll tell them we had intentions to."

Before I have time to tell Dylan that that is a pathetically lame excuse, the car finally reaches ours. I then pray that our guy will arrive even later, because I can't imagine this situation would go any smoother if an even sketchier car were to pull up.

The cop stops parallel to us. The person inside (I can't tell their gender because it's dark and I'm trying as hard as I can to not look at them and act casual) takes a few seconds to consider our car. Dylan acts like she's talking on the phone. I don't know why that would help, but it seems to satisfy the person, because they then continue down the parking lot and leave.

"Told you," she flaunts.

I can't believe it. They didn't care at all. They didn't do anything. Why was I so sure that they would? I then become increasingly angry due to a mixture of anxiety, impatience, and being proven wrong.

"I'm done," I whisper.

"What?"

"I'm done, Dylan! I don't want to have anything to do with this anymore."

I can tell she wasn't expecting this. "Look, we can find a new place or go at an earlier time," she tries.

"No!" I become quite dramatic. "I don't want to do any of this! It's time wasted, and I don't even use what we're waiting here for." I continue, "It's my car! I let you use it, and come to think of it, *I* would have gotten in trouble because of that. They would have ran my plates. They could have done anything they wanted to!"

Dylan tries to cut in, "They didn't care! They left. We're fine, and you could have told me no. I don't have to use your car, I thought you were cool with-"

"You never even asked!" I bud in.

"That's because I thought we were close enough that you'd tell me if you didn't like what was happening, Junebug."

"Oh don't do that," I sneer in disgust.

"*What?*"

"Don't make it my fault."

"Wh- I'm not! Look, I'm sorry. That's not what I meant. We can go, okay? I can tell him I don't need it."

"Oh, been here half an hour, might as well just wait another. And even if you did tell him, you would just ask him for it again tomorrow," I accuse.

"What's wrong with that? You've never had a problem with this before," she claims.

"That's because I never say no to you. How could I when you control everything?" I start to get scared that this is being blown out of proportion, but I can't seem to stop my sudden burst of pent up anger.

"Is that what you think? June, I do that because you let me! I've wanted all along to teach you how to stand up for yourself."

"Teach me? I have to be taught? Oh, thanks. I can, Dylan. I can and I am right now. Ever think I just went along with things because I felt pity for you? That I thought it would help, letting you do things you wanted to? Well, I guess I was wrong, because look at you now. Fucking drug addict!" I stop yelling and my voice gets low, "I'm just waiting for the day that you become your mother."

I angrily open my door, get out, and slam it shut. I instantly review, and regret, what I just said as I walk towards the back of the parking lot with my hands to my head.

I realize that she doesn't have a marijuana addiction because that's physically impossible, but she has started buying pills more often. I usually don't object because she shares a few with me, but I know that I'm not addicted; I have *never* felt like I needed them. Her, on the other hand, could easily develop an addiction just by looking at her mother. I guess if anything, it scares me, and I let it out in probably the worst way possible.

I hear her door shut and her footsteps running toward me.

"June, stop!" she yells. "Junebug, please."

I stop, but don't turn around. She catches up.

"June, I'm sorry."

I close my eyes and grab my hair. "No, I am. I'm sorry. I didn't mean that about your mother. I shouldn't have gone that far." I finally face her.

"No. Don't submit," she demands, but then she pauses and suddenly starts to hastily fiddle around with her pockets. It looks like she's searching for something, and she has a worried look on her face.

"Oh shit," she says, "you know what I forgot?"

Still angry, I stubbornly ask, "What?" and try not to sound like I care.

"To be a good friend," she states.

I don't smile even though that was kind of cleaver.

She continues, "You were right. You were right and I didn't see it, and I'm sorry. I'm sorry that I drag you along in *your* car and put so much time and money into things I shouldn't need or want. I didn't think it was a hassle because it's normal, but it shouldn't be." Her hands frantically move around as she speaks, so I know she means it.

"I'll try to cut back," she promises. "I should be saving my money anyway."

I look at her gently, but I don't know what to say. My indecisive thoughts are interrupted however, because finally, our guy shows up. We silently make our way back to the car to meet him.

He rolls down his window and says, "Just the gram this time? I'll make you a deal if you get three."

"No thanks, just the one," Dylan replies, and she pays him.

He then leaves without commenting on the fact that he was nearly an hour late, and Dylan and I get back in my car.

"I won't buy anything until Tate and Tanner come. I know they'll want to, and it'll give us something to do. How about that?" she offers, thoughtfully.

"That works," I say and mean it. "You might as well smoke tonight," I continue, because I know she had intentions to and what harm would it do now?

"Thanks," she says as she digs through her never-ending bag in search of her bowl. While she does, I turn up the radio and rest my head on the side of the door. "The Gates of Hell" by The Features is playing.

+

The next week is better. With school being over and work picking up, Dylan and I don't have as much time to go out and do things together because our schedules never match. Dylan does, however, spend the night more often than usual because it's easier that way.

By this point, my mom is aware that Dylan practically lives with us, but she doesn't ask questions. I think she likes having another set of hands that's willing to help around the house. Dylan realizes her presence could be considered a burden, so she tries hard not to make a mess and cleans up the ones she can.

My mom and Dylan get along really well, often sharing the same type of humor. Although, I must concede, sometimes it gets old. But that's to be expected. Dylan and I give each other privacy when we need it because at some point, we both become unbearable.

("Can you *please* stop humming?" I asked Dylan, who was across the room.

"What?"

"You hum when you read," I insisted.

"Seriously?"

"Yes. How do you not notice that??"

"It's a good book. . . ."

She stopped for about ten minutes.

"Oh my god, get out.")

("June. What are you doing?" Dylan asked, angrily.

138

I used my elbows to perch my front up while in a laying position. I had about six chins as I looked at Dylan across the couch.

"Trying to nap," I said.

"Well, can you manage do it without kicking me in the face?" she asked and proceeded to shove my legs off the couch, after which I lost my balance and fell with them. My hip made a loud thud on the floor.)

("Why are perfume commercials always *so dramatic?*" Dylan asked to no one as we watched TV.

I glared at her. "Why do you *never* stop talking?")

("Hey, Dylan, where's your charger?" I yelled from a different room.

"I told you, it's in my backpack!"

I may have asked her a few times before that. I looked around the room, but saw no backpack. I hesitantly yelled back, "Um. . . where's your backpac-"

"Oh my god!" I heard in a loud grunt before I could finish the question. I then heard the sound of a door being forced open.)

I have no siblings, but I assume this is how it would feel to have a sister. Or at least a college roommate. It would never be okay to kiss my sister, which Dylan and I did do that one time. I asked her once if she thought she would ever regret that. She couldn't understand why I would've even thought to ask.

Right now, I'm lying in bed next to Dylan who's rereading one of her dozens of books. My eyes are closed even though I have no intention of sleeping yet. There's only three days until Tate and Tanner show up and I'm trying not to worry about it, but I can't refrain from asking questions. Despite me knowing for a long time that I'd be meeting them, I know next to nothing about them.

"So, what are they like?" I ask, but then remember that Dylan hasn't been reading my mind, so I add, "Tate and Tanner, I mean."

She takes a moment to finish her page, "They're fun," she says. "They're fun, and they understand, and they're quirky, and. . . an odd duo."

I don't know if that helps me at all, so I push further, "Well, can you be more specific?"

"Well, as I said before, Tanner's a vegetarian. He's very aware of the world, but he's not annoying about it. Tate doesn't care as much, but he's kind of a protector; he works out a lot."

I silently worry that Tate is going to be more of a douche, but then I shame myself for stereotyping. I still feel like I don't know them. Considering I've slowly been learning about them, they seem more like characters in a book rather than real people. So basically, Reader, we're on the same page right now.

I consider their short descriptions in silence, but I soon start to wonder about the extent of their relationship to Dylan.

"Have you ever dated one of them?" I ask, quickly adding, "Or *been* with one of them?"

Dylan represses a laugh. "No. I'm sure I've kissed them both at some point, but the furthest I've ever gone is pretend that I was dating Tate to ward someone else off. It was his idea." She smiles at the memory of it. "We're strictly platonic."

"Well, are they dating anyone?"

Dylan breaks her devotion to her book to look at me. "Why are you so interested? You lookin' for someone?" she jokes.

I blush but am sincere when I say, "No. I'm just curious. I don't know how the visit's gonna' go."

"Well, don't worry so much. If I like you, they'll like you. It'll be fun."

I try to believe her, and she turns back to her book. But barely a minutes later, she acts as if she's made a profound realization: "Oh!" she turns to me, "I forgot to mention, one of them is gay," she pauses, "but I'm not going to tell you which one."

I'm both surprised and annoyed. "What! That's so unfair. What am I supposed to do, just hope it comes up in conversation?"

"Well, why should it matter?"

"I mean. . . it doesn't. I just don't wanna' accidentally be offensive or anything." My argument is illogical, but never getting confirmation on who it is will bother me immensely.

"Then don't be offensive. It's quite easy," she says in an obvious manner.

"Well. . . can you at least give me a hint? It's just. . . good to know."

She looks up as if to think of a defining characteristic and replies, "No."

"Okay, that was anticlimactic."

"Just wait until they come," she insists. "Now, let me finish this page. I've read the same line like four times."

I sigh and turn back over, now with the intention to sleep, but it doesn't come.

Not 5 Foot 7 [12]

=

"These are my Tits," Dylan joyously declares with her arm outstretched, presenting her two best friends.

"I used to call them that because of the T's, ya' know, Tate and Tanner," she clarifies.

"Yeah, no, I get it," I say as I observe the two tall boys standing with grins behind Dylan.

They have just arrived, and we're standing in my kitchen at the moment because it's the easiest destination and my mom's not home.

Dylan hugs them both as I watch from behind my kitchen island.

"This is Tanner," Dylan clarifies, pointing to the boy to her left. "His middle name is Oakley, by the way. Always good to know."

Tanner is wearing a dark blue sweater over a grey shirt with blue jeans. He has dark brown hair that's shaved on the sides but hangs over his forehead. He's taller than Tate and has on white Adidas. He has to crouch a bit to hug Dylan, and his lengthy arms display a tattoo of a geometric bear and some thick, string bracelets.

"And this is Tate," she points to her right, "middle name Matthew."

Tate, on the other hand, is the same height as Dylan and has on a short sleeve, maroon button up with cream joggers. He has longer dirty blond hair and is more muscular than Tanner. He has a big smile and gives a tight hug.

I feel awkward. I hate meeting people for the first time.

"Alright guys, this is Junebug," Dylan introduces me. She's obviously excited that they're here, and that we're finally meeting.

143

"It's actually just June, but call me whatever," I lightly correct.

I learn quickly that they aren't nearly as shy as I am as they approach the island and lean over the side opposite of me. Their faces, suddenly far closer than they were before, display characteristics I hadn't noticed. Tanner has light brown eyes, while Tate's are grey-blue. Tate looks like he'd be able to grow a beard while Tanner's face is nothing but smooth.

I instinctively lean back due to my personal space being invaded, and Tanner notices. He looks at Dylan and she says, "I told you." I look at her questioningly, but she only returns a smile. I hate the fact that they must have been talking about me before this.

"Okay, June, I have three questions," Tanner states. I appreciate him using my real name.

"Okay," I reply, a bit apprehensive.

"Are you supposed to eat Pop-Tarts one or two at a time?" he promptly asks.

Well, I was expecting anything but that, and it shows on my face. However, his childlike demeanor gives ease to his presence and therefore his question, so I answer, "One," definitively.

"Wrong," he plainly states, and quickly continues with, "Do you eat macaroni with a spoon or a fork?"

I take a second to reply because I have to visualize the last time I had macaroni, "Um, fork."

He scoffs. "Wrong again. Okay, last one, pill before water or water before pill?"

I easily answer, "Pill before water."

Tanner is overly excited about my answer as he sighs in relief and gives me a rather hard high-five. I try to play along as he says, "Was worried for a second, but don't sweat it, Tate here didn't get a single one right, and I've never met a better friend." He pats Tate on the back and Tate agrees, "He's right."

"What about me?" Dylan asks, offended.

"Well, you don't count," Tate steps in. "You got them all right."

"That doesn't even make sense," Dylan nags.

I stay behind the island as I watch them interact. There's no question that they've been friends forever. They mumble, and joke, and laugh, and simply enjoy each other's presence. I don't feel like I belong. I suddenly wonder if Dylan considers my relationship with her to be as meaningful as all of theirs. I know I shouldn't be comparing, but I've never seen our relationship from an outsider's point of view, and I don't know if it looks like this.

"Are you guys ready to check into the motel?" Dylan asks, ready to start their staying process.

"Yeah, everything should still be in the car," confirms Tanner.

"Are you sure you guys are okay with spending the money?" Dylan asks, concerned. I can tell she feels bad that visiting her could be viewed as an inconvenience.

"Between the two of us it should be fine. Don't worry." He smiles, and they head for the door.

"It was great to finally meet you, June!" Tate yells as they exit.

"You too!" I manage to yell back before they're completely over the threshold.

They're going to get checked in and then hang out while I'm at work. I work until 10:15 so they have about five hours to think of plans for tonight. I can't tell if I'm excited or not, but I know that I'm trying to be.

Work is slow, yet time seems to be traveling fast. (Maybe he's late for something.)

It's 9:46 when I start closing concessions down.

9:53 when a group of young adults come in, fifteen minutes late for their movie, and make me get everything back out again. I hate those people.

10:02 and my manager says he'll just be minute.

10:19 and I'm finally in my car, reading texts from Tanner since Dylan still doesn't have a phone.

"Hey Junebug, [must be Dylan] *let us know when you're home, we're gonna longboard."*

145

I don't know where they plan to go, but It's certainly a nice night to be adventurous. The atmosphere is dense with a muffled, purple-grey sky littered with stars. There's a slight breeze, and It's the perfect temperature. A t-shirt with shorts or a sweater with pants, either one works, so I go with a mix as I let them know I'm home.

They arrive shortly after in Tate's car.

"Okay if I leave my car parked here?" Tate asks as he opens his trunk, pulling out two longboards.

"Yeah, that's fine."

"Cool, thanks," he says as he hands the yellow longboard to Tanner.

Dylan and I head behind my house to retrieve ours from my shed. Once we get out of earshot, and the boy's laughter has faded away, Dylan becomes very serious and makes a point to ask, "Are you okay with all of this?"

I wasn't expecting her to be concerned, and I've been trying to suppress my anxiety, so her forcing me to think of it makes me hesitant to reply.

"Um. . . yeah, I mean," I unlock the shed, "they seem great, and I bet I'll have a good time once I get comfortable."

"If it's ever too much, let me know," she says, making eye contact. I can tell that she means it, but considering my comfort level has never been of much concern to other people, it feels moderately strange to be cared for.

"Why do you say that?" I ask.

"Because I know they can be a lot, and I know you. . . so just don't forget that, okay?"

"Well, thanks. I won't," I say as I lock the shed.

"Good."

We then silently walk back to the boys, and I'm thinking of all the things there are to be nervous about. Since Dylan is aware that they can be a lot, then I can't imagine what we'll be doing. But my thoughts are interrupted when, suddenly, Dylan screams and nearly knocks me over due to a jump in my direction.

"Oh my god, what!?" I frantically ask. Her scream startled me, but my concern is soon masked by laughter once I fully realize just how high-pitched and girly her scream truly was.

"Did you see that? It jumped out of the bush! God, that scared me. What the fuck was that?" As she goes on, I look across the street and see a little, white tail quickly bouncing away.

"Oh my god, Dylan," I say, slowly, just to make sure she knows I'm mocking her, "that was a bunny." I'm laughing.

"No way," she defends herself but can't help but laugh as well. "That was not a bunny."

But she knows it was a bunny, and the sudden comic relief sets my nerves at ease as we reach the guys and relive what just happened. They laugh at the image of it, and after, we all mount our boards and head out of my neighborhood.

Although I'm the one who's lived here the longest, I'm not the one leading. I can tell they have a destination in mind, but perhaps they don't know how to get there because after many twists and turns, down only smooth roads, we end up at my old daycare, which happens to be a church.

(Side note: Yes, I went to daycare at a church that doubled as a school, but my daycare years completely ruled [contrary to presumed popular belief], but it didn't have an effect on me religion wise. I don't understand how people have the capacity to devote their life to God, whatever God they believe in. But I do know that I have no right to shame them for doing so. I should support them, and I do, and I hope they support me too because I met some pretty boss-ass people in that daycare. Including Oliver.)

We stop at the edge of the grass. They need to mow.

"What are we doing here?" I ask because I still haven't figured it out.

"Didn't you once say that you could get on the roof?" Dylan asks me.

"Well. . . yeah, but the priest literally lives in that house," I point to a small, white house down the hill, "and he's always busting people for doing it."

"It's eleven, do you really think he's watching?" she questions.

"I guess not."

"Well, good. Lead the way, Junebug."

And so I do. We carry our boards as we cross the grass and venture through the park. Our shoes and my socks are wet with the night's dew as I lead them to the back of the building, where the roof is low and the ground is high. It's a bit of a climb, but the path to the top is obvious, so Tate goes first.

I know this degenerate act isn't particularly risky, but I feel convinced that "I Think We're Alone Now" by Tommy James & The Shondells should be playing in the background.

We try to be quick, but we're rather dysfunctional, especially with our longboards. I'm continuously worried that we'll be caught, but when I think about it, nothing serious would happen if we were. So when Dylan helps me up, and we're out of sight, I relax.

Tanner had been prepared. He lays out a blanket and gives everyone an Arizona Tea that he had in his bag. I thank him graciously because he didn't need to do that, and it must have been difficult to longboard with such a heavy backpack.

Dylan supplies the weed, and I'm not bothered by it because we had agreed that it was okay. And she was right, Tate and Tanner accept it casually and are also quite grateful. They pass it in a circle, and when Tate passes it to me, I'm hesitant, but I accept. It's been so long since I've smoked pot that a couple hits is enough for me to feel the effects. I decline after the fifth round. I can tell their tolerance level is far above mine, so they continue to smoke while I look at the stars above. It gets me thinking.

There's a certain misconception that I wish to correct – or maybe it's something that I need to clarify within myself – but I'd like you to know, Reader, that we are not doing this because we think it's cool. We didn't climb up this church and smoke weed because we think we're being daring, devious teenagers. We did it because it's a great view. We did it because it's peaceful, and secluded, and once we're up here, there's a far less chance of being caught smoking. Which brings me to another point: we don't smoke because we think it's a novelty that gives us rep. We smoke because it's an escape. I, however, know that I don't need it. To me, it's merely fun on the right occasion, and a paranoia on any other. But for Dylan and perhaps Tate and Tanner, it's a preferred state of mind.

What I've noticed by observing those who devote a considerable amount of their life to drugs, is that they've lost some sort of ability to make their life one that they are willful and satisfied to live in. To them (but not to all - I am generalizing), it seems that life's only potential is to provide them with a plant that allows them to leave it. But once the plant life starts to feel like the life they had before, they need an even better one. Eventually, each life they try ends up feeling like the previous one, and by the time the potential for each life has diminished, they've been brainwashed into seeing only one solution: find a new life. And so they do, but this time, they can't return to the life that provided them with the plant that started the journey in the first place. I can't tell if they thought it was a good or bad idea at the time, and I think that's the saddest part of their search for a new life with potential.

I know that they can be defined as addicts who have developed chemical dependencies, built up tolerances, and more terms that define perpetual bad habits, but I can't help but view it as a helpless search for something more tolerable than where they stand in their lives. So as I observe the three beautiful people around me, I simply hope that the lives they've been given haven't withheld any of their potential, because I don't want them to go searching any further than they already have.

That being said, I know that they're not far. I know that this can even be viewed as a minor recreation. And I know that this is merely the start, but I hope that it can double as the end. I don't tell them this, however. I don't see the point because I know they're not ignorant. Perhaps careless, maybe reckless, but not ignorant. So I wait for them to be done smoking and to stop discussing pills, because I know that it's not their greatest concern. I know this because once they're done, and we're all laying down, Tate breaks our silence by saying, "Goddamn - would you just look at that sky."

Even though we're already looking at it, he continues, "Like, do you see that? Those billions upon billions of stars, and planets, and galaxies, and who the fuck knows - what is that? All I can make of it are small, bright dots, but it's the most amazing thing I've ever seen, and we're right in the middle of it because space is infinite! I can't even comprehend that. We are literally just a spec. Even smaller than a spec! Yet I know that I'm five foot seven, but really, I'm not."

He says it all as one, big sentence with hand gestures to the sky, and we all shift our view in his direction as he rambles. I'm in awe of what he says, and love to know that he thinks about that; I love to know that I'm not the only one who lets their mind ponder over those kinds of things. Tanner on the other hand, seems to be used to Tate's commentary because he says, "Dude, don't try to overthink it. Just appreciate it."

There's a long pause before Tate finally murmurs, "But I don't like to feel so small."

Dylan then replies, "You're only small if you think of it that way."

"Well, I can't help but think that way," says Tate.

"Sure you can," Dylan says, confidently, "that's why I know that I'm *huge*." Her arms shoot up in the air and go down as a horizon as she demonstrates how huge she is.

"Why is that?" I ask, and they all look at me because I haven't said much of anything yet.

"Because there's no point in thinking otherwise," she says, definitively, and I can't think of a quick counter argument, so I reply, "I guess so."

"You know you're an idealist, right?" Tanner tells Dylan.

"Is that a bad thing?"

"I'd just rather be realistic," he reasons.

"Well, I'd rather die a utopian than die believing that life sucked," Dylan argues.

"A realist knows that life is somewhere in between," claims Tanner.

"But where's the fun in being in the middle?" Dylan inquires.

"Well, you don't need to worry about being at the end."

"But you don't get to enjoy the front."

Tate cuts them off, "I don't think your metaphor is working, and I still feel small."

We think it over.

"Well, then, at least you feel small in the midst of something beautiful," Dylan says, ending the conversation.

After a long pause, I break the silence by commenting, "*Deep*," in a half-sincere, half-mocking voice. Everyone starts laughing because we know how cheesy that conversation actually was, but yet it meant something. I think that's the best thing about the situation: the awareness.

When it comes down to it, I think if we can remain aware of who we are, who others are, what we're doing, and what's going on in the world, we're pretty well off. I hope I never become unaware, and I strive to always be present. Especially in these moments, because eventually, our backs start to hurt, our high wears off, and the night hits its peak as we climb off the roof to start our journey home.

The air is utterly still, and the silence of the atmosphere makes the compression of wet grass under our feet sound like a waterfall as we make it to the street. And if I thought the grass was loud, then the contact of our wheels on the road sounds like cannons as we glide on its smooth surface. I feel as if I'm disturbing the night, but I can't help but smile as I look ahead at the three people helping me disturb it, because I know that I am lucky.

I'm lucky because in a world that provides millions of questions – but only a few answers – I've been given three people to help me ponder over our makeshift solutions. That's as good as it gets, really.

FABRICATED LINES [13]

=

The next day we have an open schedule with no plans, so we decide to make use of the crappy pool at the motel that the boys are staying at.

Due to its crappiness, it's often deserted, so we have the place to ourselves and the encouragement to use it by the scorching sun. (Which reminds me, I'm one of the unfortunate people who gets burnt two seconds after walking outside. So to mention something they wouldn't show in a movie, I put on a shit ton of sunscreen. There's no point in denying it.)

Once again, I'm subjected to wearing a swimsuit, and although I'm aware that I have a fairly average body, I still can't help but feel insecure. I think it's mostly because of the boys. Even though I have no interest in being with either of them, and one is even gay, I still feel the need to impress them. It's as if I want to feel desired, but only for that purpose – only to receive validation, but I know that that's bullshit. God, am I mad at myself. Their opinions shouldn't matter.

Their opinions shouldn't matter.

Isn't it funny how the people who always say looks don't matter, are usually the ones who aren't deemed "ugly" by society? It's easy to say you don't care about looks if you don't need to care about looks. I know there are some people who would shame me for saying this, but looks *do* matter. If we see a stranger from across the room, and are dumbfounded by their beauty, are we talking about their beauty within? No. We're talking about what we saw on the surface, they are a stranger to us otherwise. And if we didn't deem them attractive, we would've never had that thought, simple as that.

Here's my redemption: the only thing that we've got wrong is the definition of beautiful – or attractive, or hot, or *whatever*. We seem to think there's a singular definition, that everyone's beauty could be ranked on the basis of society's view, but we're wrong. We've never been so wrong.

Each and every person has their own definition of beauty, some much more broad than others. But when it comes down to it, it's not society's fault; it's the people who choose to blame society when they call someone ugly, and I think that's what needs to change, for *we* are society. It is our doing.

"You ready?" Dylan asks.

I had been staring into the mirror. I wrap myself in a towel as we exit the bathroom.

The boys are already in the water. I see them for the first time without shirts. They easily fit into my definition of beautiful, both inner and outer, for most people do.

Dylan keeps on her bright yellow t-shirt. Even though we all know her situation, she still feels the need to cover herself up. Sometimes I wish she'd show me the damage, so I can stop guessing, but it's the one part her she refuses to reveal.

I, too, would have kept on my shirt, but I despise the feeling of wet fabric. I also regret coming out in a towel because when I take it off, I feel even more exposed than what I would have felt if I had just started without it. This is a mess in my head, but if you were to view it objectively, it would simply be me walking out to the pool and nothing more. Weird how that works.

"Is it cold?" Dylan asks.

"No!" yells Tate, just as Tanner yells, "Yes!"

"Thanks guys, know I can always count on you," Dylan sarcastically remarks. She then breaks into a short run and leaps nearly on top of the boys. They all come up laughing and coughing up water.

I stand at the edge of the pool as Dylan comes over and stretches out her hand to me. I grab on, knowing what's to come, and she yanks me in head first. I'm happy to get a clear invitation, but Tanner was right, it's certainly not warm.

We then do normal pool things, which are quite difficult to explain. Swimming is such an odd form of entertainment, but I can't say that I don't enjoy it. The water slows me down, both physically and mentally, and I'm fascinated by its clarity. It feels like silk. Silk that is thick, yet when I submerse myself underneath it and don't move a muscle, I feel as if I'm floating in midair. I've never fully understood it's consistency.

After we've been frolicking around for a while, I start to notice that Dylan spends long spans of time underwater, so I follow to observe what she's doing.

It hurts my eyes, but I see her in the deep end, completely still, sitting on the pool's ground. She seems peaceful as her arms float to her side and her hair dances above her head. She hasn't noticed me, so I resurface to get some air and move to where she sits. I submerse myself, blow all of the air out of my nose, and sink to the bottom next to her.

Once grounded, she turns her head towards me and smiles. Her face is flushed with the abstract patterns of water as I smile back. But shortly after, it seems I'm already short of breath and am forced to resurface before she does.

"How do you do that for so long?" I ask with a gasp after she follows me up.

"I'm part fish," she explains. "My late uncle was a flounder."

"What?" I ask, confused at her sincerity.

"I'm kidding," she says. "Practice," she adds.

"From what?" I ask.

"When I was a kid I used to hold my breath when my parents fought. I don't know why. I just thought it would help in some way."

"I see," I say, staring at her.

"It's a nice perk," she says with a smile, and then goes back under with her hands above her head.

I'm left standing, slightly dumbfounded at the pure lunacy that is my best friend. I then turn to look at the boys and wonder if they have the same perception of her. They probably do, but obviously 'lunacy' is not on our list of deal-breaking qualities.

Apart from this thought, I see that they're sitting on the stairs, talking. When Dylan comes back up, they call us over.

"So I heard June here doesn't know which one of us is gay," Tanner states.

"Oh yeah!" Dylan exclaims as she nudges me.

"Would you like to guess?" asks Tate.

"No, I don't want to guess," I insist.

"Come on, we won't be offended or anything. We're just curious about who'd you pick," Tanner tells me.

"Take a guess," Tate encourages.

I have never been asked to guess someone's sexuality before. I know they want me to, but I can't help but feel that it's wrong in some way.

I look them both over and see no distinctive, stereotypical characteristics of a gay person. It's quite terrible that that's what I'm basing it off of, but I don't know what else to.

After watching their eager anticipation for much longer than I would like, I blindly decide by gesturing to my right, where Tanner sits.

"Dammit!" yells Tanner as he pounds on the water. They're all laughing.

I don't appreciate his response so I quickly say, "You shouldn't think it's a bad thing that I chose you."

"Oh, no," he starts, "that's not it. I don't care that you thought I was gay, but we made a bet on who you'd choose," he explains. "Now I owe them each five bucks."

"I'd like mine in the form of our next meal," Tate joyously declares.

"Me too," adds Dylan.

After they stop celebrating their proven prediction, Tanner address me, "Can I ask why you chose me, though?"

Considering I wasn't confident in my decision in the slightest, I say, "To be honest, just because you're tall and slim. I know that's extremely stereotypical, but I had no idea."

"Fair enough," he says.

"But nope, it's me," Tate declares with a big grin. "Big and burly me."

"But aren't we all a little gay?" Dylan says as we exit the pool with a new desire for food.

Once we're dressed, we head to a local food truck with wet hair and smudged makeup. (One of the most unrealistic things about movies is when the characters are completely dry and perfect two seconds after being wet.)

We thank Tanner because he buys for all of us, even though I wasn't included in the bet. He's quite generous that way, and I'm reminded that he's a vegetarian when he orders the only salad on the menu for himself.

"You look like a raccoon," I tell Dylan as we eat our tacos.

"I think raccoons are cute," replies Dylan, and she continues eating.

Once we're done, we sit for a while longer simply people-watching: one of my favorite pastimes. It reminds me of when I used to have big family reunions, and I'd sit in my mom's car with one of my cousins, because my family was a bit overbearing at times. We'd watch them from behind the windows and narrate what we thought they were doing. It was quite enjoyable and rather humorous.

I watch someone at the next table struggle to get their taco in their mouth. I see a couple across the park kiss before one of them gets in a car. I see a woman walking her dogs and failing to pick up its shit. I see a man sitting on a bench all alone, and a woman who has one of those *I'm a dog that looks like a cat* faces. I see a kid picking up a cigarette butt, and their mother quickly swatting it out of their hand. But mostly, I see a sea of phone-absorbed people with headphones and a destination on their mind. I'm not saying our technology dependency is a bad thing, but I'm not saying it's a good thing either. All I'm saying is that some people should really watch where they're walking.

A bit later, while Dylan and Tate are discussing the presidential election, I notice a group of teenagers approach the food truck. I believe we went to the same school. I think they're Sophomores, but I can never keep that straight.

The group consists of three girls and one guy, and with a quick glance they could easily be identified as a "goth" or "emo" group. They have multi-colored hair, dark clothes, and some facial piercings. I think one even has a tattoo, but they all share the same depressing vibe.

Dylan notices me looking at them. "Don't judge them," she tells me.

"What?" I look at her. "Oh, I wasn't -" but I don't get to finish.

"I know, I just. . ." she says as she stops to look at them. I see a flash of pity stretch across her face. "It just means they've had it rough. And it's not fair for us to be prejudice against them because they have problems we don't know they deal with. And I hate that they dress like that because it just makes it easy for others to label them, and then they're bullied on top of it all for being different. But they *should* have the freedom to dress however they like, and they just do it because it reflects how they feel. And it's not "attention seeking" or "desperate," it's depression or anxiety or any other form of mental disorders that they have no control over, and it's fucking stupid that it's viewed as anything other than a person who could really use a permanent pick me up!"

Dylan said this all in a fury of desperation, and when she spoke, she spoke to the sky rather than to us. Tanner, Tate, and I look at each other with nervous expressions.

After a moment of almost awkward silence, I softly say, "Um. . . I promise I wasn't thinking that," as I try to make eye contact with her.

Tanner then asks, "Are you alright, Dylan?"

She finally fully acknowledges us and says, "Yeah, sorry about that. . . . I could go for some ice cream now."

We aren't fully convinced, but I suggest, "I've got some frozen yogurt coupons if ya' wanna' go there."

158

"Sounds great," she says, and we all stand up, pretending to move on from her mini-breakdown.

When we get into Tate's car, I look back at the table we had deserted. It's now occupied by the group of misconstrued individuals that Dylan had defended. They look just like us.

+

Considering there isn't a ton to do in our moderately small town, we quickly run out of ideas over the next few days. However, it never seems to hinder our moods, because we all share the wonderful quality of being entertained by simplicity.

We spend some time in the boys' motel room, and Tanner watches the Discovery Channel while Dylan draws, I read, and Tate plays a video game on his laptop. None of us need to ask if the others are okay with it, and we all know that we're enjoying our time.

There are numerous sun rays seeping in from the behind the curtains, and a quiet murmur from each of our activities. We don't communicate with words, but with the contentment on our faces as we keep to ourselves but share our space.

It's as captivating and effortless as "Idle Town" by Conan Gray.

As I think about it, this may be one of my favorite memories with this group so far, because I couldn't ask for better company, and my life feels whole. There's an unmistakable glow in my stomach that tells me that this is right, and I can't help but thrive in its benevolent glory. And on top of it all, I love the fact that I feel this way by doing next to nothing, and as I look up from my book, I hope that they do too.

The afternoon turns to evening, and after what equates to a relaxing day, Dylan becomes adamant about trying something she discovered on the internet: paint twister.

"You got a twister board?" I ask, doubting her plan.

159

"Well, no. Don't you?" she asks.

"There are only two people in my house, do you really think we play twister together?"

Twenty minutes later, we return from Walmart with a new twister board. We made Dylan pay.

I have paint at my house, so we decide to do it in my backyard. By this time, the sky is a mixture of navy watercolor, and the horizon glows orange. We lay out the tarp and pour a considerable amount of paint on each dot. I then venture to the deep downs of my basement to find a bucket of old clothing I wouldn't mind ruining.

Once I manage to dress everyone, we look like we've either come off the street or are some far-fetched art students – sometimes there's not much of a distinction, but I'm happy with the collection.

We then stand two to a side on either end of the tarp, and Dylan does the honor of giving the first spin.

"Left hand, blue," she informs us, and we all find a dot.

The paint is cold, but I love the feeling of it slipping through my fingers as I press my hand hard against the tarp. We all smile with enjoyment, and I can tell from that moment that this is going to be fun.

By the time Tanner manages to flick the spinner with his barely-free hand, announcing, "Right food, red," we are a tangled mess of colored limbs. Instead of red, blue, yellow, and green, we are now purple, and orange, and variations of brown. We cannot keep to ourselves. This is, physically, the closest I've ever been to a group of people without it being weird, and I appreciate our disregard of modesty.

"Your balls are in my face," Tate informs Tanner as he retracts his neck.

"Oh come on, you like it," Tanner jokes.

"Not yours," replies Tate, and he flicks the spinner. "Right hand, green."

I'm stretched across Tanner's waist when I put all of my weight on my left arm and lift my right. As I reach for the green, my left hand slips on the slick surface, and I land hard on Tanner's lap while the rest of them fall in a domino effect. We laugh as the paint squishes under our bodies.

This signals the end of our game because we then get up and start chasing each other with colorful hands. Dylan lays on the tarp and does a snow angel in the paint.

"Have a fun time gettin' that out of your hair!" I yell at her as I dodge Tanner's grasp.

She doesn't reply, and the scene ends with a jubilant scream of childlike enjoyment.

Or, at least that's how it would happen in a movie. In reality, there are a few hours to follow of us in the bathroom peeling dried paint off the majority of our body, and vigorously scrubbing our hair in the shower. No regrets, though.

+

The days string together as a spindled spider's web, and we often get caught in its adherent qualities. But only with joy does this happen, because remorse only comes after you've walked through it, and so far, we've only expanded its endpoints.

Eventually, the weekend comes, and even though most days feel like the weekend because it's the summer, we want to do something bigger. So Dylan steals some of her mother's alcohol and we plan a night. It will be at the motel so we can have privacy, drink without worrying about driving, and can spend the night.

Dylan and I plan to help the boys pay their bill because we're using their space. Technically, we're not supposed to be there in the first place because we're not guests, but it's not difficult to sneak us in. So after Dylan and I get done working, the boys come and get us and we head over – it's 7:42.

The sun is low and it casts long, defiant shadows over the door from the black railings. Somehow, I feel older. It's as if I'm on a vacation with my friends, and we've just returned from a day out, ready to make a memorable night. I feel

161

as though I've handled some sort of business, and the night is mine to direct because I'm in a new setting with no set rules. Of course that's not true, and I'm actually breaking the law, but at the moment, I don't care. I'm finally getting a glimpse at what it means to make my own footprints in the world.

We see no point in binge drinking, so we each get a cup and drink it casually with no pressure of being rushed. We find a comedy on TV and lounge around the room. The bright orange streaks of sunlight, dancing on the walls, slowly depart. We're on our third drink by the time the light is gone, our lamps are on, and our walks get wobbly.

I don't think we are unhealthy for choosing this form of entertainment. I don't think we are naive, foolish, irresponsible, or stupid for drinking. Of course we can be, but we do this knowing it's not important. We do this knowing what we're doing, and I think there's a difference between that and doing it purely because it's fun. But what I will say, is that we don't appear our smartest, but duh, we're drunk.

We decide to turn off the TV and play some music. We then gather in a circle on the floor as Tanner announces that we're going to play Never Have I Ever.

Again, for those of you that don't know (and please don't feel lame if you don't), Never Have I Ever is another popular game among teens. You each take turns making the statement, "Never have I ever _____ ." Obviously, the blank is filled with something you have never done, and if anyone else participating *has* done the thing you have never, they either have to drink, take off an article of clothing, or for the most innocent version, simply put down one of their fingers to see who gets out first. Really, you can make the consequence anything you want, these are just the ones I've heard about.

We are playing the stripping version. Normally, I would most certainly object, but in this case, my drinking has turned off the part of me that cares. And I really do, wholeheartedly, trust these people.

We each have a pillow and a few blankets with us as a form of protection, and we all make it very clear that no one is being forced to do anything. And with a smile of anticipation, we start.

"Never have I ever been to a concert," Dylan says. We start out easy.

"Oh, come on," Tanner complains as he and the rest of us take off our accessories first. We all know we want this game to be long.

"We can do whatever we want," Dylan reminds him.

"Fine, then never have I ever totaled my car," Tanner sneers.

"Hey, there's no targeting!" Tate steps in. "Especially with that," he adds after a moment.

Dylan doesn't think it's fair, but she takes off her only bracelet anyway.

"I can say it if it was her fault," Tanner defends himself. "She shouldn't have taken them before getting in a car."

"But still–" Tate is cut off.

"Okay, okay, okay! We are *not* talking about this right now," Dylan declares. "Junebug, your turn."

"Okay. . ." I start after everyone's settled down, "never have I ever slept naked."

Tate gives a giggle. "You've gotta' try it, girl." They all take off an item – mostly small things like socks.

"Seriously, I'm the only one who hasn't?" I ask, mainly looking at Dylan.

"It's actually quite comfortable," she tells me.

"Well, I'm glad you haven't tried it while you've been at my house," I reply. "Hate for my mom to find you on the couch one morning."

We all laugh even though it wasn't that funny. To be realistic, being influenced by alcohol simply makes our interactions more enjoyable and our attitudes more ballsy. I'm thankful it can be used as a device to make me more outgoing. Although I know not to be dependent upon it, after all, alcohol is a depressant.

"Your turn, Tate."

"Never have I ever. . . taken shrooms," he tells us.

We all look at each other, waiting for someone to move, but no one does.

"Proud of us," says Dylan. "But that doesn't count then, so think of something else."

"Ummm, never have I ever peed in the shower."

Tanner immediately takes off his other sock, but once he notices that no one else has taken anything off, he says, "What? Why don't you guys do that?"

"Because I'd rather not stand in my piss?" Tate tells him like it's obvious.

"Do you know how many gallons of water a toilet goes through? Some old toilets can use up to seven gallons of water with each flush," he says, very dramatically, and makes a point to emphasize every word.

We all give him blank stares.

"What??" he asks.

"Why the fuck do you know that?" Tate asks while laughing. We all join in.

"That's beside the point," Tanner reasons.

"Okay, let's keep it going," Dylan encourages. "Never have I ever been with a girl," she says.

"*Beeeen?*" Tanner draws it out and makes it sound slurry. "Like slept with, or made out with, or been to a base with?" he mumbles on, asking for clarification.

"Like done more than kiss with," Dylan explains.

Tanner takes off his sweatshirt while Tate gets his sock halfway off, but then stops. "Would like – touching covered boobs count, or is that implied with making out? I don't know the steps."

"Oh come on, you're gay, not oblivious," Dylan says.

"I was in middle school!" he proclaims. "I don't remember."

"You were touching boobs in middle school?" Tanner asks, mostly to himself, with a very stiff posture and little mouth movements. "Why didn't I get

164

game in middle school? I was cute. I was *boob-touching-worthy*." I seem to be the only one listening to him because Tate and Dylan are still arguing about what counts.

"Just take it off," she finally says.

"Fine." He gives in and takes it off.

The game carries on and our confessions lead more and more into sexual categories. I don't know why we find these things entertaining, but they never fail to be the resolution of these games. At this point, Tanner proves to be the most. . . experienced (seems to be a nice word for it) because he's sitting in his boxers and a t-shirt while Tate and Dylan are tied with their underwear, pants, and shirt still on. I come up, technically first, with my underwear, pants, t-shirt, and bra. Dylan had taken off her bra before she took off her shirt. She still seems to be hesitant to show her abdomen. (I must say though, I was quite impressed with her ability to swiftly take off her bra in what seemed like one movement.)

"Never have I ever had sex with someone within the first week of meeting them," says Tanner.

Tate reluctantly takes off his pants.

"Seriously, dude?"

"I don't need to explain myself," Tate replies as he throws his jeans aside. His legs are just as muscular as the rest of his body.

It's my turn, but I'm struggling to think of something I've never done. It can't be too far-fetched that no one else has done it either, and it can't be lame because that's boring. We're all a bit distracted with ourselves to really care that I'm taking a long time to say something, but our anticipation is certainly growing stronger as more parts of our bodies are exposed to the slight draft in the room. I have never presented my body to multiple people at one time, and I'm trying not to view it that way, because I don't want to chicken out right before I'm supposed to. I know that I won't be judged, but it's nearly impossible not to have an opinion about something, and I know that I will be curious as to what they think. Although, I doubt there'll be any verbal commentary about the appearance of our bodies considering we're all doing this through free will.

I know there are some of you out there who would doubt the validity of these events, but I ask you, how many lives have you not lived? I'm certainly not an expert, but I can't help but conclude that there must be one like this. And I can be particularly confident in that statement considering I happen to be living this one. That is why, I then truthfully state, "Never have I ever been in love."

They're slightly taken aback by my change of category, and they take a moment to decide on their responses.

"I'm assuming you don't mean friendship love," Dylan asks.

I shake my head.

Tanner then takes off his shirt, and Dylan and Tate are not surprised.

Knowing Tanner is single, I ask, "Where is she today?" I do this before realizing that that's quite personal, and it's maybe not the appropriate time.

Tanner looks me in the eyes and says, "She died of Leukemia last year. Her name was Lily, and I will never regret the nearly three years I was lucky enough to spend with her."

It was as if he had rehearsed the lines, and he said it with a sincere face of gratitude. I stare back at him, and in my intoxicated state, I instantly visualize an epically sad love story. I had no idea that he had such a heartbreaking past, and I don't know why I'm just now hearing about it. I can't prevent my eyes from welling up as I stare into his. I can feel my lips slowly morph into a quivering frown, and I naturally shove my face in my hands as I start to quietly weep.

I can hear laughter around me, and I feel pats on the back before I finally look up. Apparently they are amused at my response.

Tanner leans over and gives me a tight, one-arm hug and says with a simile, "It's okay June, really. I remember her only with joy, and we all knew what would happen."

"Are you sure?" I look up at him, vigorously wiping my cheeks.

"Yes," he says with certainty.

I manage to pull myself together, and I give twirling hand signals to Tate, informing him to carry on. They're still enjoying my reaction.

"Ya' good? Okay. . . never have I ever blacked out because of drinking."

Tate's innocence leads me to the confession of the first time I ever drank. I ended up taking shots of mixed, hard alcohol. I was stupid and binge drank. I feel like that's the story for many first time drinkers, and I wish that wasn't the case. But needless to say, I take off my pants, leaving me in my underwear, shirt, and bra. No one else takes anything off because they're much more stoners than drinkers – probably because of the wonderful role model they had growing up.

Dylan's turn. "Never have I ever had sex in a public area."

I was really hoping none of us would be taking off an item for this one, but Tanner puts his thumbs under his boxers and hesitantly starts to pull them down. We all give him scoffs of disapproval.

"Hey! Lily couldn't always get to places easily, and it's not like anyone was around us. It just happened to be a place where the public was able to go sometimes." He says it as if it was nothing, but we put aside our judgment because we're all still waiting for him to get naked. I can tell he's not pleased to be the first one exposed.

"Oh god, guys. I really don't want to do this," he tells us with his boxers inching down. We're all snickering.

"Just do it quick and then grab a pillow," Dylan suggests.

I feel like I should tell you, Reader, that we're not overly eager to see each other naked. I really don't know why we have a desire to do this in the first place, but I think it's derived from our excessive curiosity and limited amount of exposure to other people. Many would argue that this type of behavior is not suitable for people of our age, but is it really suitable for any age? And if there isn't a *prime time* to do this, then why not do it now? I think if we do things like this, and de-sexualize our perceptions of others and their naked bodies, then being promiscuous doesn't seem like such a desirable thing anymore. If we're desensitized and accepting, I think we're less likely to expose ourselves to unsafe or uneducated sex at a young age, because the "*I'm gonna' do it because you told me not to*" factor is then practically irrelevant.

But I know there are exceptions, like people who expose themselves to all sorts of sexual situations, yet never learn to be smart about it and don't bother with proper contraceptives. I don't necessarily understand these people, but I wish someone would talk to them about it.

Although it may not appear this way, we are approaching this game rather maturely, with no pressure, and no intentions of having sex. That is why, Tanner is then able to quickly swipe off his boxers and cover himself with his pillow. We all laugh and applaud his bravery, and he bounces his legs up and down on the ground in a spur of adrenaline.

I had gotten a quick glimpse of his privates, and although I have never liked the appearance of a penis, I have no uncharitable judgments of the human anatomy. I'm simply happy we're comfortable enough with each other to do this.

It is now down to Tate, Dylan, and I, and after skipping Tanner, it makes it my turn.

Once we settle down, I take a moment and say, "Never have I ever skipped school."

Tate takes off his shirt, and while explaining that it had been in middle school, and that she would have never done it in high school, Dylan takes off her pants.

"Never have I ever had a legitimate boyfriend," admits Tate. He then adds, "Not much to choose from back at home," downheartedly.

Dylan takes off her underwear, leaving her in just her t-shirt which is long enough to cover herself. I take off my shirt because I don't want another experience like my towel at the pool. And although being in my bra and underwear is exactly the same as being in my swimsuit, I feel even more exposed now.

I start to grab my pillow tighter, and after thinking for a while, I say, "I don't know what else I haven't done," which is stupid because now that I think of it, there are many things I could have said.

168

"Well, then let's open it up," suggests Tanner. "Anyone can say anything they think of."

"Okay then, never have I ever pierced anything below my face," Tate says as he grins at Dylan.

"You said no targeting!" Dylan yells back.

"I'm not targeting," Tate slyly states. "I have no idea whether June has been adventurous in that area or not."

"How cheap," Dylan says, grumpily.

"Yes, now let us see those sexualized milk cartons!" Tate exclaims.

I can see the hesitation on her face, but Dylan leans her pillow over her stomach, lifts her shirt off over her head, and we all see her boobs before she turns the pillow vertically and hugs it close to her chest. There's another round of applause for her bravery.

"Your nipples are pierced!?" I ask in astonishment even though I just saw that, yes, they are. It feels like I'm reliving the level of stupefaction I got when I realized that "a Capella" is two words, or when I found out that chameleons don't actually change color to match what they're touching.

"Yes," Dylan says, kind of shamefully.

"When? Why?" I'm flabbergasted.

"I don't want to talk about it," she mumbles.

"I like 'em," I decide.

She tries to smile.

"Next," says Tanner.

"Never have I ever broke my left arm *and* leg by jumping out of a tree." Dylan is obviously targeting Tate, but he doesn't object. Off goes his plaid boxers, and on goes the pillow. We cheer in his honor and he rubs his hands together and says, "Now for you, June. And congrats on being the most innocent." He gives me a nod.

"Let's just think of one more," Dylan decides.

"Never have I ever had sex before I was sixteen," says Tanner.

"Fifteen," I reply and feel a sudden doom brought on by the commencement of my undressing. It gives me the same kind of anxiety that I get when letting go of a balloon outside. I lay my pillow over my lap and manage to take off my underwear. I then look up at their kind faces and find the courage to unhook my bra. Quickly after, I hug my pillow just as Dylan had, and lean forward in ecstasy. It's such an odd thing to be proud of, but I am, and their cheers are a wonderful song.

"Okay – okay," Dylan gets our attention, "we'll turn off the lights, and on a count of four, we'll all stand up and drop our pillows."

We look at each other for nods of approval. Tanner leans back and flicks off the lamps. It's dark enough that our features will be blurry, but there's enough light in the room that our eyes can adjust to know what we're looking at. The anxiety hasn't gone away, but I'm able to tell that it's mixed with excitement as well.

"Ready?" Dylan asks.

"Four...."

"Three...."

"Two...."

"One!"

We all stand up with shrieks of exhilaration. We drop our pillows and quickly look each other over. I am filled with nerves, shivers, and joy. I can't get over how weird it feels to be doing such an odd thing with people I've just met this week. And even though I've known Dylan for quite a bit longer, this is the first time I've ever seen her fully undressed.

We stand for about six seconds, six *long* seconds, and quickly descend once Dylan initiates it. We all have huge smiles and loopy motions as we sit back down and start to find our clothes. It's a rush, but it's also relieving.

I'm not going to comment on their bodies because, after all, they're just bodies; we all know what they look like. What I will comment on, is something that shocks me even more than the fact that Dylan has her nipples pierced: as I reach for my shirt, I get a closer look at Dylan's stomach and side. Although I see no bruising – because it's been a long time since Dylan has spent a night at home – I do see dozens of crisscrossed, white, puffy, scars. I know instantly that they are self-inflicted, and I have an epiphany about why Dylan has always been so adamant about keeping on her shirt.

As I stare for as long as I can without her noticing, once more, my stomach drops, but this time it's with sorrow.

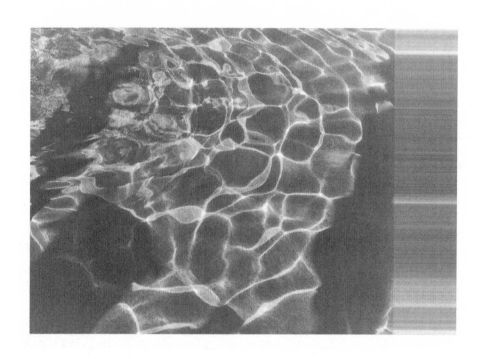

DICKS & PRICKS [14]

=

The night doesn't end there. The music seems to have stopped, but I know that's only in my head. I'm in a trance of frantic thought, and it's only interrupted when I notice that everyone is laughing at Tanner.

The music comes back, and I look to my right. Tanner is holding his pillow to his crotch and bouncing up and down, trying to get on his pants.

"Oh come on, dude!" Dylan says while chuckling.

"It just happens sometimes!" Tanner yells backs. "I can't help it!"

"Get in the bathroom," Tate manages between laughs.

Tanner hops his way into the bathroom to. . . take care of himself. It turns out he had gotten a boner, but we find it nothing more than humorous.

I then try to force the thoughts of Dylan out of my head because the night is moving on without me. The boys had either not noticed, or had already known, but no one brings it up.

Once we're all fully dressed, and Tanner has returned from the bathroom, I succumb to my thoughts and pour myself another drink. I don't believe I'll be able to move on without it. The rest follow in my footsteps as Tate goes to his phone to pick the next song.

I nearly down my drink as "Golden Years" by David Bowie bursts out of the speaker.

"Yes!" Dylan cheers, approving the song. She then dances her way over to me with her arms outstretched. I put down my drink and meet her hands. She starts pulling each of mine, one at a time, forcing me to move. I let her take me

173

because seeing her in such a pleasant mood is far better than thinking of her past.

The boys join in with sporadic dance moves that would receive, at most, a 3 out of 10 if being judged, but no one cares. Once the chorus hits and we theatrically lip synch the lyrics, no one really cares about anything, including me.

My last drink kicks in and we dance in what feels like slow motion, all around the room. I turn my head, but my vision doesn't follow. I blink my eyes, but don't miss a second. I flop on the bed, beaten with exhaustion, flushed with well-used energy, utterly dumbstruck with the discovery of two more properly told stories, but find myself elated. Elated because I'm not in the dark anymore. Elated because we were able to dance our asses off to a song way before our time, and forget what we'll be forced to worry about someday; I think that's as much as *in the moment* as I can get.

The rest flop down next to me, out of breathe. Dancing while drunk has never proven to be effortless, so Tanner takes off his shirt and Dylan takes off her pants to get some air. It's also getting late, so we get as comfortable as possible as we prepare for the night.

The boys struggle to hook up Tate's laptop to the TV as Dylan and I lay on the bed together. I can see the small imprints of her piercings under her shirt. I don't know how I hadn't noticed them before. It's similar to when you've driven down a road for your whole life but suddenly notice that there's a giant tree at the end of the street, and you have to ask someone if it's always been there, because for some reason, you can't remember having seen it before. But of course it's been there, it's a tree.

As I'm looking at her and thinking about that, she turns her head to face me, cheek smooshed on the pillows, and says, "One day, long from now, I'm gonna' call you up and ask, 'Hey, do you remember that one thing?' and I want you to know that that *one thing*, is this, right now. It's us sitting on the bed together in this cheap motel room, doing practically nothing. And when I ask, I want you to tell me, 'Yes, I do remember.'"

I stare at her for a little while. "I promise I will always remember."

174

"You better," she says, pointing a finger at me.

"I will," I say, grabbing her finger and bending it around.

"Good." She pulls her finger out of my grasp, and Tate yells, "Got it!" as they join us on the bed.

As we wrestle around with who gets to put their limbs where, the intro to *The Breakfast Club* comes on the TV. We mindlessly watch it for as long as we can, but all I can remember is seeing the iconic clip of the unlikely group dancing on the library table, before I fall asleep. And of course we all love this movie because we're a perfect example of a cliché, but it's a cliché for a reason, now isn't it?

The next morning, I'm the first one to wake up, and it's due to my sudden urge to puke all over the place. Luckily, I have good aim.

When I emerge from the bathroom, disgusted with myself but feeling much better, I see a jumbled mess of bodies entangled on the bed, and the pale shade of morning sun reaching their visible skin. I go to their mini-fridge and get a bottle of water; gotta' love a hangover.

I shouldn't have slept in my contacts.

I silently read, waiting for the others to wake up. They make stupid noises in their sleep, but it makes me smile.

Reader, what's your favorite book?

If you're anything like me, you'd think that's a terrible question.

They finally wake with fuddled expression, baggy eyes, and nests for hair.

"Food," is the first word uttered, and we all agree as we make ourselves semi-presentable. We then find a small coffee shop down the street, and enjoy pastries for breakfast (or should I say lunch, because they let the morning come and go as they slept).

We spend the rest of the day lounging around the motel, because no one feels up for activities. I've always thought a hangover was a fair tradeoff for drinking, or at least a good reminder that there are consequences to prevent over usage. I guess it doesn't work for everyone, however.

Periodically, I remind myself of what I saw on Dylan's abdomen. I have no idea how, but I have every intention of talking to her about it. I wait for a time that we're alone, but it never seems to come. Even though we hit pretty hard last night, the boys don't plan on ending this ride until we go to a "real party." I'm sure all they mean by that is going to someone else's party, but it doesn't look like I'll get to talk to Dylan until we end up back at my house together. And with that, I try my hardest to shove it to the back of my mind. But of course, making the conscious decision to do this, makes me think of it.

"I could go for some lunch," says Dylan, breaking our zombie-like state.

"You mean dinner?" I ask, looking at my phone. "It's seven twenty-five."

"Oh. . ." she says, wrenching her head back to look out the window, "yeah."

"Well, the party starts at nine, so now's a good time to eat something," says Tanner.

"How is it that you can find a party after only being here a week?" asks Dylan, suddenly more energetic than before.

"I know some people," he says, immersed in his phone.

"That makes you sound like a douche, ya' know," Dylan replies.

"Okay fine, you remember Emma? Graduated a couple years ago?" he asks.

Dylan nods.

"Well, she lives here now, has her own place. And she's friends with some people who are throwing a bonfire party out at an old campsite. And me being my charming self," he puts his hands to his chin and gives a fake, cheesy smile, "got us invited."

"Do you have directions?" Dylan asks.

"Working on it," he says, returning to his phone.

Dylan then turns back to me, picks up a pillow, and chucks it at my face. I barely manage to catch it.

"What the hell??"

"Wake up!" she says. "Let's go get some food."

She drags me off the couch and I see a window of opportunity to be alone, but it's quickly ruined when Tate says, "I'll come with."

By food, she meant the vending machine on the level below, but I'm not complaining because I'm cheap as hell. We make sure to buy something for Tanner too because he always buys for us.

When returning, Tanner informs us that the party's about twenty minutes away, and we have to drive.

"So. . . who wants to be sober cab?" he hesitantly asks.

We all look at each other, but when no one says anything, I volunteer. (Wow, I feel like Katniss [but not really though because I'd be that bitch that trips off the platform before the countdown is done, and die before it even starts.)

"You sure?" asks Tanner.

"Yeah, I don't mind," I reply, and they're very appreciative, but to be honest, I wasn't looking forward to drinking anyway. And if there's a fire, I'll be entertained just looking at that. So all in all, it's kind of a relief.

So we waste some time like it is ours to waste, but I don't really think it is. Often times, I think of all the productive things I could be doing, and then proceed not to do them. Instead, I sit where I have sat the majority of the day, and have pointless but revolutionary conversations with Dylan and her Tits.

(Oh-my-god, I apologize, I'm never calling them that again. That felt so weird even typing it. I got the same feeling I get when I'm out of a school setting and I hear one of my teachers being addressed by their first name, how bizarre.)

Anyway, we leave at an appropriate time and arrive fashionably. I think that's just a fancy way of saying we're not confident enough to be the first people there, which is most accurate, because when we get there, I don't know a single one of the faces around me, and I'm suddenly a lot more apprehensive than I was before.

The campsite required a bit of a walk through the woods, but after seeing the space, I decide it was worth it. There's a huge, blazing fire with a random assortment of chairs and logs surrounding it. There's an old set of picnic tables under an awning in the background that bares the alcohol and some food. Someone has managed to string lights in and out of the nearby trees, and has taken the time to make a big banner displaying the words *Your Favorite Kind of Campfire.* There's also a stereo with appropriate music playing, and a bunch of older people holding drinks, roasting a variety of food over the fire, and mingling about. Atmosphere wise, it's the prettiest party I've ever been too, but I'm starting to regret agreeing to be the sober cab because having a few drinks would certainly help me warm up to these intimidating people.

Tanner, Tate, and Dylan, knowing Emma, don't seem too worried about it as they're greeted with high fives. Their presence seems to be appreciated, and I hope that includes me as well. After our introduction, we drop off our contributions, and they get started.

Dylan stays close to me the majority of the night, and although I'm very thankful for it, I still wish to talk to her about what I saw. But knowing that this would be a terrible time to do so, I'm simply left thinking about it as I watch her slowly become increasingly more inebriated.

Throughout the night there are several guys who approach her, trying their hardest to flirt, but Dylan has never been particularly accepting of pick-up lines. It's honestly quite humorous to see them get knocked down, but I do applaud their guts; there was even a girl who tried.

Tanner has been talking with Emma. She's actually Vietnamese with jet black hair and cute cheeks. It was unfair of me to assume she was white before meeting her. She's considerably shorter than Tanner, but it looks like they're having a happy conversation.

I don't know the whereabouts of Tate at the moment, but I'm sure he's fine.

Dylan soon finds a seat at one of the picnic tables and pulls out her mini sketchbook to add to her collection of *Assisted Will* drawings.

I watch her fluent hand in awe. I've always liked watching people draw, but it frustrates me because I don't know why I can't get my hand to do that. I can tell she's drawing the aftermath of a group of people to our right who seem to be playing a game of quarters, but I don't watch for long because I know she'd prefer not to have an audience. Instead, I grab some marshmallows and find myself a vacant log.

After having my first attempt at roasting a marshmallow fail, I try another. Then, out of nowhere and after a long span of semi-quiet sanctuary, Tate comes up behind me and takes a seat on the other end of the short log.

"How's it going?" he asks.

"I kind of suck at this," I say, observing my marshmallow start to droop.

"Here," he says as he picks up my graham crackers to help me make my s'more.

"Thanks."

We sit for a while watching the fire and listening to the hustle around us. Tate is by far my least acquainted friend out of the group, so this is one of the only times we've been alone together, and I start to wonder if he's thinking about that too.

"Dylan was right about you," he says, all of a sudden.

"What do you mean?" I ask, finishing my s'more.

"She said you like to watch."

"Watch what?"

"Everything." He gestures around.

"Well. . . that's true," I admit. "But doesn't everyone sometimes?"

"I don't know," he starts. "I'd rather be doing things, so I don't miss out."

"I don't think I miss out," I say, and he looks at me in question, so I continue, "I mean," I look around, "see that guy over there? He failed the majority of his college classes and hasn't told his parents yet. And that girl

thought she was pregnant for two weeks, but really, she just gained some weight."
I point to another person. "He's going into the military next year. The ginger
over there got laid last night, and she, the one in the red sweater, binge watched
Orange Is The New Black all of yesterday."

Tate looks at me, rather impressed. "You got that all while sitting here?"

"Yeah," I say. "You know, alcohol affects your hearing, and with the
music, everyone here is practically screaming." I laugh. "It's not that hard."

"Well, maybe I should pay attention more often," he says.

"Maybe," I concur, and there's another nearly awkward silence.

"Hey, do you know how Dylan's been doing? Like actually?" he asks,
looking back at her. By him saying this, it implies he knows that her jubilant
persona doesn't always account for her internal feelings. I consider what she's
been through, what I now know about her, and how she's been lately, and reply,
"I think she thinks she's doing well."

He's fixated on the fire for a while, but finally says, "Yeah, I thought so."
He opens his mouth to continue, but it's suddenly interrupted by a loud shriek
coming from the woods.

"What was that?" I ask, knowing he can't give an accurate answer.

"Sounds like someone's having fun," he says.

A few people look in the direction of the sound. It maintains little
attention, however, because it's hard to tell the type of scream considering
everyone's buzzed, and screaming isn't that uncommon. But after we've all
returned to our business, I hear it again. This time it's much fainter, but it's now
obvious that it's not a scream of enjoyment.

"I'm gonna' go check that out," I tell Tate as I stand up.

"Check what out?" he asks.

"You didn't hear that?"

"Hear what?"

"Come with me," I tell him. I then hurry over to grab Dylan.

"Hey, come with us for a second," I tell her. She's still immersed in her
drawing.

"Where?" she asks.

I don't feel up to explaining because I could be wrong, so I vaguely say, "The woods. Just come on," and they do. I don't know what I'll tell them if I'm wrong, but I want help if I'm right, so I lead them in the direction of the second scream.

We walk aimlessly over roots and leaves.

"Where are we going?" Dylan asks, a bit behind. I hadn't considered how difficult it may be to do this drunk. I start to get discouraged because, if I'm being honest, I don't know, but I shush her and keep my ears alert. I then hear what sounds like a muffled argument to my right. I immediately change direction, and Tate follows close behind; I think he caught on.

The noise gets louder, and eventually I'm able to decipher that there's a boy and a girl fighting viciously a few yards from us. They finally come into focus, and I see a tall guy in a white shirt messing with his jeans with one hand, and holding a small blond against a tree with the other hand. It's instantly apparent what's going on, and I'm infuriated. I quickly yell out, "Hey!" to make ourselves known because they hadn't heard us approaching over the girl's loud pleas to stop.

The guy turns to look at us, alarmed. He slowly backs off the girl who is now crying. As he messes with his underwear and tries to zip up his pants, he says, "Hey, it's not what it looks li-" but before he can finish, Tate rushes out from behind me and decks him across the face. He hit him so hard that Tate nearly falls over from the momentum of his swing, and the guy is forced to the ground, cupping his nose, trying to stop the newly gushing blood. I step around him and hold out a hand to the girl. She accepts, pulls up her shirt strap, manages to get a hold of her undergarments, and tries to suppress her crying. She has thin hair and dark makeup. She's a twig and has obviously been drinking.

The bastard on the ground gets up, tilting his head back and pinching his nose. Dylan then arrives, and her hands cup her mouth in astonishment.

The guy, now vexed and dealing with pain, spits blood to the side and yells, "Fucking asshole!" to Tate in disgust.

Tate starts towards him again. "Are you kidding me!?" he asks, stopping right in front of him. The guy pushes Tate before he can continue, and Tate trips on a root and falls backwards to the ground. The guy laughs and says, barely audible, "Stay down, faggot." Apparently, he either knows Tate, or is prone to using gay slang as an insult (even though gay is anything but). This, however, doesn't work in his advantage, because Dylan lunges forward and kicks him in the balls before Tate can get up. The guy gives a low grunt of pain, and again, hunches over.

"You fucking piece of shit!" Dylan says, nearly spitting with anger.

The girl I'm supporting flinches every time someone is hit and holds my arm tightly. The guy, evidently refusing not to have the last line, says, "Oh come on," he's nearly laughing and on all fours, "she was asking for it!"

That's the last straw for Dylan; her fists clench, and with all the power she can muster, she kicks him in the ribs. The girl cries into my shoulder, Tate leads Dylan away, and the guy falls to his side in pain. We turn around, ready to leave, but Dylan makes a point to yell back, "Oh, *sorry*! I thought you were asking for it!" in a fake, girly voice, and Tate pulls her along.

Due to the shock and how abrupt the situation was, we find ourselves short of words as we make our way back through the uneven terrain. I continue to support the girl who hasn't managed to stop crying, so I decide to start a conversation.

"Hey," I say in a soft voice, "what's your name?"

She sniffles and tries to focus on me. "It- It's Chloe."

"Chloe? Okay Chloe, did you come here with some friends?" I ask because I'm not sure how to handle this situation, and it'd be nice to consult with someone who knows her.

"Yeah. . . but I think they left already."

Great.

"Well, we can take you home, okay?" I offer with the hope that she lives somewhere safe.

She manages a small nod, and we find our way out of the woods. When we emerge from its edge, Tanner notices us from across the campsite and hurries to greet us.

"Hey! I have great news!" He then realizes that we all look distraught, and that I have a small, teary-eyed, blond hanging onto my shoulder. "Wait, what happened?"

Dylan, Tate, and I glance at each other, but no one feels up to explaining the outrageous and infuriating situation we had discovered. Despite rape being common, I have never expected that I'd be exposed to it, and that's because I have the *"but that can't possibly happen to me"* mentality that most people have about serious things. But realistically, this is a frightening first glimpse at college life, and a sad reality that is only now being given a spotlight.

"We'll tell you later," Tate says, finally.

Tanner's still concerned, but he tells us that Emma will let them stay at her house for the rest of the week. "She said she has an extra room because her roommate's in the process of moving or something, I don't know, but we can check out of the motel and move in tomorrow." He tries to contain his excitement. Tate doesn't share the enthusiasm however, and he pats Tanner on the back as he leads him away from the rest of us. Dylan and I then bring Chloe to an empty table to get her address and discuss bringing her home. I have a cigarette to calm myself while she talks. Dylan gives me looks of disapproval.

Chloe has managed to stop crying and now seems overly tired. She's a sweet girl, but not necessarily the brightest, and although that could be due how much alcohol she has consumed, we decide it's time to bring her home.

We contemplated for a long time bringing her to the police to report what happened, but considering she's underage and has been drinking, Chloe insisted that she couldn't risk it. Plus, none of us feel capable of dealing with such a daunting process, and it's devastating to think that this is part of the reason why the majority of rapes never amount to be rape cases.

When we get Chloe back on her feet, we round up the boys who are further collaborating with Emma about sharing her place, and all head to Tate's car where I will be driving. I've never been fond of being the driver due the responsibility I have over the passengers' lives, but I put in Chloe's address and manage to find my way to a run-down set of apartments. Apparently, she's renting it with some roommates, but those roommates didn't bother to check where she was before they left the party, so already, I don't have a positive image of them.

Dylan wakes up Chloe because she had fallen asleep on the long drive here. Chloe had to sit nearly on top of Dylan because there wasn't enough room in the car, so she's a bit startled when she wakes up. We then help her up the stairs, and she drowsily tells us which door is hers. It's apartment 6B, and it has a dingy, grey-green door with nothing but a peephole and doorknob. When it's opened, a loud mix of party girls fill the doorway – along with my eardrums.

"Chlo-Bear! Where've ya' been?" one girl yells with a drink in her hand. Apparently, they had brought the party home with them. I can't imagine who they deemed sober enough to drive them home, and can only hope that they had enough sense to get a cab (or should I say Uber).

We reluctantly hand over Chloe. None of them ask who we are or why we're bringing her home; they drag her in, and I can see a girl in the back pouring Chloe a drink. When Dylan sees this, she makes a point to say, "She's had a rough night. If you have any brains at all, you'd put her to bed and help her if she throws up." Dylan sounds like an angry mom.

The remaining girl in the doorway gives a high pitch, "Uh huh," with her mouth buried in her cup and proceeds to close the door.

We stand for a second, looking at each other.

"Idiots," Dylan says as we make our way back to the car.

"Do you think Chloe will tell them what happened?" I ask.

"Not sure she'll even remember with how much she drank," Dylan replies.

"Maybe that's for the best," I say, but I don't know if that's true. I don't know if there's any efficient way of coping after a rape, but at the very least, I hope she gets support if the memories flood back tomorrow morning. I know I'll never forget, and I wasn't even the one it happened to.

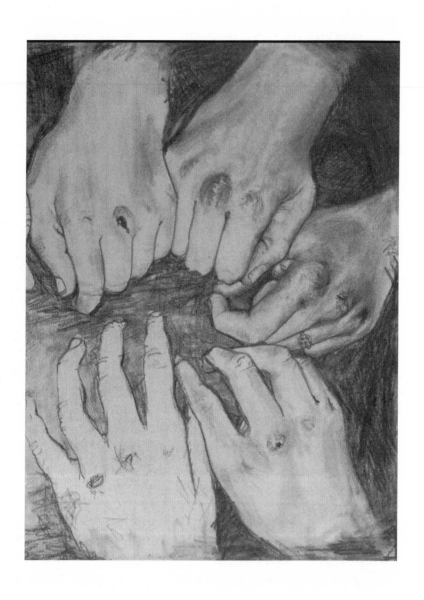

THE ANIMALS [15]

=

"You know, if someone likes the vagina that much, you'd think they'd respect it rather than abuse it," Tanner says in anger the next day after we explain what had happened.

We all agree, but eventually we have nothing more to say on the topic because its brutality wears us out. So we help Tate and Tanner gather their things and check out of the motel, because they have accepted Emma's offer to be roommates for a week. At this point, it's obvious that Tanner has a bit of a crush on Emma. It's cute, but it's never addressed, so we all arrive at Emma's place with knowing grins across our faces and nothing more.

"Thanks for doing this," Tate tells Emma. "It saves us a lot of money."

"Of course," Emma replies. "Always good to see an old friend, and I have the room."

It doesn't require four people to move the few items the boys traveled with, but we all go in anyway. Upon entering, my jaw unintentionally drops.

"Jesus Emma, you didn't tell me you were rich," Tanner says, with his mouth equally agape.

"*I'm* not," she stresses. "My family is."

From the outside, it looks like an ordinary house, but what it disguised is art from who knows what century, walls as white as a redlined suburb, furniture you'd only see in some futuristic Facebook video, wool rugs probably hand sewn by the sheep themselves, and mirrors so spotless, you'd believe there were actually two of you. (Okay, obviously I'm exaggerating, but it's a nice house.) It's the type of place that makes me feel like I can't touch anything. I'm not sure I'd like to live in a place that isn't inviting.

Once we stop gawking at her pristine dwelling, Emma feels as if she should give an explanation: "My family owns a lot of businesses, and they don't think I should be '*deprived in my young years.*' Whatever that means. I actually feel foolish for being so spoiled," she says as she stares at a rather ostentatious chandelier. "Does that make sense?" she asks, not necessarily looking for an answer.

I have never been poor (or should I say my family has never been poor), but I've also never been privileged enough to have a house like this all to myself. I still marvel at fancy things, despite how many fancy things I've seen. Does that make me humble? Does it make Emma humble if she knows that her house is overdone? Is Dylan ever envious of places like this considering she's by far the least financially equipped? Maybe, but I can't picture Dylan ever wanting to own a place like this, nor can I picture a place like this in my future.

"Don't feel foolish," Tanner tells Emma. "Money doesn't define a person."

"But it sure does help," Dylan says, quietly, as she flicks the knob on some sort of desk pendulum.

The amount of money someone has doesn't affect my opinion of them, but how they treat that money does. For Emma, she's still cute and sweet, and she shows us where the boys will be sleeping. It's a big room with pale-blue walls, containing furnishing that match the quality of the rest of the house.

"You guys can hang out for a while if you want," Emma tells Dylan and me. "Always nice to have company."

Although I wouldn't mind staying, I'm still waiting for an opportunity to talk to Dylan, and seeing that I haven't been home since Friday, I tell Emma that my mom would want me back, and she's understanding. Dylan on the other hand, doesn't owe anyone her appearance, so she decides to hang out with the three of them instead. I'm not mad at her decision, because I never made it obvious that I wish to speak to her, but I can't help but be disappointed that I'll have to wait even longer now.

I thank Emma for being kind, say goodbye to my friends, and exit the lavish door. But when I get to the street and see only Tate's car, I remember that we all drove together. I sigh from my stupidity and contemplate my options: either walk home or go back and ask for a ride. Although I feel childlike and slightly embarrassed for no reason, I return to Emma's house. When I enter without knocking, I find them sitting on a leather couch together, scrolling through movies on an Apple TV.

"Um - hey," I say, making myself known. "Tate, I forgot that we all came together, so unless you'd like me to leave you without a car, I kinda' need a ride."

"Oh yeah, sorry," he says, getting up from the couch. "I'll go get the keys."

When he returns, Dylan volunteers to drive me instead, so he throws her the keys and we head back out together. Of course, the first time we're alone together, it's not nearly as long as I need and doesn't promote serious talking. So when I sort my thoughts, and the music is low, I casually ask, "Are you staying at my house tonight?"

"Uh, yeah. Why wouldn't I be?" she asks, genuinely looking for an answer.

"Just checking," I reply, but I think me questioning it makes her question it herself.

"Do you not want me to? I don't have to. I mean my mom's not always bad," she says in a rushed sort of way.

"No, no, it's not that," I assure her. "I just didn't know if you'd end up staying at Emma's or something."

"Oh," she says, "no, I'd feel weird there, and I don't want to make a fuss about it."

"Yeah, no, I get it. Just let me know when you're coming home. I'll stay up," I tell her, not trying to sound too suspicious, but most likely failing.

"You don't have to," she says. "I know where you keep the key." We then pull into my driveway.

"Yeah, okay, well – I'll see you later then, alright?" I don't want to make a big deal out of this, but I can't keep it from bothering me. I hate that there's a part of Dylan that I never knew about, and I regret to say that, in some way, it affects the way I think of her. I have never viewed her as anything less than strong and put together, but the fact that she has physically and intentionally harmed herself, makes the part of my mind that is wrapped around my perception of her, unfold a bit, and I don't know how to deal with that.

"Okay, Junebug," she says, looking a bit confused at me. I then break my stare toward her, and exit the car. I watch her drive away as I go inside. I don't know what to do with my day because it's now dedicated to merely wasting time in hopes that my waiting doesn't drag, but I know that it will.

When I go inside, I'm surprised to see that my mom is home.

"Take off today?" I ask her.

"Lunch break," she says as she pulls leftovers out of the microwave.

"Oh, yeah, duh." I often lose track of daily schedules when I don't have one myself.

"I can heat some up for you too, if you'd like," she offers.

"I'm good, thanks," I say, because honestly, I can't tell what leftovers she's eating, and that's a bit disturbing.

Reader, I haven't talked about my mom that often, and that's mainly because this story isn't about that. But I don't think I can properly display my life if I don't talk about her at least once. After all, she's the reason I can write any of this in the first place.

I can start off by saying that my mom never sang me to sleep as a kid. Now, that sounds like a sad story, but in reality, she's just a terrible singer and thought it'd make manners worse if she did sing, so really, I owe her gratitude. But this minor truth has taught me something other than the fact that I, too, am a terrible singer: it's taught me the value of perspective.

(I feel like I'm starting to give some speech that people would roll their eyes at, but I don't know how else to say it. So I give my regards to your attention span, which may not wish to undertake my potential bullshit. But whatever, here I go.)

Growing up in a house that has its flaws, such as a faucet that won't cease to drip unless turned predominantly on the hot side, a kitchen light that hasn't worked in nearly three years, and a basement that becomes a pool whenever it rains, has taught me to expect these things throughout the rest of my life. I have come to love these imperfections because I'd rather learn to tolerate a few flaw, than be surprised that the world won't be handed to me.

My mom has fallen into the vast majority of middle-class-tolerants: people who have a job, but don't have a job that they love. And although this does pay the bills, I hope I won't follow in her footsteps, so to speak. My mom has done a good job at not complaining, nevertheless, because she knows that it could easily be worse.

However, disregarding finances, because that doesn't matter anyway, my mom is quite sufficient on all of the qualities of a good parent. She doesn't prod, she doesn't disregard me, she cares if I'm doing poorly, but doesn't punish me in return. She laughs at the same things I do, she swears when it's called for and even when it's not, and she doesn't shove a religion down my throat, or anything for that matter – besides equality of course – but she never told me to think that. She never *told* me to think anything because she knows that my thoughts aren't hers to decide. And I think, just based on that fact, I can classify her as a good human being because she has that rule for everyone, despite their beliefs.

Although there are things I dislike about my mom at times, as there are for every kid, I've never been tempted to say that I hate her. Yes, it's annoying how whenever we enter a building together, she makes me go in first, but she claims that's because it's a motherly instinct to keep one's child in eyesight. With this, I try to remember that there's usually a reason behind the things that she does that I dislike, and I think that's why our relationship works.

To end my tribute to the woman who grew me inside herself (what a disturbing thought), I will give to you, Reader, one piece of advice that she gave to me: when purchasing cups, never buy a set that you can't fit your hand into, because you'll never know when you need to hand-wash shit, and have fun drinking out of it the next time if you can't reach the bottom of it when cleaning. I don't know why that's the first thing I think of, but I'll never forget it.

What have you learned from your mother? What have you learned from your father? Even if you've got a parent like Dylan's, she's still learned what not to do as an adult, and sometimes that's just as effective.

My dad is probably the only person I know who likes his passport photo, and I laughed when he told me this. My dad's not afraid to pick up spiders or even befriend them. He's selfless in ways that aren't usually recognized, and although that sometimes gets the better of him, I know he means well. My dad is a whole other story however, and it's not one that I can relate to this one, so I'll leave it short. But to make a final point, my mom is always early and my dad is always late, so in a perfect world, and mathematically speaking, that should make me right on time. However, I've undoubtedly proven this to be wrong, so before we go around assuming things, I think we need to remember that there will always be a margin of error in life - or rather - we should just know by now that we aren't our parents. For some people, that's really hard to accept.

I've never had that much of a problem with it, but as I sit next to my mom, eating a bowl of cereal and watching a rerun episode of *Friends*, it dawns on me that I'll be alone next year. This cereal (which is so loud due to my crunching that I may as well have the subtitles on) will be what I live off of when I get to college. And that's true because my bank account is not what I want it to be, yet I work more than I'd like to already, and I dread every time I have to go there, even though it's not that bad. But in this day and age, I see countless examples of young starts, doing exactly what they want before they even hit the age requirement for working, and everyone says, "*You can be whatever you put your mind to!*" but that's not true. We're easily fooled, and if we truly believe that if we work our asses off it'll get us to where we want to be, than boy, am I sorry to the many who didn't make it, because they were lead down a mightily misleading road.

I may sound melodramatic, but I'm a teenager, writing a book, hoping that it can one day enable me to list 'Author' as my occupation, and be a ticket out of a minimum wage job for the rest of my life. But do you know how many books actually make a profit? Not that fucking many! Not to mention, I am wholeheartedly trusting that my life experiences are enough to convince you, Reader, to read them. That's a whole lot of trust, but I'm a trusting person, and some say that that'll bite me in the ass, but what's the point of life if I don't give a little?

I don't know the answer, but I do know that I sure as hell won't get anywhere if I become a writer in hopes that it'll make me a lot of money. I know that's not the point.

I'm too eager to start my life, but too scared that it won't work out. So as I sit here, finishing my cereal, I ask myself *how long do I think I'll live?* And all I can say is that I hope it's long enough to make me okay with dying, but that means that I have to be okay with my timeline, and I need to stop trying to rush it. Do you rush yours? Or worry about it, or wish it would slow down? If you were asked to put a pushpin precisely on the timeline of where you were, where you are, and where you hope to be, could you do it? Sometimes I don't think I could, and that's the main reason I'm ranting to you. But I'll stop now because I'm kind of grossing myself out with how annoying I'm being.

It's amazing where the mind can wonder.

I get another bowl of cereal.

"How was your weekend?" my mom asks me.

"Fine," I say at a minimum, because that's what we always say.

"Where'd you stay at?" she asks because she knows that it wasn't at Dylan's. I've explained to my mom that Dylan shouldn't live with her mother, and she understands, to say the least.

"With Tate and Tanner," I reply without explaining that it was at a motel, but she doesn't ask. My mom has never been strict on my interactions with males. I'd like to think that it's because she trusts me, rather than her not caring, but your guess is as good as mine.

"I need to go to the store later, want to come?" she asks after a while.

Although I normally wouldn't, I accept because sometimes it feels better to get out of the house and at least pretend to do something productive.

"I'll be home at five and then we can go," she says as she rinses off her plate and grabs her purse.

"Okay."

"Love you, bye."

"Love you too."

I think we're normal.

I spend the remaining time trying to convince myself that it's okay to be lazy. This includes copious amounts of binge watching on Netflix, and making food because there's a part of me that's bored. I don't hate it, though. There are some days that I'd kill just to be doing this, but I feel bothered by something nearly the entire time, so it's hard to relax.

At 5:00 I go to the store with my mom. I wonder what Dylan is doing. I wonder what Stephen Hawking is doing. Do you ever do that? Everyone's doing something at this very moment, but for most people, we can only guess.

At 6:00 I unload the car and put away the groceries.

At 7:00 my mom tells me to pick a movie, so I do.

At 8:00 I'm consumed.

At 9:00 I return to my life.

At 10:00 I wish I could go back.

At 11:00 my mom's in bed and I'm waiting to hear from Dylan.

At 12:00 I'm still waiting.

At 12:29 I hear the front door open.

"Hey," I say, just as I see her emerge.

She jumps. "Oh! Jesus, you scared me. I told you, you didn't need to stay up."

"I was up anyway," I lie because I was about to fall asleep minutes before she came in.

"Okay, well, I seriously have to poop, so move it," she says, throwing down her stuff and jogging past me on her tippy toes.

"Glad you can be so open about it," I joke quietly to myself. It then dawns on me that in the entire time of me doing practically nothing, I didn't even prepare myself for bringing up what's been bothering me to Dylan. How stupid. What am I supposed to say? *"Oh hey, I saw something you didn't want me to see, and by the way, thanks for not telling me about it."* No, so what am I going to do? I'm going to wing it.

"I hate using the bathroom at other people's houses, so I had to wait a long damn time to do that," she says when she comes back out.

"Lovely," I say in return. "Hey, did you guys drink or anything?" I continue, casually.

"No, just hung out."

"Okay. Well, did you have fun?" I ask.

"Yeah I guess," she pauses. "Why?"

"Just wondering," I reply.

"You've been doing that a lot lately," she says, knowing that I'm acting weird.

"Yeah. . . ." I stand and stare at her for a while. "Hey, can I talk to you about something?" I then decide to ask.

She looks at me funny. "Well, considering you already are, I'm assuming this isn't going to be good, but yeah."

I head into my room and she follows. When we sit on my bed, I become oddly aware of what she's wearing, because it's what's under it that concerns me. She has on her yellow hippie shirt with a blue vest over it. It makes her look old and young at the same time.

"What's up?" she asks in her everyday voice, but when I simply continue to stare at her, she adds, "Seriously dude, you're acting weird. What is it?"

"I know why you never want to take off your shirt," I say before consulting myself.

"Oh, are we getting sexual now?" she jokes.

"No. . . Dylan, I know why you hide your stomach, and it's not just because of your mother."

She stops joking as the slightest flash of fear shows through her eyes. I can tell that she feels uncomfortable, but her voice doesn't waver from casual when she says, "Those are from a long time ago. It's fine, don't worry." But for some reason, I can't accept that.

"When?" I ask.

"I don't know," she says, trying to remember. "It was a weird time span."

"Well, when did you start and when did you stop?" I'm not sure why it matters that much, but I really want to know.

She's hesitant to reply, but she purses her lips and easily says, "I started in the summer of sixth grade and went until sometime after my Freshman year."

"Four years!" I exclaim, and can only manage to ask, "Why?" even though it wouldn't be that hard to guess. But there's a part of it that I've never understood: how could someone think that that was a solution? How could someone as smart as valedictorian Dylan, think that that was going to help?

"Isn't that obvious?" she asks instead of answering.

"Well. . . yeah, but like. . . why that?" I don't know how else to phrase it.

"Look, you're not going to understand unless you've been driven to do it yourself, and I don't really want to talk about it," she says, almost angrily, and starts to get up off the bed.

"Wait, wait, wait." I grab her arm and make her sit down again. "If you explain it all right now, I'll never ask you about it again. I promise."

There's a slight roll of her eyes. "I don't want to sound all depressive, and gross, and shit."

"Oh who cares, everyone's depressed, just tell me." I say this lightheartedly to get her to talk to me, but I do know that this is not something that should be normal, and I don't want to give the impression that I don't take this seriously. So just know, that in no way do I view this as okay.

"Well, you gotta' ask me something, I don't wanna' just talk about it," she says, but agrees.

"Okay, then. . . how'd you get the idea to do that in the first place?" I start.

"Honestly, I saw it on social media, and from there on - I really don't know. I just kinda' did it."

"But how did that help?" I ask without realizing that this sounds like I'm judging her for it.

"I told you, you wouldn't understand."

"Yeah, but like, for four years, how-"

She cuts me off, "Look!" I can tell that she's frustrated. "Will I admit that not every part of it makes sense? Yes. Will I admit that it seems completely counterproductive from an outsider's perspective? Yes. But what I won't admit is that it didn't help." She struggles to get the words out because it doesn't seem to be an easy concept to grasp, but she explains, "When everything is shit, and you have no control over what is happening to you, you search for something easy. And the fuck if I know why, but for some reason, doing that to myself relaxed me. It was a type of destruction, a type of. . . pain," she rolls her eyes, obviously disgusted at her words, "that I had complete control over, unlike all the other crap in my life. I could just sit there, and focus on that, and feel free for just long enough to get me to the next day." Her hands are moving all over the place, and she's barely looking at me because she's living in a memory.

"I couldn't even feel it!" she continues. "If I was truly sad enough, I literally didn't feel a thing. And hell, I don't even like blood! Like that shit makes me woozy, but if I caused it, it didn't affect me whatsoever. Does that makes sense? No. Does that make it okay? No. Is it something that people should be doing to themselves? Fuck no! But I did it. For *four fucking years*. It's the only true addiction I've ever had, and the saddest part is that I don't regret it." Her voice is finally back to its normal volume, and she ends with saying, "It's just a part of me now."

She had gotten up off the bed in the midst of her rant, so I stare up at her as she waits for me to say something. My eyes start to pool, although I'm not entirely sure why. I ask, "What made you finally stop, then?"

I can tell this isn't the question she was expecting because her set expression changes, and she has to think about it for a while.

"I - I don't know. I guess I just kinda' slipped out of it. Just like I slipped into it."

I silently nod my head.

"Why didn't you tell me?" I ask once she decides to sit back down.

She shrugs her shoulders. "I've been so used to keeping it a secret that I just didn't know how to."

I nod again. I don't know what compels me to want this, but I ask, "Would you show me?"

"So now you want me to take off my shirt? Back to the sexual are we?" she jokes to lighten the mood. I manage a smile, but she knows that I'm being serious.

After slight hesitation, she lifts up her shirt to reveal her abdomen. In this light, I get a better view of the variety of puffy scars. It's obvious that there are multiple years' worth of damage. Some are pink while others are ghost white. Some were much deeper than others when first created, and there are some areas that are nearly all scar rather than stomach. She doesn't show me for that long.

"Satisfied? Can we go to bed now?" she asks, lowing her shirt.

"Thank you," I make eye contact with her. "And yes. I was about to before you came home."

"You should have," she says as we get up to go get settled.

Reader, I just noticed that I unintentionally called it "home" when talking to Dylan, and neither of us found it weird even though my house isn't technically her home. I don't think it gets much more real than that.

The next morning is normal, and I put what happened in the back of my mind because that's how life works. One thing I've learned throughout writing this is that nothing is ever about *just one thing*. This story isn't about Dylan's life. It's not about how her mother affects her. It's not about what she teaches me, or how she changes my life. It's not about me, or Tate, or Tanner, or even Dylan. I don't know what it's about because I don't know why it's happening. Everything just *is*, and I've learned to accept that.

"What are we doing today?" Dylan asks as she heats up a pack of Pop-Tarts.

"You're asking me?" I question.

She nods.

"I'm probably the last person to decide that," I say.

"Exactly why you should," she remarks.

One of her Pop-Tarts comes out burnt.

"What do you want to do?" she asks as she sits down across the table from me.

"I don't know," I reply without giving it much thought.

"I'm making you pick," she says, stubbornly.

"Seriously?"

"Yes!" She's determined.

"Fine," I try to think of something that requires some extra work, "I want to go to a zoo."

"Zoos are cruel," Dylan declares.

"Oh come on! You told me to pick, and I did. I want to go to a zoo, and it's not like the wild isn't cruel either. . . ."

"Yeah, but that's natural cruelty," she makes a point.

"Well, think of it this way, the zoo isn't going to close down, so we might as well support it by giving it money, so that it can use it for getting better care for the animals."

She stares at me for a while. "Fine. I'll tell the boys."

I smile as she leaves the room. It was kind of a long shot, but I'm glad she agreed. I haven't been to a zoo in years, and I think animals are extraordinary. And although I don't like that they're in captivity, I can't necessarily help that they are, so I might as well help them make it a respectable zoo. Perhaps I'm just telling myself this to deal with feeling guilty. Excuses are probably one of the most widely used coping mechanisms, so I'm not surprised if that's the case.

"They're asking how far away it is," Dylan tells me, reading from her laptop. She uses Facebook Messenger as her form of communication since her mother will likely never give her her phone back.

"About an hour and a half," I reply.

"Can Emma come?" Dylan asks. "Tanner's wondering." We both smile and I tell her that I wouldn't mind, and within an hour, we're dressed and ready, so we head over to Emma's to embark on our short road trip.

Tate drives, Dylan sits passenger, and I manage to share the back seat with Tanner and Emma. The music is loud and I'm entertained by watching the people in passing cars. They all have a destination, probably miles away from ours, yet we end up on the same road at the same time.

You can tell a lot about a person in the five second glance you manage to steal when passing. Some sit stiff like boards; some dance like they're not in control of a motorized killing machine. Some sing, but it looks like they're just mouthing the words. Some talk with their passengers; some argue with their passengers. Some are carrying a family while others are carrying a dog. Some text; some put on makeup; some just sit there. And then there's some that look over at the same time you do, and through eye contact you make the awkward realization that you're doing the same thing but aren't connected in any way. That always creeps me out a bit.

When we're halfway there, Tanner and Emma smoke. They roll down the windows, but the smell doesn't leave the car. Dylan takes a pill, but don't ask me what kind because there's no doubt she was trying to be discreet about it. She knows that I don't approve of how often she takes them, but who can miss the distinct toss of her head, followed by a sip of water? I decline when Emma offers to share her weed, and Tate doesn't take anything because he's driving. I wonder if any of the neighboring cars are taking part in these types of activities as well.

Despite it being a weekday, the zoo's parking is horrendous. It seems to take us just as long as it did to get here to find an empty spot. When we do manage, we make the long walk to the entrance, and my stomach fills with childlike glee as we pass bronze statues of animals.

We don't know where to start, but we want to see it all, so we grab a map and head to our left.

The zoo is a proud holder of all that we could be, but nothing we'd like to admit.

The Monkeys: they're kept in kingdoms of trees and ropes. They swing with arms as long as their bodies, and legs as long as their arms. Some have beards, some have mustaches, and some have eyes that I can almost relate to. They are humans once removed, and although I can't say I fully believe in evolution, I can't seem to convince myself that we're not at least on the same page.

The Birds: plucked from a rainbow, they never seem to stop singing. Although the glass muffles their tunes, I know that they do it because they want to. Some say it's sad that a bird can be caged, but we all know it's just a metaphor.

The Fish: they never seem to know what direction they're going in, but who ever does when they're in school? With eyes that never blink, they live in a sea of colorful confusion. What wonders I could do if I could breathe underwater.

The Snakes: feared by many, they're misunderstood. Although riddled with patterns of vibrancy, it's only skin deep. Despite their ability to move swiftly,

201

they remain resting in areas not big enough for their tethered bodies. With forked tongues and missing limbs, it's hard not to be viewed as an outcast.

The Tigers: a symbol for strength and an unlikely companion, yet I've always wanted to pet one. When you're the king of the cats, I still view you as a cat; when you're a celebrity of the people, I still view you as a person. But isn't it hard not to marvel at their power?

The Tortoise: they say it'll beat the hare, but that's only because the hare is stupid.

The Hare: they say it'll lose to the tortoise, but I've never met a stupid hare, and I've never met a fast tortoise, so maybe we should just acknowledge that the race is unfair in the first place and know that conditions won't always save us.

The Giraffes: they have necks I could climb, but they use them as weapons rather than a form of elegance. I think I'd hate to be that tall, but I'd love the view.

The Bears: I watch them fight – or maybe they're playing – but either way, they're massive. They can survive purely off their brute force, and are fast on top of strong, and burly on top of frolicsome. They remind me of Tate.

The Sloth: my inner self – but we all say that.

The Zebras: they're the most popular answer when asked, "What's a word that starts with Z?" I wonder if they know that they're so popular. They're the outcome of a donkey and a horse who had to compromise on what their favorite color was. But who's to blame them? We're terrible at making decisions.

The Butterflies: they're kept in a dome, hidden by plants of many. We walk around, hoping that they'll land on us, but due to their silent presence, we probably wouldn't even notice if they did. With wings that make statements, they live a beautiful, short life.

The Camels: being a trademark for cigarettes, they start at a low bar. But with what they've lost, they make up for with their efficiency. They are walking water bottles with a stamp of transportation and a symbol of patience. They are the ones that are prepared.

The Frogs: their beauty is a poison.

The Penguins: they were set up to fail. They have wings that don't fly, but are nothing less than a bird. As a minority, they've persevered, and made use of their wings in the water. When shown doubt, they're smart enough to know that it's merely a guess; it doesn't define anything.

The Ostrich: brother to the penguin, their legs have never failed them; they are what makes them great, and they know that to be ashamed would only prove their existence unjustified.

The Wolves: I can't help but think that if I met them in the woods, I'd treat them like a dog. The severity of their bite, the ruthlessness of their grit, and the knowledge that they bestow are nothing but whispers in the back of my mind when I hear them howl.

The Whale: I don't have words that can fill its monumental vitality. I fail to comprehend how massive they are, and am bewildered even further when thinking that from the perspective of the ocean, they are small.

The Meerkat: perched on the highest ground, they have a better view than even the giraffes. With no defense other than an eye, they are a sniper. Finding sanctuary underground, they prove that size doesn't matter.

The Bison: equipped with a hide able to withstand any weather, the strength to stomp its enemies, and horns to prevent some from even daring, they are herbivores. Gentle does not have a body type.

The Gazelle: swift, stealthy, smart, and speedy, they glide over the earth. Often viewed in a run for their life, they prove that a sprint can be worth it.

The Fox: often paired with "sly" or "clever," they are the robbers. It seems that before they slip into cracks, they have to check if they're wanted or not - and if they aren't, they feel validation to do so. But don't get me wrong, their ginger fluff and long faces are enough to convince me to house one for myself. I could make use of a robber.

The Elephant: what can I not say about the elephant? All the wisdom that they possess is woven throughout the grooves of their skin, and they're worn because of their longevity. Longevity that allows their imposing memory to prosper, and they vouchsafe their good fortune through a lifted trunk. Who's to say what can be true, but pink tusks is the least we can do for the great who walk amongst us.

Sometimes we forget that we're their greatest enemy.

Although I don't like to admit it, throughout the day, I find myself occasionally prodding at the glass that restrains these animals. I do it because I like them a lot, but they don't know that. They don't know much of anything other than what slot their food comes from and the cycle of fixation and rotation. I wonder what they're thinking. I wonder what they're capable of thinking.

Tate likes the giraffes. He says they make him feel the good type of small.

Tanner likes the bears. He says he wishes he could have a domesticated one, but he knows that that's unrealistic. Maybe that's why he's such good friends with Tate.

Emma likes the sloth. She says she relates on a spiritual level.

Dylan likes the otters. She says they know what love is.

I like the sharks. There's a huge misconception about sharks, and I wish people knew what a threat we are to them. However, I'd be scared shitless if I saw one in the ocean, so I'm a hypocrite to that extent.

After exploring the zoo in a very disorganized manner, we stop to get food. I can't restrain myself from buying one of those rainbow-stick-swirl-sucker-things because the nostalgia beckons too loudly. Even though it's overpriced, it makes my lips turn ugly colors, and I'll never finish it, I'm satisfied.

As we sit at a crosshatched table (the type I used to shove my fingers though as a kid, and receive the sudden strike of fear when they seemed to be stuck), Tanner and Emma share some fries, Tate enjoys a cheeseburger (seems weird to eat meat at a zoo), and I watch as Dylan walks back from the food stand. Halfway through reaching us, Dylan stops dead in her tracks and a flash of anger stretches across her face.

"Hey, June!" she yells, walking a bit faster.

"Huh, that sounds like I'm the girl version of a Beatles' song," I joyously say when she reaches me. "I feel special."

Dylan looks at me with a *you're stupid but it's amusing* type of face, and then says, "Well I don't. Do you have a tampon?"

"Oh. Yeah." I dig through my bag and give her one.

"How do you not have one in that bag of yours?" I ask, genuinely astonished.

"None at my house," she replies and quickly walks off to find a restroom.

Five minutes later Dylan returns looking even more pissed than before.

"Didn't go well?" I ask.

"Riddle me this," Dylan say after she aggressively sits down, "the U.S. is capable of possessing mind boggling technology, right? Like cars that drive themselves and phones that know your fingerprint, yet for some reason, we've somehow not figured out how to make the bathroom stall door line up with the wall. Like what is the purpose of having that mile long gap?" she asks, not looking for an answer.

"The people who are waiting in line to use the bathroom should not be able to walk past my stall and know what color my underwear are. If you want to know if a stall is occupied, you should have to bend the fuck over and check for a pair of shoes – not make eye contact with me through the door that was obviously designed by Satan. But I only say this because in the midst of shoving a plastic tube up my vagina, I look up, and what do I see? A small child shoving their fat little fingers through that very gap, and looking at me with their beady eyes. Apparently, the mother, the only other person in the bathroom at the time, who chose to use the stall *right next* to mine despite the *numerous* other options, had just let this kid run free. Not only is that annoying, but it turned out to be an invasion of my privacy as well." Dylan crosses her arms and turns so that her back is to the table. "Not to mention, I also ruined my favorite pair of underwear."

I look at her with big eyes and an open mouth, somewhere in between repressing a laugh and slightly scared of her intensity. But I can't help it. I laugh, and so does the rest of our table, because they couldn't help but listen in halfway through her bluster.

"Some shit to be a girl," Tate manages.

"Yeah, but urinals sound awful," Emma makes a point.

"But we have an unspoken rule that you never choose the one right next to a dude if you can prevent it," says Tate.

"Alright, let's stop talking about urinals and shit, I'm eating," Tanner tells us.

Dylan turns back to us, still grumpy, but starts to eat.

"You going to be able to manage the rest of the day?" Tate asks without mocking her.

"You got more tampons?" Dylan asks me.

"Yeah."

"Then yeah," she assures Tate.

She then reaches into her bag, opens a pill bottle without revealing the label, and pops one in her mouth without showing its color.

"What was that?" I ask.

"Ibuprofen," she casually says, but for some reason, I don't believe her.

ANYWHERE [16]

=

Dylan's birthday is on Friday. With it being Wednesday – and the fact that she has no reason to be at home – we figure we should visit her house while her mother's working in order to grab the belongings she'll be bringing to the cities. Dylan's plan is to be home for the day it takes to get her inheritance and then never return. I fully support it.

"She leaves at six, so she's gone by now," Dylan tells us as we throw on some clean clothes. The boys, who didn't bring a lot of luggage, seem to never be short of a new outfit. I wish I was as stylish as them; I've worn the same raggy, old, burnt orange sweatshirt for practically half the week, and I have a whole closet to choose from.

"You guys don't all have to come," Dylan tells us. "I can manage."

"Shh," Tate smooshes his hands against her lips, "we're coming with."

"How much stuff do you need to grab?" Tanner asks.

"Taking everything I can get my hands on. I'll either use it wherever I move, or sell it," Dylan informs us while putting up her hair (she failed to take a shower last night or this morning).

"So should we take both cars? You've got like a dresser and stuff," I point out.

"We're only talking one car to drop her off, though," Tate makes another point.

"Okay let me rephrase: we're taking everything we can fit into Tate's car. Sound good?" We all nod and bustle out of the door.

I feel like we're taking one of the first steps into adulthood: packing and moving, figuring it out by ourselves, finding a place for Dylan to live - I don't think I could do it. Dylan's going to travel to a place she's only visited and find an apartment and a job to support it with no guidance from an adult. But what amazes me the most is that she's excited for it.

I've always had a support system or people to fall back on, so that's probably why I'm scared simply to go to college, but Dylan - Dylan thrives on her independence and longs for a life under her sovereignty. I'm happy that I'm helping her get there, in the smallest of ways, but when we pull up in her driveway, and I look at her crummy house, I know that she's not leaving her life behind.

A lot of people are applauded for their courage when "leaving their life behind" to pursue a dream, but Dylan isn't doing that. She's not sacrificing anything; she's starting over because she doesn't *have* anything *to* leave behind, and with that, I don't know where I stand. But that's a lie. I'm standing on her dull, concrete driveway, feeling small in the presence of her house, even though I know that I'm valued more than it. I'm standing on the driveway which will one day be the red carpet to freedom as she backs out of her past, and into her future; where this house, this town, and even these memories, will simply be words and nothing more. I can't help but feel that *I* am a part of the *nothing* she's leaving behind. I don't know if that makes sense, and I'm probably just scared to lose a friend, but it's as if I can't hear the others rummaging through the car to make room for her belongings as I stand and stare at the house.

"Ready?" Dylan asks me when they're done.

"Yeah," I smally reply, and I wonder what she would have to say about the same topic.

We then enter her house (it's never locked), and within seconds, we know that our anticipations were falsely promoted. Apparently Dylan's been away for so long that she hasn't memorized her mother's schedule correctly, because when we all get through the door, we find her standing across the room, staring at us with eyes I'd lose a fight to.

209

Dylan doesn't know what to do. She stumbles forward and leans against the railing of the stairs. "Um. . . what are you doing home?" she tentatively asks while the rest of us stand awkwardly by the door.

Her mother is wearing a pair of considerably old jeans with a skinny tank top that looks like it's gotten a decent amount of use as well. Her hair is untamed and grey at its roots. She has bags under her eyes big enough to take to the store, and her cheeks are small and tight as she sucks on a cigarette. There's an empty bottle on the table.

"Hardly think you have the right to call it a home," she says in a raspy voice as she takes a drag of the cigarette. She's standing across the room, but even from there, she feels like a threat. The image of her is so gripping that I hardly notice what has changed about the room since the last time I had entered this house through the front door. There's nearly nothing to look at, and the walls are dulled – along with the atmosphere – from what seems like a persistent cycle of decreasing care. The garbage doesn't seem to have a designated area, and the carpet is a ragged mess of who knows what.

"You're never here, and you take what isn't yours. . . use it at your convenience," Dylan's mother says as she slowly walks closer to us, touching the sparse and random furniture in her path with one hand, and carelessly holding up the loosely held cigarette with the other. "Don't respect it. Don't respect *me* – your own mother. Won't help with money. Won't follow my rules." Her words pierce the still, sultry air, and she stops about five feet in front of Dylan. Her menacing glare painfully sweeps through the boys and me.

For a moment no one talks, but then the most unnatural laugh I've ever heard breaks the silence. "*Ohh* - I remember them." Dylan's mother lifts up a crude finger and waves it in our direction, but I know she's referring to the boys. "Big. . . now, aren't you."

She doesn't break her stare at them until Dylan says, "Hardly think you have the right to call yourself a mother." She says it with hatred and derision and then turns to us. "Come on guys, let's do it quick."

"Dylan, we can just come back another time," Tanner whispers while keeping an eye on her mother, but Dylan doesn't reply.

"Probably doin' em'!" cracks her mother, nearly hysterical. "Don't know why else they'd still be around."

Dylan is infuriated. She storms down the stairs, and considering we'd much rather be with Dylan than keep company with her mother, we follow.

Once we catch up with her, Tate pleads, "Seriously Dylan, we should leave and come back another time. She's not going let us take anything."

"I am not letting her dictate what I do," Dylan replies, more obstinate than I've ever heard her. Tate knows to back off.

She starts ripping off her bed sheets along with the few blankets and pillows she has. She goes to every drawer and empties their contents into her bag. We can tell that nothing we say will hinder her determination, so we help her gather all of her art supplies and roll up the posters on her walls. We put her books in a box, unplug her lamp, roll up her Christmas lights, and move everything we plan to bring to the center of the room. Dylan's mother hasn't come down or even made a noise from upstairs.

"Don't think we'd manage to get the mattress up, huh?" Dylan asks, knowing the answer - not to mention the fact that it would never fit in the car - but she's determined to get what we've gathered out of the house. We all grab a box or bag and Dylan leads the way. We'll have to take two trips.

I don't know what to expect as we slowly climb the stairs. There's still no indication that her mother is doing anything, and I can't tell if that's a good thing or not.

Dylan reaches the top and doesn't even bother to locate her mother. She walks straight to the door and successfully gets outside and to the car. We follow, but before I exit the house I see that her mother is sitting with an utterly blank face in a chair facing the wall. Her expression suggests that she isn't present, and her droopy eyes focus on nothing as her cigarette burns slowly in her hand. I can only assume that the ashes are falling to the ground because there isn't an ashtray in sight, and she hasn't acknowledged that it needs to be flicked.

"Jesus, she looked dead," Tate says as we load his car with Dylan's possessions.

"She's not dead," Dylan says with a huff. "She just drank too much, and at this point, who knows what else."

"Surprised it hasn't killed her yet, though," I say as I hand her my pile. The sight of Dylan's mother was disturbing. This is the first time I've truly seen her illness in its entirety. Until now, her near-comatose state has only been a thing I've heard about from Dylan. I could only picture it in my head when she would tell me the stories, and if they're only stories, it's easier to disregard their impact. If they're only stories, it's easy to view it like we do a book. It's something you read or something you hear, but its influence is only as sterling as the quality of the writing or the passion of the speaker. But this is real. It's never felt so real, and it hits me like Dylan's mother hits her. The only difference is that it's not illegal when it happens to me, and I won't grow up with mental health issues because of it. It's hard to believe that this is a reality in someone's life, especially one that I view so dear to me.

"One can only hope," Dylan says as she shuts the trunk that is now full.

When we go back inside to get the rest of Dylan's belongings – the rest of her life – we find her mother sitting in the same spot as she was before. I think she thought we had left for good because she looks as us with a confused face when we're all through the door again. As we descend down the stairs, she watches us intently until we're out of sight. I hope she stays where she is.

We grab what's left, and I watch as Dylan looks around her barren room. Its personality has been taken away, and I wonder if she'll miss any part of it. I don't see how she could, but it's often hard not to let a part of you linger in the places that make up your past. I hope that someday this one can be resolved within herself.

We don't leave until Dylan initiates it, and despite this being a good thing, the atmosphere is somber.

When we reach the top of the stairs, I know that my hopes have amounted to nothing more than exactly that, because her mother has since left the chair and has become a barricade in front of the door.

"What do you think you're doing with those?" she asks, gesturing at the contents of Dylan's room with the hand that still possesses the cigarette that is now burning its last breaths.

"They belong to me," Dylan states, but doesn't move.

Her mother is in a forced, manic state of hysteria as she scoffs at Dylan's statement. "Takes my things, disrespects me. . . " she mumbles to herself, doubling over. I can't tell if she's laughing or crying and it's quite disturbing to watch. Tate, Tanner, and I stand slightly behind Dylan, looking awkwardly amongst ourselves. The boys obviously have a history with Dylan's mother if she was able to identify them, but I don't know how much they've been exposed to her insanity. This situation is as uncomfortable as having a friend that has parents who aren't afraid to complain about their child bringing you over, right in front of you. I've never understood people who don't know the boundaries of what's socially acceptable when it comes to having personal conversations.

"Don't make this a problem," Dylan says, trying to remain calm in the presence of her ill-sighted mother. There's a tone of plea in her voice. I wonder if she finds this embarrassing.

Her mother stands up straight and regains a stern, menacing posture. "Oh- *I'm* not the problem." She crosses her arms but continues to support the hand with the cigarette even though it's clearly not lit anymore. It seems that it's just a habit at this point.

Dylan doesn't know what to do. I can tell that she's livid, but I know that she doesn't want to cause a fight worse than whatever is happening right now. I don't know what's happening. I can't tell if being outnumbered will subdue her mother, or if she actually has the audacity to make a scene. But like they say in health class, the first thing to be impaired after drinking is your judgement.

After too long of a silent stare down, it seems that her mother has decided.

213

"*You ungrateful little brat. . .*" she says in a loud whisper as she advances toward Dylan at a faster pace than I would have thought possible. Dylan braces herself, but doesn't have time to react due to the load she's carrying, and her mother latches onto her wrist with her free hand. Tate then yells, "Hey!" out of instinct and tries to step in between them. Tanner and I stumble on our feet and don't know how to react.

Dylan's mother wrenches on Dylan's wrist as she tries to pull away, but it seems that her mother's bony hand has managed to sustain quite a tight grip.

"How dare you take from me! How dare you come into this house and take all my money! You shitty little. . . ." Her mother roars at Dylan through the struggle of resistance, but Tate forces himself between them and uses the box of overflowing books to press Dylan's mother against her torso to separate them.

Tanner rushes to the door, Dylan trips to the ground after being released from her mother, and I grab under her arm to help her up. Tate has her mother nearly pinned to the wall as Tanner gets the door open, giving us the opportunity to hastily leave.

Tanner goes first but turns to wait for us.

"Come on!" he beckons.

"*I wish I never had you!*" Dylan's mother spits as she pathetically beats on the box of books. A few of them fall to the ground as Dylan and I make it through the door while Tate aggressively releases his pin. He dashes behind us, but when I glance back at him, I notice that one of the books that had fallen out of the box is *The Complete Tales of Winnie-the-Pooh*.

I remember Dylan talking about her cherished memories of her father reading her that book. I remember that her fondness of it is so prevalent that she plans to get a tattoo inspired by it. I can't let it be left behind, ruined by the sickness that is her mother.

I make the rash decision to set down my box and quickly follow my glance and lunge toward the book. I swiftly bend down to pick it up, but as I turn in the process of running back to the others, my head is jerked back by the pull of my hair. I can't believe it, but Dylan's mother has managed to grab me before

214

I've reached the first step. I let out a shriek of pain and shock, but quickly turn around and instinctively beat Dylan's mother with the book.

I think because she must know that abusing not only her child, but her child's friend, is taking it too far, it doesn't take much for her to let go of my hair. I throw the book in my box, sprint to Dylan's side, and we hurl ourselves and what we've managed to bring with us into Tate's car.

The engine starts, and we're soon on the road with a better view. I breathe heavily from pure shock and forced exertion. I don't look back at Dylan's mother. I have absolutely no desire to.

As we get further and further away, nobody knows what to say, and having the radio on feels too normal for this type of situation. So for a while, we sit in silence while glancing at each other for some sort of sign or clearance to engage.

Tanner takes one for the team: "Lovely weather we're having, huh?" he jokes as he leans back to look out the window.

I smile at him, Dylan gives a small huff, but no one responds. At this point, we don't expect each other to, but Tanner has eased the ambience by treating the situation as merely trivial. Although we know it's not, it somehow makes it easier to move on. Instead of stressing over the dozens of ethical questions circling my head in regards to how we should be treating this, I focus on the elegant curves of the passing oak trees. I notice a little girl in a blue dress playing basketball with her brothers. I see two squirrels chasing each other up and down a tree. I look at the cloudless, beaming sky that does not serve as a metaphor for the tone of this story, but instead – just a sky; as it always is, just a sky.

One good thing I'll say about a shining sun, however, is its ability to bring out the beauty in what's more or less a broken person (even if she would never admit it). Its yellow-orange glow leaks through the window and stretches itself across Dylan's face. Her normally almost jet black eyes are illuminated and turn a golden brown that consists of patterns that are neither symmetrical nor abstract. Her faint freckles are amplified, and her hair glows despite hiding an emotionless face with stagnant features. I never have a guess of what she's thinking. I wonder how different this story would be if it were told from her perspective. I guess that's the beauty of living within ourselves: our experiences are the true definition of unique.

The sun licks a part of Tate's skin as well, and his blond hair turns white over his ice-blue eyes. His face is scratchy and unshaven, but it works for him. He looks up in his rear-view mirror to check on Tanner and me in the back. We make secondary eye contact and he's never looked more gentle.

"Where to?" he asks us all, but we know that it's up to Dylan. We try not to stare at her, but once she realizes we're waiting for her answer, she simply says, "Anywhere," and we accept that.

I wish Anywhere was a place. I wish we could hop in a car designed to go for miles without eating gas, designed to carry minds that aren't satisfied with the destinations they've been shown, designed to find an undiscovered place just waiting for a group of people who think they could handle the abyss that would be Anywhere. It'd only take in people who knew that an abyss is not a place for the damned, but instead a room with white walls and a marker sitting in the corner. And if you cannot draw, you need not worry, because Anywhere isn't a place that has standards. It's a place where you can sit in blissful solitude, far away from burdens we create, far away from the burdens we don't create, but must endure. Anywhere is a place that everyone in existence could use once in a while. It's a place that I can only hope for after I die, but it's a place that isn't real, so I don't know why we have minds that are capable of thinking of it.

If we were to go somewhere – Tate, Tanner, Dylan, and I – I'd like to think we'd go to the same place. I'd like to think we wouldn't need to discuss which roads to take or what music to play, because we'd know that "Geographer" by Sydney Wayser would fuel our journey to somewhere – Anywhere – much more tolerable, much more inviting, much more scintillating, just much MUCH MORE, but that's not the case. We're restricted by Grove, Lynn, Maple, and Dale, and they've never been known to invest in expansions. Maybe that's why we have minds that can wonder. Maybe that's why we've been

216

given a time scale for life, so that when we die, we'll know exactly where we want to go. But maybe I'm just getting philosophical again because car rides with clear windows have that effect on me. I don't know.

What do you think about when you have time to acknowledge that you're thinking?

We let Dylan down because we don't go Anywhere. Instead, we go to a movie because it's the closest we can get to escaping our lives for a while.

Seeing a good movie can embed a light within me that continuously grows throughout the plot, and I leave with a refreshing feeling of triumph and a surge of inspiration. The only downside is that it's short-lived. It usually subsides by the time I wake up the next morning, but in that short time, what I'm able to accomplish - or simply what I *believe* I'm able to accomplish - feels life changing.

We go to the movie *La La Land*, and I don't feel like I can talk about a current movie when writing a book, but I don't care. I don't care because we're sitting in a theater accompanied by a majority of elderly people, who are all experiencing the same story at the same time as I am. I become overly aware of this because I'm listening to a gorgeous tune that is prevalent throughout the movie by serving the purpose of being a form of structure. Structure in a way that does not promote stability, but rather the structure of the informality of living. It's the truth - the blaringly obvious, painfully obstructed, Truth - that knows an aesthetically pleasing viewpoint doesn't change the content of what you're looking at.

I become incredibly immersed in the story because I feel like it's talking to me. It *has* to be talking to me. It *must* be talking to me. And I repeat what I say a lot because it means something. It. Means. Something. It's a call to all the dreamers. It's a call to those who know too well the feeling of "No." It's a call to the ones who would find the story worth telling, because if you didn't get the point, then you didn't live the life. And if you didn't live the life, then you wasted eight bucks on a movie.

But oh well, right? Sometimes we lose the structure of our life because we're too accustomed to saying "Oh well." I don't want to be like that.

Throughout the movie, I laugh at the funny parts and cry at the sad parts. Although I'm not ashamed of crying, I try to be discreet about it because when I look at Dylan and the boys, none of them seem to be shedding any tears. Despite this, I'm sure that at least Dylan is being influenced by the movie because she, most of all, fits the category of being a dreamer. I don't say it as a bad thing, I say it as a hard thing. But it's also one of the most rewarding things when you realize you no longer need to be one.

I don't feel like moving when the movie ends, but the lights instruct our departure.

I pick up the trash others leave behind out of habit.

"Half-popped popcorn kernels had so much potential," Dylan says as she looks into our nearly empty bag. "They could have been a big, white, puffy corn, but just didn't get there."

"That's the part of the movie we didn't see," Tanner says as he props open the door.

"I liked it a lot," Tate says after we've silently exited the theater.

Getting in his car, shutting the door, and buckling my seatbelt doesn't feel real. I feel like a part of me was left in the movie, and now I have to work on getting it back. I feel elated to be free for a while, but the lost weight makes me feel heavy with the pressure that it will return. I think that's how movies are supposed to make you feel: heavy but free. It gets us talking about what we liked, what we didn't understand, and what we wished would have happened, but none of it's the same.

"Alright, where are we going? Because I really have to pee," Dylan announces after our conversation has subsided, and we've driven aimlessly.

"Why didn't you pee at the theater?" Tate asks.

"I didn't have to go then," Dylan claims.

"What? That was like two seconds ago," I say.

"I don't have control over my bladder," remarks Dylan.

"We could go to Emma's," Tanner suggests. "She got off work a little bit ago."

"As long as there's a bathroom, I don't care," Dylan declares, and with that, it's decided.

We head down roads I've seen a million times, but for some reason they seem longer than I remember – yet the ride feels shorter, and I feel further away. I don't think I should feel sad after seeing a movie I loved, but I don't know what I'm doing. I don't know what any of us are doing. I know what our goals are, and I know what we dream of, but the future is only an idea, and ideas almost never turn out the way we expect them to.

When we make it to Emma's driveway, we talk for the first time since deciding our destination. It seems we have all been stuck in our thoughts.

"We all good?" Tate asks once he's taken the keys out of the ignition. I make eye contact with him in the mirror again.

"Yeah," we say, because it's what everyone always says, and we exit the car with soft slams.

The day is hot and my walk is slow as we approach Emma's house. Emma's cute smile greets us when she opens the door, and Tanner returns an excited one. I don't know what they plan to do with their flirtatious meetings if Tanner is ultimately going to go home, but we don't question it.

Her house is just as amazing as it was the first time I visited, and we leave our shoes by the door when we come in.

"How was the movie?" Emma asks.

We give our input as we wander into what must be deemed a living room. It's big with a lot of natural light, comfy chairs and couch, a grand TV, and some undefined statues. While they discuss the movie, I notice something I hadn't seen the first time I was here.

In the corner, there's an animal's bed with a small, black cat resting peacefully on top of it. I disregard all inclinations to be present in the others' conversation, and head off to disturb the cat's sleep. I think the fact that we can pick up cats whenever we want, even when they're sleeping, justifies the fact that they can walk on us whenever they want.

It's body simply goes limp when it realizes it's being removed from its bed, and I cradle it in my arms, smooshing my face on it. I love cats, but my mom's allergic to them, and that's probably the only thing I hate about her.

"Oh, that's Vladimir," Emma says as she sees me. "Or Vlad for short."

"That's wonderful," I say, still cuddling him.

"He's my company when no one's around," she continues. "He kinda' sucks at it, though."

"Why don't you ever have any family here?" Tate asks.

"They travel a lot, and I have no siblings. Work calls," she says at the slightest, but we understand.

I sit down on her couch with Vlad on my lap, and he's just as content as he was in his bed.

"So what do you guys want to do?" Emma asks.

"Will someone play me in pool?" Tate offers. I didn't know she had a pool table. I'm assuming I will continuously be impressed with this house.

"Only if you don't mind getting your ass kicked," Dylan instigates. Tate accepts the challenge by coaxing her out of the room.

"Can we play your video games?" Tanner asks Emma, and she agrees, but since I know that they are usually a two player game, I stay on the couch with Vlad. Although no one here is dating, I suddenly feel like a fifth wheel, but it's not their fault, I just don't have the motivation to include myself at the moment and I don't know why.

"You can take whatever you want from the kitchen!" Emma yells before Dylan and Tate are out of sight. They thank her and leave to play pool. I take Emma's invitation to search the kitchen as an opportunity to make myself look occupied, so I get up to exit the room. Vlad makes a small plop when he hits the ground and curls up once more.

The house is big, so it takes me a couple turns to find the kitchen. When I do, it feels like I'm entering the set of a cooking show. It's so clean it's hard to believe it's ever actually been used. There are pots and pans hanging from a rack attached to the ceiling, and stools that belong in a high-class restaurant. There are dozens of spices I've never heard of, and a stove with way too many knobs. I'd have no clue where to start if I were to make something, and no confidence in what I was using. I start to feel inferior. I start to feel inferior to a kitchen, how stupid is that?

Instead of discovering the contents of the pristine, varnished cupboards, I notice a small door to the side of the kitchen. When opened, I find myself facing her backyard. I take it as an opportunity for solitude, so I close the door behind me and sit on the step to have a smoke.

If I were to consider this anything, a backyard would not be my first choice if viewing it from the typical, American-family standpoint. It's cut clean and has a spherical water fountain in its center. Other than the decorative accessories to the fountain, and a trimmed hedge surrounding the perimeter, it's quite vacant. It's like the most narcissistic fountain ever surrounded by bodyguards who all go to the same barber. It's as if the area was solely made to be something pretty to look at, and I can't help but view that as a waste of money.

As I observe my surroundings, I continue the process of, essentially, destructive breathing. I feel like the toxins of my cigarette are ruining the atmosphere. I should be more worried about them ruining my body, but I'm not, and I don't know why.

I stare at whatever catches my eye until I have nothing left to smoke. I then realize I don't know where to put the butt, so I simply set it next to me as I watch the flow of the water being thrown over the fountain. It glimmers as it rolls to the ground.

The sun makes me tired.

I hear a shriek of joy coming from somewhere in the house. I assume it's Dylan making a good shot and rubbing it in Tate's face. It doesn't make me jealous, and I'm not sad, but I can't bring myself to sit and listen to it. I get up and walk to a spot in between the fountain and the hedge. I take off my

221

sweatshirt and bundle it up like a pillow. I lay down so the shadow of the hedge covers my eyes but the rest of my body can bask in the sun. Its warmth floods over me as a form of comfort despite the prickly grass.

The sun makes me tired.

The narcissistic fountain looks even bigger from this angle, and the hedges are dauntingly tall, but what's even bigger are the clouds. They don't have identities, but those I give them. I contemplate whether they're moving or not. I squint to watch their progress, but the sun makes me tired.

I'm in an empty bathtub with my clothes on. I'm in my house, but it isn't my house. I don't question why I'm here. The lights are turned off and I'm examining a cut across my wrist. I know that it's from a battle, but I don't know who was fighting or how it started.

I have not a single urge to get out of the bathtub. It's deep and long, and it fits me perfectly. As I rest my head on its side, giving me a horizontal view of the room, a mouse approaches. It hops on the ledge of the tub and runs to meet my eyes. He's tan.

"Have we won the war?" I ask him because I do, however, know that we're on the same side.

His mouth doesn't move, but I know that he replies, "Yes, but at great cost." We make sad eye contact. "We have to go now," he tells me. "They're clearing out the house."

"What about my room?" I ask, sitting up. I haven't had the chance to get what I want yet.

He looks at me for a while. "Do you remember when you were a kid, and your mom would ask you what you would grab if there was a fire and you have to leave?" the mouse asks me, standing on his hind legs.

I nod.

"Do you remember what you told her?" he asks.

I think hard. "I – I could never decide. She said it could only be one thing."

"Well, that's why you don't get to pick now," he tells me, and runs to where my arm touches the ledge. He climbs up my sweatshirt and stops on my shoulder. "I'm sorry it had to be this way," he says. "But I suspect you knew it would happen."

He's right. I knew the war wouldn't result in any type of win, so I stand up and slowly get out of the tub.

I then exit the dank bathroom. Down the hall is my room, and I sorrowfully pass it as I get one last look at everything I have to leave behind. I turn before entering it and go downstairs. The mouse grips tightly to my sweatshirt. "Oooh, I don't like heights," he says.

When I reach the bottom, I find only a door, so I have no choice but to open it. I walk through with no question, but suddenly, I'm in my school, looking down an empty hallway.

"Where is everyone?" I ask the tan mouse.

"You couldn't have expected them to stay. Not after that," he says, sounding sad, but I understand. I stand firm in my position for a while, simply starting down the grey-tinted hallway. I then feel compelled to look to my left, and out of all the dusty-blue, metal lockers, there's one that's destroyed with crude writing and chipped paint. I walk over.

"*KKK*," "*Whores*," "*Faggot*," "*Pussy*," a swastika, a drawing of a noose, the anarchy symbol, and everything else you could imagine that would accompany such bigotry is revoltingly littered across the locker.

"I hate people," I tell the mouse, but I only say that because I actually love people.

I look for a way to fix it. Conveniently, there's a can of red paint sitting next to a trash can. I bend down to pick it up, and the mouse climbs further up my shoulder to stay level. I grab the bottom of the can and breathe heavily as I stare at the disgraceful profanity. I then angrily throw the paint across the lockers. It's heavy but drips down the metal and onto the floor. It pools in the crevices and stretches across five of the lockers. It looks much better.

I continue to hold the can, and its remnants drip on my pants and over my hands.

"June!" I suddenly hear coming from the hallway to my right.

"Junebug! Where have you been?" Dylan asks when she reaches me, but she doesn't let me answer. "You have to take this," she says, urgently. She's holding a plate of what looks to be lime green Jell-O wrapped in Saran Wrap.

"What?" I ask.

"You have to take this Jell-O to room one twenty-nine!" she tells me, thrusting the plate forward. I drop the paint can and accept the plate. Dylan then runs down the rest of the hallway until she's out of sight.

"You have to hurry," says the mouse, calmly.

My stomach drops as I feel the pressure of delivering this Jell-O.

"Where's room one twenty-nine?" I frantically ask.

"It's your school," replies the mouse. He then leaves my line of vision as he crawls into my hood. The hallway suddenly looks much longer than it did before.

Even though this is my school, I can't seem to recall where the room is. I run to the end of the hallway and climb the flight of stairs, two steps at a time, with the Jell-O in front of my chest. I take a right at the top and look at the room numbers. *405, 406, 407. . . .* These aren't right. I turn around. I take a left, and I start to sweat out of fear of not getting there on time. *260, 259, 258 . . . .* "Where the fuck is one twenty-nine?" I ask no one, considering the mouse is still in my hood.

I stop and spin in a circle but none of the rooms are right, and they're all empty. I then spot a hallway that I don't remember seeing before. I head towards it in a pleading hope. *127, 128. . . 130.* "Oh, you've gotta' be kidding me!" I say, still gripping the green Jell-O tightly. I turn around in anger, but to my relief, I see *129* posted next to the only door present. I quickly lunge at the door knob and open it with glee due to finally finding it.

I rush forward, but stop abruptly when I realize what room it is. I find myself staring at my old History class. My seat in the back is empty, but Dylan

224

and everyone else in the class is present, and they're all staring intently at me along with the teacher. My stomach tightens from feeling utterly embarrassed.

I think to the mouse, "*What do I do?*" He thinks back to me, "*At least you remembered forks.*"

"*What?*" I look down at the plate, and the Jell-O is suddenly accompanied by about a dozen forks.

"How nice of you to share with the class," my teacher says in a sweet voice as she walks to my side, "And happy birthday." I look at her with confusion as she puts her hands on my shoulders. Half the class then stands up and starts to sing "Happy Birthday" as they come to grab a fork. A girl who I used to be best friends with in middle school, who now hasn't talked to me in five years, and leaves me guessing as to whether or not she even remembers our relationship, grabs the plate from my hands. I step to the side as they start to unwrap the Jell-O. The class is halfway through "Happy Birthday" when Dylan, who had remained in her seat, starts to yell over them to get my attention.

"June! Hey, June!"

"June!" I blink open my eyes after being shaken forcefully.

"What are you doing out here?" Dylan asks as I sit up. "And why don't you listen to me?" she interrogates, waving the cigarette butt I had left on the step in my face.

"You're one to talk," I say under my breath as I grab my sweatshirt. Dylan stands up and lends me a hand. She looks at me for a response.

"Wanted some air," I say because I don't know what else to say.

"Okay. . . well, if you're tired you don't have to stay," she says.

"I'm not," I truthfully state. "The sun made me tired," I explain.

"Well, are you good to come back in? We're all just hanging around still. Didn't know where you were. Didn't expect to find ya' here, though," she says, looking around. "What an ugly fountain."

I look at her and laugh.

"What?" she asks.

"Nothing," I say, and we start to walk back to the house. "I had a really weird dream, though."

We get inside and Dylan leads me to the room with the pool table. Emma and Tanner are playing while Tate watches. The room isn't as big as I was expecting. There's a couple chairs, a big wooden trunk, and a bunch of notebooks and folders sprawled out in a bay window.

"Ya' know, I *have* extra beds," Emma jokes when she sees me enter.

I laugh, but don't know how to respond because I'm moderately embarrassed, so Tate does for me, "I'm sure she was just observing her surroundings." I assume he says this reminiscing on our conversation from the night of the bonfire. It makes me smile.

I abandon the topic of me falling asleep in the middle of Emma's lawn by asking, "So who's winning?" Tanner and Emma burst into a light-hearted argument about who's better, despite the clear advancement of stripes which happens to be Emma.

"I'm gonna' get some drinks," Dylan tells me and heads to the kitchen. I go to the chair by the bay window to watch the rest of their game.

The room is brightly lit, and Tate cheers on Emma who clearly has more experience than Tanner. Dylan returns shortly with a handful of red soda-pops. I say soda-pop because they're in tall bottles instead of cans, and I feel like that deserves an old fashioned name.

I thank Dylan and she goes to sit in the chair across the room. She hands Tate a bottle and he puts his big hand on top of her head. She looks up at him and then rests her head on his hip. I think that's what true friendship looks like. And I think Tanner and Emma are what a crush looks like. So what do I look like?

I drink my red soda-pop and examine the notebooks that are resting on the ledge in the bay window. One of them is open and on lined paper it reads:

"Just keep walking," said the snickering friend to his blindfolded buddy.

"Just keep walking," said the women to herself after being cat called on the street.

226

I read it twice before asking, "Hey, Emma, what's this?"

"What's what?" she asks in the middle of hitting the cue.

I grab the notebook out from the pile and hold it up. She squints at the writing. "Oh, that was an assignment for a class. About perspective or something. I've been going through my old school work to decide what to keep. I never know what to do with it all," she explains.

"Shouldn't need any of it," Tate comments from the wall. "Should all be in here." He taps his temple.

"Yeah, coming from straight C's over there," remarks Tanner.

"Hey, it's not my fault I couldn't memorize the periodic table of elements. Like that'll get me anywhere."

"I guess that's true," Tanner admits.

They humorously chat a while about the useless things we've learned in school like how to say and spell antidisestablishmentarianism which is the longest word in the dictionary, the "i" before "e" except after "c" rule, long division, the tongue taste map, prime numbers, and so on. I get why we learned them at the time, but I can't say I've effectively used those things in my life outside of school.

Like Emma, at the end of each year we end up with stacks full of notes and worksheets that have accumulated over our learning process, but what are we to do with them? It feels wrong to throw them away, and keeping them could fill a dozen backpacks, so we shove them in a corner of our room and they sit there over the summer, accumulating dust. And then the once-a-year-cleaning-endeavor comes along and we pick up our old, chicken-scratch notes, and we toss them in a garbage bag because we've moved on and don't have the motivation to sort them.

I can't imagine the information in our head is any different; the unused gets shoved to the back of our memory and eventually it becomes the forgotten. Yet I ask anyone what's the one thing they remember about science class, and they confidently spew off that "the mitochondria are the powerhouse of the cell."

227

I don't understand how our learning works, and I never seem to remember what I need to. But they ask us how confident we are that we'll do well in college, and it leaves me feeling glued to the vandalized, wooden desks I've been forced to sit in for the majority of my life, desperately trying to recall all of the answers to every test I've ever taken, but falling short when the ceiling provides nothing but the ceasing of my thoughts, and my neighbors are just as clueless.

School boils down to memorization, but as human beings, our memory goes when we get old. And I promise that when that happens to me, it won't be the mitochondria that I'll be holding onto; it won't be the quadratic formula or the fact that the acetabulum is the socket of the hipbone; it won't be Newton's second law: F=ma, or that Joan of Arc was burned at the stake for "witchcraft;" it won't be that red, blue, and yellow are the primary colors, or that to show plural possession of a regular noun, you put the apostrophe after the "s;" It won't be anything I've ever been forced to learn for a high school test. So as I look at the pile of Emma's notes, I know that the majority of it will one day be forgotten, including this assignment on perspective. So when Emma's focused on making a shot and her back is turned to me, I rip out the page, fold it, and put it in my pocket, because I know it'll end up in her garbage if someone else doesn't value it.

"Ooooooh!" A loud stampede of cheers erupts from the pool table. "What'd I tell ya'?" Tanner gloats in Emma's face.

"That's unfair! You can't deny I'm better than you," Emma insists.

"Oh, the mighty and powerful *Emma*, with no dubiety of her skill, yet trounced by measly ol' me," Tanner performs.

"Man, what the fuck are you even saying." Tate laughs from the side.

Emma crosses her arms but can't help but smile at Tanner. "It's a stupid rule."

"It's the best rule," Tanner says as he puts his arm around her shoulders, and they leave to get some soda-pops for themselves. It turns out Emma had gotten the eight ball in rather than her last stripe, how frustrating.

"You wanna' play a round?" Dylan asks me.

"Nah, I'm trash at pool."

"Let's go meet Mr. Green," Tate suggests, happily.

"What?" Dylan asks.

Tate downheartedly sighs. "Let's go smoke," he explains.

Dylan stares at him for a while. "That was terrible. That's not a thing. You're not making that a thing."

"Wha-, oh come on."

"I'm ashamed to call you my friend."

They bicker out the door and I follow, rather amused.

Tate finds Tanner and Emma and they leave to get their weed. Dylan then turns to me and asks, "You want to at all? I think Emma actually has some joints."

"Is that better?" I ask.

"It feels more like a cigarette," she reasons.

"Sure, I'll try," I say because I don't feel like being the only one sober.

"Really?"

I nod.

"Okay, cool. I'll get ya' one."

When they come back, Dylan hands me a tightly rolled joint and it makes me feel like I'm in a stoner movie. It feels like I'm an actor playing a role I only got because I was the understudy, and the real actor was out sick; I'm honored to have the part, but it doesn't feel like it was meant for me.

"Ah - should I go outside?" I ask Emma.

"Nah, it's just me here. We can do it in the house."

"Oh, okay." I'm pleasantly surprised, and I light the joint. Oddly enough, I do prefer it in this form. It's smoother, easy handling, and I don't think about it as much. It makes time move faster, and the smoke rises in the room, catching the orange sunlight of the slowly setting sun. I've never smoked inside a regular house before, and with no possibility of getting caught, I feel comfortable for the first time in a long time. Because of this, I smoke more than I have in a long time. Because of this, I smoke more than I have ever.

We watch a movie. I don't know what it's called and I don't remember how we picked it, but it has actors I recognize and I say, "Oh, it's that guy," and, "Oh, it's that girl," like we do with most celebrities. We watch for a long time, and the others keep going back and forth from the kitchen, bringing food and drinks.

I have another red soda-pop, and I stare down into the bottle. It glimmers when I swirl it, and it captures my vision, and soon, I'm swirling too. But really I'm not because I'm glued to the couch, and it feels like the cushions are swallowing me. I'm thankful that they're soft, and my feet continuously rub over the texture of my blanket.

Tanner and Emma are cuddling in a chair, Dylan is eating a bag of chips by herself, and I can't remember the last time Tate blinked as he watches the movie.

As I watch the movie, I focus on only the actors, and I become overly aware that they are acting. I become so aware of it that no matter how superb their acting is, all I can see are some people reciting lines and projecting emotions. Suddenly, they aren't characters anymore, they're people doing their job, and the movie feels two dimensional and just *weird*.

I rub my eyes partly to see if it changes anything, and partly because it feels really good. I rub them for longer than I should and my contacts get screwed up, leaving me teary eyed and blinking rapidly.

"Dude, are you crying?" Dylan asks me.

"What?" I look at her, suddenly shocked back to reality. "What, no. It just feels nice."

She gives an odd nod and a crunch of her chips.

I look at her chips. They look good. I realize I'm hungry.

"Could I have some of those?"

She tosses me the bag.

"Thanks."

I start mindlessly eating the chips while focusing on the weird movie.

I eat three chips. I eat four chips. I eat five, and suddenly, I realize that I'm swallowing them. I realize that they're going down my throat. I realize that I have a throat, and that it's small. And then the worst realization you can possibly make comes: I realize that I'm breathing.

In and out. In and out. In and . . . . My breathing stops being natural. I think about every inhale and exhale, and I force myself to do it, but then I worry about not doing it. What if I forget? What if my throat is too small? What if it closes? What if the chips are making it close?

I give the bag back to Dylan. I rub my eyes. I rub my neck. The couch is swallowing me, and the movie is weird. The lights are dark, and the screen is blinding. My drink makes me swirl, and I can't breathe. I can't breathe.

I get off the couch. I put my hair up as I try to find a bathroom because I feel like it's restricting me. I don't know where a bathroom is. Why is this house so big? How have I not used the bathroom yet? Where the fuck am I going?

I get to the kitchen. I go to the sink and get some water, but it just makes me feel my throat again. I shouldn't be able to *feel* my throat.

I pace around the kitchen breathing heavily. Is this how Dylan felt on top of the roller coaster? Is this a panic attack? Thinking about it makes it worse.

I try to focus on my steps, but they're heavy and far away. I don't know what to do. I don't know what t--

"Junebug?"

I look up, startled. I stare at Dylan with my hands to my head, and she stares back. I can feel my mouth start to quiver and the next thing I know my face is wet from tears.

I get caught on my inhaling sobs. "I started - started eating chips - and. . . now I don-don't know what's happening," I try to explain.

Dylan doesn't say anything but instead walks toward me and grabs one of my hands down from my head. She leads me to little door to the side of the kitchen, and we're back to the view of the narcissistic fountain.

She leads me to where I had fallen asleep. "Lay down," she says, and I do, still a mess.

She lays down next to me. We have our backs on the prickly grass, and there's a cool breeze.

"Look at those," she says, and points to the stars. "Focus on them."

My breathing still isn't steady, but I look at the stars. The sky is cloudless, and it looks like a population map full of constellations I can't identify, and stars too far away to comprehend.

"What do you see?" she asks.

"Stars," is all I can say.

"Well, did you know that there's more than a billion trillion stars in the observable universe?" she starts, and I turn my head to meet her eyes. "With each one of them, there's a collective gravity of its mass, pulling it inward. But there's a pressure pushing back on the collapse, and that's light."

My crying turns to sniffles. She talks slowly and collectively.

"They're balanced, and the sun is the closest star, but it's certainly not the biggest. The bigger you are, the faster you burn. The sun has used up about half its life, but eventually, its core will run out of hydrogen, and then helium, it'll contract while its outer layer expands, and it'll become a red giant. It'll form a planetary nebula, become a white dwarf, and finally, when the rest of its left-over heat has dispersed, it'll be a cold, dark, black dwarf."

My breathing is slow.

"And there'll be no sun, or heat, or life, or us. At that point, maybe the human race has learned to live on a different planet, or maybe something else has already killed us off. But no matter what, the sun has lived its life, and it's done its job well, and we won't have to worry about it."

We look back up at the sky. I feel as calm as "Wild Child" by Elijah, and I'm in the presence of a speckled beauty. But I can't see the sun, so I ask, "What about the moon?"

Dylan laughs. "The moon is just a satellite of the Earth. We can only see about sixty percent of it, and it's always the same side. We'll never get to see the side that's hidden." She sits up. "Besides the tides, it doesn't do much for us. The sun is much more vital to our survival, but I'd rather look at the moon than the sun any day. Weird how that works."

She looks down at me, and it breaks my devotion to the sky.

"You okay?" she asks.

"Yeah." I sit up. "Don't know what happened."

"You're high as fuck," she declares, and we both laugh, kind of exhausted.

"You have too much anxiety to smoke," she continues.

"I thought weed was supposed to help with that."

"Not with everyone." She has kind eyes.

I heavily sigh. "I blame the chips."

"Well, unless you're allergic to Cool Ranch Doritos, I'd blame your mind." I look at her with admiration, and she knows that I'm thankful. So after we spend some much needed time with the sky, Dylan once again leads me back inside the house.

No one asks about us leaving, and Dylan doesn't bring it up. I appreciate the privacy, and the night is finally peaceful once the movie has ended, our appetites have subsided, and we grow tired.

We decide to sleep at Emma's.

By the time everyone's high wears off, no one has the motivation to bring us home, but we don't mind. We sleep wherever we end up last, and no one makes anything official, so Tanner sleeps next to Emma on a fluffy pile of pillows and blankets on the floor, while Tate, who had fallen asleep long before the rest of us, sleeps alone on a big recliner. Dylan and I lay at either end of the couch with our feet in the other's face, and an undefined ownership of blankets. I'm the last to close my eyes and that's mainly because I'm trying to coax Vlad to come and lay with me.

He's standing in the middle of the doorway, looking at me with his big, glossy eyes that manage to catch the little light in the room. I pat my fingers on the side of the couch, and he slowly trots his way over, rubbing his head on the objects in his path. He makes it to the end of the couch, so I reach down and scoop him up. He purrs softly in my arms, and I feel a comforting rush of relief.

I still don't know what I'm doing, or why Dylan never shows any emotion towards her situation with her mother. I don't know how college and being apart from Dylan will be like, or why I feel alone at times. I don't know what the boys think, or what Emma will deem worthy of keeping out of her notes and papers. I don't know how successful I'll be in life, or if Dylan will make it as an artist. I don't know why cats purr, and I don't know when the sun will die, but I do know that the couch is comfy and the blankets are warm; the air is still, and the light is dim.

So as I look at my surroundings, I remember that when I was a kid, I used to stare into the fuzzy darkness of my room and watch as the darkness would pixilate. I could see thousands of little specs that made up the colors of the room, and I would conduct them wherever I wanted. They'd follow the direction of my eyes, and they'd only quit when my lids could no longer support their endeavor.

It's been a long time since I've acknowledged them, but I do tonight. It reminds me of how, in the grand scheme of things, I'm still a kid. Even though I've been deemed legally an adult for a good few months now, I don't feel any different than when I was seventeen. And when I turned seventeen, I still felt sixteen. They blur together like Dylan's swift brush strokes and the passing of the world through a car window; I feel no different than I did when I was a kid. Only this time, I have taxes to anticipate rather than the next Disney episode. But I confide in the pixilated darkness, and reveal to myself that I still sleep with my baby blanket. I still wait for the new episodes of my favorite shows; I still have sleepovers; I still leap to my bed in a fleet of fear when I turn off the lights, and I still dream of what I want to be when I'm older. Only now, I'm actually deciding.

Seeing *La La Land*, experiencing what Dylan is going to be leaving behind, and looking at all of Emma's school work had me convinced that time was moving too fast for me. But as I softly pet the tuff of Vlad's neck, and I hear the muffled snores coming from the people I'd be lost without, I remember that time is a human made concept, and that it is not – in any way – the burden I wish to bind my life to.

So as my lids lose confidence in their ability to support this endeavor, I become okay with where I am. I become okay with it all.

HIGH HOPES & PREDICTABLE OUTCOMES
[17]
=

We wake slowly, one-by-one, around 12:30. We don't care that it's late, and despite that it is indeed *afternoon*, to us it's the morning, and therefore, it's time for some breakfast.

"I'm outta' Bisquick, so we gotta' make it from scratch," Emma yells from the kitchen as the rest of us drag ourselves out of our less-than-qualified beds. We had slept in the simplest form of whatever we had, so the boys throw back on their shirts while us girls just continue to go braless, because let's be real, who keeps their bra on for longer than they have to? Plus, boobs are boobs just like an arm is an arm; I shouldn't have to say more.

"You know, I've never actually made pancakes," Tate says in the middle of a yawn.

"How have you never made pancakes?" Emma asks, shocked.

Tate shrugs. "Big family."

"Well, there's a first for everything." Emma grabs a big yellow bowl and hands it to Tate. "Mix one and a half cups of this, three teaspoons of that, one tablespoon . . . ." Emma lays out all the ingredients, and we watch as the young Tate learns how to survive in the real world. All the while, Dylan is rummaging through Emma's cupboards when she stumbles upon some food coloring. "Hey, can we eat colored pancakes?"

Thirty minutes later the table is set, displaying a grand heap of *blue* chocolate chip pancakes.

238

"You know, blue is considered to be the most unappetizing color for food," Dylan declares as we pour ourselves some juice of varying sorts.

"You're the one that picked the color," I point out.

"Wanted to see if it was justifiable, but I think these are beautiful pancakes."

"Thank you." Tate smiles and passes them around.

We had decided to go all out with breakfast because Emma's kitchen is so beautiful that it would have been a shame not to see it used properly. Tanner made sausage and bacon. Even though he's a vegetarian, he doesn't find it necessary to shame us for eating meat, and he bragged that he's a really good cook, so we let him prove it to us. Dylan and I tag teamed the eggs while Emma set the table, which now leaves us sitting in a loquacious circle with wonderful food and good people. What more can I ask for after a day of uncertainty?

The room suddenly becomes filled with the typical clinks of silverware and small conversations as we enjoy our breakfast. These things are commonly viewed as inevitable conditions of life and sometimes even annoyances, but I find them reassuring. If nothing else, I can always count on the small bustle of having a meal with someone, and its simplicity is something that we shouldn't take for granted.

"So what are we doing to be going -" He stops. "Wow, no, that was wrong. What are we *going* to be *doing* for your birthday?" Tate asks Dylan after he takes the last drink of his orange juice, and we give a small laugh at his struggle.

"Aren't you guys supposed to be planning that?" she asks in return.

"But I want to do whatever you want, and how am I supposed to know what *you* want to do?"

"Oh, I don't know, friend for half my life, I'd hope you'd at least have an idea," she jokes.

"I didn't even know how to make pancakes, I mean," he throws up his hands, "what more do I have to say?"

Dylan laughs. "Alright, to be real, I kinda' just wanna' go to a fancy restaurant and chill. Because I can't remember the last time I was sober on my birthday."

"Sounds great." Tanner smiles, and thus, our broad plans are made.

When we finish breakfast, we all help with the dishes because we all contributed to making them dirty. We load the dishwasher and hand wash the annoying few that don't fit. My hands feel pruny with soap and water.

"Thanks for this," Emma says, and we all claim that it's no problem, and that she's generous to even let us stay. She really is humble despite the riches she's been accustomed to, and I'm glad Tanner made friends with her in his short visit, otherwise, I would have never had the pleasure of meeting her.

When we're done, she looks at the clock and says, "Alright, I gotta' be at work in twenty minutes." She continues slightly under her breath, "Because I refuse to be coddled in every aspect of my life." She dries her hands and puts away her towel. "So you guys can hang around if you want, or whatever, doesn't matter." She goes to her room to change, and the rest of us go back to the living room to pick up a little after last night.

When Emma comes back in her waitressing uniform and is halfway out the door after saying goodbye to us, I quickly stop her. "Hey, Emma!" I yell from across the hall. She looks back at me. "What's college like?" I ask.

She thinks it over for a second. "It's the most expensive hell you'll ever love to buy," she says.

I grin, and she closes the door behind her. I asked right before her leaving because I wanted the simplest answer possible, and I'm certainly not disappointed. Maybe I should stop worrying so much.

When the living room is back to its classy self, the day becomes a day like any other. We hang around Emma's for a while longer, but don't wish to overstay our welcome, so we go to my house to take a rotating cycle of showers (because you can only pass as *I'm just not trying that hard* for so long).

My bathroom is quite small, so we occupy it one at a time. After Dylan, Tanner, and I have successfully cleansed ourselves, we watch TV as we wait for

Tate. The episode of *Adventure Time* that we happen to be watching (with no shame, may I add), is suddenly interrupted by a low and disturbing scream coming from the bathroom. We all exchange quick, worried looks and get up to see what's happened to Tate.

We hurry down the hallway, but right before Tanner has his hand on the doorknob, Tate comes rushing out, barely holding his towel around his waist, and dripping all over the floor. "Fuck, man! Fuck."

"Wha-, what?" Tanner says, stabilizing Tate.

"What happened?" Dylan demands.

"There's a fucking spider in the shower!" Tate says, aggressively, and points back into the bathroom.

We all release an amused and relieved sigh. "Oh my god." We burst out laughing. "Are you kidding me?"

"Oh, fuck you," Tate defends himself. "You go see that thing. It's big and black, and right by my head, and it's fucking legs. . . ." He gives a shiver of disgust, reliving the experience.

When we manage to control our laughter Dylan says, "Go kill it, Tanner."

"What? Why me?"

"I don't know. You seem capable."

"No way. I don't kill, and nobody fucks with that many legs."

"Then you go," Dylan says to me.

"Why not you?" I justifiably ask.

"It's *your* house."

"Will someone just please get it? I still have shampoo in my hair," Tate says, still dripping.

"Fiiinne," I submit.

I head into my bathroom and they closely follow. With boisterous anticipation behind me, I swipe back the rustled shower curtain.

"There." Tate points to the corner just above eye level.

"Oh, *come on*," I let out. "That? That tiny thing?"

"Hey, it's a lot bigger right next to your face," Tate points out.

I give him a look of fake disappointment and step inside the tub.

"Whoa, whoa whoa. You're just going to kill it with your hands?" Dylan stops me.

"I'm not gonna' kill it," I say.

"So you're just going to pick it up?" she asks, astonished.

"Yeah?" I reply and return to the spider.

I put one hand, cupped, right below it, and use my other to coax it into my palm. It goes easily, but there's an uproar of horror behind me.

"I'm throwing up. Right now. That's disgusting."

"Howwww?"

I step out of the tub with the spider in front of my chest. I can feel it's legs on my palm, but it doesn't move.

The group's reaction amuses me, so I decide to take it further and shove my hands near their faces. They retract as quickly as they can, and Tate nearly drops his towel. I laugh at the numerous curses I get in response, and I leave the bathroom with the spider. I make it to my back door and slide it open with my elbow. I put my hand to the grass, and it seamlessly crawls away and ventures to where my eyes can't find it.

"Happy?" I ask. "Ya' know, spiders are actually good for our environment, and are a great form of pest control," I point out, kind of disappointed in their lack of appreciation.

"You disgust me," Dylan says in reply, and with that, we head back inside my house where Tate tentatively returns to the shower to rinse his hair.

"You know the type of spider that's practically a clear piece of string, that just sits in corners and never does anything?" I ask the group.

"I guess," is the reply I get.

"Well, my mom calls them friendly bathroom spiders, and I think they're adorable."

"You're crazy," Dylan declares. "Makes me love ya', though," she adds.

I scrunch my face into a happy one.

242

"I appreciate you not killing it," Tanner says, and I give him a nod.

It's sad that if given a choice between killing a caterpillar or a butterfly, we'd most likely chose the caterpillar, because it's hard to kill a beauty. But what beauty would it have been if it weren't for the caterpillar?

The day is still a day like any other. It's filled with mindless activities that keep us occupied, and irrelevant but enjoyable conversation.

I find it disappointing that our "go to" conversing topic with strangers, or people who aren't qualified past small talk, is the weather. We choose it because it's something we all experience, and we can be objective and unbiased about it because none of us control it. But who genuinely enjoys talking about the weather besides meteorologists?

Why don't we talk about the fact that we all breathe the same air, or that us having long appendages is actually pretty creepy looking? Why can't we complain and rant about the exasperation of having the hiccups? Why don't we talk about the ground we all walk upon, or that the bees keep us alive, or the feeling of water; the sensation of a sneeze, the annoyance of a cold, or the pure exhilaration of music? Why not the fact that we bleed when we're cut, or the torture of unrequited love? Hell, we could even talk about going to the bathroom because it's all just as universally known as the weather and a whole hell of a lot more interesting – but we don't. We talk about the weather because that's playing it safe, and we live for the feeling of security.

Dylan and the boys are not ones to play it safe. I think that's why I like them so much, and why they're good at getting along with people: they're down for any conversation and not afraid to start one. I wonder what would happen if we all got rid of that fear for a day.

The contents of a day like any other: we scour Netflix in the hopes of finding something new and exciting, but end up settling on an old favorite. We play a couple rounds of chess once I dig out the nice marble set that was hidden in my mom's closet. We spend a lot of time exercising our thumbs with our phones, and making each other watch funny videos we find. We eat rounds of food because snacking is basically a habit at this point. We do whatever because we have the privilege of doing so. That's probably why I hate it when people tell me they're bored. That and the fact that it puts the pressure on me to entertain them. Like, no. Be happy you're bored, and if it's because of me, then by all means, leave. (Sorry, pent up emotions brings out language conducive to a stereotypical teenager's.)

By the time the sun isn't as high, and my house feels like a cage, we decide to go for a walk. The breeze is blissful, and our legs are free as our feet caress the pavement of the old, beaten roads. As I walk, I think, and it reminds me of a funny little story of when I was in daycare:

On the sunny days, we'd get in a big line and everyone at the daycare would walk to the local pool together. I remember knowing a girl named Elizabeth, and I noticed that she was behind me, walking alone. I thought to myself *I wonder if she feels bad that she's walking alone.* So I contemplated for a long time whether or not I should go back to walk with her. But as I was doing that, she unexpectedly came running up behind me and met me at my side. I was startled and she asked, "Whatcha' thinking about?"

I thought for a second that she could read my mind because it was such a coincidence that she would ask that at that time. But she couldn't read minds; she was just curious, and then it dawned on me that I had been thinking of her, and how she was walking alone. I didn't want to make her feel weird or embarrassed, so I decided to answer, "Nothing."

She laughed at my response. "That's not true," (I got even more nervous that she could read minds), "You're always thinking," she insisted. "It's impossible not to."

She was dead set on convincing me that I must have been thinking something, so eventually, I made up a lie and said I had been thinking about the trees that were hanging above us, and that seemed to satisfy her.

I don't know why I remember that walk, and I'd bet money that she doesn't remember it, but I think about it a lot. And in the end, she wasn't walking alone anymore, and I think that's the best part of the story.

We walk all the way to the Library and hang out under our deformed tree. Over time, the area's become a bit more decorative. The bare branches have accumulated old trinkets tied with string, that normally people would deem "junk," but if used right, they're nothing short of wind chimes. They occupy the space for sound along with the occasional song of a bird or chirp of an insect. It's nice. It's peaceful.

We set our bags on our numerous painted rocks, and dig through their contents for entertainment. Considering tomorrow has been set aside to be a sober day, the three of them smoke the rest of what they have. I'm content with sharing my time with the characters in the book I'm reading. And considering smoking has proven to be a bit of a lost cause for me, I decline the opportunity.

"I think I've got a pill if you'd prefer," Dylan offers, and I'm surprised at her decision to address them.

"When'd you get em'?" I casually ask, hoping for a chance to confront her with my concerns.

"While back. Not sure," she vaguely replies.

"What are they?"

She shrugs.

"Dylan," I say out of disappointment and surprise.

"What?"

"Why would you buy pills not knowing what they are? Do you know how stupid that is?"

"Oh, come on. It's not like that," she defends herself.

"Then what's it like?"

"You know our guy. He's not going to give us anything dangerous."

"It's all dangerous, Dylan."

She falls silent.

"Look. It's fine." She turns to meet the boys. "It's fine."

I shake my head but return to my book. She's smart enough to know why I'm mad, yet I'm left blankly staring at the pages because my mind is too occupied thinking of what I should have said. But like every other situation in my life, I submit to the failed authority that I perpetuate and try to move on.

When the ground is no longer comfortable to sit on, the weed is gone, and I finish my chapter, we continue through the woods to visit our lonely dock. As always, there's no one in sight, and the water calmly licks the shore.

"If this was a boat landing, where's the road you'd use to get here?" Tanner asks.

"Used to be over there," I say, pointing to the far left of the lot. "It was really small and inconvenient, and since the fishing sucks over here, no one really came. Trees kinda' filled it in. See?"

"Ahhhh, yeah. Okay."

Dylan goes to the end of the dock while Tate digs through his bag. I watch as he pulls out a football.

"Tanner, go long," he instructs.

"Oh, come on, dude. You know these gangly arms are good for nothing."

"Just do it," Tate persists.

"Okay *Nike*," Tanner mocks and gives in and goes long. But just as he said, when Tate throws it, he extends his arms to make the catch, but ends up doing what looks more like the Macarena than playing football. We laugh as he claims that he was right.

I watch a few throws and then go to join Dylan on the dock. I decide not to bring up the pills again because I don't want to start a fight the day before her birthday, so instead I ask, "Do you think you'll feel any older?" I sit down.

"Ahh, no. I mean. . . I only *now* feel seventeen because I know that I won't be tomorrow."

"Weird how that works," I comment.

"Yeah."

We look at the water and the trees across the river as our hair blows in the wind. We have squinty faces because of the sun, and everything glows as we share the loud silence.

The dock starts to rumble, and we look back to see Tanner jogging toward us. "Dylan, do you have any sunglasses?" he asks.

"Ah, yeah. Look in my bag, there," Dylan tells him, and points to her bag that's sitting by the next pole back.

He rustles through its never-ending contents, but instead of pulling out a pair of sunglasses, he pulls out the small brown cow figurine.

"You still have this?" he asks, amazed.

Dylan nods.

He gives a small laugh. "Wow, that's insane. I completely forgot about it."

"Well, you *were* wasted," Dylan points out.

"Ahhhhh, well, about that. . ." Tanner starts.

"You weren't?" Dylan asks, feeling lied to.

"No. Funny story. Um," he looks to the side to recall the memory, "I was actually just walking around with it as a joke or something, and I put it in my pocket to look at something else. But by the time we left, I forgot it was there. So, I did steal this cow, yes, but it was completely unintentional."

"Why didn't you tell me that?" she asks.

"Well, that makes for a pretty lame story, now doesn't it?" he makes a point.

We laugh, and he puts it back in her bag and finds her sunglasses. "Means a lot that you kept it, though," he says and then runs back to continue throwing the ball with Tate.

"Wow, you just never know with anyone," Dylan jokes.

"I think it's even a better story that he felt the need to lie about."

"Yeah, you're right."

We fall back to silence, so I ask, "So how does the whole legal process work with you getting your inheritance?"

"Ahh - it's kinda' confusing. All I really know is that this guy, Adam, who was my dad's best friend at the time, took the responsibility of dealing with it. And considering there wasn't any family or a proper will and stuff, the court had to get involved. . . I don't know. I talked with Adam for a while, and I gave him my address, and he said he'd be here as soon as he could on Tuesday, the week after my eighteenth birthday, to deliver whatever I get."

"Oh, I see," is all I offer up.

"Yeah, I haven't been able to talk to him since my phone was taken, though. And he's one of those weird people that doesn't have Facebook, so I'm kinda' just hoping it all works out at this point," she explains.

"Well, are you sure it's alright that I'll be gone? I mean, I could come back early in case something doesn't work out," I suggest.

"No, no, it's fine. It really shouldn't be that bad. I mean, yes it sucks that I have to come back here just for that, but it's whatever. Plus, you haven't seen Oliver in forever, so you should really go," she insists.

(To make it official, it's time for me to tell you, Reader, that I'm going to be visiting my other best friend, Oliver, through Wednesday, leaving Thursday morning. I feel guilty for doing it over a time where Dylan has to be home, even if it's just for a day, but we've been planning it for a long time now. It sucked when he moved away, and the most we've done since then is video chat.)

"You're one hundred percent sure?" I ask.

"Yessss." She smiles, but I'm still not convinced.

"Well, why can't the boys just stay until Tuesday, and you all go back then?" I ask.

"They have to work over the weekend. They could only take off for so long, and I'm keeping all my shit at Tate's house for a while," she explains. I knew that, I just had a small hope that something could be arranged.

I nod, trying to think of some other solution.

"Seriously, Junebug, it's fine. I promise. Tate will let me take his car Monday night, your mom's cool with me staying over, and then in the morning I'll wait at my house for Adam. My mom will be at work, and I'll be able to go back right after." She leans over to give me a sideways hug. "Come on, let's go get in on their game," she tells me, and with that we stand, grab our bags, walk back to the boys, and I try not to worry.

The dock ends and we watch Tanner who has the ball in his hands. He gives an exceedingly lame attempt to throw it, and it hits the ground about four feet in front of Tate, bouncing away in a completely different direction.

"Come on, dude. You throw like a girl!" Tate yells at him as he runs to get the ball. But when he turns back around, he realizes he's made a mistake. Tanner crosses his arms and comes forward to talk to him. Tate, who must know what's coming, says, "Oh, you know I didn't mean it- " but he's cut off.

"You say I throw like a girl?" Tanner starts.

"You don't need to-"

"Did you mean to say," he pauses for emphasis, "that I throw like a completely justified women playing a sport that is executed with an equal amount of talent to that of a man, and even does so without being sexist? Yeah, I know. Thank you. That's actually quite the compliment considering how I'm playing right now," Tanner spews off, and my mouth drops in awe.

"You know I didn't mean it like that," Tate finally says with a bit of a roll in his eyes.

"Then don't say it," Tanner says, simply. "You should be on top of this. I mean, you're gay for God's sake," Tanner points out. Even though he's serious, we all find it humorous.

"I'm *sorry,*" Tate says, realizing he's not going to win the argument.

"I'm not the one you should be apologizing to," Tanner says.

Tate turns to Dylan and me, and in a grand gesture with arms flailing, he says, "I'm sooorrry."

"You better be," Dylan jokes. "Because I'm gonna' kick your ass." She runs and jumps on his side, trying to get the ball. I watch in amusement and eventually we start to play.

I don't know the rules of football or what position does what (because after all, I play *true* football: soccer), so we basically play monkey in the middle with teams, and yet again, Tanner proves to be the least athletically inclined, but we don't mind. We don't mind anything because the physical exertion provides us relief from our thoughts, and an outlet for the energy we've suppressed while in my house. I've never liked football more, and we walk home with sweat stained clothes as proof of our activities, and the blissful feeling of happy anticipation for the day devoted to the freedom of our friend.

EIGHTEEN [18]

=

Friday morning. Hurried arrivals. Groggy responses. Persistent celebration. Uncooperative participation. Incomplete sentences.

"We should make a cake," Tate says as he tries to pull Dylan out of my bed.

The boys slept at Emma's but woke up early in order to come barging into my house to "surprise Dylan." But considering they have nothing to surprise her with, other than their presence, Dylan's not too enthusiastic about her early awakening.

"I think pancakes were enough of an adventure already," Dylan replies with her face buried in her pillow.

"We have to do something that's festive," Tate insists.

"*Festive?*"

"We'll just order dessert at the restaurant," Tanner suggest.

"Oh, where are we going?" Dylan asks, suddenly encouraged to sit up at the mention of food.

"We will be attending the Olive Garden," Tanner announces dramatically. "Because one, we can afford it, and two, that bitch is tasty."

We laugh hearing this come out of Tanner's mouth.

"Oooh, no, you made it weird." Dylan pushes him.

"Yeah, maybe it'll get you guys up. Come on!" he beckons as he springs off my bed and to the door.

The boys leave, and I turn over to Dylan, still strangled by the bird's nest I call hair, and in need of toothbrush and face wash, but I say, "Happy Birthday."

"Thanks, Junebug." She gives her humble grin: the one I know to reflect her true size despite her occasional show.

We roll out of bed and throw on whatever comfortable clothes are within arm's reach. For me, it's my burnt orange sweatshirt over some pajama shorts, and for Dylan, it's her vintage Beatles t-shirt and baggy sweatpants. We obviously dress to impress (that is, if you consider it necessary to impress the broad population of *who gives a fuck*).

My mom has left for work, and we raid my kitchen, slowly scouring the cupboards and fridge for an unofficial breakfast.

"Why are we up early if we don't have anything planned?" asks Dylan in the midst of spooning cereal into her mouth.

"Because we didn't wrap your present," replies Tanner as he finishes his first Pop-Tart.

"What?" Dylan asks.

"It's hard to move around without you knowing what it is," I explain.

"Wait, what? You're in on this too?" says Dylan, suddenly bombarded with the realization that the boys actually *didn't* arrive empty handed, and that I am a knowing accomplice, which I suppose makes it time for me to inform you, Reader, of what's going on.

Last week, in the few hours that Dylan was at work, Tanner had called me and asked if I had gotten anything for her birthday yet. When I told him I hadn't, he suggested we all pool our money to get one big present. I agreed, and we went to a local store to buy a gift of good quality. It was then a mess in attempts to hide it from Dylan because there aren't many places in my house that she doesn't venture, and there were certainly none at the boys' motel. So they stored it at Emma's when they moved and brought it here today.

(I'm sorry that I didn't tell you, Reader. Don't take it personally that I didn't trust you with the secret. It's just – I don't actually know you.)

254

"Well, what is it?" Dylan asks, not yet departing from her cereal.

Tate then joyously leaves the room as Dylan looks at Tanner and me for hints. We give none, and when Tate comes back smiling around the corner, he holds up brand new, darkly varnished, acoustic guitar complete with a small blue bow on its body.

Dylan's face morphs into a reserved form a glee as she attempts to balance her gratitude, surprise, and humble objection to what appears to be an expensive gift.

"You guys, you shouldn't have gotten me something so big," she insists as Tate hands her the guitar.

"We know your old one could never been tuned right, and the strings were shit," Tate explains.

"It was a good price," Tanner reassures her.

Dylan puts the guitar in playing position and lightly strums it.

"Your dad would have wanted you to continue," I softly say as I recognize the fragmented rhythm that has reached my ears once before, in the Antique store.

She looks up with admiration. "I love it, you guys."

"Well, good. Promise us you'll send videos of your progress," Tate says.

Dylan replies with a frown, which he was not expecting.

"What?" he asks, concerned.

"I just don't wanna' be away from you all," she says in a pouty manner.

"We won't be that far away," I say, unconvincingly, because I too am a mixture of sadness and hesitancy thinking of our separation – which will shortly be followed by a mass of new people with little direction.

"We'll still be friends," Tanner states, resolutely.

"Yeah, but you'll be at the other end of the state, studying the environment," she claims and then points to Tate, "And you'll be playing football and learning about engines." She gestures towards me. "And you'll be writing it all down with all the English majors, too far away to drive there and back in a day. And then there's me, working in the cities, alone, without a fucking clue of what I'm doing," Dylan states, out of breath.

We're slightly taken aback because this is the first time Dylan's expressed her worry regarding her plan. She's always been fixated on the idea that everything would fall into place when she was able to leave her mother, but it seems she's finally sharing my concern.

"If anyone could attempt something like that, it's you," Tate says, definitively.

"You're only saying that because you have to," she gives a rebuttal.

We scoff.

"You're not one I peg as someone who asks for compliments," Tanner says, lightly.

Dylan looks incredulous. "Wha–? I'm not!"

"Dylan," I address her sincerely and sit down at the table across from her, "you're amazingly smart, you understand art in every way, and you can even freaking sing." I forcefully gesture at the guitar. "You're strong as hell and nothing in the cities is going to be as bad as what you've already been through."

She stares at me with disbelief.

Tate steps in. "What do you think will happen?"

She attempts to reply but fumbles a bit before proclaiming, "I don't know! I just. . . I've never been completely alone before."

"You'll meet people. And you're always welcome to stay back at my house if you need. It won't be too far away, and you know my mom would love it," Tate offers.

"Yeah, I know," she replies, quietly.

"The city will love you, and we'll help you find somewhere cheap. Maybe it'll be with a roommate, and you'll make friends, get a decent job, and be able to afford college in a year. I mean, you're bound to get scholarships with your grades, even after a gap year," Tanner reasons.

"And we'll visit whenever we can," I insist.

She doesn't say anything. The room is lit white with the morning sun, and the guitar still rests on her lap.

She looks down. "My cereal is mushy."

We give small smiles of amused sympathy and try to make the conversation happy again. We're determined because there's no way we're going to let sad talks of moving away ruin Dylan's birthday, no matter how accurate her fears may be.

Reader, were you ever warned that your friends in high school wouldn't last? I know I've been told that a handful of times, but I distinctly remember that on each occasion, I refused to believe it. I was adamant about proving them wrong, and I was extremely confident in my determination because of the friends I had. However, notice the word "had."

I don't mean to be a downer, but I must concede that on some level, the ones who said that were right. It's a common knowledge that friends come and go, but it's a bit harder to swallow when that friend has earned the title of "forever," but doesn't follow through. I've had friends in the past who have shared the deepest parts of my life, and theirs to me, but today, if I see them out in public we either avoid acknowledgement, or go for the short, slightly awkward, few-lines catchup. We could sit and talk about how our relationship dissolved into casual friendliness and nothing more, but I don't know if our stories would be the same, or if we'd even associate blame. I'm not sure what would happen, really, because not once have we tried.

What I've learned through various friendships is that clockwork friends only work when the time is right, and teammate friends aren't always there when the season is over. Friends by association require work, a friend of a friend can ruin a relationship, and friends with benefits can work, but not on every level. An old friend can't always accept a new friend, and a new friend might not approve of an old one. A convenient friend isn't committed, and a committed friend isn't always there to be convenient. And a convenient friend who used to be a committed friend, well boy, they walk a thin line. But what astonishes me most of all, are lying, cheating, jealous, drama-seeking, flat out *mean* friends. They're inevitable, but yet we're always surprised when we have them. Is that because we assume the best of people, or because we're naive? Either way, it's partially our fault, but if we were to assume the worst of everyone, we'd have no friends. Wow, what a fucking predicament, huh? So my point is, following the trend of every math equation I've ever learned, there's always an exception.

With each profound friend to come, we try to convince ourselves that they are that exception, and that's what Dylan, Tate, Tanner, and I are doing here. But I used variations of the word 'friend' 16 times in one paragraph, and I don't even know what the true definition of 'friend' is. That being said, as I look at Dylan looking at her guitar with Tanner's lengthy arms hugging around her neck, and Tate coaxing us to smile for the camera, I just hope that it's them, because I can't imagine what I'd be left with if they were ruled out.

"You're doing it again," Tate tells me.

"What?" I ask, suddenly coming back to life.

"Just watching," he says with a smile.

"Well, then don't be so fun to watch," I joke.

"Where do you go when you do that?" Dylan asks from across the room. She had gotten up to clean out her cereal bowl.

"I don't go anywhere," I tell her, because I wasn't aware that this was considered "a thing that I do."

"Well, okay then. Do you want to go anywhere? Because I assume we're eating right before we leave, right?" she asks the group, and we nod. "Then we've got time to kill. So what weapon do you guys wanna' use?"

"What?" Tate asks, not catching on.

Dylan rolls her eyes. "What do you want to do?"

"Well, I still haven't packed," I admit.

Dylan frowns. "Me neither."

"You guys are unbelievable," Tanner comments.

"Then we'll go find something to do while you guys pack, how about that?" Tate asks.

We agree and the boys clean up what they used for breakfast and depart. Dylan and I then head back to my room to change and pack.

Dylan leans her new guitar against my wall and looks at it intently.

"Probably the best gift I've ever gotten," she says.

"Really?" I ask, not being able to decide if I'm surprised or not.

"Family never really had a lot of money," she says.

"The price of something doesn't make it a good present," I remind her as I dig my duffle bag out from my closet.

"Okay well, yeah, I guess I mean. . . if all their money went towards something else, their attention did too. Or -" She looks dissatisfied with her answer. "Like, my dad would sometimes. . . I mean. . . he meant well -" she can't finish a sentence.

"Dylan," I stop her, "I understand."

She stops looking at the guitar.

"Yeah, no, of course you do," she says in an almost embarrassed tone, which is rather unlike her.

"Okay, what's wrong?" I ask as I stop my quest through my dresser and sit down on my bed.

She sits on the opposite end. "I don't know. Things just - they feel different, like I should've been more appreciative of. . . whatever I had. I don't know."

I'm genuinely confused as to where this is coming from so I question, "You should've been more appreciative of a mother who beat you? Of a childhood of fighting parents? Watching the horrors of an alcoholic? Dealing with your father's death? Dylan, what do you mean *more appreciative*? *I* should be more appreciative. *I* didn't have any of that and I still complain about things. I. . . you don't have to be, Dylan. Why would you think that?"

She doesn't have a response right away. She looks back at the guitar. "I loved my dad."

I can tell that she's just as confused as I am, so I try to redirect her attention. "I know you're scared," I lean over in her line of vision to get her to make eye contact with me, "but I know you're going to get through it. For him. Because you're just like that, and there's no way you're going to let *freedom* be your downfall."

I'm not sure either of us know if we're on the same page, but it doesn't seem to matter. She manages a small huff of a smile and admits, "I guess you're right. I wasn't looking at it that way." She gets up, sighs, stretches broadly, and runs her hands through her messy hair. "I have to find all my shit," she proclaims, thus changing the subject.

Our clothes have been through the wash and mixed together dozens of times, so by now, Dylan's clothes are just as buried as mine. But I take her initiative to move on and start digging. Within the hour, I've managed to over pack for my stay at Oliver's, and we've found what we think are the rest of Dylan's belongings. But just before she shuts the suitcase I'm lending her, she digs through it once more and asks, "Did you see my hippie shirt?"

"The yellow one?"

"Yeah." She looks under the blankets and around my closet once more.

"No. Um, the last time I saw it was. . . the day before we went to the zoo, I think."

She digs a bit longer. "Well, I don't have it."

"Maybe it's in the wash or something," I offer. "I'll find it at some point. It'll give me a reason to come visit you right away," I say in response to her dissatisfied glare, trying to look on the bright side.

"You better. I love that shirt."

"I know. I'll find it"

"Okay." She closes the suitcase and I look around my room. It's a mess, but I can tell that it's only my mess now, and despite how littered it is, it feels empty. Maybe that's how Dylan feels too, and it's conflicting because she shouldn't be sad that she's picking up her mess, but for some reason it's harder than she thought it'd be. But I never really know with her.

We leave my mess and watch random TV in the living room, waiting to hear from the boys. After a rather disturbing episode of *Law & Order: SVU*, I get a text from Tanner: *"Put on your swimsuits under some clothes. We'll be there in 10."* I read it to Dylan.

"Swimsuits?" she quotes. "What does he think we're going to be doing?"

Obviously, I don't know the answer, so I shrug. "You up for it, though?" I ask, not quite sure if *I* even am.

"Well, now I'm curious," she states and we get up to, once again, annoyingly dig through my room and her bag to find our swimsuits.

Once they're concealed under our clothes, and Dylan has packed her never-ending bag as accordingly as she can, the boys arrive as promised.

"Where are we going?" Dylan asks as we greet them outside.

"You'll see, get in," Tate orders with a conniving grin on his face.

We're not reluctant, but I do have my doubts. Not knowing makes me nervous, especially with the potential of it being a place that requires me to be surrounded by people in my swimsuit. We pry them for hints, but they're not susceptible to nagging. So instead, I watch our trip, trying to determine our destination, but with each turn they make, I'm more confused.

After nearly a half an hour of driving, Tate takes a left off the mainstream road and heads down a gravel one that I've never seen before. We're in a wooded area going uphill. I look for a sign stating our destination, but there isn't one. Dylan and I look out the windows in silence as anticipation builds in my stomach – or is that anxiety?

Tate follows the narrow road until he comes to what ultimately looks like a dead end. He swings the car around, so we're facing the way we came in, and parks.

"Okay seriously, where are we?" Dylan asks. "I have no reception and you're kinda' givin' me a serial killer vibe."

Tate laughs. "Chill. We found this spot online. It's nothing special, really, just thought it'd be fun." He gets out of the car and we follow. His explanation was certainly not a description, so Dylan asks further, "So this is it? Just this circle here?" She gestures around herself.

Tanner looks at her as if she's slow. "Why would we ask you to wear swimsuits if this was all we're doing?"

Dylan crosses her arms, obviously feeling slightly stupid for having overlooked that point. "Okay, then where's the water?"

"Relaaax." Tate puts one arm over my shoulder and the other over Dylan's, and we smile at his fake, boy-ish charm impression. "You'll know eventually."

We give in to their secretive approach to the event, and watch as Tanner opens the trunk of the car. To my surprise, he pulls out an Aztec style blanket and what looks to be a traditional picnic basket. He sets the basket down and sprawls out the blanket parallel to the car. He sits down with his back resting on the door, and we watch as he opens the basket and pulls out paper plates, juice boxes (which are really juice pouches but who the hell calls them that), some containers of various fruit, and many small cut sandwiches.

"Aww, this is cute," I say as we sit down on either side of him, all grabbing a plate.

"Bit of lunch since we're not eating until seven," he explains. "I've got peanut butter and jelly, ham and swiss, and pepperoni with. . . whatever sauce this is." He opens the bread to examine it.

We give our orders and he passes them around.

"This is all thanks to Emma," he says once we've received full plates. "So we should stop by to say thanks before we go."

"Well, of course. We have to say goodbye too, after all she's done for us," Dylan agrees.

We peacefully eat our sandwiches, and I look around at our surroundings. It's rather elevated, and has low trees that hang close above our heads. I know there must be water around but this isn't an area I'm familiar with. I suppose, now that I think of it, we did pass a lake on our way here, but it didn't strike me as important. Nevertheless, I'm just happy we seem to be this destination's only occupants.

When the sandwiches are gone, we've finished the fruit, and our juice boxes are shriveled, we pack away the garbage and roll up the blanket. Tanner brings it back to the car, but before he puts it away, he pulls out the remaining contents of the trunk: four deflated inner tubes, some towels, and a couple of pool noodles.

"Where'd you get those?" Dylan asks.

"Well, these are June's," Tanner says, holding up the towels.

I squint. "Oh, jeez, yeah. How did I not see you take those?" I ask, but don't receive an answer.

"And these we got at the Dollar Store," Tanner says, holding up the rest of the inflatables.

"Wow, safe and reliable, huh?" Dylan sarcastically asks, but we don't actually care. Tanner gives a fake laugh and throws us each an inner tube which we begin to inflate.

Tate leads the way. The boys must have visited here before bringing us because the path Tate takes to get to wherever we're going is not one I would have ever chosen. To be honest, I wouldn't have even found the path due to the heavy underbrush blocking its entrance. But once we diligently but ungracefully hobble our way through the shrubs, the path becomes quite clear. We still seem to be walking uphill, and after a few meters I start to understand where the water is: far below us.

I think Dylan is catching on as well because she looks over her shoulder to shoot me a worried glance. Perhaps she's giving the boys the benefit of the doubt, however, because she doesn't object, and we silently continue our walk in Tate's wake.

We take a sudden sharp right, and a few yards later find ourselves emerging from the crowded path. At this point, there's no doubt that my predictions were right.

"Oh, fuck no," says Dylan, not daring to walk any further from the edge of the path.

The trees and soft ground had turned to rock, leaving us now standing a few feet away from the edge of a cliff.

"It's not that bad," Tanner reasons. "It's only fifty feet."

"*Only fifty feet!?*" quotes Dylan with an air of astonishment.

"That sounds worse than it is," Tate says, trying to soften the shock.

"You don't even know if it's safe or not!" Dylan points out in disbelief of the boys' decision to bring us here.

"Sure we do," Tate starts, but before he can explain why, Dylan jumps to the question, "Then why is there no one here?"

"And why have I never heard of this place?" I chime in, also slightly skeptical of the validity of Tate's claim.

"Well, to be a bit blunt, June, you're not necessarily the most adventurous person out there," Tanner answers.

I shrug. "Fair enough."

Dylan seems flabbergasted at her loss of an ally and demands some further explaining.

"No one's here because there are a few spots twenty or so minutes away that are way more worth their time if they actually like cliff jumping. Plus, like. . . let's be real, this is a small town," Tate explains.

"Okay, but how do you know it's safe?" Dylan presses further.

"Because I've already jumped," Tate says, confidently.

Dylan crosses her arms. "When?"

"Before we came and got you," Tate says, easily, but when Dylan doesn't look convinced, he continues, "Boy hair dries fast." He gives a flick of his head, but it has no improvement on Dylan's posture.

"I trust him," I offer.

"Thank you, June," Tate says loudly with a gesture in my direction and a nod at Dylan.

"Just walk towards me and take a look," Tanner says, taking a few steps closer to the edge, coaxing Dylan, in the hopes of helping ease her through her fear of heights. She's hesitant, but sighs and takes a few half-steps forward, but before she reaches Tanner, she thrusts her hands down with a loud grunt of defeat. She crosses her arms again, safe at the edge of the path, and questions, "What on earth made you guys think I'd be willing to do this?"

"Well," Tanner says as he walks back toward Dylan, "we just thought that if you could get over this fear," he gestures to the edge of the cliff, "you'd be less afraid of starting your life in the cities, essentially alone."

Dylan doesn't move or talk for a moment. "You do know that those two events are completely unrelated, right?" she says simply but not with judgement.

Tate and I give a laugh.

"Yes," Tanner drags. "But you know what I meant. . . I mean, humor me," he insists.

"Well, do you know what would happen in a movie?" Dylan asks.

"What?" Tanner says, looking beat.

She takes a deep breath and says, "I'd be in eye-opening awe of the metaphor you've so insightfully presented, which represents the conquering of all of my fears with a single jump. And I'd be so inspired by your ability to even *think* of something so caring and clever, that I'd be racking up all the courage I could muster in order to follow through, in honor of you, in honor of me, and in honor of the deeply cheesy plotline that people end up paying way too much money to see," Dylan performs, and then adds, "Oh, and it'd be in slow-mo.," to top it off.

Tanner stares at her downheartedly. "Well, that was kinda' mean, but I can't deny I'm impressed."

"Look," Dylan says, back to reality, "it *is* very caring, and yes, rather clever, it's just the simple fact that there's no way in hell I'm jumping off a fifty foot cliff into water I've never seen before."

Tanner accepts defeat. "Then will you at least swim with us at the bottom?"

"Gladly," Dylan states. "So give me the tubes and your clothes and I'll meet you down there."

We hand them over with a bit of reluctance. I don't blame Dylan for not jumping after seeing her on the roller coaster, but I do view the cliff as a bit more daunting now that I don't have someone to confide in, regarding my apprehension. I'm not afraid of heights, but that doesn't mean I'm not afraid of hitting dark water at a high speed. I've never jumped more than ten feet, but I don't want to disappoint the boys even further.

"I'll go first," Tate declares, and we're not surprised.

Tanner and I step back to give him room as he lines up for a running start; he has not a single nerve of fear.

"Back flip or front flip?" he asks no one in particular.

"Bullshit," Tanner says. "I've never seen you do either of those in my life."

"Well, you gotta' stop blinking at the wrong times," Tate replies, on the brink of moving. Tanner gives him a confused, you're-stupid, *I don't know what's going on*, kind of look as he starts to run.

We watch intently as he takes his last, forceful leap off the edge of the cliff, and to our utmost surprise, Tate manages to execute a rather lopsided backflip. We run to the edge to see how he lands. When we look down, we get a quick glimpse of his feet breaking the surface of the water, quickly followed by the rest of his body. He's submerged for a few seconds but comes up with a flick of his hair, smiling, and finishes with a dab. We laugh as Dylan gives him a hand out of the water.

"He lied," Tanner says as we recede from the edge.

"What?" I ask.

"He didn't jump before we went to get you guys. He just said that to try to convince Dylan."

"Seriously?" I question even though he's obviously telling the truth.

Tanner nods. "We knew it was safe, though. He didn't lie about this being a real spot."

"Well, thanks for telling me, I guess." I don't know what to say.

"You wanna go next?" he asks.

"Oh. . . sure - yeah," I say, feeling slightly pressured despite him having a completely indifferent demeanor towards the question; I haven't mentally prepared myself yet.

He steps to the side as I look at the drop off. *It's going to be fun* I tell myself, *it's just air and water.* I'm a few paces from the edge. *Think of a song.* Tanner's watching and I hear Tate distantly yell, "The water's great, come on down!" *40 Day Dream by Edward Sharpe & The Magnetic Zeros.* "No pressure," Tanner says from behind me, probably sensing my hesitation. *It's only a few seconds in the air, and a grand song makes for a grand jump.*

I start to move. Slow, and then fast, and then forceful, and I close my eyes as I push off the rocky edge. My stomach drops before I do, and I look down only to see my feet inches away from colliding with the water

What is discovered in those inches: I know that there wasn't a right place for my arms while I was in the air, and I know that my muscles were knots and my hair couldn't keep up. But I didn't know that I wouldn't have time to think about the water below me, or that I'd feel weightless. I didn't know that it'd be silent, and that the music would only truly start when I was no longer in the middle ground, but plummeting into the comforting density of billowing water. If only I could see how far my legs ventured toward the deep dark, and how miniscule it might have looked from below, would I understand the significance of my resurfacing.

It all happened in a few seconds, and I wipe my wet hair from my eyes as I swim to the side, serenaded by the buoyant approval of my friends. I smile as they reach down to help me up. I'm glad I jumped, but I wish Dylan had as well.

Tanner's turn. We can't see him from where we stand, so when Tate yells, "You're next, greenbean!" I squint into the sun waiting for movement. Moments later, Tanner leaps off the edge with a bit more speed than Tate and I, and kicks his legs in the air, evidently trying to straighten himself out, but with little success. He hits the water, nearly sitting, with great strength and a loud splash.

When he comes up he spits out a large amount of water and yells, "Throw me a floaty!"

Dylan tosses him a tube and follows by attempting to land in the middle of one herself. This time she's wearing her thick, navy blue, Harvard shirt. She says she wears it ironically, but considering she'd actually have a decent shot at getting accepted there, it makes it even more ironic.

Tate fastens himself a pool-noodle diaper of some sort and hops in with them. I grab a remaining tube and collide once more with the silky water. I still don't understand its appeal, but I give in to it and enjoy the time with my friends. We float on our backs, gazing up at the brilliant, yellow-green, lit leaves and broad sky. We see who can remain floating the longest without the aid of a device, and even though I failed that portion of the test in swimming lessons, I feel like I could stay on the water's surface forever. Maybe it just took the willingness to give up my weight.

Tate takes a few more jumps off the cliff, and we let our minds drift away with the small momentum of the water. We lay on the smoothest rocks we can find to air dry with the anticipation of leaving soon. The celebration of Dylan's birthday is still in its youth, and we have yet to stop by to thank Emma before dinner.

Around 5:00 in the afternoon we use the towels for what the air couldn't manage, and gather the remaining floaties. We deflate them so they'll fit properly in the trunk, and load up. We leave with contentment, but also with a sense of displacement for we discovered a place worth remembering right before leaving it behind. It feels wrong to make memories in places that have not been used to their full potential, but it seems that that's going to be inevitable with a schedule that has a closing time.

We stop back at my house to change out of our swimsuits and put on some respectable clothes. Once we've managed that, we head to Emma's.

Even though we live in the same town, I'll probably never see Emma again after Dylan and the boys leave. Some people probably don't understand that considering we're technically friends, but our relationship was a friend of a friend of a friend basis, and, like I said, those don't always work. I valued our time together, and I still have the English assignment that I tore from her notebook, but she'll go down as a good memory and nothing more. Sometimes that's okay.

We arrive around 6:00 and the driveway is quiet as usual. Emma greets us with a boisterous, "Happy birthday!" cheer. Dylan thanks her, looking slightly overwhelmed.

"You guys look nice," Emma says as we follow her inside.

"We're pretending to be sophisticated when we go out to dinner," Tate explains.

"Well, I'm convinced," Emma declares as we enter her kitchen. It's now when I notice that there's an arrangement of items sitting on the middle of her table.

"What's this?" Dylan asks.

"This is a taste of what it's like to be eighteen," Emma presents.

It appears that Emma has gone around and picked up everything she could find that is a privilege of being a legal adult, which includes: a single cigarette, a lottery ticket and scratch off, an "I voted" sticker (that appears to have been peeled off of something and reattached to a piece of paper), a shot of some sort of alcohol, a small firework, and one of those tattoos you get for a couple quarters out of a machine (this one happens to be a particularly swanky ladybug).

"Why the shot?" Dylan asks.

"Why do the Brits get to have fun?" Emma questions.

"Well, in that case. . . ." Dylan gives her best impression of a British accent and swiftly downs the shot.

"Oh, fuck," she says, putting down the glass, "that's nasty." She looks like she's swallowed an entire lime.

"That's how you know it's good," Emma remarks.

"Hey, I thought this was supposed to be a sober day," I suddenly remember and protest.

"But the Brits. . . ." Dylan murmurs.

"It's only one shot, but I do think you should have to put on this tattoo," Tate says, picking it up off the table. "Very stylish."

"Oh, yes. I think it would look best on my forehead, don't you?" Dylan jokes.

"The gambling's all yours," Emma informs Dylan. "But I hope ya' remember where ya' got it if it happens to be a jackpot," she says with a smile and a nudge.

"I've got shit luck, but I promise I'll remember," Dylan says and gives her thanks for the courtesy Emma has shown us. Emma plays it to a minimum and assures us that she was happy to share her house, and that she'd love to have us all over again if we were ever together. Emma's only a few years older than us, but it shows. I wonder if I'll ever be in a situation like this. I wonder how I'd handle it.

Dylan pockets the cigarette, but I'm sure she'll never smoke it. She probably took it to prevent me from taking it, but I've been getting better at sparsely smoking. I do promise that I'll quit. I hope you trust me.

Dylan wins five dollars on the scratch off and puts the ugly tattoo on her wrist. We're all happy with the outcome of the day, so around 6:45 we gather our belongings in preparation to leave.

"So you guys are driving to the cities after you eat?" Emma asks, clarifying our plans.

"We are, yes. June's driving to her friend's house. We figured there'd be a lot less traffic at night," Tanner explains.

"Well, drive safe," Emma says.

"-ly," Dylan interjects.

"What?"

"'Drive safe*ly*.' Grammar bitch," Dylan corrects, casually.

Emma laughs, "You're right. My apologies." She gives a fake praise.

"Thanks again for letting us stay," Tanner says.

"Any time," Emma insists as her cheeks puff with a smile.

We slip on our shoes and open the door, but right before we're out, Emma says, "Oh!" as if she's just remembered something.

"June," she addresses me, "I got an B plus."

"What?" I question.

"On the perspective assignment," she answers. I get a hot rush in my face from embarrassment. She must know that I took that page from her notebook, but she simply grins. "They said it needed more, but I argued that more was less."

Dylan and the boys look at us with confusion. Obviously, the event of me taking the paper wasn't as pertinent to them as it was to me.

"Deserved an A," I state, sincerely. She looks at me with thankful eyes but then turns to Tanner, who's standing to my right. She gently tugs on his shoulder, leaning him closer. She then swiftly kisses him on the cheek, and he blushes and can't help but smile. They give a telepathic goodbye, and we close the door behind us. The driveway is humble as ever. What a pleasant end to a small fraction of my life.

We're at the restaurant in ten minutes and are thoroughly prepared to eat. I'm not going to talk about the meal however, because frankly, I don't like talking about food. But I will say that it's the perfect way for us to share our departing thoughts that have previously been aches in the crinks of our minds.

We say things like, "I can't believe how fast it went," and, "It still doesn't feel like it's actually happening." When really, it's been eighteen years, and all the while, it's been real. I don't know how I'm supposed to feel at this age, but I know I'll only feel worse if I try to figure it out. I can't come to terms with the fact that when our stomachs are full and our bill is paid, we'll be heading our separate ways for an undefined length of time. Of course, I'll be returning to my house for the remainder of the summer, but this time it'll be with a mindset devoted to preparation rather than delectation.

Reader, this book may feel like a story that's stuck predominantly in rising action, or a pointless lecture, a temper that hasn't broken, or a road that doesn't end, and if that's true then 1) I'm sorry, and 2) I'm not actually sorry. I say this because I think that's how the majority of life feels. We go to preschool to go to elementary school to go to middle school to go to high school to go to college. We go to college to get a job. We get a job to buy a house. We buy a house to fill it with a family, and we have a family to start the whole process over again. But what if we don't want kids, and what if we're not passionate about our jobs? We do everything to ensure that we won't be left hanging, but even at the prime age of eighteen, I can't help but view that as a pipe dream.

I don't know how I'm supposed to feel, but I know I'll never figure it out if that's all I focus on. So I shame myself for, yet again, spacing out and having to be brought back to reality by the persistent calling from Tate.

"June!"

"Oh – sorry, what?"

He gives a little laugh with mocking eyes. "Your bill." He presents the black fold which had been delivered to our table without my notice.

"Thanks."

We pay, leave a tip, and depart from our table. When we make it outside, the air brushes our skin and the sun is shining its last breaths. The soft, unified murmur of the restaurant is left to trail in the wind, and we stand on the quiet ground that knows nothing but depth as it supports our heavy hearts.

We get in the car and turn up the music – never has there been a better device to tune out the unwanted uncertainties of our lives. There aren't many words on the drive to my house. I'm not sure what would be worth saying, but I'm hoping that the few minutes it takes to get home will drag – that I'll get to stay in the perfect bubble of sanctuary that the car provides – but they don't drag. We pull into my driveway and I know that it's only me who's meant to get out, but a proper goodbye deserves more than an over-the-seat hug, so the rest follow.

"It was amazing to get to know you," Tanner says, flinging his arm around my neck. "Even if you do eat macaroni with a fork."

I look up at his towering features which includes a broad smile, and I know that I'll miss the lanky vegetarian.

"There's no other way to eat it," Tate steps in. "He doesn't know what he's talking about." He gives Tanner a small push and me a big hug. I wasn't prepared for the hug, and I wouldn't have considered our relationship to be of that kind, but it's nice, nonetheless, and I'm certain that my mind will be trailing away more often than I'd like without the grounding aid of this gentle grizzly bear.

"I'm with Tanner," says Dylan. "But I still love you." The boys step back and Dylan and I walk toward each other with open arms. I didn't presume I'd be this sad to see Dylan starting a better life, but it feels as if I've got mechanical cables attached to her maze of a mechanism, and pulling away is harder than I thought It'd be. I guess being fearless to be personal can pay off.

"You're going to be fine, right?" I ask.

"Better than fine," she says with a sad smile.

"We need to Skype or something," I insist.

"I don't have Skype."

She makes me laugh. "I don't either. We'll get Skype."

"And you better bring me my shirt!" she warns.

"I will." We look at each other endearingly.

"If we go now we'll still get some of the light," Tanner mentions, smally.

"I love you," I tell Dylan as the boys get in the car.

"I feel like we should have something to say that's better than that, like they do in the movies," Dylan says, and I give her a slight roll of my eyes.

"But I love you too." She grins, and with that, she opens the door to the back seat and gets in the car that will carry her all the way to a new chapter of her life, and thus, a new chapter of this book.

YOU STILL CALL ME UP SOMETIMES [19]

=

The drive to Oliver's feels long. It's only a couple of hours, but the roads are dark and my mind has a million places to be, and not enough time to dwell in any of them. (I find personification gives ease to my problems. If I think of them as beings, they're easier to understand.)

Too busy thinking about my present friendship, I forget to be nervous about seeing my old friend until I'm only twenty minutes away from his house.

Reader, seeing as how you're going to meet him soon, I should give you some background about Oliver:

Like I said, we met in a daycare that took place in a church. I can't remember how we started our friendship, but I'm almost certain it was instigated by him. Perhaps I'm drawn to this type of personality, but similar to Dylan, Oliver is one of the most fearless people I know. Being a moderately short, stubby fingered, ginger, you'd almost have to be.

Oliver is the most accurate definition of a social butterfly. His willingness to interact with anyone and the support he receives from carrying it out, is quite astounding. Which is why I am dumbstruck at the fact that, to this day, he calls me his best friend. Perhaps I beat out some of the others because of our early partnership, but I've always been amazed that my reserved personality is enough maintain such a stature.

Childhood friends get their own category because their outcomes can vary from despising one another, to being lifelong companions. For Oliver and me, the adventurous, dream-like world we created was enough to instill our relationship today. We were the type of friends who "started a band together,"

275

and planned a life where we'd live on an island and provide for ourselves (we even had the island picked out). We inspected houses that were rumored to be haunted, and ran the front on a bug-catching epidemic. We designed video games in notebooks, and were convinced that we were dating, but really, that's just something we said. I used to give him the new name of Olivia so he'd be able to play on the girls' team, and we were infamous for running the daycare. It sounds ridiculous, I know, but even typing it now makes me smile.

As we grew up, he became the class clown with his charismatic, jokester disposition, and things like girls and tests started to matter. He was one of those people who never did their homework but still passed because they were great at taking exams. He used to make fun of me for doing my work and titled me "dictionary girl," which is anything but creative.

But what came even easier to him than tests, were girls. When it was acceptable to be "dating" multiple people at one time, he'd have up to seven girlfriends who'd hang out with him at recess. I have to admit, it made me jealous at times that I wasn't one of them, but I know now that dating would have never been the best suit for us.

After being fought over by girls for the majority of his life, you'd think it would make him believe that he deserved them - but it didn't - and I think that's one of the best things about him. Not once did he view them as a possession, item, or entitlement. He'd make a point to consult with me and ponder over what he should do about them. He was the most diligent boy I knew, and, hopefully, still know.

Today, we'll comment on social media, text about wanting to see each other, sometimes pick up the phone, but mostly, we'll just live our lives. There'll be times where I'll remember something small that's been shoved to the back of my mind, and I'll feel as if I've fallen short on the commitment we once had. In which case, guilt will compel me to get him on the phone, and to my relief and my astonishment, we'll simply pick up where we left off.

I don't know what I did as a kid to deserve such a guy, but I'm sure as hell glad it happened.

I park next to the curb in front of his house. It's dark, there's no one in sight, and I text him letting him know I'm here, but there's a slight fear that no one will come to the door accompanying my initial nerves. Before I get the chance to knock, however, the door is opened and I'm greeted kindly with the familiar smile I had forgotten means so much to me.

"Hey!" says Oliver.

"Hey," I reply through my small, delighted grin.

He steps aside and a small dog trots over to inspect my feet.

"Ross," Oliver declares as I bend down to pet the blurry-eyed dog.

"He's getting old," I observe as his tail slowly flops back and forth. The aging Ross puts time in perspective, and I feel the sudden weight of how long it's really been resting on my shoulders.

"How was the drive?" Oliver asks, casual as ever.

"Good," is all I can muster, and I grab my things as Oliver prepares to lead me through the rest of his unfamiliar house.

"My dad's sleeping, and who knows where Sam is," explains Oliver.

Sam is his younger sister. We used to wrestle in the grass and pick fights. We made nearly everything we did together a challenge. She's only a year younger, but that year was the only thing that made me feel dominant. I could never gain the confidence to thwart her.

"You can sleep in my room. My dad doesn't care and I've got a futon you can stay on," Oliver says as we climb the narrow steps leading to his room. His house is tall but not wide. There's miscellaneous objects scattered in places they don't typically rest, and there's framed pictures of the Oliver and Sam I remember. We walk the same walk, just simply on a different ground.

He opens the door to his room and it's obvious that he's the one who decorated it. Contrary to what I've previously said, the only objectification of women he partakes in is obtaining the stereotypical hot-girl-next-to-a-truck posters. I'm certainly not a fan of them, but I know they don't define him.

"Nice room," I say, simply because it's new and seeing anything of his is nice after such a long time.

"Thanks, just changed it up. Gonna' get some new stuff, wanna' see?" he asks as I put down my bags. He walks to his desk where his computer sits, illuminated by his lamp. He opens an accumulation of tabs and shows me things he's been considering, have already considered, and are on their way to his house as we speak. He's always been a big spender, and I've always been baffled at his ability to never be broke. I know he'll go far. I've thought that ever since I can remember.

We spend time with dry eyes, looking at his computer, and it leads to topics that can be unraveled and explored because catching up is broad. I was worried that we wouldn't connect like we used to, but I forgot that talking is his forte. Our conversations flow and he tells me about school and his parents, his job and girls. It's soon 2:00 a.m., and although there are still mountains to hike, we call it a night.

He sleeps on his bed (which is really just a mattress on the floor), and I sleep on the futon. The surface is stiff and short, but that feels right. The familiarity of being in an unfamiliar dwelling area – resulting from staying the night at new places – rushes over me, and it's comforting. I get a direct view out of his window from where I lay, and I watch the slow movement of the leaves blowing in the breeze. I listen to the inevitable motion of the world, and my feet move back and forth under the heavy blanket – as they always do when things are matchless.

Beauties are double-sided.

That same window allows the sun to blind me when it finally rises in the morning. I wake with squinted eyes and a quick sense of displacement, but when I look to my right and see Oliver tangled in his blankets, it all comes back to me.

I get up to go to the bathroom. I check my phone on the toilet (like I, and most people, usually do), and I have a message from Dylan: "*Made it to Tate's. Great to see his family again. How's Oliver?*"

I'm happy to know there haven't been any complications and I fill her in. When I'm done in the bathroom I exit into the hallway. But before I make it back to Oliver's, Sam comes out of her room and we nearly run into each other.

"Oh, hey," I say.

"June?" She's a bit startled but comes to terms. "Hi."

"Long time, no see." I'm not sure what to say. We've always had a perplexing relationship.

She gives her usual, nearly-mocking, small laugh and I swear there hasn't been a day in between the last time I saw her. We continue on our ways with no further words, but with an unspoken agreement that it's nice to see each other again.

I reenter Oliver's room and find that he's now awake.

"Good morning," he says as if he were the first to wake up.

"G'morning," I reply. "Just saw Sam, she looks the same."

"She's still a mess," Oliver declares.

"Figured." Sam has always been a fan of objecting the construct of authority, and if I'm being completely honest, Oliver's not far behind. However, I've never felt the need to change that.

"So what do you wanna' do today?" Oliver asks my least favorite question.

"I don't know, what do you do around here?"

He crawls out of bed. "I actually made a list," he says, and I'm pleasantly surprised as I dig through my bag to find my toothbrush and some clothes to change into.

He returns with a piece of paper he grabbed from a stack on his desk. "Um, there's a paintball range. We could take out my go-kart, visit part of the State Park, see a movie, meet up with some of my friends at this barn we've renovated. Um. . . oh, and there's this forest that's known to be haunted if you drive your car by a certain tree at night. I was gonna' try it a while ago, but haven't yet," he finishes.

I look at him with a mouth slightly agape, but how could I have expected anything less? I nearly laugh, "Um, how about we worry about breakfast first?"

"Yeah," he smiles, "my step-mom usually makes something."

He's always understood my definition of adventurous compared to his, but it's his disregard of it that's made our friendship the quality that it is. I love that I've never hated him for making me a passenger in his life. And I love that he knows I like to roll down the windows.

I get ready in the bathroom and he gets ready in his room. We then head downstairs to discover that he was right: his step-mom is in the process of making eggs and bacon.

When we fill the kitchen, I expect her to acknowledge that I'm in their house, but she doesn't. Oliver pours me some coffee as his step-mom continues to silently stand over her steaming pan. Although I wasn't thrilled at the idea of meeting her, this would almost be less awkward if she would say something, or at the very least, look at me.

When we exit the kitchen to sit in his living room, I discreetly attempt to ask Oliver about his step-mom's behavior.

"What's with. . ." I gesture my head towards the kitchen and scrunch up my face.

"What?" he asks, completely clueless.

I sigh at the frustrating fact that I can't express what I mean without being louder, and that he's not catching on. I try again. "Didn't say anything. . . ." I aggressively gesture in her direction with gritted teeth.

There's a second before I can see the gears click. "Oh! My step-mom?" he asks, way too loud. I give disappointed hand movements and look at him incredulously.

He laughs. "What?"

"She's right there!" I whisper-scream.

He's still laughing, but he manages, "Dude, she's deaf."

I open my mouth with hesitation, not knowing what to say. "Well. . . how was I supposed to know that!?" I ask, still in a whisper out of habit.

Not yet composed, he says, "She barely ever talks out loud because she doesn't like her voice. Which I don't understand because she can't hear it, but we use sign language mostly."

Finding it hard to believe simply because I expected anything but that, I question, "You know sign language?" in a dubious manner.

He rolls his eyes, but instead of talking, he puts down his coffee and signs out a response with about four different hand movements.

I'm amazed. "What did that mean?" I ask because only the first and last movement looked the slightest bit familiar.

"It means 'I'm going to hang with friends,'" he admits.

"Well, that doesn't pertain to the context at all," I reason.

"*Pertain to the context*," he mocks. "Who talks like that?"

My incredulous look remains. "What? That's not weird to say."

"*Pertain to the context*," he repeats with a huff. "You haven't changed at all."

I laugh. "And neither have you."

We sip our coffee, I pet Ross, and his step-mom eventually brings us some breakfast, where she acknowledges me with a happy smile. It was soon after Oliver moved that his parents got divorced, and even though he never talked about it much, I feel like I should have known that his step-mom is deaf. When we finish our breakfast, I'm still wondering what else I'm behind on.

"Thought about what you want to do today?" he asks, interrupting my thoughts.

"Oh, no. You're the host. You should decide," I insist.

"You're supposed to treat your guests," he reasons.

"Well, *your guest* doesn't like to pick, so I'm making you do it."

"Fine." We rinse our dishes in the sink. "Then today we're going for a walk," he declares.

"Sounds grand." I smile.

I soon discover that the state of desertion I found his town to be in when arriving was not due to it being night, but because this is simply and utterly a shitty little town. Regardless, it certainly has its beauties.

We walk over a river and through the woods, however, his grandmother's house is not our destination. He brings me to a small clearing, in which an old train track rests vacant.

We follow it, and all the while it reminds me of the movie *Stand By Me*. However, our reason for trailing it is far less harrowing. We stand on either end of the lifted rails, balance to the best of our ability, and converse.

He asks me about my life, and although I've mentioned Dylan to him before, he's still far from knowing the extent of her situation or our relationship. I don't know how to talk about her. It would simply be easier if he could just read this, but since that's impractical, I sum up my life in a way that doesn't do it justice but gets the point across. He accepts it.

"So you're going to college?" I ask, changing the subject.

"Yeah. . . I guess. My dad really figures I should," he tells me, sounding unenthusiastic in every way possible.

"I mean, it's logical," I reason. "What's your major?"

"Undeclared at the moment," he admits.

"Well, that's okay. Most people are, really."

He shrugs. If I'm being honest, I never pictured him going to college, so it's surprising that he's agreed, and I wish him the best.

"Thanks." He manages a pleasant smile.

"Where does this end up anyway?" I ask, pointing to the tracks.

"Who knows?"

Scene jump - because that's how I'm going to remember it - and you don't need the whole picture to get the point: with the sun setting, we call it a night. We return to his house to find that its occupants are either sleeping or out, but we don't wish to partake in either activity. Instead, we see which pizza place is still delivering, and we ransack Oliver's video game collection.

By the time we've gone through two games, the doorbell rings, and after giving the miscellaneous assortment of change and small bills that we could muster as a tip, we have ourselves a late-night feast.

What proves to be the most amusing part of the night is that Oliver had asked the makers of the pizza to draw on the box. And when it arrived, we found a largely exaggerated sketch of an axolotl drawn on the inside cover in red marker. Never have I been more satisfied with a service.

Scene jump: We go to a movie, and I hate that I have to pay full price. While in line, I have an odd desire to let the employees know that I work at a movie theater too. It's as if they're in on some secret and I wish to announce that I'm qualified to hear it. I don't know why I feel this way, but the desire goes unfulfilled as we buy our concessions and enter the movie.

It's the type of theater that has big, puffy recliners. I almost fall asleep.

Scene jump: When the moon is high, we go for a drive. Oliver plays "Hollow Moon (Bad Wolf)" by AWOLNATION, and I don't know how I haven't heard the song before. It makes me feel cooler than I am as my hand rides the waves of a lowered window. It makes me think about what I consider to be cool, and where on the spectrum I fall. I know I've been as cool as the intro to "Devils" by Say Hi, but I'm not cool enough to deserve a movie that opens with "Gansta" by tUnE-yArDs. Do you know what I mean?

Scene jump: While sitting in Oliver's living room, Sam enters the house with a handful of cash and her signature grin.

"What's that from?" Oliver interrogates.

"None of your business," Sam declares, defensively.

"Well, where were you?"

"What's it to you?"

"Dad's not gonna' be happy," Oliver warns.

"Dad doesn't give a shit about what I do."

"That's bullshit and you know it."

"Whatever. Piss off," says Sam, ending the conversation by going to her room.

"What was that about?" I ask.

"I think she sells drugs," Oliver plainly states.

"What!?" I'm flabbergasted at his casual accusation.

"Where else would she get that cash?" he asks. "And she smokes all the time. My dad keeps telling her she needs to get her act together."

"Okay, but that can't be the only logical explanation. She has a job, right?"

"Yes, but what kind of job hands you a wad of cash at the end of a shift?" he asks, making it obvious that that's impractical.

I don't know what to reply. Instead, I sit and consider the possibility that Oliver's right. In all reality, I shouldn't be surprised. Oliver smokes, I've known that for a long time, but it's hard to accept that most of the people I know are somewhere on the same path. What's even stranger is that I'm somewhere on it too, and therefore have no right to criticize. I wonder, however, whether or not we'll decide to take the same turns – or is the destination the same regardless?

Scene jump: Oliver introduces me to Larry, a boy with skin as black and lustrous as a panther's. He's got big lips and short hair, and quickly earns the title of being the funniest person I know to date.

Scene jump: "How much further?" I ask, squinting at the blurry road ahead.

"They say it's the second tree to the left of the lake," Oliver tells me while he cautiously continues driving.

"Who is the 'they' you're referring to?" I question.

"What?" he asks, absentmindedly. But when I continue to look at him inquisitively, he catches on. "Oh. . . I don't know. They! The people who live here. Anyone, whoever, why does it matter?"

"I just think 'they' gets too much credit. We quote them without even knowing who they are," I say.

"You think too much." He shakes his head. "Here! It's this tree."

He pulls off the gravel road and aligns the car so that its headlights illuminate the dark wood of the abnormally large tree. He leaves the car running.

"So what's supposed to happen now?"

"It's supposed to get all foggy and then there'll be handprints on the window," he tells me.

"Handprints?"

"Yeah, of a child. Apparently a little girl was kidnapped many years ago and they found her body under this tree," he informs me.

"That's disturbing."

"Very," he agrees while intently watching the window.

However, after fifteen minutes of asking each other, "What was that?" at the slightest hint of a scurry beyond the car, we come to the conclusion that nothing's going to happen.

"Well, then let's go out and see," Oliver says as he unbuckles his seatbelt.

"What? Why?" I ask, trying not to sound too apprehensive. Regardless of whether I expect anything to happen, I can't deny that merely the woods at this hour puts my nerves on edge.

"To check out the tree," he claims.

"You'd die in a horror movie," I assert.

He scoffs. "Well. . . then you'd die in an action one." And with that, he opens the door and vacates the car, leaving me feeling slightly pathetic and overly inadequate. But inadequacy is simply a state of being, and certainly not an infinite one, so I get out as well.

By the time I close the car door Oliver is already to the tree. He's standing under its mass, looking up at its spider web of a coverage. For a moment I find it beautiful, but then I remember its rumored allegations and the scene turns cold.

285

"Nothing's going to happen," I say.

"And you think I'd be the one to die in a horror movie?" He looks at me. "The doubter always dies," he claims, but I know that at this point he's just humoring the night instead of waiting for expectations to be fulfilled.

I simply smile. "You ready to go?" I ask at last.

"Yeah." He slowly turns from the tree, and the final opportunity for a spectacular, supernatural, *something* passes like the falling of a leaf.

We get back in the car with barely a story to tell, but I wear a grin of satisfaction. This was the same outcome of the numerous ghost hunts we went on as kids, yet with each one, it was somehow thrilling enough to convince us to do it again. So at the prospect that there will be another, I must say that I couldn't have asked for a better ending.

Scene jump: It's Monday night, and as I lay on the futon I get a message from Dylan. It's a picture of her and my mom watching a movie on the couch. I'm happy to know that she's made it there safe and I hope that tomorrow goes just as well.

Scene jump: With our mental alarm clocks kicked in, our eyes open automatically around 9:30, Tuesday morning.

While in the bathroom, I ask Dylan when she plans to head over to her house, and soon after she informs me that she's already there. She explains that she went over around 8:00 because she still didn't know what time Adam would show, and she didn't want to miss him. Her mother had left for work soon before, and Dylan agrees to send me updates.

After breakfast and some lazy dog petting, Oliver gets excited over his sudden inspiration regarding the plans for the day.

"Did you bring a swimsuit?" he asks me.

"Oh, um no. I went swimming soon before I left so I didn't have time to dry and pack it," I explain.

"Cool with borrowing something from me, then?" he asks.

"Why not Sam's?"

"They won't fit you. Just wear a sports bra and a pair of my trunks."

"What for? Where are we going?" I ask before committing to such an outfit. I'm completely in support of breaking the societal rule of gendered clothing, but I can't deny I'd be self-conscious if viewed by bystanders.

"The State Park barely reaches this town, but I know a spot there that's nice. You down?"

"Will there be a lot of people there?"

"I never see anyone."

"Okay, then sure."

We go to his room and he tosses me a pair of purple swim trunks. I thank him, change, stare at myself for way too long in the mirror, and finally get the confidence to go back to his room.

Upon entering, I find Oliver in his own swimsuit, packing a drawstring bag on the floor.

"Holy shit," I unintentionally say. He looks up at me inquisitively. "Since when did you get buff?" I ask, looking at his muscles with astonishment. "You have like twelve abs."

"Started working out." He shrugs.

"Paid off," I admire.

He stands, slings the bag over his shoulder, and says, "Not bad yourself, even in my shorts."

I blush, but not because of romantic inclinations. It's simply nice to still have approval of one another after all this time. We leave the room ready for the day.

Oliver drives far above the speed limit to a small parking area. From there we walk to the park's entrance, and as he said, it appears we're its only occupants.

When we make it down the wooden steps, I'm amazed by the beauty of the flowing creek, scattered with glistening rocks of all colors.

"This isn't even the good part," Oliver tells me with a smile.

We hop across on the rocks that protrude the silky surface of the water and make it to a clearing. It's covered in sand with the consistency of clay. I take out my phone with intentions of sending Dylan a picture, but I soon discover that I don't have service.

"Hey, do you get reception here?" I ask Oliver who has started to walk adjacent to the creek.

"Not for miles," he replies.

I don't tell him that it would be ideal to keep in touch with Dylan today because I know that that would involve abandoning our plans, and he's obviously excited to show me his spot. So with a swallow of trepidation and bit of guilt, I put my phone on airplane mode to conserve its battery and stow it in the pocket of my shorts (yet another perk of being a guy: you actually get clothes with real fricken pockets). I then hurry to catch up with Oliver.

We walk for what feels like a mile over the clay-like sand, taking the time to cross the creek either by rock or fallen tree. With each turn there's a new beauty, and by following in Oliver's wake, I get the feeling that he would be good friends with Tate and Tanner.

Once we cross a particularly narrow ledge around the bank of the creek, we come to a steep drop-off. Oliver braces himself on a nearby tree and starts to descend.

"We're almost there," he tells me as I mimic the path he takes.

When back on level ground, with shoes two-thirds full of sand, he takes a left around the large rock wall we've just descended from to present a roaring waterfall.

"Damn," I comment as I stand parallel to Oliver.

He smiles at the impressed look on my face. "Care to take a dip?"

"We're going to swim in there?" I ask, slightly intimidated.

"Yeah, you can't go directly under it, but all around is nice."

"What's with all these water activities?" I say, partially to myself. "Wettest summer so far," I comment, suddenly realizing how often I've put on a swimsuit.

"That's what she said," Oliver laughs.

"Oh my god. I hate you." I move to push him but he runs ahead. He sets his bag on a rock and kicks off his shoes. I watch as he diligently walks toward the water.

"There are rocks, so be careful," he yells over the sound of crashing water.

I take off my shoes and shirt, put my phone in his bag, and attempt to follow him. The water, which is colder than I expected, has a current from the waterfall, requiring an effort to keep from falling. After tripping a few times, I make it past the rocks and suck in my stomach from the cold. My hands hover over the water as I slowly walk toward Oliver, who is now fully submersed and swimming freely.

"Nice, isn't it?" he asks, flicking back his hair.

"Cold."

"You'll get used to it," he says, and he's right. Eventually I go under and we happily tread water, dazed by the constant drone of the waterfall. We touch the bottom at the shallow end and lazily talk about all that we can.

At some point I start to get cold again, as I always do when in water for an extended period of time, so we venture back out to air dry, seeing as neither of us brought a towel.

We sit in a crevasse of the rock wall and look up at all the initials that have been carved by people who came before us. Many of them are circled with a heart. I wonder how many of those couples are still together today, and if they'd regret seeing their commitment displayed here.

"Should we put ours up there?" Oliver asks.

"I mean, why not?"

He hops down and returns to the edge of the water. He then comes back with a small but pointed rock. I scoot over to allow him to stand, and he promptly starts to etch an "O" into the rock wall.

"Oh my god," he says once the "O" is clearly visible.

"What?"

"Our initials spell OJ. Why wasn't our nickname Orange Juice in daycare?"

I laugh, "You seriously would have liked being addressed as Orange Juice?"

"Yeah! Or at least OJ for short. Everyone knows that's the best kind of juice."

"I prefer cranberry if I do say so myself."

"I can't believe you don't support our nickname." He hops down. The "J" had been a lot quicker.

"It's not our nickname."

"You'll see," he says as he walks back to his bag. I stare at the carving for a while longer. I know that I'll never regret seeing our commitment displayed here.

"Ready to go?" he asks, handing me my shoes.

Once sand-free and on my feet, we start our hike back to the car. I can't tell if the walk back feels shorter or longer, but I know that I'm happy to see the start of the creek and the scattered rocks once again.

We take the same path we took to first cross it and ascend up the wooden steps. It's not until we enter Oliver's car that I remember that I should check my phone for updates from Dylan. Oliver turns up the radio and I switch my phone off airplane mode. It takes a moment to gather what I've missed, but once it does, my stomach drops.

"*4 missed calls from Mom*" is displayed at the top of my notifications, and when I scroll to look at the others, I see that there's not a single message from Dylan.

"Hey, turn that down."

"What?"

"Turn that down. I need to call my mom back," I tell Oliver, obviously flustered.

"Is everything alright?" he asks, turning down the volume.

"I don't know yet." I put the phone to my ear. With every tone I get more and more anxious. On the fourth ring, my mom finally picks up. "June?"

"Yeah. Hi. Why'd you call?" I try to reserve the worried tone in my voice.

"Dylan lives on eight fifty-five Alan street, right?" she asks.

"Yes," I answer, my stomach in a knot.

"That's what I thought." She sounds distant, almost guilty. "Dylan left early this morning and everything seemed fine. I. . . I don't know what happened for sure, but when I got to work my coworkers were talking about an accident that happened there. I heard the sirens, but I didn't think anything of it."

"Well, what happened!? Did they say?" My breathing picks up and Oliver looks at me, concerned.

"They just saw the ambulance and a few police cars arrive. They went inside the house. . . ." She stops, choking on her words.

"Then what!?" I frantically ask.

"They. . . they came out with someone on a stretcher. Couldn't see who it was. . . they were covered. I've been watching the news, but I haven't heard anything. I thought you should know. I didn't know if you wanted to come back or-" she continues to talk, but I don't register any of it. It's the scene in the movies where the film keeps rolling but the sound is turned down, replaced by the eerie aftermath of a bomb, ringing in my ears and my mind. But in reality, the music isn't gone. I can still hear Post Malone through the speakers, the rumble of wheels on road, and the worried questions from Oliver. I wish it would stop. I wish it was like a movie - because in a movie, she'd be fine. Right? My fear of her mother finally going too far would just be that, a fear? Right? Not reality?

Oliver would die in a horror movie. I'd die in an action one. Would Dylan die in a drama?

No.

"I need to go home." I finally find my voice.

"So you're coming back?" My mom asks.

I had forgotten I was on the phone with her. "Yes. Be there soon." I hang up.

"What's happening?" Oliver asks.

"I need to go home. Dylan. . . I don't know what happened, but. . . she could be hurt. I'm sorry, but I have to go home."

"I understand," he says. "We'll be back at my house in five minutes."

Five minutes feels like ten years. I can't imagine how long the ride home will feel, but I'm desperate to get in my car. I feel bad for rushing our goodbye, but Oliver shares my sense of urgency. We hug, which isn't typical of us, but it feels right.

I'm on the road within ten minutes. The clock reads 4:06. The sky is turning grey. I remind myself that it's not a metaphor for the tone of this story, but just a sky; as it always is, just a sky. But what if I'm wrong about how the world works? What if my best friend really is dead?

NO AMOUNT OF BEAUTY [20]

=

The sun, poking through the clouds, hits the thick trees and illuminates my car in a pattern akin to strobe lights. It seems only suitable, for my mind is racing to the same beat. I can't get myself to listen to music, so the drive is empty, longer than I could have imagined, and almost painful.

I approach a stoplight and it turns red at just the wrong moment, forcing me to break. In anger, I hit my steering wheel and my eyes start to blur. The road had been a distraction, but I can't avoid my thoughts when stopped. I rub my eyes and relentlessly repeat *it's not true* over and over in my head, but when I finally look up, I realize that I'm the only car in sight.

Why am I stopped? I don't need to be. Am I a bad friend for following the law when it proves not necessary? Why am I allowing a light to prevent me from figuring out the state of my best friend's life? I stare at the red circle, willing it to turn green, but my foot doesn't move. I can't bring myself to run the light, but it has nothing to do with my respect towards the law. I think, in my desperation, making the decision to comply to this hindrance reveals the truth that I am utterly afraid to continue, to arrive at Dylan's house and find her covered by a tarp that signifies her death, to know that I really have lost the best part of my life.

The light turns green.

My foot is no more compelled to move than it was before, but I force it to. My car is once again in motion, and so is the wet reminder that this could possibly be the worst day of my life. I cry harder than I have so far, knowing that within thirty minutes I will be faced with a single truth: my life will never be the same.

When I reach my town, numb from tears, I search for signs relating to the accident on my way to Dylan's house. To my vexation, the town seems untouched by any sort of disturbance. Do they not know that someone may be dead? Do they not care? Or is this a good sign? Perhaps what my mom told me was an exaggeration – derived from the effect of passing information from one person to the next – like the game we used to play in Kindergarten. Is that why it hasn't been on the news? There's nothing to report?

But this small hope is soon crushed when I turn onto Alan Street and see two police cars, Tate's car that Dylan borrowed, and the yellow tape marking a scene of a crime. I park as close as I can, mindlessly exit my car, and approach an officer who appears to be documenting the scene on a clipboard. I feel as though I have no insides as I tap the man's shoulder to get his attention.

"Oh, I'm sorry this is a restricted area at the moment," he says, ushering me back.

"No. . . no, I just. . . I need to know. . . ." I resist him with little strength.

"Need to know what? What can I help you with?"

This doesn't feel real. I am somewhere else.

"Did she live? Is she alive?" I can't tell if the words came out of my mouth, but the officer seems to have understood.

"The woman. . . um. . . she didn't make it. There was nothing we could have done when we arrived." He doesn't make eye contact.

"The woman?" I ask. Even though Dylan is technically an adult, it feels odd for him to address her as a woman. Or is it possible that it's not Dylan he's referring to?

"Yes. After that kind of fall it's hard to say anyone would have lived."

I'm confused. "But. . . the woman. A woman? An older lady? Dylan's mother?"

"Correct. I'm sorry to say that her mother is dead."

Her mother is dead. Dylan's mother is dead. Dylan is alive. Dylan is alive!

He continues talking, but I don't know what he's saying. I cut him off. "Where is she!? Dylan, I mean."

"Oh, um, we took her to the station to get a statement about an hour and a half ago. We're just finishing up her–"

I don't let him finish. "Okay, thank you!" I run to my car. Again, mindless, but this time as a result of relief – sweet relief, better than any feeling I've ever felt; how is it possible to be this happy? I start to cry. I start to lose my breath as I sob in my seat, knowing that I simply have to drive to the station to confirm that it's true – to hug my best friend and never let her go.

I manage to put the car in drive and head towards Main Street. I arrive in ten minutes and am through the glass doors within seconds. I frantically look around, stopping on all the brunettes, hoping that one is Dylan, but she's not in the lobby.

I approach the receptionist, and even though I would never interrupt someone who's on the phone on a regular day, I interject my urgent question: "Excuse me, is there a Dylan Rivers in the building?"

He looks up at me but doesn't acknowledge my question.

"Please, sir."

He covers the bottom half of the phone and say, grudgingly, "What do you need?" in a near whisper.

"Dylan Rivers. Is she here?"

"Curly brown hair, kid your age?"

"Yes!" I beam.

"Released half an hour ago. Left with a man," he plainly states.

"Do you know where they went?" I ask, but he doesn't answer because he's not able to ignore the person on the phone any longer.

I take it. She's alive, and I'll take it. But I need to find her. I exit the building and get back in my car. The receptionist said she left with a man. I can only assume that that man was Adam, but who knows at this point.

I take out my phone, ready to message her over Facebook, but I don't know what to say. I decide to only send, *"Where are you?"* in the hopes that she's near a device and knows that I would be wanting to contact her. But I don't count on it, so I set off to my house, thinking it's the only logical place she could be.

When I pull into my driveway, I'm disappointed to discover that there's no other car present. It is possible that Adam dropped her off and left, but my hopes aren't high. I run inside and yell her name, "Dylan!?"

No reply.

I run through each room, but she's not in any of them. Heavy-hearted, I return to my car. Halfway through pulling out of my driveway, my mom approaches in her car. She rolls down the window.

"I got off as soon as I could. Is she okay?" she yells.

"Yes, but I don't know where she is." I back out completely.

"Oh my god," she says in relief. "Let me know when you find her!"

I wave a confirming hand out the window and head towards Emma's house.

When there, I discover that neither Dylan nor Emma is home, for there's no car in the driveway and all of the lights are off. I decide to try the Library.

I reach the woods. Further disappointed and slightly sweaty from running, I see no trace of Dylan having been there. In frustration and running out of ideas, I decide to call Tate. I don't know why it's taken me this long to do so, but following in the pattern of my luck, he doesn't answer. I try Tanner.

"Oh my god, hi!" I say once hearing his wonderful voice.

"I'm assuming you've heard what's happened?" he asks, sounding more depressed than ever.

"Yes. Have you heard from her? And how did you find out about it?"

"Your mom found me on Facebook."

"Oh, wow, okay." I wasn't expecting that. "So Dylan hasn't contacted you?"

"No."

"Great. Well, she's not at my house, Emma's, the Library, dock, or the station. Any ideas?"

There's a long pause. "When her dad died she. . . acted out, I guess. She was reckless. Destroyed her room, took a lot of pills, crashed her car. All that shit. I mean, of course she didn't have the same feelings towards her mother, but I bet she's searching for something to do. I don't know, June. But please let me know when you find her."

"Of course. Thank you, Tanner."

"Sure thing." He hangs up. I feel a rush of sympathy for Tanner having to witness Dylan after her father's death, and I praise their relationship even further. I hope that I can manage this disaster with some grace, and I make my way back to my car. All the while I'm thinking of different locations she'd deem suitable for this situation, but I'm drawing a blank. Where would she want to be at this time?

I buckle my seatbelt and look at the horizon, and then it comes to me: what could possibly be more in her character than to be undaunted? Now, with the biggest obstacle in her life being sent to the grave, and no one to prove a goddamn thing to, the stage is hers. I know exactly where she is. The only problem is, do I remember how to get there?

Now that I've wasted nearly an hour in search for Dylan, I set off immediately. With the sun starting to set and a destination in mind, I head for the country. I look for the lake. I know we passed a lake. I beam when I spot it because it confirms that I'm headed in the right direction. And soon enough, I'm approaching the left turn that leads to the tall cliff where I expect to find Dylan sitting. With my confidence being this high, I'm not sure what I'll do if I find the cliff unoccupied.

I park at the rounded dead-end and quickly find the hidden path the boys had shown us not too long ago. I follow it with longing in my stomach and palms slippery from sweat. The dirt soon morphs to rock, and I break through the bushy underbrush. There, sitting with her legs dangling over the cliff's edge, taunting it as I expected, is the most euphoric thing I've ever seen.

"Dylan," I announce, barely audible.

She turns her head around, looking slightly startled. Upon coming to terms, she bursts into tears and slings her body to face mine. I've never seen her cry before, and instinctively, I do too. I walk over and sit to face her. At a loss for words, I simply pull her close and hug her tight.

"Fuck you," I say after I've gathered my breath.

She pulls away. "What?" I think I see a hint of a smile.

"I've been going crazy trying to find you. I thought you'd be with Adam. Or at my house. Why didn't you tell me? What happened?" I have so many questions, but Dylan only bothers answering one.

"I was with Adam. I told him to drop me off here."

"So this guy, after all that, just trusted to leave you stranded here in the middle of nowhere?"

"I told him you'd come. I knew you would." She wipes away her remaining tears.

"Jesus. A hint would have been nice!" I proclaim, not angry in any way.

"What fun is that?" She's exactly the same.

I look at her. We're playing it off with humor, but I need to know what happened, so I ask.

She stares at her lap when she speaks, but says, "My mother was sent home early for drinking. . . I was still waiting for Adam. Um - she kept asking why I was there. I couldn't tell her, and I couldn't contact Adam. . . I refused to leave. She came at me. . . tried to bring me to the door. . . ." She starts to cry again and looks up to the multi-colored sky. "It happened so fast. I mean, she was so wasted it's hard to say it was my fault. . . . I was fighting to get her off me, and I guess we were closer to the stairs than I thought. She fell . . . all the way to the bottom. She must have hit her head . . . lot of blood. . . ."

"It wasn't your fault," I instantly insist.

She won't make eye contact. "It was kinda' my fault," she says, almost to herself.

"Honestly, Dylan. . . it's not like she didn't have it coming." The words feel cruel coming out of my mouth.

"I killed my mother," Dylan states with her eyes closed. "I killed her."

"No! Dylan, if anything it was self-defense. She abused you for years! You can't possibly think of it that way."

"I told the police it was an accident. They didn't ask much with her history."

"It *was* an accident," I press.

She doesn't reply.

"Dylan, she was a terrible person." I don't know how to justify a death, but I've never heard Dylan speak a positive thing about her mother, and it can't be now that she finally feels some sympathy, and even worse, guilt. "You need to know that you can't take blame for this. After all she's done, Dylan. It happened, and . . . that's all there is."

There's a long stretch of silence that seems to cover the entire sky, the water below, and the air we breathe. She will have to move on, and the scene is set for her to do it.

"Why'd you come here?" I ask, knowing my version of the answer.

"I don't know. Didn't want to see anyone. . . thought maybe I'd feel different if I did something. . . thought-"

"Thought you finally deserved your movie moment?" I finish.

"My movie moment?" she asks, managing a small smile, trying to wipe away her tears.

"Yeah, like you said. Only in a movie would you jump off the cliff. Slow-mo. and everything." She continues to stare at me. "Everyone deserves a movie moment," I say.

"I really just came for the view. . ." she tries.

"No you didn't. You came to do something, and this is what it's going to be." I take charge for once in my life and stand up. She looks up at me, and for the very first time, she looks small.

I lend her a hand, and she accepts.

"You came here for a reason," I repeat, "and maybe since then you've come to your senses and remember that fifty feet looks scary, but you were able to sit on the edge of the cliff, so why aren't you able to jump?"

She's at a loss for words.

"Come on! Give in to the cheesy plotline that people pay too much money to see," I quote. "Do it for your character, because I know you, Dylan, and if you don't do something now, you'll feel this all over again later."

"Okay, but jumping won't actually change anything. You get that, right? Like, there's a reason it'd be considered a *movie moment*, because movies are unrealistic," she argues as a form of stalling.

"They're only unrealistic because we're too afraid to live our lives."

"Okay, now you're just trying to sound like a philosopher or something."

"Look! I don't care." I let go of the rope I used to cling to for security; the one that would burn my hands in the battle between *is this right* and *should I care?*

"Why is that a bad thing? Why does it suddenly become a cliché if we actually live out the things we see on screen? I want that! I want to live with a soundtrack, find beauty in sad things, and just fucking *feel.* Of course, talking about this is defeating the purpose, and maybe it won't be significant, but I don't care anymore. I *just don't care*, and neither do you. Am I right?"

She can't help but smile. "You've never been more right."

"I know." I laugh. "So do this. Do it in the spirit of *fuck you.* Your life has been shit, Dylan, but I know you're still brave enough to jump off this damn cliff - to be fucking free."

She laughs.

"What?"

302

"I've always loved those movies."

I laugh too, and by this point I can tell that she's convinced. She turns to face the cliff and begins to take off her shoes, socks, and sweatshirt, so that she's standing in a black tank top and old shorts. She wraps her toes around the edge of the rocks and sighs loudly, obviously apprehensive.

Everything is still.

"I think I loved her," she says with a blank stare. "My mom," she adds, noticing my incomprehension. "I mean, not like you're supposed to. . . but there were times. . . a few. . ."

"I understand." I stop her from struggling, and she smiles with appreciation. "It's okay."

"Well," she braces herself, looking down at the dark water below, "I suppose it's now or never."

"That's all you got?"

"Okay, fine. Here's to. . . guilt-free liberation and not giving a single fuck!"

And without another ounce of hesitation, she pushes off the rock's edge and descends towards the vast prospect of *something better*, and all the while, I swear I can hear the magnitude of "Release Me" by Corrina Repp serenading her fall.

There's a wide range of curse words thrown around when I meet her at the bottom, but I can tell that she's far from regretting the jump. She sits in wet clothes, wrapped in my emergency blanket on the ride home. She's quick to fall asleep once in my bed, and the boys are happy to receive an update.

The next morning feels hollow. My mom stays home from work and makes a big breakfast. She also volunteers to handle the legal clean-up regarding what to do with Dylan's dead mother.

After breakfast we're forced to return to Dylan's house to get Tate's car, and the view couldn't be more dismal. We leave with haste, and I follow Dylan to a gas station where she will get some food for the road and return to Tate's house.

I wait for her to come out, leaning against the hood of my car. She didn't want to say goodbye at a place with nefarious memories, and figured the Holiday would have to suffice.

She comes out bearing a wide range of junk food and says, "Still giving zero fucks," at my judgmental look.

"Well, I'm glad."

She puts the food in her car and gives me a monumental hug.

"God, I'm going to miss you," she says. "And I'm sorry that your visit with Oliver ended short."

"Don't worry about it."

Having already said our goodbyes once before, and, at that time, not expecting to have to do it again, this feels more casual.

"Message me when you get back, work on getting a real phone, and drive safely," I tell her.

"Yes, *mom*," she mocks, but then we both stop. "Oh, too soon?" she asks, feeling awkward.

"Things will be things," I say, not knowing what exactly that means, but it seems to work. Her mother's death is easiest dealt with by not dealing with it at all.

"I love you, Junebug" she says.

"I love you too." I've never had a name to call her.

"Your job for the next time we see each other," she says, getting into her car, "is to think of something better for us to say." She shuts the door and rolls down the window. "Like they do in the movies."

I roll my eyes with a smile on my face, promise that I'll think of something, and watch as she pulls out of the lot and gets on the road that will serve as the long-overdue, first step to a new life.

It was one of those days where you could see the white moon in the blue sky. The gas price was $2.14. There was a deflated Capri Sun juice box resting sadly on the ground, and there was nothing that hinted that I'd remember those things forever.

That was the last time I saw Dylan Rivers.

And no, I'm not fucking with you. I'm not saying this because it'd make for a better story. I'm not saying this because I want to say it. In any way.

I'm saying this because i once met Death - not directly of course, simply over the phone - and just from his voice I was able to tell that no amount of beauty someone gave to the world would stand a chance against his greedy ambition of ruthless vigor.

In other words, I say this because it's fucking true, and I promise I am way more upset than you.

EVERY SWEAR WORD YOU CAN IMAGINE
[21]

=

I know there are some of you who are not surprised. Perhaps you called if from the beginning, caught on that the title is "i once met" not "am still meeting," or simply just figured it would happen. Either way, I know there are a few of you who were innocent, and I can tell you that I was one of those people.

Reader, I have to explain that me writing in present tense has been a lie. In fact, everything you've read so far has happened in the past, for it's been two years since Dylan died. I have written this in present tense simply because that's how it feels to me: like it's still happening now. When in reality, I've since gone to college, am in my second year at the moment, and I haven't mentioned Dylan's name out loud in what feels like too long.

I hope you can forgive me for any confusion I may have caused, and continue to read, keeping in mind what I've told you. It is now when I'm going to write about her death, and I'm going to do it past tense – where it belongs – and how I want it to feel.

+

The day at the gas station was as normal as the day could be, and does not mark the day of Dylan's death. It wasn't on the drive back to Tate's that Dylan died, but the drive from his house.

July ended and soon August did as well. I had moved into the dorm of my college and Dylan found a job in the cities, managed to buy a crappy old car, and was on her way to finding an apartment. I could talk a lot about my early time at college and Dylan's settlement in the cities, but that's not what this story is about. So I'll skip to the weekend where I went home.

It was my first weekend back and Dylan had taken off work to come and visit. I was excited. I was beyond excited because I missed familiarity, and there was no better way of getting it back than sitting on the couch and watching a movie with Dylan and my mom, eating popcorn I picked up from the theater, and experiencing the routine of long stretches and deep sighs when the movie was over.

I longed for it, and it was planned, and I was ready. And I thought Dylan was too, but it was her misjudgment that made Friday, September 22 the worst day of my life.

I arrived around noon and my mom was thrilled to see me; I don't think her hug could have been any tighter. Dylan was supposed to arrive around 5:00, but when 5:00 came and passed, I started to worry.

My mom made a big dinner, but we were waiting to eat it. The last I heard from Dylan was a text that said, *"Leaving now, see you soon ! Junebug,"* and that's when I realized that lies can be accidental.

It was at 6:00 that I gave up on trying to reach her over the phone, and it was at 6:30 that I called both Tate and Tanner to ask if they've heard from her. Both being at college and preoccupied with their own lives at the time, said they haven't and asked if everything was okay. I assured them that it was. I don't know why I did that. Perhaps I was trying to convince myself that it was.

But it wasn't. I couldn't have been more wrong.

It wasn't until 8:43 that I got the call. I was listed as one of Dylan's emergency contacts, and it wasn't until then that the police were able to send out a notice.

Dylan had taken pills - the very same pills I had a suspicion about for so long - the kind that say "do not drive or operate heavy machinery" on the warning label. Many of us, including Dylan, seem to forget that that is not a suggestion.

She clipped a semi at 60mph.

My only hope is that she died instantly. I didn't ask for the details. I couldn't.

|||||||||

Nine lines for the nine days I stayed in my room, for there are no words that can describe how I felt, but let me try:

Dylan's death was as devastating as "The Cold" by Exitmusic, and if you have not known or been listening to any of these songs, then I advise you to at least look up this one. Sometimes it's not words we relate to, but a shared feeling evoked from occupying our minds with beautiful noise.

It was finding things I relate to that got me out of my room, and the sinking feeling that I could no longer share those things with Dylan that made me return to it.

I don't know how to say these things without screaming them, but being one of the things I've learned from Dylan, and in her honor, I do not care about the volume of my voice anymore.

At the time, I didn't care about much of anything – if not to say absolutely nothing – because my life was set to an unexpected halt, and I have never been one to enjoy waiting. During the halt I was surrounded by a hot, sticky, mess of sadness – like the air on a humid day. I was convinced that the suffocation I endured would be never-ending, and the only difference between a hot summer's day and what I felt then was that when I walked into an air conditioned room, the feeling didn't go away.

In fact, it was worse indoors; it was as if I had a pillow permanently wrapped around my face. And I have to admit, sometimes I wished there really was a pillow stopping my air flow. Some of you may read that and think that I'm being dramatic in a way, but I want to remind you that there have been many who've wished the same thing and for far less monumental reasons. And I also want to remind you that in all situations, the reasons for them wishing it are equally justifiable.

But I don't want to talk about that. I could write another book about the tragedy of losing someone you love, but I think the story about how I got to where I am now is a better one.

There was funeral, and a lot of people attended. It was utterly devastating to see Tate and Tanner cry. Dylan wanted to be cremated, so she was.

I reluctantly returned to school, and grudgingly returned to work. I had almost zero motivation to smile at customers.

People were sympathetic, but I knew, just as Dylan had when she first revealed the depths of her situation to me in the Antique store, that people saying "I'm sorry" doesn't help, and I got sick of seeing the face of pity. I tried to remember that they were being genuine, and sometimes those words were the best that they could do. But it was all the same.

Have I gotten to a point yet? I've had two years to think of a point. When I realized that I couldn't, I started writing as a form of stalling, but now the time's come. I guess that's my point: that there wasn't a point - not in Dylan's death, not in my writing, not even in us living - there is only this: I am sitting on a small, wooden chair with a pillow to my back and my computer sitting on the small, wooden desk. My lamp is on, illuminating the fraction of the room that I'm occupying and giving an ease to my eyes, because I've noticed, as a writer, that staring at a computer screen for too long makes me blink with more force than should be required. But I've also noticed that the day can be categorized as "big" when my contacts are just a little bit harder to take out - as if they've been conforming to my eyes to convince me to keep them open. And I've noticed, above all, that that is beautiful.

For me to wish, to will myself, to succeed in staying up just another hour to write, to read, to finish a movie, or even to be on social media, is a beautiful thing. Because to *want* to be awake for life is a beautiful thing, and that's what I found to be the most difficult thing to *want* after Dylan died.

But then I realized I was being stupid.

Yes, that's rather blunt, but it's the truth, and that's how the truth is best served. *I was being stupid.*

I say this because after a month of feeling bad for myself, trying to get back to my normal routine, I realized something: Dylan would have been extremely disappointed. And from the very start, that was the last thing I wanted her to be. So that is why those sublime encounters I've mentioned throughout the book did not end when Dylan's life did, because after all, the majority of the roads we take don't lead to a dead end; they simply provide a turn.

So before I speak about the near-impossible task of moving on, I want to mention three things that were by far the hardest to overcome:

1) I found Dylan's yellow hippie shirt - but not before she died. Admittedly, I had forgotten about it soon after she moved that summer, and I think she must have too because she never nagged me about it. That being said, it made finding it a whole hell of a lot worse.

I discovered it tucked away in a box I had packed full of winter clothes - clothes I wasn't planning on bringing to college right away. I must have grabbed it by mistake. I cried for hours when I found it. I still have it today.

2) Dylan will never randomly call me up one day, years from now, and ask if I remember that *One Thing*. Yet I will always know that it's referring to us sitting on a bed together in that cheap motel room, doing practically nothing. What I would do to be back there, you have no idea.

3) Rivers and Roads take me Home. I'd call her Rivers and she'd call me Roads, and that's how we'd know we loved each other. Or at least that's what I was going to tell her when she arrived at my house that Friday, because she had asked me to think of something better to say, and that was the best that I could do. And even if it was a cheesy idea, it saddens me today to think that she never got to hear it.

She would have laughed. I know she would've.

But to aid as at least a sliver of a positive outlook, I haven't smoked a cigarette since the day Dylan died.

I told you I'd quit.

I think about these three things more often than I should, and I'm hereby giving this book a secondary title (because I'm fully aware that an 11 word title is hella long for a book). So by all means, Reader, you can call this Rivers & Roads - for the ease of it, but also for Dylan, because it is her who inspired it, and her who deserves it.

RIVERS & ROADS [22]

=

All the beautiful things we temporarily forget when blinded by tragedy, and just a little more to make up for what's left:

I was walking down the street with my headphones in, surrounded by strangers, and "For the Kill" by Biting Elbows started to fill my ears. I instantly got a misplaced feeling that I was supposed to start something great – that the scene would cut to a montage of epically constructed acts of virtue, and everything in my life would've become meaningful. But as I merely continued down the street I was following, I realized that it wouldn't happen if It wasn't me who initiated it. And then I thought, *well how the fuck am I supposed to do that?*

It wasn't until recently that I discovered the word *sonder*. The word basically means the realizations that every stranger I pass has a life equal in complexity, severity, presence, and vitality. It's the realization that the act of me listening to that song, in my own world, was just as real to me as everyone else's life was real to them. We are singlehandedly taking on our own version of the world, and no one is discluded. Sonder is the realization that everyone in existence has at least one thing in common, and boy, it's one damn big thing.

While in other people's houses, I'd be in their kitchen and I'd look and their fridge, and I'd see pictures of them when they were a kid. Looking at their big smiles and chubby cheeks, I'd be reminded that they had a childhood too. And if anything, it was probably much like mine. I never think about it, but they do.

The silent communication you can have with strangers over something you're both experiencing is one of the most satisfying things we can take part in.

We ignore the homeless. Why do we do that?

There's a certain metaphor in the act of yanking on a seat belt repeatedly, while knowing that it'll only come if you do it softly, but I'm not sure what it is.

Sometimes it feels like people can only progress as far as their chargers can reach, and that's disappointing.

I woke up with "Fuck It and Whatever" by The Echo-Friendly stuck in my head, and I think that says a lot.

"What's the hardest thing you've ever had to do?" they asked.
"Know that someone had to do something harder."

I don't know what I'm writing.
It's important to be honest.

I know a little about a lot. But that implies that I know a lot to know a little about it.

I love that there's a distinct difference between the smell of a hotel with a pool and one without. And I love that they both make me feel a different way.

I wish life was as simple as the slow melody of "Beach Baby" by Bon Iver.

I hate that I kinda' like bowling shoes.

It's strange to think that there are a lot of people in the world who have never experienced snow.

Make a point to write down your thoughts. You'd be surprised at what they say.

People perform grand gestures of defining love by saying, "I'd give you the world." But I would never give you the world, for I wouldn't want to burden you with such a cruel gift.

i love You.

If this were a movie, the credit song would be "It's Alright" by Black Sabbath, and I'd like to think that that's self-explanatory.

The cover of this book was a self-portrait done by Dylan.

When she died, I couldn't decide on how I wanted to honor her; nothing felt good enough. But then I remembered her saying "you'll be writing it all down with all the English majors," and although she might not have meant this, and ignoring that she said it a worried manner, I wanted the statement to be true.

Have I succeeded?

Upon review, I've decided that there's no overarching theme to this book. But after being through multiple English classes, I've learned that that's not acceptable. So if for whatever reason you are asked, Reader, what precisely the theme is, tell them it's their own damn fault they don't know for not reading the book.

Jk, don't do that.

Tell them it's accepting the divine intricacies of living in a fucked up world that conveniently managed to omit the portion of the manual that explained why we're doing it.

But make it sound prettier.

Or, wait. . . maybe the theme is yet another broad explanation of what love looks like. Or perhaps this is just a prolonged eulogy. I don't know. You figure it out, it's your assignment.

But what I will say is that I don't read books in order to pick apart every word, decipher why they used a semicolon instead of starting a new sentence, or to fill out worksheet about the tone. I read books to fucking feel, and that's what I hope this has done for you, and if not, I sincerely apologize.

Would you believe me if I told you that I had to get up and take a shower before writing this last section? I did it to clear my head, because I couldn't stand blankly staring at the cursor any longer. I'm finding it difficult to decide if there's more to say or not. I'm sure there is – there always is – but I have to remind myself that sometimes silence is just as effective.

But I should probably tell you what's happened of the people I've invited into your lives, because that's what I'd want to know.

Tate: he is no longer able to say "never have I ever had a legitimate boyfriend." He's doing well in football, exceeding in school, and still brings me back to focus when we talk over the phone.

Tanner: he couldn't get himself to return to school after Dylan died, and I don't blame him. Instead, he got a job that helps the environment and does a lot of volunteering. He's currently on a team that will be heading out of the country to distribute food and supplies to those in need.

He still talks to Emma.

Oliver: he never made it to college, and I wasn't surprised. To be honest, I never really know what he's doing, but I'm not worried. I've never been worried.

As for me, I'm trying not to give a damn that the resolution to this story is a death. I didn't want it to be one of those books, but it wasn't my fault. There are days that I think it was, and days that when I stare into my coffee, I can't help but listen to the voice in my head that tells me I could have done something about it. I don't know if I could've.

I don't know where I'll go from here, but I figure this is a good start. After all, I will get older and my memory will grow fainter, and I'll want to return to this time. Although it'll be painful to read, I know that it's the type of pain that comes from love, and that's the best kind there is. Some would argue that it's the worst, but it hurts with the same intensity in which you loved, and I refuse to believe that that is something to be sad about.

As a few departing thoughts, I offer this:

If you were to meet me one day, Reader, and for some reason the first thing you thought was *wow, I wonder what's the worst thing that ever happened to them*, the answer would be that I lived. I lived while a girl with mountains of potential didn't. It has never seemed fair to me, but to expect fairness in this world is to be ignorant. And unless it is by their choice that they are, we can never blame the ignorant.

We can, however, blame ourselves, for it was me who refused to look at beauty for longer than I should have. But today, there is very little that I can look at and not smile at the mere prospect of its potential.

It was Dylan who feared Death and who doubted the idea of living after it, but it was Dylan who was forced to face it. I would ask her, if I could, what it's like, but I know that that would spoil the novelty of living. If we did not fear Death, we would not choose to live, so in a way I owe him my thanks. Although it was he who took Dylan too soon, it was he who kept her here before that.

I've learned to appreciate irony because it's the world laughing at itself, and it's always better to be in on the joke.

It's always better to *be*.

I grew up watching the expression of my mom's eyes in the rear-view mirror when she talked, and that's how I know what life looks like.

I have grandparents that when ordering fast food and the employee says, "Thank you, pull ahead," they reply, "You're welcome."

I'm lucky enough to have the gift of being entertained by simplicity, and the privilege of knowing others who are as well.

I know the burning feeling of having something to contribute to the conversation at the dinner table, and the disappointment of changing topics before you have the chance to say it. But remember, stop them and they'll listen.

I may be one of those people who take ten minutes to get an automatic paper towel dispenser to work. And my life-changing decision skills may be about as good as my how-many-times-should-I-hit-the-snooze-button decision skills, but I can admit that. Maybe that's beautiful.

Who knows? Maybe there's something beautiful in a cold night on the street, serenaded by the rubbing of loose change in your pocket, knowing that it's the only money to your name and not having a place in the world.

Maybe there's something beautiful in being told no, having to prove yourself, or starting with a bar so low you'd think it didn't exist.

Hell, I can even find the beauty in not being able to sleep, for you learn what time the birds start to sing.

So I figured maybe there's something beautiful in this, and although I couldn't find anything at first, I know that Dylan would have told me I wasn't looking hard enough.

So I put on my fucking glasses, grabbed a map, and got in the car, because I was going to search the Earth before I decided to give up on such a beautiful goddamn thing. And I promise, I hit every pothole, dead end, and traffic jam there was. But I visited every gas station I saw and always tried something new; I saw the sky in every color possible; I listened to all the best songs; I even found Anywhere – because as you may already know, i once met a Girl who paints the lines on roads, and now I know exactly where it is I'm supposed to go.

A THANK YOU TO PREVIOUS WORKS

Soundtrack

- Rivers and Roads - The Head and the Heart
- Pearl Jam
- Roll Me Away - Jack Symes
- Water - Jamaican Queens
- 17 - Youth Lagoon
- A Punk - Vampire Weekend
- Kettering - The Antlers
- Obstacles - Syd Matters
- White Ferrari – Frank Ocean
- Long Road to Ruin - Foo Fighters
- Sweater Weather - The Neighborhood
- Devil May Dance - Aj Roach
- Holy Toledo - Vundabar
- You Keep Me Hangin' On - Vanilla Fudge
- 666 ʇ - Bon Iver
- Here - Alessia Cara
- The Gates of Hell - The Features
- I Think We're Alone Now - Tommy James & The Shondells
- Idle Town - Conan Gray
- Golden Years - David Bowie
- Hey Jude - The Beatles
- Geographer - Sydney Wayser
- Wild Child - Elijah
- 40 Day Dream - Edward Sharpe & The Magnetic Zeros
- Hollow Moon (Bad Wolf) - AWOLNATION
- Devils - Say Hi
- Gansta - tUnE-yArDs
- Post Malone

- Release Me - Corrina Repp
- The Cold - Exitmusic
- For the Kill - Biting Elbows
- Fuck It and Whatever - The Echo-Friendly
- Beach Baby - Bon Iver
- It's Alright - Black Sabbath

Flicks
- American Ultra
- Star Wars
- Harry Potter
- The Breakfast Club
- La La Land
- Orange Is The New Black
- Friends
- Adventure Time
- Law & Order: SVU
- Stand By Me

Words
- To Kill a Mockingbird
- The Realm of Possibility
- Life of Pi
- It's Kind of a Funny Story
- The Full of the Moon
- The Man Who Was Thursday: A Nightmare
- The Complete Tales of Winnie-the-Pooh

and you

Made in the USA
Lexington, KY
28 December 2017